AN INHERITANCE OF
ASHES

AN INHERITANCE OF

ASH

A NOVEL BY Leah Bobet

CLARION BOOKS

Houghton Mifflin Harcourt

Boston New York

The author gratefully acknowledges the support of the Ontario Arts Council.

Clarion Books
215 Park Avenue South, New York, New York 10003
Copyright © 2015 by Leah Bobet

Clarion Books is an imprint of Houghton Mifflin Harcourt Publishing Company.

www.hmhco.com

The text was set in ITC Legacy Serif Std.

Book design by Lisa Vega

Library of Congress Cataloging-in-Publication Data
Bobet, Leah.
An inheritance of ashes / by Leah Bobet.
pages cm
Summary: Now that the strange war is over, sixteen-year-old Hallie and her
sister struggle to maintain their family farm, waiting to see who will return from
the distant battlefield, soon hiring a veteran to help them but, now as ugly truths
about their family emerge, Hallie is taking dangerous risks and keeping
desperate secrets while monsters and armies converge on the small farm.
ISBN 978-0-544-28111-0 (hardback)
[1. Fantasy. 2. Sisters—Fiction. 3. Secrets—Fiction. 4. Monsters—Fiction. 5. War—Fiction.
6. Farm life—Fiction.] I. Title.
PZ7.B63244In 2015
[Fic]—dc23   2015006823

Manufactured in the United States of America
DOC 10 9 8 7 6 5 4 3 2
4500573449

For Chandra,
Michael,
and my Philippe,
fixed stars all

Windtown

Dock

Beach

River

Orchard

Hay Barn

Chicken Coop

Farmhouse

Hawthorn Tree

ROADSTEAD
FARM & APPROACHES

Goat Shed

Old Smokehouse

Barley Field

Malthouse & Cistern

Hay Field

Lakewood Farm

Eight Years Before, Midsummer

HALLIE?" THE VOICE WHISPERED AROUND THE BROKEN chairs and cobwebs, and I breathed out because it wasn't my father.

Uncle Matthias edged past the snapped spinning wheel, over a pile of fishing nets set aside for mending. "You can come out, sweetheart," he said. "It's over."

My ears still rang with Papa's roaring swears, with Uncle Matthias's voice pitched low to cut. They didn't bother whispering anymore when they fought. Marthe had nudged her foot against mine — *I'm right here* — when Papa started to growl, but I wasn't half as big or strong as my older sister. When the first dish had flown, I'd run for the smokehouse — and I hadn't looked back.

Deep behind my junk barricades, I swallowed. "Who won?"

"Nobody." Uncle Matthias's light steps stopped in front of me. "It doesn't matter anymore."

I scowled. Of course it mattered. I would feel that win or loss in the weight of Papa's footsteps on our farmhouse floorboards, in whether being slow on my chores tomorrow would mean an indifferent smile or a bucket of water across the face. I peeked out from behind the scratched table leg. "Who *won?*"

Uncle Matthias sighed. "Your father did," he said, and my shoulders sagged with relief. "Come sit with me, kiddo. You'll get splinters down there."

My uncle's careful hands lifted me from my tangled fortress, carried me — even though I was much too big for carrying — to Great-grandmother's red brocade stool. He set me down gently, a thin, hardy brushstroke of a man, and I pulled my knees up to my chest. There were new islands in the mess of the smokehouse floor: clothes, tools, two pairs of walking boots.

Uncle Matthias's clothes. Uncle Matthias's tools and boots, scattered everywhere.

"Liar," I blurted, and he straightened up. "You said it was *over.*"

Uncle Matthias's shoulders slumped. "It is, sweetheart," he said, so gently. "For good. You and your sister and father are staying. I'm leaving tonight."

I gripped the sides of the red stool. "You can't." Uncle Matthias was the one who handled the goats, who could tell Papa *come on, let the girls be* without a day of screaming. Who still gave me piggyback rides along the plowed fields, neighing like the horse Papa'd always promised and never bought.

Who still, after Mama died, loved Marthe. Loved me.

"I'm sorry," he said, and pulled out a dusty leather pack. "Your father's the older brother. The older child inherits; that's the way it's always been. His name is on the farm deed, Hal. I don't have a choice."

"He can't make you go!" I argued. My voice swooped and cracked. Uncle Matthias looked down at me, red-eyed, exhausted, and we both knew it was a lie. Tears crept from my eyes: the first drops of a cold winter rain. I buried them against his shoulder. "You *can't*."

"Hallie, sweetheart," he said, and wiped my nose with his worn white handkerchief. "Just sit with me while I sort."

He'd given up. The fight really was over. I nodded, wordless, and he opened his bag.

I watched Uncle Matthias pack as slow as a lullaby. Each seed bag weighed in his palms he fixed in his full, kind attention; each warm sock tucked into the leather pack was another piece of him, vanishing; each shirt left on the smokehouse floor whispered like shed skin. He walked in tighter circles through his scattered worldly goods, and I watched him, my chapped nose buried in white cotton and the smell of his sweat. Both of us just breathing, until the pack was full.

He looked down at his warm winter boots, muttered, "No good," and closed the pack. It sat between us, bulging, full of fights and love and years: a full quarter of my world, wrapped in a slice of old leather.

"Where are you going?" I asked, too small.

The long, lonely road unwound in his eyes. "South. There are good farms in the southlands."

"But then you'll come back, right? When it's better?"

Uncle Matthias winced.

He crouched on his haunches so his serious eyes were level with mine. "Hallie. Love. I need you to take care of your sister, okay? Be good to her; be strong. You're the only sister either of you is ever going to have."

I nodded. I was crying again, crying uselessly, knuckles tight on the stained cotton hanky. Uncle Matthias kissed me gently on the top of my head and picked up the pack. "I love you," he said clearly, and then slipped out through the smokehouse door.

Behind him, through the eaves and flagstones, the endless silence poured in.

The lamps were lit in the kitchen windows when I trudged back to the house. Light shone jaggedly onto the porch. Papa's voice blasted through the orchard trees, shivered the foundations of our house on the hill.

I clenched my fingers around Uncle Matthias's kerchief. *You have to take care of Marthe,* I thought, and opened the kitchen door.

The kitchen was a shambles. Broken crockery gleamed sharp on the floor, tinkled against Marthe's dustpan as her broom went *shush, shush* across the boards. The table was still uncleared: an overturned chair and four places set for the very last time.

"Leave your shoes on, Hal," Marthe said, still the stone-faced mountain she became when Papa thunderstormed about. "I haven't found all the pieces."

I didn't say a word. I didn't have to: Marthe took one look at me and put down the dustpan. "What happened?"

My face twisted. "He's gone."

Her eyes went wide. *"What?"*

"Uncle Matthias—"

I wasn't quiet enough. "And where have you been?" Papa snapped from the next room, and my shoulders hunched high.

Marthe's expression flattened. "She checked the coop for me," she answered, oh so casual. "I thought the latch was loose."

"Well, *close* it next time," he snarled, and just like that, just like always, Marthe shouldered his fury away from me. My smart, strong sister, putting the mountain of her fearlessness as shelter over my head. *Take care of Marthe,* Uncle Matthias had said. It was a ridiculous thing to ask. Marthe was ten years older than me. How would I ever be able to take care of her?

And then it struck me finally why Uncle Matthias, the younger son, had told me to make sure I was good to my sister.

Papa and Uncle Matthias hadn't always hated each other so. And it was Marthe who would one day have Roadstead Farm.

"Hallie?" Marthe said softly. "Talk to me."

I looked up at my sister's troubled face. And for the first time—the first time *ever*—my mouth shaped the lie: "It's nothing."

Her frown crinkled as Papa stormed up the stairs. "Here,"

Marthe whispered with a new reserve, a crack of worry. "Hold the dustpan for me."

I crouched on the floor and gripped it tight. Stared at the floor while Marthe's broom worked its rhythm, *shush shush*, to clean up Papa's mess. Upstairs, his footsteps banged. His bedroom door slammed. The walls hummed with his fury.

It was only the three of us now: Papa and Marthe and me. All alone together.

Be good to your sister, I told myself among the broken dishes. *Don't fight. Be nice. And think hard about what you need in order to survive.*

So that when the day came, when it was over, I'd know what to pack.

AUTUMN

ONE

THE BARLEY WAS IN. THE STUBBLE OF IT LAY BENT-BROKE IN the fields as far as the eye could see, rows of golden soldiers, endlessly falling, from the river to the blacktop road. On a clear evening, with the harvesting done, you could see both river and road from the farmhouse porch: every acre, lined in sunset light, of Roadstead Farm.

So I was the first to see him. Everyone claimed a sighting in the stories that grew up later: a dark man, with a dark walk, striding bravely through the dying grainfields. But it wasn't like that. I was the first to see the stranger when he came to the lakelands, and he stumped up the road like a scarecrow stuffed with stones. Marthe's chimney smoke drifted to meet him, a thin taste of home fires. He caught its scent, his head tilted into the breeze, and hesitated at the weathered signpost where our farm began.

It can't be, I thought, breathless, and then he straightened—and strode up the gravel path to our door.

For a moment I forgot the argument Marthe and I had just had: every vicious thing I'd said to my sister. I leaned forward, fingers wrapped around the porch rail, and squinted at the silhouette ghosting through our fields: The fields Thom and I had planted together before the men marched off to war. The fields I'd harvested alone—and was still working alone, plowing them under for the winter, when I wasn't having pointless, nasty arguments with Marthe over nothing more than a heel of bread.

No, I told myself. *It was about more than the stupid bread.*

It was about . . . everything.

I'd known right away that asking was a mistake. Marthe had been wrestling with the autumn canning since sunrise, as behind on our winter stores as I was on the woodpile, and the second the word *bread* came out of my mouth, her face fell into put-upon fatigue. And suddenly I couldn't bear to hear her tell me for the thousandth time—like I was a slow child and not half owner of Roadstead Farm—"Hallie, I need you to try harder."

One more chore before I could taste a bite of supper, because Thom was gone and the war had killed half our harvest. Because of the November wind outside, the woodpile that wouldn't get us past January, the snarled hole in the chicken coop that let the foxes in. Every time she said it, I could see the disappointment in her eyes: *self-centered, childish, useless Hallie. Hallie, not strong enough.*

"I'm trying, okay?" I pleaded, exhausted, hungry, cold. Marthe stared down at me, sweat-smeared and impatient; no mud on her boots and no sympathy in her eyes. *She doesn't understand,* I realized, and then it hit me: *She doesn't care.*

"It's easy for you to say," I shouted, wild with hurt. "It's not you out there, working yourself dead."

Marthe stiffened. Put down her cheesecloth, slow. She didn't say anything; she didn't have to. She was just in the kitchen working herself dead, seven months round with Thom Clarlund's child. The doorway stood deadly quiet between us, as wide as the wound of Thom's missingness. And then my sister did something she never had in the six years since Papa's funeral: she shut the door in my face.

I stared at that door a full minute before it sank in: *You've finally gone too far.*

It had been eight years since the fight that ended things between Papa and Uncle Matthias; eight years since my uncle went his lonely way. Marthe and I—at this rate we wouldn't even make it to my seventeenth birthday.

But none of that—none of it—mattered if Thom was finally home.

The wind stirred my hair, stirred the edges of that ragged silhouette in the broken barley fields. *Please,* I thought, *be Thom.* Not some man two inches too tall who walked all wrong, who didn't wave to me—

I let myself believe it for thirty delicious seconds before I let the truth in: It wasn't Thom. Just another veteran coming up the road, with a family who was waiting and wouldn't have to wait much longer. Just another stranger.

The man set down his pack five feet from the porch rail, in the soft gravel and dust. He was full-grown, but not long to it: twenty-three or four and long with muscle, his brown forearms three shades paler than Thom ever got. He huddled before me in a red-checked flannel work shirt worn thread-bare, useless against the chill November breeze. My breath puffed out. It was plain what he wanted. He had a soldier's sleevebuttons, and his boots were in ribbons.

"We've nothing to spare," I muttered, too distracted to say it louder. He wasn't Thom, Marthe was still furious, and I was still in trouble. I stared into the dirt at his feet: *Please, please go away.* "You might try the Masons down the road."

He neglected to pick up his pack immediately, turn around, and never be seen again.

Instead, he took off his cap. There was a shock of black hair under it, pulled back in a cattleman's tail. "Thank you," he said, quiet for such a big-shouldered man, "but I'm actually hoping to hire on."

I blinked. The barley was in. Anyone could see that.

"I'm quick with my fingers," he kept on. He had an accent more suited to the wild country northward than our lakeland farmsteads and ruins. "And I don't eat much."

My hands tightened on the rail. "You're come from the war."

The man tucked his chin with a passable country respect.

"You by any chance pass a man on the road, shorter than you by a few inches?" I worked to keep my voice casual. "Twenty-seven, dark skin, brown eyes, name of Thomas Clar-lund?"

The stranger pressed his lips together, a hair's-width, no farther. "I'm afraid I've not passed any travelers in some weeks."

A tiny shudder moved through me, from the rib cage down. I shut my eyes against it: against the empty road and the ruin I'd made of the farm Thom, Marthe, and I had built up together.

"We don't take on help past harvest," I said hollowly. His starved face emptied like a water bucket. All I could see inside it was some black-haired mother or sister pacing behind wood walls, weeks north, her door left unlatched past midnight in case he arrived before dawn. "Look, I can spare some apples. I'll give you apples if you just go home." Frustration beat hollow fists against my temples. *Thom, if you've hired on somewhere—*"Your people don't know if you're alive or dead. You can't *do* that to them."

His smile twisted like a scar. "Don't worry," he said crisply. "No one's waiting for me to turn life normal again."

I flinched. That wasn't why I wanted Thom home. That wasn't it at all.

Something in his eyes flinched back. That anti-smile faltered. "I'm sorry," he said, humbler. "You're being kind and I was just snide."

I blinked. "Kind?" I'd done everything but run him off.

He lifted his chin and regarded me: a girl too sunburned to be pretty and too small to throw him bodily off the kitchen porch. "You looked at *this*"—and he gestured down, from that soft north country accent to tattered shirtsleeves and the reek of sweat—"and saw a man someone might wait for."

I'd done everything *but* run him off. I hadn't run him off. And for that—

No one had ever called me *kind* before.

"So if it's too late for harvest," he finished, oblivious to my surprise, "I'll help however I can."

I bit back the automatic response: *I can do this,* the ugly chorus of every fight Marthe and I ever had, with the ghosts of Papa and Uncle Matthias hovering over our shoulders. *I can run this farm. I can earn my keep if you just give me a little more* time. I *had* to, so Thom had somewhere to come home to. So Marthe and I could laugh again, could build pillow forts under the table like we did when I was young. So we could raise her almost-child together in our own house—a house where everybody knew the younger Hoffmann sister was still half owner of Roadstead Farm.

I looked down across the soft, gray fields, to the thick green of the changeable river that cradled us in its hand. Between them the cherry trees flung their branches stark against the sunset and the goats lay in their paddock, curled around each other to sleep. You could see every speck of Hoffmann land from this spot; on a clear night, you could see all the way to the stars. You could see the half-full woodpile; you could see the broken wagon wheel, sunk in mud, and one stranger, strong and grateful just for shelter—the kind who would just move on to the next town if Roadstead Farm blew away into dust.

If the man in front of me could help this farm work right, things might be good between Marthe and me again — even if he was two inches too tall to be Thom. And then it wouldn't matter if Marthe didn't understand me, because I'd never let her down again.

"You understand we can't pay you," I said.

"Room and board is all I'd ask."

"Right, then." I spun on my heel and stepped into the kitchen.

"I thought I told you to stay outside," Marthe snapped. She was baking bread after all: the air was sweet and dusty with yeast, and the dough sounded, *slap-thump,* against her good block table. *You didn't tell me anything,* I thought at her, smart enough, at least this time, not to say it aloud. We'd lived in the same house for sixteen years. She hadn't had to *tell* me to not dare cross this doorstep until she invited me back in.

My sister turned, and her brown hair slid out of its messy twist. Marthe was pretty, when she wasn't coiled with anger. And Marthe had been throwing grown men off our property since before I could walk. I bit down on a river of resentment, of curdled love. "There's a man wanting hire."

"Barley's done," she said, as if I hadn't noticed.

"He's a veteran," I added, and watched her arms stutter: *slap-trip-thump.*

She untangled her fingers from the dough and peered out the kitchen window. "Not much to look at." I winced. It was true: tall or not, he was thin to the ribs, a scarecrow with a beard like spilled ink and a nose that had definitely been broken.

"He said," I added reluctantly, "he's not passed anyone in weeks."

Marthe's hand grasped air; landed on the stewpot spoon. "What are you saying?"

I bit my lip. My sister was infuriating, condescending, endlessly moody, but — there were our fights and then there was *this*. "I want to take him on," I said, and waited for the storm to break.

Her rounded cheeks paled; her mouth set into a thin, hard line. "Why?" she said finally, too controlled by far.

"For the poultry barn." I swallowed. "With someone else around I could fix it *and* start the malting, and not worry about the woodpile or cleaning the goat pen or the fields, and then I could even *get* to dry-docking the boat and all the chores in town —"

The words ran out. Marthe stared at me with a compressed hurt that was worse than any rage. We'd lived in the same house for sixteen years. She could hear what I really meant: *Because I'm not strong enough to keep this farm* or *this family alive while we pretend Thom's coming home.*

"I thought it might be good," I whispered, "with the baby coming."

Marthe's hand drifted to her belly, dusting the old apron with flour. Unspoken words flitted across her face: linens, lifetimes, rations of small brown eggs, and it all added up to *no, no, no.*

"I know we can't pay him," I said quickly. "He just wants a place to be overwinter. Marthe, I have to. He's barely got boots."

"Charity, then?" she said, surprised: a flicker of the sister I knew—who saw me, who cared about me. Who still, sometimes, smiled.

It's just he said, I thought wonderingly, *that I was kind.* "It'd get us through the winter," I said. "And I'd want someone to, if it was—"

Marthe threw the wooden spoon clean across the kitchen. It clattered against the crockery shelf, smacked a blue clay mug, and rattled, dishes ringing, to the floor. The mug wobbled. I didn't dare steady it. Marthe's damp hair curtained down her cheek, over sheer, gutshot pain.

I swallowed.

Marthe stared at the spoon. Her right hand worked, and then she scrubbed it across her face as if she was very tired. "Put a pallet in the old smokehouse. At least with the stove he won't freeze," she said, and bowed her head over the squashed bread.

"All right," I whispered, through the sudden roar of my own heartbeat. I shoved shaking hands into my pockets and went back outside.

The soldier stood at attention five feet off the porch, as wary of the line between the house's shadow and the sun as I was of Marthe's kitchen doorway. He didn't even twitch: better at keeping a plain face, plain hands than I would ever be.

"You're to have a pallet in the smokehouse," I forced out. In a soot-stained junkyard we'd meant to clean out for six years. "My sister will give you spare linens." My hands were still trembling. I'd won the argument, but Marthe's grief, Marthe's *frustration*—

This didn't feel like winning.

"It's her farm?"

"Ours." Papa's snarl peaked, banked, and faded. "Our father willed it to the both of us."

If he was surprised, he feigned well enough; he nodded and shouldered his brown leather pack. "Thank you, miss."

"It's Hallie," I said. "My sister's Marthe. From Roadstead Farm, in the lakelands."

"Heron," he offered, and tilted his head with something finer, deeper than lakeland manners.

"Heron, from the war," I said bitterly.

His lips pressed shut for a moment. "From the war," he agreed.

"So," I asked, "did you see it?"

No reason to say what *it* was. The war was won when John Balsam, a man simple and small, lifted his dagger and cut out the Wicked God Southward's dark heart. Tyler Blakely had carried the tale home three weeks past midsummer, limping on a leg once hale and thick, his eyes blasted pale with the sight of it. We'd already realized a change, though, here on the river: Birds not known on the riverbanks since Opa's generation washed up dead and open-mouthed each sunrise. The stars rumbled nightly, too low and regular for thunder. Greta Chaudhry's hives failed, and Berkhardt Mason's orchards. By the time the Twisted Things staggered, wounded, through our fields, we couldn't tell if the war was won or lost. Half our crops had burned at the touch of their acrid wings: a whole winter's provisions gone up in noise and smoke. We shoveled their bodies into bonfires by night and prayed, among the cinders, for news.

We didn't know what it meant, then. Those three weeks, we held our breaths.

"I didn't see it," my new hired man said softly, and closed his hand around his satchel strap. "I turned my face away."

I opened my mouth. Shut it. I hadn't expected a real answer, and now I didn't know *what* to say. Not one lakelands man who went to battle with the Wicked God Southward would speak a word about how he fell, but they all saw it. You could tell it from their eyes: newly guarded, and dark as pits. They all *saw*.

The stranger's own eyes had abruptly lost their kindness. They shuttered, chilly as river ice. They made me feel young, and ignorant, and small.

"I'll show you where you're bunking," I said, unsettled, and wrapped my fingers in the dusty flannel of my shirtsleeve. There was more to a farm than a kindly face, and you still didn't shake with hired men.

TWO

HE CHOPPED WOOD FOR A WEEK. HE SAID *PLEASE,* AND *thank you,* and fixed our rotting fences.

No one shouted for seven days, but I never stopped expecting it: when thunder kicked me awake on the eighth day, it almost felt like coming home.

My bedroom window clattered in its frame, loud enough to scruff me out of sleep. Half awake, I caught my breath and held it; closed my eyes tighter and listened for the inevitable nightmare steps. If I pretended to sleep, maybe it would be all right: maybe his furious muttered swears, his heavy boots would pass my closed door by—

I swallowed hard. I was sixteen, not six, and my father was dead.

A bird called, harsh and frightened, and I dared open my eyes. Dawn light pried through my thick-paned window. The sky above it was as blue and fine as my faded bedroom walls. The thunder rattled weaker, wet leaves on glass. My heart wouldn't stop its frightened stutter. "He's *dead*," I muttered sternly, padded across the green rag rug and opened the window.

The yard stretched before me, brown and empty; the air smelled of woodsmoke and frost. I shoved my head into the chilly dawn outside, and the bare branches of trees, the barns, the gray river unscrolled sleepily into the sky. From below, from the leaf-clogged gutters, something let out a whimpered *cheep*. I reached down —

— and a small shape exploded in a fury of wings.

I shrieked.

It staggered and shrieked right back at me, a harsh, uncertain caw. Battered brown wings struggled for purchase on the sill; tiny claws scrabbled closer. I grabbed the window handles and jerked them down between us. The thin cry muffled as wood and glass slammed down — and then it rose to a scream. A dark smear fluttered between the thick panes and the white sill: *the wing*. It was nothing more than a stunned bird, and I'd just crushed its wing.

"Oh," I breathed, and brushed river stones and hair clips messily off the sill. Bile stung my throat: *You've killed it. It can't even fight back.* I shoved the window upward fast, hands clutched under the bottom frame.

The wing slapped my hand so hard that *everything* stopped.

"*Ow!*" I cradled the hand close to my chest. Furious, ragged squawks trailed me back into the bedroom. "Sorry," I whispered over and over, an exhausted litany of *sorry* that beat in time with my throbbing hand. The wing had left a red spot, as red as a bug-bite burn. I brushed it with idle fingernails.

They caught on something, hard.

The thinnest edge of a cobweb was growing out of my left hand. It seared my window frame brown where it stuck, and the line it burned led straight to the bird's desperate talons. I'd been too rattled, too guilty to see it: those eight black sparrow-nails were sticky-coated with web.

It wasn't a bird. It was a Twisted Thing — one of the Wicked God Southward's pet monsters.

"Not possible," I whispered to myself, and Papa's mocking ghost sneered *not possible* back. We were supposed to have seen the last of them. John Balsam, by magic, skill, or cunning, had killed the Wicked God and the world had ripped itself shut again; we'd burned the dead Twisted Things that had fallen from the sky. We'd grieved our tomatoes, our chicken hutches, our fields, and watched the real birds migrate south with the weather, into the newly gap-toothed constellations. The Twisted Things were supposed to be over, just like the Wicked God who made them. Just like the war.

The burn on my hand throbbed, red as a stove coal and condescending as Papa could ever be: *Well, explain this, then.* I scrubbed it hard on the paisley curtain. Outside, a wisp of sour black smoke rose from the Twisted Thing's acid feathers. *It'll burn down the house,* I thought, sharp as snow, and slammed the window down on its body — three terrible bangs.

The thick bottom pane of my window misted and cracked.

The brown wing flopped uselessly against the frame, and there was silence.

I unclenched my teeth and peeked through the clouded pane.

The Twisted Thing lay crumpled against the sill, its tiny chest wreathed in smoke. It was impossible to mistake for anything real now: Its hooked black beak threw sparks against the old glass; its body stank of ash and dead violets. Four eyes stared sightless back at me, spider-round and white, nestled in feathers that wilted at the very touch of air. *It's dying*, I realized, with a pang of shame. *It'll be dead soon.*

I grabbed the wooden comb off my dressing table. You had to burn Twisted Things: they rotted the stones off their own graves overnight. I cracked the window wide and nudged it gingerly with the comb, but there was no reaction left in the Twisted Thing—just a pause in the beat of its downy chest and a weak *caw*. A plea.

"Sorry," I whispered, one last time, and shoved it to the brown grass below.

The dawn breeze ruffled the feathers on its body and coaxed goose bumps from my bare arms. The sweat on my nightgown had chilled into ice.

The burnt-out imprint of the Twisted Thing's body smoked on the sill before me: a craned, tortured neck, sketched in ancient wood and brick. A pair of violent, outstretched wings.

Kitchen. Get a coal, I thought, quick and shaky, and reached blindly for my trousers.

Marthe was already dressed when I clattered down the stairs, my hands scraped raw with scrubbing. She'd been milking; our thick glass milk bottles stood on the kitchen counter, stained weirdly by the rising light. The sunlight wrapped her so privately, so *normally* that I almost expected her to turn, smile *good morning,* and slop extra cream into my tea like she would when I was small. The kitchen doorway stood, impassable: a portal back to the years when she was my protector, my best friend, my world. I couldn't bear to move. The slightest rustle could destroy that spell.

Marthe didn't say good morning. She didn't even turn her head.

Time snapped back into place. I was sixteen years old, not six, and my sister was nothing, anymore, but angry. "Marthe," I started, and crossed that unmagical threshold.

She looked up with red-blotched eyes, and my stomach did a flip. She'd been crying onto the counter, head turned to keep the tears out of the milk pail. "Marthe, can I—" I started, softer.

She cut me off with a jerk of her rounded chin. "That's your breakfast and the hired man's. Take it out to the fields when you go."

No, I translated. *Whatever it is, you can't.*

I closed my hands tight. The left one itched and burned. "I need a hot coal," I said, smaller now, and Marthe raised one thick eyebrow. "There was a bird. Not a real one, a Twisted

Thing." The runnel of milk from pail to bottle slowed. "It's dead."

Marthe set the pail down. "Just the one?"

"I only saw one." My voice quivered at the memory of the window slamming, slamming in my hands. "It landed on my windowsill."

Marthe finally met my eye with a cool, clear determination: her version of panic. "We'll check the barns," she said, wiping milk and sweat off her hands. "Rake the garden. Sweep the dock." I sucked in a breath. I could almost hear the crack of dying seeds; taste rot and burnt feathers from the midsummer fires.

Marthe's hands stilled on her towel. "You've got it?" Asked like that protective sister of old would have: *Do you want me to handle it?*

I bit down on the urge to hug her and sob 'til I couldn't breathe. "I can do it myself," I managed. I was a youngest child, and part owner of Roadstead Farm. Not handling it was an indulgence I could no longer afford.

The gentleness in Marthe's face went stiff. "I'll lay a fire in the yard," she said, and turned back to the milk.

I grabbed our meager breakfast and fled.

The tea was weak but still warm: one mug for me and one for quiet, unobtrusive Heron. Their heat blanketed my fingers as I rushed out into the morning, into a plume of my own exhaled breath. Roadstead Farm by dawnlight was all soft blues and grays, the crisp smell of autumn soil and the foggy calls of geese southbound on the river. The mugs steamed as I hurried, head down, across the farmyard, scanning for gray-bleached soil; for places where the rakes would bring up ruin-seeds and bone.

Inside a week, Heron had made the smokehouse barely recognizable. He'd scrubbed a circle of flagstones clean and laid out his stranger's things as tidy as a barracks inspection. I counted a cookpot, plate, and canteen; a stack of half-mended clothing that looked three sizes too big. His straw pallet was made neater than I ever kept my bed, its corners sharp and tight. He'd made more progress with the place in one week than Thom and I had in two summers.

He wanted to, my head countered dryly. I gulped down a yearning to *fix* the smokehouse: to put back the junk and curled cobwebs and settle safe under my table, among the knickknacks and dust.

"Good morning, miss," Heron said, and blocked my view with his own long bulk. "More carpentry today?"

"Morning," I answered, and shoved his breakfast at him. "We've got to eat quick. There's a Twisted Thing dead in the garden."

His face blinked into wary blankness—everything except for those sharp gray eyes. "A Twisted Thing?"

"The Wicked God's creatures." I squinted up at him. "You said you were in the war."

Heron's hands tightened around the mug until his brown knuckles pulled smooth. "We called them something different there," he said, and looked away. His fingers didn't lie right about our good Windstown pottery. They'd been broken too, in jagged, twisting lines.

Fingers broken, I realized with a shiver, *more than once.*

I tore my eyes away from that jigsaw hand. "Hurry up. It'll scorch the soil dead," I said, and took off down the smokehouse steps.

The burn mark lay right beneath my bedroom window, a small, seared shape in the deep brown soil of Marthe's vegetable plot. I traced its outline with my metal rake: a pair of outstretched wings rucked and hilled where we'd grown the snap peas.

It was hard to ignore the bit where the outline was empty.

"It was right here," I argued to nobody, and hugged the long rake handle.

Heron's rake parted the browning grass stalks like hair. "You're sure it was dead, miss?"

"It's dead," I snapped back; glared it into being true. "It had a broken wing. It couldn't halfway breathe."

Heron shaded his eyes and scanned the sun-drenched grass. "Well, it can't be far," he started, and then my morning went from bad to worse.

Marthe came around the corner, her arms speckled with sawdust, and asked, "So, do you have it?"

"We'll send for the Blakelys," Marthe said. "It can't have got off the property with a broken wing." Her hand rubbed slow circles across her belly, soothing herself or the child squirm-ing inside. What she did when she was nervous, now. I'd some-how liked it better when she'd just bit her fingernails.

Heron nodded. He had no idea how to read the words beneath Marthe's words. Roadstead Farm was fifty acres, half of it unfarmed wilderness.

The Twisted Thing could be anywhere.

I dropped the rake into the dirt. "I'll get my coat."

"*You* won't," Marthe corrected, and eyed Heron, stand-ing haphazardly at attention with a rake two feet too short for him. "Lakewood Farm's half a mile up the old road: the white-painted house with blue trim. Just tell James or Eglan-tine Blakely what's happened. That we need to cover ground."

I swallowed. She was angry at me for losing track of it. She had to be, if she wouldn't even let me make good.

Heron set his rake against the redbrick wall. "I'll be as quick as I can, ma'am."

He took off at an easy, swinging walk, one that didn't get quicker as he met the path toward the old highway. Mar-the watched him go with grave, sober eyes. "That man's been walking a long time."

She sounded tired. She sounded . . . infinitely sad. I stared, bewildered, and she pointed at the road with her softening chin. Heron was not much more than a detail upon it, another pine made tiny by distance, waving in the breeze. "Look at that: he'll go only so fast as a walk."

"I'd have run," I said, resentful.

"Exactly," Marthe said softly. "You don't set your pace that steady if you think you'll ever get to stop walking."

She's telling me something, I realized. Something important about her and me and winter, and everything that *wasn't* what time Heron would arrive at Lakewood Farm. Marthe waited, expectant, and my mouth emptied of every profound word. I had no idea what she meant. I had no idea what she wanted from me.

Why can't we just talk, *like we used to?* I thought, and turned away too fast to hide the sudden tears in my eyes: to the farm buildings and the orchard beyond them. Once, we'd talked all the time: in gestures, in whispers, in messages written in river stones and hidden by the apple orchard when Papa's rages made it too dangerous to speak. Away from her, the sky was cloudless and cold, perfect weather for turning a field among the last of the red autumn leaves.

I'd imagined a thousand ways I might lose Roadstead Farm. But they always ended with the road south, a backpack, and a home I could never again have. None of my doomed futures had held a missing Twisted Thing and seas of endless, spreading gray dust.

I fumbled the rake into my hands, fumbled for words. "Marthe, what do I do?"

Her expectation dissolved into pure exhaustion. "There's chores," she said sharply, and rounded the corner without another word.

I stared after her, mouth open. If I chased her, there'd be a fight: *Clueless, self-centered, childish, useless Hallie.* If I demanded she just *explain* what she'd meant, in plain language, we'd go at it all morning, and—

There were chores.

I picked up the water buckets from the kitchen porch. The sun was well into the sky, and the malt was two weeks late. Maybe if I filled the cistern, hauling water 'til my hands ached, I could forget how to think until the Blakelys arrived to save us.

THREE

CHORES.

I flung the bucket into the well and hauled it up with blistering fingers. I'd forgotten one thing about forgetting how to think: how hard that is to do when you are alone inside your head. I fought the urge to jump every time the grass trembled; every birdcall raised shivers on the back of my neck. And my head kept *circling* on all the things I should have said, devastating comebacks and perfect replies to Marthe's disappointed face that came so easily now that she wasn't here.

Chores, I thought viciously. *Of course, Marthe.*

The ache in my left hand beat a cranky pulse as I hauled the bucket to the malthouse. The cistern beside it glowed dully in the sunlight. It was built of scavenged tin and Papa's erratic ingenuity, connected with ancient piping from before the old cities fell. Papa had been tall, and it had never been his way to think too hard about others: I had to hoist the bucket shoulder-high to pour. My hand twinged under its weight, the burn stretching wide. I gritted my teeth and braced the bucket higher.

Pain hissed through my nerves like a riled snake.

It only touched me for a second, I thought, and gingerly poked my throbbing hand. It was redder than the worst sunburn I'd ever had, violent red, tender under my fingers. Holding a Twisted Thing was suicide: they'd rusted the metal teeth off our rakes. But one touch wasn't supposed to lame you. Lots of people had been *touched.*

"Come *on,*" I muttered blackly, and shook my wrist. I had to work. Marthe was already angry at me. I lifted the bucket, and my hand tingled, ached—and quit.

All my rage—at Marthe, at that stupid Twisted Thing, at Thom's absence and my useless hand—crawled up my throat and *boiled.* "*Damn!*" I reared back and kicked the tin bucket clear off the steps.

Suddenly there was water everywhere—on the steps, on my shirt—and metal ringing like a bell. The bucket hit the dead grass with a thud and rolled smugly into the dirt. *There's that Hoffmann temper,* Papa's voice rumbled approvingly, and I shuddered. "Damn."

Distant, a chorus of raised voices answered back.

I'm the only one who gets to shout around here, I thought sourly, but I knew those quick, squabbling voices. The anxious pecking in my chest blurred into blinding hope: the Blakelys. Nat was here.

I clattered down the malthouse steps and raced around the corner, and there they were: Nat's whole family tumbling off their wagon, work shirts and sheep-stink and clean hair and limbs. Her uncle Callum unloaded rakes and their shepherd's crook, and two of the Blakely sheepdogs, Joy and Kelsey, circled the wheels, jumping and snuffling the leaf-sharp air. We'd sent for the Blakelys, and we'd got them: everyone except the sheep.

"Oh, my poor Hallie. We got here as soon as we could," Mrs. Blakely said, and came off the wagon in a flurry of skirts.

I dropped an awkward curtsy in my stained work pants. "Mrs. Blakely," I said. "James. Callum."

Heron perched atop the wagon like a river buoy that'd tangled with too big a thunderstorm, his long elbows and knees crammed together between the tools and James Blakely's broad back. He straightened haphazardly—"Miss Hallie?"—and in the blur of motion, someone stopped.

Nat, her hands full of housedress and her hair flecked with straw.

Nat I couldn't curtsy to; she wrapped her arms around me tight enough to push the air out of my lungs. We'd stuck closer before this summer. She'd been trapped with the sheep on Lakewood Farm just as surely as I was tied to Roadstead, and the end of the war hadn't changed that. Her two uncles had come back aged five years in a summer, her brother Tyler wounded for life. But her father hadn't come back at all. There was a vial of ashes on the Blakely mantel now: the John's Creek ash the regiment gave for every broken body they'd been unable to bring home. The family had held a service, and made a stone. And I hadn't seen Nat since.

She looked different: same careless red hair, same brown-greenish eyes always watching much too sharply for anyone's own good, but she was — not skinny, but *lean* now, lean down to her shoes.

She sized me up in the same way, half baffled at the change in me, at the seams between strange and familiar. *What do I look like now?* I thought suddenly, but then she laughed a little, and the shake and shudder in my chest eased. *It's Nat*, I thought joyfully. *She's still my Nat.*

I looked up when she loosed my arms, and fidgeting beside the cart, not just lean but outright gaunt, was Tyler Blakely.

"Ty," I said, and Nat's older brother took my hand and squeezed it. He was tanned and hair-combed, and nearly swimming in his best shirt: clean linen, all the fresh starch in the world not enough to keep it from slopping above his belt. His buttons were different — not wood, but cool-sheened smoothnesses rough-cut about the edges and ridged like fallen trees. His army buttons, engraved with John Balsam's sigil: the crest the Great Army had, once their hero vanished, made in his name. Nat might have been the same as she ever was, deep down, but Tyler Blakely was back from the war.

"It's good to see you," I managed through all the awkwardness in the world. We hadn't spoken since the funeral, since Marthe and I swept too quickly past the chair his injured leg confined him to, his head down, bristling *leave me alone.* I squeezed his hand. It had never before felt so tenuous in mine.

"It's good to see you too," he said, and his gaze stuttered and dropped, enough to hide his white eyes — and the shreds of hazel left to them. Tyler had looked upon the Wicked God dying, and five green-ringed blotches, as irregular as ink spots, were all that were left of his normal eyes. The rest was white to the pupil, white as the Twisted Thing's spider gaze.

I tried to pull up a smile for him and failed in the glare of that twisted hip, those broken eyes. His fingers slid cool against my palm and pulled away. Tyler, looking for the familiar in me, just like Nat — just like we all were, rattled and odd.

"And how are you, Miss Halfrida?" James Blakely said mildly. His smile, courteous as ever, pulled at the half-healed, dotted wounds that covered him cheek to shoulder. The shallowest cuts had already scarred, a sick pink that pulled his cheek into strange angles. Those wounds stared every problem I had down into the gutter. He didn't need to hear me whine about my stupid bucket.

"Fine," I said faintly. His husband, Callum, shook his head once, resigned.

Color bloomed around the smooth pink scars. "Well, we're ready to beat the bushes," James pressed on. "Show us where you saw it?"

Marthe had heard the Blakelys' racket. She was waiting on the kitchen porch, wrapped in her thick wool jacket. Warmth spilled out of the kitchen window behind her: not just the oven running hot, but a kettle on the stove set to boil.

"Chores?" I hissed into her ear.

"We can't ask someone's help and give them nothing in return," she whispered crisply, and her face opened up into warmth and worry as Eglantine Blakely rushed up the steps.

"Marthe," Mrs. Blakely said, and kidnapped both her hands. Mrs. Blakely had made a practice of being totally overbearing since the moment our mother was buried, and she felt that practice made perfect. "Brave girl. Don't you worry; we'll get to the bottom of this."

"You're very kind," Marthe said, and Mrs. Blakely poohpoohed it, and I scowled behind my hair at both of them. Of course Marthe was warm gratitude and manners now that company was here. Of course that cutting voice was kept only for me.

I turned away to where Cal Blakely squatted beside the burn mark. "No tracks around this, hey? Just the one mark in the dirt."

Nat frowned. "It didn't struggle."

"Or walk. Or fly." Cal's long finger hovered over the seared soil and the normal, rich brown that outlined it. "Either it was lifted or it just disappeared."

James's frown pulled his scars into whole different constellations. "Right. We pair off and comb out, from here to the fencelines. Marthe, you're with me. Cal, Eglantine, take the field road."

Mrs. Blakely cast a quick, involuntary glance at Tyler. No: at Tyler's bad leg. "James, I should—"

"Good. We'll go down to the river," Nat cut in, shuffling

behind Tyler so it was clear who *we* meant. Tyler's shoulders went rigid. Their mother's eyes narrowed as she took Callum's arm — and the look he sent Nat, over Eglantine's head, absolutely brimmed with complicity. *Not my regular Nat after all, then,* I thought with a shard of despair. There had never been this many secret alliances in the Blakely house, or such an edge to their bickering.

"Hallie, you'll come with us?" Tyler asked tightly.

"Yeah," I said without thinking, and looked up — right at Heron. He trailed the search party, dust on his tattered boots, behind even the nervous, whining dogs. He watched the small crowd of Blakelys as if they were a reflection from another world. *He called me kind,* I remembered guiltily, *and we just shut him out.*

"Heron too," I said firmly, so they'd all hear it. "It'll go faster with four."

Heron blinked, and fled instantly into that sheeting, blank expression.

Tyler's face fell, fractionally. "Fine," he said, and limped hurriedly down the path with Nat striding at his heels. Mrs. Blakely stared at her children's backs, all her fussing and mothering snuffed out. The hole it left behind filled slowly with a desolate pain.

"We'll find it," I stuttered, and rushed off after them.

Heron was behind me, though I could hardly tell. He carried the distance between us, five feet back and steady, like the borders of a whole universe. *This is what the open roads do to you,* I told myself, and thought of Uncle Matthias and the half-packed bag I kept in the smokehouse. Even when I was ten years old and grieving, I'd never been that alone.

Nat's garden rake scraped the roots and dirt clods; Tyler's bad leg dragged an uneven counterpoint beside her. No one spoke as we slipped around the goat pen, eyes scanning the soil, and gained the orchard trees. The branches hung still and naked above us and fallen fruit oozed under our boots, over the crannies where Marthe and I used to write. Ahead, the ever-present rustle of the river rose and rumbled louder.

Tyler squinted through the dust and the orchard trees — and his white-stained eyes narrowed. He leaned forward, just as focused as Joy hunting rabbits, and unease shuddered through my belly. Tyler was looking *at* something.

The thing was, there was nothing there.

"What is it?" I asked, a fat pebble thrown into that silence. He startled, but didn't turn.

"I don't know yet," he said, and hobbled faster toward the river.

"Ty, slow down," Nat said — Nat, who *never* got nervous, scrambling right on his heels but not one step farther. *She doesn't want to get ahead of him,* I realized. *It'll remind him he can't run anymore.* She looked back at me, her lower lip bit hard between her teeth, and I shrugged helplessly. Heron paced sentry behind us, blank as new-laid snow.

"Come *on*," Tyler snapped, and we hurried through the last dregs of orchard shade, down the steep, stony hill that led to the river.

The path faded into shoreline: a breath of weedy water, the crunch of shoreline stones, and our lonely dock, stretched out into the gray river ahead. At the end of it, our two-seater rowboat huddled empty in the current, nuzzling the ancient concrete piles: our only way to Windstown or Bellisle now, what with our wagon's back wheel broken for good. "Well, the boat's still here," I said into the strained silence.

Nobody answered. They were watching Tyler pace.

Bent awkward at the waist, he followed a looping, invisible trail, his shepherd's crook planted between the stones for balance. "Ty, what're you looking at?" I asked carefully. I wasn't seeing much: rocks, sand, weeds. The debris of coming winter on the shore.

There was no answer. Tyler Blakely stared past me, down to the river, one hand on his short shearing knife — and his eyes went wide.

Nat flung her hands into the air. "Tyler, for God's sake, cut the drama out. *What?*"

"There," he said darkly, and pointed far down the beach. "There's the bastard."

He curses now, I thought, inappropriately, before the next thought overtook it.

I was wrong: Tyler Blakely could still run.

Shuffling and lopsided, he dashed down the beach, slipping

on slick stones, his waist twisting to keep him upright. *"God!"* Nat shouted, and sprinted after him, her arms flailing against the blue sky. I took off after them, my long rake ready across my chest. The rocks bumped and bruised as I drove myself along the riverbank, a sick lump hardening in my belly.

Tyler stuttered to a stop just before the river curved, his unearthly eyes flaring. He sagged and lowered his knife.

I dropped the rake to my knees and bent double after it. My lungs burned. The ache in my hand burned. Nat pattered to a stop ahead of me, her face blotched red with fury. "I'm *trying* to keep Mum off your back, okay? Do you have to act so *insane*—"

Tyler wasn't listening. He paced a circle around the featureless rocks, his knife held low and mean. His chest heaved just as hard as mine—mine, which couldn't hold a breath. I coughed, and black spots swam in the corners of my eyes. *What on earth,* I thought in fragments. I'd run that fast and more. I'd run longer without breaking a sweat. The choke under my ribs hardened, grew tight. I coughed helplessly, and the tightness ripped, and tore—

And then there were hands at my elbows, pulling me back mere inches across some invisible border where my lungs became whole again: Heron's hands. The unfamiliar sourness of his sweat clogged my nostrils. "Miss Hallie, you all right?"

"Out of breath," I said, and leaned elbows-to-knees forward, my field rake loose in both hands. The line of it swam before my eyes. "The Twisted Thing's there, isn't it?"

The crease between Heron's eyebrows deepened. "It is."

The tearing feeling was fading. I coughed into my pant legs again and straightened. "Let me see?"

The tumble of brown wings hid beneath a cairn of what had once been rocks. The touch of the Twisted Thing had worn the rocks, in hours, to gravel. Its feathers peeked up now, unearthed again, from the dirt of a troubled grave.

I brushed the crumbled rocks aside and the body of the malformed sparrow emerged, broken-winged, web-tangled. Its good wing and breast were bloodily marked by a small, delicate, familiar mouth. My hands curled into useless fists. "*Stupid* cats."

"Of course," Nat said sourly, and kicked the sand.

Heron's black brows rose. "What do you mean, cats?"

"We have a family of them in the barn. Marthe's pets," I said, and shook my head. "And *that* is one of them being too damned lazy to mouse and just picking up a Twisted Thing for its supper." Lucky for them there was no way to know which one was responsible. I'd have flung it into the river and let it swim its way out.

Heron eased around us and crouched over the Twisted Thing. "I'll dispose of this," he said, and tipped Tyler one of those nods that passed between grown men. "Good eye, there."

Tyler ducked his chin and shrugged, uncomfortable, the knife loose in his hand. His color was coming back, sun-brown instead of pale, but he still looked like he'd watched his house burn down and been fed the ashes.

I glanced between him and his fuming, frightened sister. My stomach churned with adrenaline; my arms were absolutely freezing. "We'll catch up," I said, and rocked back on my heels. All the fear and rage that had kept me going were drained dry. I had to sit. I had to *breathe*.

"Miss," Heron said, with that automatic dip of his chin, and lifted the Twisted Thing onto his rake. It settled between the tines, light and lifeless. He held it out before him, as far away as he could, and started back to the house.

The rocks where it had lain crumbled into gray-stained sand. The wind rose—*the air's moving again,* I thought; I hadn't even realized how still the shore had been—and dust curtained down the beach. I leaned away from the gray flecks, my hand outstretched to the rocks to counterbalance.

My left hand. My burned hand.

Pain shot up my palm and fingers, lingering in each knuckle. I peeked down at the redness below my sleeve. The burn had settled into a solid lump, hot under the skin, concealed in the shadow of my own shirtsleeve. I tilted the hand into better light. It wasn't a shadow. The burn had spread in long, streaky lines, and the lump at its center was a purply black.

"What's that?" Nat asked. I covered the burn with my palm, but personal space had never stopped Nat Blakely. She lifted my right hand off my left and held the wound up to the light.

I flinched a little at the pressure, but even the touch of

another person's skin felt amazingly cool. "The Twisted Thing touched me," I said, and behind her, Tyler's breath hissed out through his teeth.

"It *what?*" Nat said.

Her fingers dug into my swollen flesh, and everything went bright white.

FOUR

COLD, WAS MY FIRST THOUGHT, AND IT CAME WRAPPED IN soft irritation. The sand beneath my head was cold. Rocks dug into my back, through my flannel work shirt, and they were freezing.

Because I'm on my back, I realized, and a worse chill shuddered through me. I was on the shore, flat on my back, my ears roaring louder than the river. I opened my eyes and the world unfolded above me, an empty stretch of blinding sky blue. My left hand felt twice its normal size. My left hand felt like fire.

I twitched, and the blue was split by Nat Blakely, her mouth a little open, braid swinging like a well rope. "Hallie?" she said in a high, tight voice that wasn't my unflappable Nat. "I'm sorry. I'm so sorry."

"Mm," I mumbled, and wet my lips. They tasted like I'd licked a shovel. I'd passed out. I'd never passed out before in my life.

I lifted my head off the stiff, damp sand, and the roar in my ears became a waterfall. "No, wait," Nat said. Delicate hands lifted my arm below the elbow, and I shuddered.

"When did it touch you?" Tyler's voice floated somewhere outside the cloudless edges of the world.

"This morning," I said, and Nat's eyebrows flinched together. The fingers paused a long second on my arm. "It hit me with its wing when I slammed —" I swallowed. That crunch of wings breaking; that was Papa's way, too. The Twisted Thing hit me, and I'd hit back *hard*.

"I didn't mean to," I finished weakly, and rested my cheek on the sand.

Tyler's fingers braced my wrist, tracing the edges of the burn. "It's fevered," he said, and set the arm down atop my belly. A sickly-sweet odor rose up from the wound: rot, and old violets. "We have to get back to the house."

His face was strained and ancient, all sharp-shadowed hollows. *You came back old,* I thought, and lost the thought's sleek tail. I *was* feverish. Every idea I dredged up scattered like a flock of birds.

"How?" Nat shot back. "I can't get her back to the house *and* find Marthe —"

"No Marthe," I mumbled from the world of birds and blue. She'd put her hand on her belly and pace, and I'd have upset her one more time.

"We don't need Marthe," Tyler said urgently. "I did this in the field, twice. Just get me bandages and hot water."

Nat's head came up. "There are bandages in the smoke-house."

"Why in *there*?"

Because it's dangerous on the road south, I thought, and looked away. Nat's mouth crimped above me. Nat was the only living soul who knew about that packed bag, and she'd sworn in blood not to say a word.

"There's strong alcohol, too," she said blithely, and stood. "That's better than water. Help me get her on her feet."

"I still need to boil the knife."

"What do you mean, *knife?*" I said, and struggled upright. The ground tilted like a sinking boat, and Nat's arms caught me. Her touch traveled all the way down my bicep, down into the misery that was my wrist. Pain shot straight to my sour stomach.

"I'm going to throw up," I said distinctly.

"Okay," Ty replied, as calm as houses, and gathered my hair off my face.

My breakfast tasted worse coming back up. I retched, aching, onto the riverside stones, and Nat paced a circle in the sand while I coughed, my shoulders hunched, spitting bile and tea. *This is bad,* surfaced in the whirl where my head used to be. *I'm making her scared.*

"Ready?" Tyler asked, and I nodded tinily. He cleared every strand of my hair from his fingers and stood.

Nat stared at me helplessly for a second, fists clenched. And then her jaw set, and she crouched down beside me. "I'm lifting you up now," she said, and slid both arms under my own. She hauled me onto her shoulder silently, her wool carder's muscles holding me straight.

"I'm sorry," I said. It sounded too young: scared and small.

"Don't be. You're lighter than my brother," she said grimly, and her arm tightened about my waist as we dragged up the path to the smokehouse.

The smokehouse door had no latch. There'd never been a reason to bother. Before Heron and his privacy, there'd been nothing of value there for anyone but me, and I'd secreted those things away. Tyler pushed the door open with a *pop*, and Nat hauled me inside.

"Sit," she said roughly, and sped off into the maze of chairs and boxes, coughing: my stumbles had kicked the dust into gnatlike clouds. I sat. Everything was predawn dark inside, the gloom of rubbed-smooth memories and too many blurred nights.

Tyler turned a circle in Heron's scrubbed flagstones. "What is all this stuff?"

I ran my gaze over Oma's ancient spinning wheel, the legless kitchen chair beside it, full heaps and boxes of wax meltings never recast into candles. Uncle Matthias's ghost moved among them always, lifting each shard of our family tree and weighing it for the pack in his left hand. "Just stuff," I said. "Stuff that's broken."

Tyler cast his eyes through the dim-lit peaks and valleys. "That's not broken," he said, crouching beside a leather pack slumped against the stonework.

My breath caught. I knew its contents by heart: a bar of homemade soap, a bedroll, a striker for campfires, a bottle for water, and a pan to heat it up. Space left, on top, for four changes of clothes that would be good in all weather, and strong winter boots. And bandages, because the road south was dangerous and long.

"That's Heron's," I lied quickly, and Tyler pulled back his hand. I leaned my aching head against the red velvet stool and sighed.

Nat swore under her breath and twisted out through the narrow debris trails. "Found it," she said, slammed the bandages down, and swept Heron's cookpot aside. It clattered into the wall, and I made a small noise of protest.

"I'll clean it up later," she sighed, and unwrapped cotton strips from around the alcohol flask.

Tyler slopped alcohol on the edge of his shearing knife. The fumes scorched my parched throat and I coughed, my gaze hooked on his short, sharp blade. There was no light in the smokehouse past the edge of sun creeping around the doorstep, but that knife shimmered like fresh water.

"I hope you know what you're doing," Nat said.

Tyler stiffened. His good shirt was soaked down the back with nervous sweat. "Cross my heart, Hal," he said quietly, and looked down at me through mussed, sweaty hair. "Let me see your hand?"

I untangled it from my shirtsleeve and held it out, trembling. Nat caught my left wrist much more carefully than before and pinned it precisely, fingers spread apart, on the cool flagstones. Her free hand laced through the loose fingers of my right hand. "Squeeze if it hurts," she said shortly. Papa's voice rose, a furious echo, behind it. That knife hovered over my tendons, close as his sour breath in my face, bleeding violence onto my skin. My throat went dry as fireplace sparks.

"They're your friends," I told myself, breath hitched, arms shaking.

"Yeah, we are," Tyler said, and pressed the tip of the blade to my skin. I shut my eyes.

The knife, coldly burning, dug into my swollen hand.

It wasn't a knife; it was a live coal. It seared through my hand and exploded in my head, shaking all the little birds of my thoughts into nothingness. Pain kindled orange behind my eyes. I gasped, and my squeeze around Nat's fingers tightened into a death grip.

Be brave, I thought raggedly. *Be brave. Don't make a sound.* Tyler turned the knife, and all my courage drowned in the flood.

I yanked my hand away, but Tyler's palm held it firm; Nat clamped down on my wrist. Tears leaked into my mouth. Thicker, rotten liquid seeped through my fingers—infection and curdled blood—and I let out a long, begging moan. "Just another second," Tyler said tightly. His knife caught everything that ever hurt in the universe and *pulled.*

The world narrowed to a dark tunnel: my hand, the wet stone floor, the pain. My gasp hit the walls, echoed against the mortared rock. Nat flinched and dropped my free hand, and

I slammed it instinctively toward the wound. "No —" she said, and caught my wrist inches from a mess of bloody pus and swollen, black-edged flesh. I stared at it, speechless.

"Do *not* infect that again," she said fiercely, and pulled my wrist back against her palm. "We're almost finished. I swear."

"We *are* finished," Tyler said. The dirty knife drew out, from the spattered wound, a tiny wisp of brown feather. It smeared against Tyler's shearing knife, bathed in thin, streaked blood that was already darkening from bright red to a reeking, rotten black. A bubble boiled up, rusted before our eyes, and burst.

I gagged. I had nothing left to throw up.

"That's all?" Nat said, faint.

"That's all it needs," Tyler replied shakily, and dropped the knife into an empty wicker basket. The smell of death and violets rose out of it like a stain. "You did great."

Nat passed my free hand to him. His touch was lighter, all fingertips and hesitation. "You ready for the next bit?"

I shook my head, breathing hard.

"It'll only last a second," Nat said conversationally, and poured the alcohol over my hand.

I had no more noise left in me. The world blacked out for a long, long moment, and then the pain faded, muttered its way down. There was air in my lungs again, drawing in, flowing out, all the automatic gestures of a body that was well.

"You'll be okay," Tyler said, small and oddly breathless.

"You're okay, Hal. I promise." He looked even ghostlier than before. His awkward hand squeezed my own, light as dandelion.

I looked down at the fleck of brown feather on his blade. My spilt blood had charred into black, ashy flakes. The metal beneath it was pitting with rust. "That was inside me," I said unsteadily.

Tyler nodded.

I curled into a ball. I needed to get back in control. I needed to be invisible, untouched, contained. The battered table back in the dust was too small to hide under now, and Nat's eyes were on me, Tyler's eyes. My friends. They'd given me so much, and I had nothing to repay them: no tea on the boil or hospitality to even the ledger between us. As if tea or words would keep them from reacting just like Marthe if they saw me *truly*: Needy. Messy. Frightened. *Weak.*

"Hey," Nat said. I looked up, and there were tear tracks on her face: thick ones beneath her fierce eyes. She put a hand on my shoulder, and I shuddered free. Nat's fire retreated behind her eyes. "Tyler," she said. "Bandages."

Tyler passed the faded bandages without a word.

I wiped my nose on my shirttail — *forget laundry, and forget propriety too.* Anything to get the disemboweled strings of my emotions back into my belly. Nat's touch came again, through the cotton fabric, and Tyler's veiled eyes stared at us and then fled past to Heron's jumbled belongings. Tyler was harder to read now, without the color in his eyes. The two darting green blotches in his left eye, the three in his right were as good as a beekeeper's mask.

"We should burn this," he said, and shoved the wicker basket. It was blackening slowly, like the first frost over the fields.

Nat's scowl deepened. "Right." She snugged the bandage tight where my thumb met my palm. The pressure gave me something besides my own shame to think about. I almost wept again for the gift of *normal* pain. I inspected my tender, wrapped-up hand: still red, the wound seeping, the veins of infection already gone. "So fast," I murmured.

Tyler got painfully to one knee. His balance wavered. I bit my lip hard. "It's like that with the Twisted Things," he said, out of breath. "Once they're gone, you heal fast."

If you heal, I filled in silently, and didn't let myself shiver again.

I braced myself on the red brocade stool and got up to my knees. My legs were dangerously wobbly. The muscles above my knees felt like an earthquake each. I pressed down on the stool, and rotten old-cities stuffing gave beneath my palm — around something lumpy, ungiving, and hard.

Something that was not supposed to be there.

"What's wrong?" Tyler asked.

I prodded at the stuffing. Something was hidden in the stool's ancient cushion, and I hadn't put it there. I dug two fingers into the hole, pried through the yellowed wool in layers and chunks, and brushed something as cold as the January trees.

The shock of it went up my fingers, into my palm. I jerked it out and held it up to the light: a bundle of bunched-up leather wrapped around metal a handspan long. A ridge of old iron peeked out the top and faded into a mess of what might have once been leather binding. The shreds remaining were darkened and slick with sweat, in patterns that spoke of one owner, one hand.

I unwrapped it and dropped the leather strips to the floor. It was a hilt: the iron and leather pommel of the strangest hunting knife I'd ever seen.

The hilt was twisted, nearly wrenched off the line of the scarred-up metal blade. The blade swept down from it in a spiral, a hot-forged ringlet curl. I turned it with two careful fingers. Despite the nicks and use marks, the knife's blade shone like new forging.

"You couldn't cut a thing with this." I touched a finger to the edge. "But it's sharp."

Nat leaned forward, eyes narrowed. "Who sharpens a knife you can't use for anything?"

"Who sharpens a knife you can't sheathe?" I said. "Unless you carry around a stool."

"Oh, God," Tyler said, sudden and strangled, and he slumped against the wall.

"What?" Nat whirled. "What is it?"

"It's mine," came another voice, quietly, from the doorway, and this one I knew without seeing. Nat paled. I turned slowly to face long, lean Heron, standing silhouetted on the smoke-house step.

"Miss," he said, perfectly without emotion, "please don't touch that thing."

My throat prickled, and my cheeks: hot and ashamed. "We weren't looking to go through your things—"

"That's not the issue," he said, and took two long strides inside. The smell of bonfires followed him: sweat and the stink of feathers crisped to ash.

A ripple of slow tension ran up Tyler Blakely's back. "That isn't yours."

"Ty—" Nat started, high and scandalized. The tingle in my finger where I'd touched the knife's edge grew itchily stronger.

Heron smiled: a sick, sad thing. "I'm sorry," he said. "It is."

"You got it somewhere," Tyler snapped. He looked ready to burst into tears.

The hilt dangled between my fingers like the tail end of a snake. "Tell me what it is I'm holding."

Silence pooled across the floor like snowmelt. Neither of them looked at me. Tyler's fingers brushed once, twice, over John Balsam's sigil on his shirt.

"That," Tyler finally said, "is the knife that cut the heart out of the Wicked God Southward."

FIVE

THE KNIFE HIT THE FLOOR LIKE A BELL BREAKING.

I backed away fast. Three paces away was too close to a broken piece of magic, a vanished man's dead weapon — something that stopped a war nobody, before or after it, even *understood*. *That killed a god,* I thought, my mouth dry. *It killed a god, and I* touched *it.*

The knife wobbled to a stop, and Nat leaned in, her mouth open.

"Don't —" Tyler started.

Heron snorted. "It's just a knife."

I laughed so tightly I choked. "Just a knife?" John Balsam had vanished: slain the Wicked God Southward with his own common hands and disappeared without a trace. Every general and veteran who'd renamed his homestead Balsam Farm this autumn — and there were thousands of them — would descend on our sleepy little farm for this knife, and there'd be no convincing them the Godslayer wasn't hid in our garbage too.

"It's not *just a knife*," Tyler spat. "I was there. I saw the Wicked God die."

Heron turned sharply. He took in Tyler's bad leg, his

God-struck eyes. "It's just a knife," he repeated softly, and leaned back on his split bootheels. "Steel and leather; no more and no less."

"How do you know?"

"Because all the time I've carried it"—and Heron's eyes sagged shut with the weight of it—"all the way from the battle-field at the burnt-out town of John's Creek, it's never done *one damn thing* that was magic."

A bird called somewhere outside, in the bright and endless distance. Tyler stared for a long moment at Heron, at the miles of grief written on his face. "You know where he's gone, don't you?"

Heron's hands closed softly around thin air. "No," he said, and Tyler sagged in on himself. "I don't."

Heron studied the three of us: me with my good hand grasping my bandaged one; Nat, gravestone-still and sharp as a blade; Tyler, a ruined, caving building of a boy. My hired man stepped around Tyler with a woodcarver's delicacy and picked up the twisted knife.

I caught my breath, expecting thunder, mayhem . . . something. Heron flipped the shredded leather grip gently into his hand. Outside, the birdcall faded, and wind rustled the trees.

Nothing happened. It was just a knife.

Heron's mouth crimped with a disgusted affection. And then he shook his head, picked up the leather wrapping, and looped it carefully about the curves and whorls of the knife that killed a god.

I scrubbed my good hand across my eyes. "How is this here? How is that knife on my farm?"

Heron wrapped the shining blade; checked his knots twice. "It was given to me," he said quietly. "I'm carrying it north."

"You've had it the whole time?" Tyler exclaimed. "Why didn't you tell anyone? The Great Army's tearing apart the countryside for even a *hint* of John Balsam. That knife's the most important thing in the *world*."

Heron's studied blankness slammed up like a fence. I caught my breath: I'd lived too long with Marthe's anger, silent and cold, to believe his stillness was sincere. "I'm taking it north," he said, his eyes viciously bright. "Back to his people, where it belongs. Not to sit in a shrine to bilk pilgrims, or go to the highest bidder, or help some general set himself up as mayor-for-life in some backwater town. *Home*."

Tyler flinched. I swallowed and tasted burnt wicker and feathers. The family of John Balsam would have no regimental memorial. No one would have brought them a vial of ashes from John's Creek. Just like Marthe and me, they had nothing.

They needed something to touch and hold, so that they could finally grieve.

Heron hefted the leather wrapping and turned his stiff dignity onto me. "Miss, I'll understand if you'd rather not have this on your land."

"Other people didn't," I guessed, and his eyes fell.

"I left the town of Jasper through a window, by night, ahead of a full western regiment. Three farms by Ball Creek were overrun entirely by Great Army soldiers after rumor got out of my passing." Heron winced, but his voice stayed low and steady. "No, I won't flatter myself: *its* passing."

Nat scowled. "That's bull. The army mustered up to *protect* our land."

"Never underestimate," Tyler put in softly, "what men do when they're desperate."

Heron looked him over again, this time quietly appraising. "Or what they'll do when they're that thirsty for hope. I learned fast to pretend I was just another veteran, but I've never stopped for shelter for more than a few nights since."

The rest went unspoken: *Not until now.* Not until the coming winter forced him to ground.

I shook my head. This was too big for me. This was bigger than my whole world: our crooked fields and the riverbend that held off the hills and forests north. I turned to Nat in mute appeal, and she crossed her arms. "We can't tell anyone about this," she said.

I nodded. Not Mrs. Blakely, not James or Callum. Not Marthe, and I bit my lip against how dangerous it was to keep things from Marthe. To her, even more than to me, this farm was everything. She'd fought Windstown to a standstill to keep it, strained both our bodies to the breaking point, broken with every friend who questioned whether we could run Roadstead Farm alone. If she knew John Balsam's knife was here—and the whole Great Army keening for it like kittens orphaned at birth—she wouldn't hesitate: she'd throw Heron off the farm by sunset to starve in the coming snow, and if she did, I would fail. We'd already fixed the fences; the wood-pile was stacked full. One week, and Heron was already giving Roadstead Farm a chance. He was giving me a chance to keep this family alive.

I snuck a glance at my half-full pack. It sat ready against the stonework, as it had for eight long years, a waiting spider in a web of dust. *Not yet,* the still, small voice in my head wailed. I hadn't failed *yet.*

Heron stood before me, stiff and unshaken, his peculiar grace bleeding into the very air. It wasn't just northern man-ners, it was his sense of *calling:* the way a person held themself high when they were devoted, without compromise, to some-thing greater than themself. He hadn't failed yet either. He *couldn't fail.*

And abruptly, I wanted him to bring that funeral knife home.

"Leave it in the stool," I said quickly, before I could take it back. "Nobody comes here; nobody but me. Leave it there and don't move it 'til springtime."

Heron's dignity broke. "You're serious. You'll hide me. Hide *this.*"

I straightened my spine and felt that sense of calling through it, so proud and rich. So brave. "We won't breathe a word of it."

"We swear," Nat added, and I tossed her a grateful glance.

Her cheeks glowed hot with determination. "We are not *like that* to folks in the lakelands."

Tyler stared at us for a long moment, right across the space where Heron cradled the twisted knife. His lips parted, and his face was so full of warmth and indecision that it threatened to flood. "I swear," he repeated after a moment. "I give you my word."

Heron's shoulders sagged. When he lifted his head, the hunted cast was gone from his eyes. "Thank you," he said, his voice ragged and a little wry. "All of you. I won't forget it. And you won't regret it, I swear."

A hollow promise from a man with three patched shirts and a cooking pot to his name. But it filled the room with such bright and enduring force that my bones knew it was true.

Heron checked the knots on his makeshift sheath and set the knife down on the stool. Its hinges creaked under the slight weight: an altar or an opened grave. Heron blinked and looked between us awkwardly, once again a man not much older than I was: far from home and friendless in a pair of broken boots. I wet my lips against the silence. The memory of John Balsam's knife in my hands made *time to milk the goats* feel trivial.

"What's in the basket?" he asked hesitantly.

Nat's expression hardened. "Something that needs to burn." She scooped it up, abrupt as weather, and slipped past me out the door.

Tyler took one step after her and then turned back, shame-faced. "Sir," he said, and took a deep breath. "I'm sorry."

Heron sighed. "It's all right." He tentatively held out a hand. Tyler hesitated and then shook it, sharp and crisp.

"It's Heron?"

"It's a family name," Heron said, and his eyes ran down Tyler's polished buttons. "You were a corporal?"

"A private," Tyler answered, with the same defiant pride as when I said *I'm half owner of Roadstead Farm.* "Under Captain Sanchez, Lakelands Division. Private Tyler Blakely."

Heron's mouth curled in a bemused, bitter smile. "Private," he said, and his eyes lingered on Tyler's leg. "Thank you for your service."

Tyler nodded, suddenly stiff, and limped out the smoke-house door. Heron dropped his outstretched hand slowly, and the hitch of Tyler's gait faded down the graveled path.

"I should help Nat with the basket," I said after a moment.

Heron shuffled, and his arms pulled in behind his back: standing at attention. "What would you like me to do?"

Chores, I thought ruefully. The most sought-after relic in the world was in my smokehouse, and he was worrying about the morning's lost work. *He wants things to be normal again,* I realized, and settled into my boots with a breath. "Fill the malthouse cistern with water. It's halfway done, and the buck-et's outside the malthouse." I paused, reddening. "It'll need washing first."

"Miss," Heron said, and dusted his palms on his trousers, wiping away the touch of destinies. "I'll find you when it's done."

I nodded and pulled myself down the steps, out of the trapped smell of smoke and secrets and my own spilled blood. The sunlight hit like cold water. I wrapped my arms around my chest and hugged my flannel shirt close.

Heron's silence followed me down the path, hung dog-like at my heels. I stopped, turned my head, regarded him. He stood shadowed in the doorway with the knife laid flat atop his palms, or as flat as it would ever lie again. A shy stranger with a distant accent and the knife that leveled gods, who watched me with the same wary respect you gave a temper, a fist. Who expected no kindness. And who'd taken my scraps of it as gifts, each and every one.

When the Wicked God fell, I thought, *he looked away.*

"Who *are* you?" I asked softly.

A thin expression flickered across his face. "No one," he said, and wrapped the twisted knife in both hands. "I'm nobody."

Tyler Blakely was waiting for me at the poultry barn tree, his shoulders high as fences. "Nat's gone ahead," he said to my boots.

"Always does," I replied, putting a palm against the wall. My legs were still wobbling, still wouldn't stop shaking. Tyler gave me one long glance and took my arm. I leaned on him precariously, and he eased me over until we were both braced, side by side, against the chestnut tree. "Most of what I remember from when we were kids is the back of Nat's head."

Tyler's mouth crinkled in a genuine smile. "Don't forget being pushed in the river."

"We never pushed me in the river," I pointed out. "Only you."

Tyler elbowed me lightly, and I smiled—a smile I didn't have to force for the first time in a long time. He chuckled, and then his face shadowed into uncertainty. "You're all right?"

The chickens clucked softly through the wall behind us, troubled by the noise and strange voices; by the smell of Marthe's pyre on the wind. There was no point in trying to hide my weakness. He'd already seen. "Still shaky," I muttered.

He offered his browned arm. "Walk with me?"

I hesitated. I couldn't tell if he needed the help or was offering it, and I couldn't take his weight, feeling like this. *It doesn't really matter*, I decided. *It's not like he can take mine either*, and I hooked my arm gingerly through his.

It pressed warm through my shirtsleeve. I noticed its every move, starved for human touch as I'd been all summer long. *It's just Tyler*, I reminded myself as we staggered, the worst three-legged race in the world, around the corner of the farmhouse.

The pyre in the kitchen yard glowed high, hot, and

ravenous. The smell was stronger here: split wood, burning leaves, the sweet, metallic nastiness of death. I coughed hard into my sleeve, and two doggy heads perked up by the porch steps. All of a sudden the world's worst three-legged race was fighting to stand upright in a pile of tumbling, wiggling worry.

"Kelsey, down," Tyler said helplessly, too unbalanced to move. Joy snuffled at my bad hand with worried intensity until Nat materialized and grabbed her leather collar.

"Puppy, *no*," she said, and Joy grumpily subsided.

"Thanks," Tyler said. Kelsey's tail twitched. He glared impotently at her panting smile.

Nat looked at him, at me, at the way we leaned together like a barn about to cave in. "Maybe you two should sit down."

I stumbled gratefully to the porch steps, Tyler beside me, and the dogs paced protectively at our feet. Cal Blakely, perched on the other side of the crackling pyre, gave us a compact wave. "You're all right, Halfrida?"

I flexed my palm inside the bandage. "Yeah," I answered. The knife that killed a god was in my great-grandmother's parlor stool. After the fight we'd had and how I'd lost the Twisted Thing, my sister might never speak to me again. But I was breathing. It was a start.

Cal nodded. "Marthe and James want to talk backup plans. They're waiting on us inside."

I thought longingly of the smell of Marthe's baking, buried now in death and ash, and my stomach growled. I climbed the steps, caught between hunger and duty and the temptation to sleep for a week. "Here, hold on," Nat said, and skipped ahead of us to get the door.

Tyler and I glanced at the back of her head, at each other, and grinned.

"What?" Nat said, and then the knob turned and Marthe opened the door.

"There you are," she breathed, blocking the doorway with the pained roundness of her belly. Her spine sagged a little at the sight of my bandaged hand. "What happened?"

"We got—" I stopped cold. *Caught with John Balsam's knife in our hands.* I wiped my fingers against the sweat-stiff hem of my shirt. I *didn't* keep secrets from Marthe. Not secrets that actually mattered.

Not secrets that mattered, except for what Uncle Matthias had really said the night he left.

"Hallie?" she said, edged with strain.

"Just took a moment to get back," Nat broke in, as confident as ever: the real reason she was always five steps ahead of us. "We didn't want to set too hard a pace."

Tyler's cheeks bloomed into two spots of furious crimson.

Nat looked back at us, and the upbeat, responsible face she'd put on for Marthe slipped. *Don't*, she glared. Tyler's fingers tightened on my arm. I bit my lip, feeling like a traitor, and impulsively added, "We're both a little wobbly. Tyler helped me back."

Nat's eyebrows shot up to skyscraper peaks. Tyler turned

to stare. Marthe looked between us and read something in that silence that satisfied her, or at least made her not want to ask. "There's tea," she said finally. "You can wash up in the kitchen sink."

Nat held the door wide for us, and we dragged into the kitchen, kicking off boots and thick hiking shoes. "I can see your back teeth," I muttered, and Tyler shut his jaw with a snap.

"Thanks," he said after a moment.

I swallowed an obscure embarrassment. "It's just what happened," I said, and Tyler shook his head.

"Don't," he said, and looked me in the eye, his white-bleached hazel to my brown one. "Just . . . thanks."

The adults at the table caught sight of us, and Mrs. Blakely came half out of her chair.

"Tyler, look at you, you have to sit—" she started, and his shoulders sagged like a prison sentence.

SIX

"WHAT ARE THE CHANCES," JAMES SAID, "THAT THERE was just one?"

"Make plans, Jim. Don't catastrophize," Marthe replied, and refilled our rose-painted teapot.

James leaned forward, his elbows on the table in a way Marthe only tolerated from him. "I'm not catastrophizing," he said, and surveyed the table: cooling sweetcakes and stray crumbs scattered beside a double handful of our good teacups—Oma's fine china from when the old cities fell. It was a proper neighborly visit, if you watched it from the neck down. But the strained eyes and sour mouths told a different tale: this was a council of war.

"Nobody ever sights just *one* Twisted Thing," James continued, and took a molasses cake. "We prepare for more. A lot more."

"We shouldn't have to prepare at *all,*" Marthe said icily. "They said the war was over—"

"It is," James cut in, a hair less calm. Tyler stared at his plate uncomfortably. "But you know that nothing about the war was certain."

"No, I don't," Marthe snapped. "I know the recruiter said if I gave him my husband, the world would be safe again. He seemed mighty certain, that man from John's Creek."

A thin hiccup noise escaped Mrs. Blakely's lips, and Nat took her hand, tight.

Marthe leveled a cool stare at James Blakely. "The Wicked God's dead. You were all at least willing to tell us *that*. If the Twisted Things are still loose on the countryside, don't you tell me it's *not certain* and we should just be afraid when you tell us to. I paid too much for that." Her hand drifted to her belly; made a fist. "It was too much to have bought nothing."

The kitchen door opened, and Cal Blakely clattered inside. "Fire's out," he said. He dropped a kiss onto James's head and clapped Tyler's shearing knife onto the table. It was clean now—dull, scratched metal once again—but a sprinkling of rust still remained where the Twisted Thing's feather had fallen. "What's the plan?"

"Blame and recriminations," Nat said dryly, and her mother shot her a reproving look.

"We are discussing," Mrs. Blakely said, "how Twisted Things might have got into the Hoffmanns' yard."

"Tea?" Nat said, and poured Cal a cup.

"The funny thing is, it's supposed to be settling down out there." Cal took the teacup, blew on it to cool it off. "I spoke to a traveler down at Prickett's last time I was in town, and he said the land's coming back in the southern townships. The Wicked God's desert is sprouting new grass. John's Creek is never going to be a normal town again, but things're starting to grow."

"It's all over down there," Tyler said softly. "Why're they *here?*"

James stirred a speck of honey into his tea. "Right. Fine. Marthe's right: we're getting ahead of ourselves. We don't know if they're here in numbers. We don't even know if this is the first sighting here since the war."

"You want to talk to the neighbors?" Cal asked.

James looked down at his fingernails. "I want to talk to Alonso Pitts."

I sucked in a breath. That weather sense I'd grown in the years before Papa died, tuned to my family's thunderstorm moods, roared to life.

"James," Marthe said warningly.

"You don't have to like him," James said, with the edge of an old, bitter argument—and it was definitely the oldest argument I knew—"but he's still mayor, and he's got a right to know."

"I'm not disputing that," Marthe said through gritted teeth. "But I won't have him poking his nose around here, and I *won't* have him speaking for this farm." She took a gale of a breath. "My father is dead. I am not taking on replacements."

James Blakely, finally, winced.

Because that, of course, was the problem: Most of the loose talk about what Marthe and I would want—what we were capable of, and what Roadstead Farm needed — in the months after Papa's death had come from Mayor Alonso Pitts himself. To whom Marthe had not spoken for the whole six years since he tried to cheat us of our land.

And that had meant no Windstown harvest balls, no meals at Mrs. Pitts's Travelers Rest, no afternoon tea visits when we bought our supplies in town — for six long, silent years.

"You don't want to deal with Pitts, that's fine. Have Hallie go," Cal put in mildly. "She saw the Twisted Thing come down. It'll beat Jim bringing half the story and Pitts showing up here for the rest. Or worse yet, calling in a regiment and setting quarantine because we didn't explain the thing first."

James shot his husband a grateful glance. "And it sends a clear message to Pitts and the Windstown Council: Bad blood or no, Roadstead Farm respects its neighbors and the law. That'll matter to the old guard among them, Councilor Thao and Councilor Haddad."

"Because of course," Marthe finished sourly, "those thieves ever respected us back. Hallie, is that something you want to do?"

I slid down in my chair. *Too late.* Every eye in the room was on me, and no matter what I did, someone would be disappointed. There wasn't love lost between me and the mayor, but when Alonso Pitts fought his epic battle against Papa's last will, I'd only been ten years old. It was Marthe and Thom — still newly courting, together but a year — who'd fought right back;

Marthe and Thom, who still felt every drop of the bad blood between us. They kept me from it, and all I remembered of that time was shadows: whispered arguments in the parlor, conferences with the Blakelys and our few allies in town through long Sunday afternoons. Nat and Tyler and I, turned out into the fields to play alone because the Mason kids and the Sumners didn't come around anymore.

I couldn't tell what Marthe wanted: my sister, who'd fought tooth and nail for my right to half of this farm, knowing full well that one of us would have to buy the other out someday. Declining would just rub it in, in their minds: *selfish, childish Hallie.* But I couldn't tell if saying yes would be another treachery.

"I'll go," I said, hesitant.

Marthe's face didn't change.

"We need supplies from town," I added. "We're almost out of soap, and the butcher —"

Marthe closed her eyes. "I'll make a list," she said tonelessly. Her hand circled her belly before she stood.

"Good," James put in just as I decided to take the whole thing back. "We'll start with the current tomorrow. Cal or I can row you across."

Tyler straightened. "I'll do it."

Mrs. Blakely waved him off, a nervous flutter. "Tyler, you can't strain —"

"I can still *row*, Mother."

Mrs. Blakely turned a slow, burning red. "Tyler," she said,

"I know you're eighteen and think you're invincible, but your hip is nothing to trifle—"

"Eglantine—" Cal warned.

"I'm not broken," Tyler cut in coolly. "I can row Hallie to Windstown and back without making Nat drop everything to mind me." He held the edge of the table with both hands, and his bleached eyes were as bright as sparks. I swallowed and rested my own hands on the tabletop to somehow hold it, hold him still.

"And," he added, "I've got more than enough proof that I'm not invincible."

The air in the room stuck like hard frost. Mrs. Blakely blinked at Tyler as if she'd been hit. *I should've kept to Marthe's chores,* I thought bitterly. My family arguments were horrible. Apparently other people's could be even worse.

"Mum," Nat said distinctly, "leave him alone. It's town, not the other side of the ocean."

Mrs. Blakely huffed out a breath. Nat was Eglantine Blakely's only daughter, and Eglantine Blakely had grown up in a house full of girls. As stubborn as she might be to her brothers-in-law, her son, and the very soil and air, she never truly denied Nat anything. She looked between her two children, one deceptively mild, one blazing, and narrowed her eyes. "If your brother goes over into the river, so help me, Nasturtium Blakely—"

"You'll dunk me in after him. I know," Nat said sharply, and her mouth rose in a crooked smile. "And then you'll have to spend the rest of your life wearing black and mourning your lost children, and it will be *all my fault.*"

The angry flush drained out of Mrs. Blakely's cheeks. "I'm glad we understand each other," she said hoarsely, and a matching smile tugged at the corner of her mouth.

"I'll be here tomorrow, then," Tyler said. His eyes still snarled like foxes.

"Thank you," I said tentatively. The world felt more like thin river ice than ever.

James folded his napkin and set it on the table. "Marthe, we should head home. We left the sheep penned up." As if they'd been waiting for permission, two generations of Blakelys raced to pull on their boots.

Marthe inclined her head to James. "Thanks," she said, rough and genuine. "Again."

"Of course," he said quietly, and kissed her on the cheek. And added even lower: "Chin up, kid."

"I'm trying," I thought I heard her whisper, but under the clatter of kitchen chairs and fall coats, there was no way to be sure.

Courtesy dictated that you walked a visitor to the roadway, or at least to their waiting cart. I pulled on my boots and kept pace with the Blakelys as they straggled out past the gardens. The blue cart was waiting at the edge of our nearest field, guarded by the now-napping dogs. James Blakely boosted his sister-in-law onto its worn leather seat and pointed the horses to the highway, back to the soft clover of Lakewood Farm.

"I'll see you tomorrow," Tyler said, still quiet and frostbitten. I nodded. I didn't know where to look. The injured leg stood out like a bruise; the cool anger on his face was worse. Everywhere, like fingerprints, the marks of the world outside the lakelands stood out on his skin—a constant reminder of how much he'd walked through to come home. How much he'd returned a stranger.

He glanced over my shoulder, and a memory dredged loose. "Back on the beach," I said, trying to be casual, "what was that you saw?"

Tyler blinked, his injured dignity forgotten. He looked at me sidelong, wary. "The bird."

He's lying, I thought, shocked, and shook my head. "No, before that. The bird was on the ground. You looked up."

He looked down at his hands, then back up at me, his face a small torment. I swallowed. Tyler was *afraid.*

He opened his mouth, and I realized: *He's going to lie to me again.* I suddenly could not bear to hear him lie.

"It must have been a deer," I said, too loud. The terror on his face froze and stuck. "They've been straying in all summer. I'll have to check the fences."

"Right," he said in a strangled voice. His shoulders slowly came down. "Right."

And then: "Tyler!" Callum called, and Tyler hopped up onto the cart like a marionette. One crackle of the reins and they were gone, rushing down the pathway past our empty fields, shrinking into a small hard knot against the sky.

I stared at the dust cloud they left me, and then at the slanted sunlight as it settled. He'd seen something for certain, something too terrifying to tell me about. Or thought he had, out of his broken eyes.

A throat cleared soft behind me, and I jumped.

Heron stood a full ten paces back, his hands up cautiously. "The cistern's full, miss," he said. And then, apologetic: "I said I'd find you when it was done."

I rubbed my eyes with my unbandaged hand. "Right," I said, and pushed down the urge to scour the riverbank. *The goat pen,* I recited. *Firewood, and a start on the malt.* Whatever Tyler was hiding, ferreting it out wouldn't feed us through the long winter.

What did that was chores.

"Come on," I said, and shook myself, and sighed. "I'll get you a shovel."

SEVEN

I WOKE INTO THE GRAY DAWN LIGHT TO DRESS FOR WAR. My town dress had sat unused since springtime, buried in work clothes and mothballs. It was already an inch too short. I ignored the shamefully high hem and fished under my bed for Marthe's old town boots. Nat was a girl in a family of men, and her mother bought her new boots for the Windstown dances, but Marthe and I made do with creased hand-me-downs, the kind that made men like Alonso Pitts sniff with aggrieved charity. *Let it go,* I told myself, and swiped at the musty old boots. Everyone already knew Roadstead Farm was poor. We told them with every stitch.

My denimless legs felt light and strange as I clattered into the kitchen; my hair trailed down my back like spiderwebs. One summer contained in braids and buttons, and I'd already forgotten how town clothes felt. In town clothes, I could almost remember visits to Prickett's, holidays, the quiet pace of life before Thom marched south. I swallowed and pushed all that aside. I was sixteen; I lived here and now.

We had chores.

Marthe was at the kitchen table, awash in a storm of paper.

Before her, the farm's thick accounts book gleamed with fresh ink between snowdrifts of debt slips: goods due to us, goods we owed, all from the last trip into Windstown in the spring. I pulled in my skirt to avoid sending the papers flying, and looked around for breakfast.

"Sideboard," Marthe said, and there it was, wedged against a half-used jar of pickles. "Wait," she added, and beckoned me into the sunlight. "Your hair."

I did a little turn, crammed between the sideboard and the table. Marthe frowned and adjusted my part with two fingers. "We'll have to find a hat. You look like a nest the crows fled."

The nerves in my belly hardened into ice. "There are plenty of combs in Windstown."

Marthe visibly fought the urge to smooth down a rebellious curl. "Not for us, there aren't. Mackenzie Green still owes us for two sacks of last year's flour, but that's all the credit we have. I've written it all down." She handed me a scribbled list. "Do what you can with her."

I scanned my sister's crabbed handwriting: Tea, salt, honey, nails; talk to Thao Pa about the goats. Alonso Pitts's name wasn't there. The blank space where it should have been ate the morning light.

"And—here." Marthe dug out our smaller town book: full of years of little contracts for cheese and salt and rice, negotiated while Prickett's oldest, Janelle, hauled me on pirate adventures under the taproom tables. I cradled the book in my hands and felt suddenly, overwhelmingly too young.

"What do I tell Alonso Pitts?" I asked softly.

Marthe pushed her chair back and stalked to the oven. "As little as possible. Focus on getting enough salt."

"Thanks," I said bitingly, and put down the accounts book to rub my aching hand.

Marthe stopped, and her shoulders winched tighter. "Let me see?"

I held out my wounded hand, curled up and chapped in its white bandages. Marthe's warm fingers unwrapped the cloth, and the cold air hit, as sharp as river water. I swallowed, remembering the oozing blood and pus, and looked down.

The Twisted Thing's mark had shrunk overnight from a vicious, messy wound to angry red skin, puffed up in the middle. Marthe pressed a calloused finger to the swelling, and I hissed. "You cleaned it?" she asked, and I nodded.

Her face fluttered, a sickly wince. "Be careful with that," she said shortly. "Don't push."

"Right," I drawled. "Thanks a lot. I thought I'd go lift weights, but you've told me."

Her eyes hardened. Her hand went to her rounded belly. "Hallie, good God, don't prickle at me today."

"I'm prickling?" I said before my head caught up with my tongue. "You didn't even say good morning. The first thing you *did* say was how awful I look, and the second was how I won't remember our supplies and I'll probably break off my own hand while I'm at it."

Marthe threw up her hands. "Just because I don't want

that man sneering at you because you haven't cut your hair this summer—"

"I am *sixteen years old,*" I hissed. *"I can figure out combing myself."*

Pain built in my hand—no, both my hands. They were curled into fists.

Marthe stared at them, her eyes hooded, and then she slammed the account book shut. "Don't forget the nails," she snapped, and flung the kitchen door shut behind her.

Tyler found me ankle-deep in the malthouse, ruining my hair gloriously with work and the autumn damp. "Hallie?" he said from the doorway.

"Don't come in with those boots on," I snarled.

He froze mid-step, caught between surprise and naked hurt. The guilt was instant. "I'm sorry," I said lower. With everyone else those two little words came so easy—everyone but my own flesh and blood. "Marthe thinks I can't do anything right, and we bickered *again,* before I'd even had breakfast, and it just makes me so—*agh.*"

Tyler shoved his hands in his pockets. "Yeah," he muttered. "I understand *that.*"

Mrs. Blakely's furious stillness flickered across my memory: the way she'd so casually decided what Tyler could and couldn't do. "I'm sorry," I said again, quieter.

He looked away and nodded. "Ready to go?"

I caught the hint: *I don't want to talk about it.* "I'm ready, yeah," I said, and pinched some brightness into my voice. "Unless whoever drove you wants a cup of tea."

His mouth quirked. "Nobody did. I walked."

I blinked, and instantly wished I hadn't: his wariness set like frost. "Oh," I managed—*say something, anything!*—"was that spite or pride?"

Tyler startled—and let out a brilliant laugh. He leaned gasping against the malthouse door, and when he looked back up, the Tyler I remembered was in his shattered eyes: so fond and quiet and patient that it took three days to recover when he climbed through your window and put a toad in your bed.

"Well," he said, wiping his eyes, "I'd have to give that a yes."

I sagged with relief. "I hear it's good to have more than one reason for things."

His grin widened. "How 'bout you? Spite or pride?"

I pulled a sweaty strand of hair off my forehead. I felt like a mess, and what with Tyler wearing his good shirt again, freshly pressed and laundered with the buttons glimmering in the sunlight, I was starting to regret that. "Yes," I concluded. "My sister used to treat me like a person, and this hurts my pride, and now I am feeling very spiteful."

"So we're agreed," he said lightly, and held the door for me. "We'll fly to town on the smoke billowing from our ears."

"Better than rowing," I added. I sloshed out of the wet malt, wiped a stray grain off my ankle, and slithered into my boots.

"That reminds me," Tyler said, jumpy all over again. "Nat sent these."

He pulled a pair of gloves from his pocket. They were a fitted blue fabric—Nat's favorite color—as deep and smooth as the sky in springtime. Much too fine for hauling cheeses and crates of salt. I squinted. "Not even Marthe makes me cover my hands in town."

"No," he said, reddening. "It's for your hand. I mean, of course they're for your hands," he rushed on, "but to keep dirt off the bandage."

"Oh," I said, embarrassed. "Thanks. I mean, tell Nat thanks." I smiled, but he didn't see it. He was gone again, a stranger again, tucked behind silent walls.

I clicked my mouth shut, arms around myself. That flash of the old Tyler, the one who was my friend, made his pull away even lonelier. "We should get going," I said. "Or we'll lose the light on the way home."

"Right," Tyler said distantly, and he levered down the malthouse steps.

We reached the house red-cheeked and tingling with cold, Tyler puffing out his chest to hide just how hard he was breathing. Marthe was nowhere to be seen, but draped across the porch rail was a clump of rust-red fabric. *Mami's winter shawl,* I registered. I'd been ready to rush off in nothing but a housedress. "Thanks," I said softly, and spread the shawl about my shoulders. It was soft: thick homespun worn smooth by years and hands, and it no longer smelled like my mother. The wind at my elbows was immediately less cold.

She'd left it out there because she loved me. And she'd left it out there as the sharpest rebuke: *All your hollering about being old enough, smart enough, and you can't even remember a winter shawl.*

I hugged the shawl to me and thought, *Oh, Marthe. How did we ever get so mixed up?*

"Marthe's not coming?" Tyler asked. Didn't quite ask.

"She's not," I said shortly.

He hesitated and then delicately said, "If we're bringing back heavy cargo—"

I looked at his heaving chest, at my injured hand, and nodded bitterly. "Come on. Let's go find the hired man."

We pushed into the river half an hour later: Tyler, me, and Heron in a clean shirt, creased faintly from days or weeks spent folded in his leather pack. He'd wiped the goat muck and dust off his boots, but they were still ragged, their soles worn through at the heels.

"We aim past Bellisle," I told him, and pointed out the low, browned island midway through the sleepy river. "Round its tip to the other shore."

"Bellisle's the nearest town?" Heron asked, awkwardly shipping his oars.

"No, Windstown," I said. I wrapped Mami's shawl tighter around my shoulders. "And there's nothing after it for miles."

That soldierly shroud of attention dropped over Tyler again. "Mister Heron," he said, every inch strain and a new, military reverence. "Mind your left oar?"

Heron's nod was terse. I was learning something of his expressions: that *Mister* made his flesh crawl like a nest of live spiders.

"I can take the oars," I said, and Tyler shook his head.

"Your wound's still fresh. A strain might burst it right open."

The nettled feeling Marthe was so good at giving me started to prickle. "I'll be careful."

"Hallie—" he started, and then said almost apologetically, "spite or pride?"

I winced. "It's not like that." He didn't reply. I closed my hand tighter, felt it twinge. It was exactly like that. My sister wasn't even here, and I was arguing with her.

I sucked in a breath. Forced it out and settled back into the rowboat's middle seat. "Pride," I muttered.

"I'm sorry," Tyler said, and he meant it. He dipped his oars into the water, a steady heartbeat stroke. Heron picked up the rhythm, and we glided across the current of the wide green river, out of the shallows, into the world.

I hadn't just watched the river go by since I was too small to take an oar. We slid toward Bellisle through a blanket of bright water, fringed by the browned shoreline and the sweet smell of pine trees. I perched on the middle bench and watched the shapes along the shore: wild dogs, listening prick-eared for rabbits to drag back to their dens in the empty towers of the ruined city. They looked so much like Joy, Sadie, or Kelsey—at least, until they *moved*, and you understood, truly, that they were something wild.

The shattered arc of the Windstown bridge curved over them, its steel beams and cables rusted, impassable for years. Its roadbed had cracked and shifted so badly that they'd forbidden travel on it when Papa was young. Old-city workmanship was peerless, far beyond the things we did and made now, but there was no knowing how to recreate that work—or how long it might last. The bridge ricketed up there, abandoned before its time: a giant's dusty bones.

The northern tip of Bellisle sharpened before us, and I dug my nails into my palm. "Careful," I said. "The Beast is coming up."

"The Beast?" Heron asked, and then we saw it.

The Twisted Thing we called the Beast rose to the left like a derelict ship, an island of old flesh and dead, rotting carrion eaters. Color rippled through the shreds of hide still left on its broken body. It shimmered like a soap-bubble rainbow, moving and hypnotic, around the red of exposed muscle and huge, splintered bones. That hide had been covered in soft feathers when it first tumbled out of the clouds, but the Windstown Council had skinned it at the end of summer. Too many fishermen and awestruck children had rowed out to pluck those shimmering plumes even after we knew the cost of a Twisted Thing's touch. Its dangerous attraction still hadn't subsided:

my oarless fingers twitched to hold those colors in my palms. I put both hands securely under my legs and looked away.

"What *is* that?" Heron asked, hushed.

"It fell from the sky," I said, and sat harder. The pain in my hand was a wonderful deterrent to those oiled, magical shreds of skin. "When the war ended. I don't think it knew how to swim."

Heron's voice came low and awful. "It drowned?"

I shook my head. "Just fell. It thrashed there for a full day and night before Windstown sent the boats out. It was before you came home," I added, in Tyler's direction. "Don't look at it." His hands had stilled on the oars.

Tyler stared at the tea-stained horns where they rose out of the river, curling like the twisted roots of trees. The near one had splintered at the tip in its fall; the burnt shreds of a white-bellied osprey's nest twined between the jagged edges. Tyler shuddered sharply and turned away. His ruined eyes glowed luminescent in the morning sun. "*That* we never saw on the battlefield."

"It was different," Heron murmured, "all over."

The oars dipped into the water and whispered river-things against the rowboat's hull. We came close enough to touch it, for just a moment, and then the river shoved us protectively away. We glided slowly past the body of the Beast, our war memorial, past the smell of rot and dying birds calling into the breeze.

The far shore came on us quickly once we passed the

Bellisle strait. Out of the air, the hulked ghosts of gray buildings sharpened: Windstown, worn down by a century of rain. The Windstown barricade curved a protective half circle around them. Inside that wall of brick and dirt and ancient furniture lay the safe, sleepy township I'd grown up visiting, the world of small courtesies and sticky buns and salt. Outside it was no man's land, another dead, ancient maze of ruins that grew like brambles between our lakes and the soft farmlands of the north.

The Windstown piers were empty, all the fishing boats already gone upriver into the lake for the last of the autumn catch. Tyler and Heron shipped the oars, and I hopped onto the dock and looped the mooring rope around the piling.

"Welcome," I said, "to Windstown."

EIGHT

THE GROUNDS BY THE WINDSTOWN DOCKS HAD BEEN parkland, once. When the world fell, our great-grandparents turned them into vegetable gardens. I led Heron and Tyler along ancient brick paths, through the familiar smell of hay and fish bone fertilizer — the same paths I remembered from being four years old, learning to touch and taste and smell that nebulous thing Marthe and Papa called *town*.

There were burn scars on the white-columned buildings now. They smudged ghostlike through layers of whitewash, put the smell of old ash into the air. All of them looked ancient, faded into the brick. Some of them had wings.

Heron's gaze flitted nervously. "So they fell here too?"

"I guess we'll find out," I said, and Windstown opened before us like a flower.

Even stripped of its leaves in late autumn, Windstown was grand. The brick path spread into a wide concrete roadway lined with bright red and white awnings and ancient mirror glass. In the shadow of remade skyscrapers and the softly turning windmills, the shops sat snug behind hand-stenciled windows: Green's General Supply, Thao's Butchery and Meats, shops for hats and tools and fine wildflower paper. Old men flocked outside the café with small cups of bitter tea, gossiping over backgammon tables. Pigeons swarmed fearlessly around their bootheels and bickered for crumbs. I tilted my nose up and inhaled greedily: bakery loaves, roses, and mint. They turned the crisp air drunken.

Tyler stopped in front of the General Supply. "Which way first?"

I turned a full circle on the Main Street pavement: from Mackenzie Green's warm, wood-polish window to the mayor's distant chimney and back. "Pitts," I said hollowly. "If I put it off, I'll be sick. Heron, can I give you this?" I pressed Marthe's shopping list into his hand.

Heron's face lapsed into that bland, armored mask. It covered his unease almost perfectly. "Miss." He twitched his cap lower over his face. "Where do I meet you?"

"In the general store," I said, and squared my shoulders. "We won't"—*I hope to God*—"be long."

Heron shouldered his way down the street, slower now, scanning for Thao's window. I turned to Tyler. "Can we get this over with?"

He nodded, and we set our awkward pace up the avenue.

Tyler raised a hand here and there to men, older men, who I'd sworn the Blakelys didn't visit: Councilor Haddad's brother and the Kims from the Windstown mill. They stared at us with blunt curiosity, dragging their eyes from my face to my too-high hemline. I swallowed and raised a hand to my hair without thinking—and then angry blood came into my cheeks. It didn't matter if my hair was frizzing; I wouldn't *let* it matter. I set my jaw and strode faster past the Main Street shops, head held high, until the bustle of Windstown tapered into small vegetable plots, fruit trees, and fences—into the quiet, modest houses that ringed the town market, their backs stubbornly turned to the barricade.

The Pitts house was anything and everything but modest. Its walls of red old-city brick were always scrubbed to a shine, its porch braced by white pillars and wrapped with shrubs and decorative cabbages. It wasn't a subtle message: *We are far too rich to grow our suppers in our yard.* "It looks smaller," I said softly. In my memory it was a mansion, a glowering castle that blotted out the sun.

Tyler stuffed his hands in his pockets. "Well, you haven't been past Main Street in six years."

I rearranged my woolen skirts; the folds were hopelessly wrinkled. Marthe had been right about the comb. The thought of her waiting at home, *knowing* that, felt hateful.

"You ready?" Tyler asked.

"No," I said, ten years old again, and pushed past him to sound the bell.

The door opened to an older Hmong woman, stout and steady, with gray streaks in her glossy black bob. Her dress was extravagantly fine and her shoes too soft a leather to even think of work outdoors. *Mrs. Pitts,* I realized. Mrs. Pitts grown six years older.

"Good day, ma'am," Tyler said, and "Young Mr. Blakely," she replied. Her eyes drifted to me: to my terrible hair and down to Nat Blakely's gloves snug about my hands. "I don't believe I'm acquainted with your new lady friend, though."

Tyler startled, his color suddenly high, and went, "No, no —"

I blinked, and he turned an even uglier red. Dodged my eyes —

—and I *got* it.

"Oh," I said, surprised. "No, that's not it at all. I'm not. I mean —" I started, and there was no good place to go. Tyler had practically curled up with embarrassment. Mrs. Pitts's polite puzzlement was turning to alarm. And I —

I'd never even *thought* how I might feel about that. And Tyler, from the stricken look on his face . . . had.

I shut my mouth, absolutely stunned. Tyler hadn't been acting so mercurial, so *odd,* because of the war alone. He wanted to court me. Tyler, who I'd known since I could barely walk.

He recovered well before I did. "You know —" he said, slightly strangled, "Miss Halfrida Hoffmann."

Mrs. Pitts's dark eyes widened, and not a little bit. "Little Halfrida," she said, my name an old, lost language on her lips. "Well. I haven't laid eyes on you since you were a child."

"Six years," I agreed uncomfortably. Tyler shifted, and it

set off thunderstorms in my head. He didn't want to look at me. All the strength I'd summoned to face down this doorstep was already wilting away.

Get it together, I scolded myself, and I dug my nails into my gloved palm until the pain brought focus back. "We'd like," I said in my best high, strong voice, "a meeting with the mayor."

Mrs. Pitts glanced over her shoulder, into the depths of her shrunken house. "I—well," she said, entirely taken aback. "I'll see if he's available. Please come in."

Mrs. Pitts flung the double doors wide, striping shadows on the floors, and showed us into the one house both Marthe and I had sworn never to set foot in again.

Mayor Pitts took his appointments in his personal parlor, a bright, wide-windowed room that looked out on the back garden. There were vegetable beds out there, battened down for the winter. Whoever gardened for the Pitts household had tried to hide them with roses. The dead brambles reached up across the windowsill.

Tyler shifted on the edge of the stuffed couch, his bad leg sprawled corpselike down to the carpet. He still wouldn't look at me, and what I could see of his face was blotchy, half hidden behind his collar.

"It was just talk," I said, desperate. "Windstown would sink into the river without gossip."

My voice vanished into the green plush couches, the high

bookshelves, the antique old-cities carpet. Tyler buried his face in Alonso Pitts's expensive teacup and didn't say a word.

"Tyler?" I asked, smaller.

There was no time to reply. A narrow chestnut door opened at the other side of the parlor, and there he was: Alonso Pitts, in full waistcoat and chain of office.

Mayor Pitts took us in, one and then the other, and nodded with fine, fatherly benevolence. The seething anger started, comforting, in my belly: Alonso Pitts, always presumptuous. So kindly and firmly smiling while he ripped out your guts.

He looked older. The years didn't wear on people the same way, but Pitts had taken the last six pretty personally. His hair had thinned in a stain that spread from his crown, and he looked smaller, less fiery, less like the voice of hell. There were stitches on his plum waistcoat where the seams had been let out, and vague gray circles under his eyes. "Miss Hoffmann," the mayor said, and leaned against the fireplace mantel. "Young Mr. Blakely."

"Private Blakely," Tyler corrected, and I abruptly understood why he'd worn his soldier's buttons.

"Private," the mayor amended. "I won't say I expected to see either of you."

No kidding, I thought, and the whole thing seeped up again: Papa's funeral, rainy and cold. The mud of our burying ground caked on the last pair of new boots I'd owned, while I clung to Marthe's strong fingers. The look on her face when she returned from the Windstown land office, drenched with rain, hat twisted in her hands, and told me Papa's will would not be proved.

I put my hands behind my back to stop their sudden shaking. "This isn't about—" *the argument, our family, your awful, high-handed meddling.* "We've sighted a Twisted Thing on Roadstead Farm."

Pitts's elbow slipped off the mantel. "Twisted Things? When?" The ease fell from him like a stolen suit. I glanced at Tyler. He stood very straight and still, arms at ease behind his back as if to hold himself in place.

"It fell against my window yesterday at dawn," I said. I heard that frantic, weak scrabbling again and shivered. "A bird with spider eyes and webbed talons. We burned it. But we haven't seen one since the end of the war. We just wanted to know if you've had any here, or if it was the only one."

The mayor drew himself up, six feet of retired muscle and ease. "Of course we haven't had Twisted Things in town," he said, much too fast. "We won the war. It's over."

He cocked an eyebrow and stared: a blatant dare to argue. I drew back. The man I remembered, Mayor Hellfire himself, simmered in his eyes. *I said something wrong,* I realized, too late. *I messed up, and now we're going to get it.*

Pitts's gaze traveled from Tyler's leg to my bandaged hand, and burned them both in the cauldron of his head. "We'll quarantine your fields ourselves until General de Guzman can be found. The militiamen will escort you back to pack your valuables. And Miss Hoffmann"—he pinched the bridge of his nose as if terribly weary—"I'll find you and your sister somewhere to stay."

"Excuse me?" I started. All I'd asked was if they'd sighted Twisted Things, and suddenly Pitts was snatching all our choices right out of our hands.

Pitts raised an eyebrow, as if I'd interrupted. "A place to stay. I'm sure Darnell Prickett has a room or two free."

"You want us to leave the farm," I said slowly, shaping the words to make them real. And then they were real: a bag in hand, no land beneath your feet, the dubious charity of others. "How can you be picking fights about the will *now?*"

"Don't be foolish," Pitts snapped. "This isn't about the will. The Great Army always puts infected land under quarantine. The war in the south killed hundreds of men." His eyes flicked, uncomfortable, to Tyler's hitched hip.

"You *just said* the war was over!" I sputtered. "There's been one Twisted Thing. How can you say this isn't about the will when you go straight to—quarantine, eviction, tramping our fields into mud, when we're just trying to find out what's wrong?"

His face went hard, utterly cold. Alonso Pitts and my papa had one thing in common: the word they most hated to hear was *no*.

"This is how it started in the southlands," Pitts said louder. "The Twisted Things showed up, one here, one there. Nothing to worry about; perfectly safe to stay at home. And then it wasn't." He faced us full on, pale with rage. "And nobody'll ever come from John's Creek again."

The sheer wrath keeping me on my feet faltered. John's Creek and its foothills, three hundred acres of green land, were dead now, and so was everyone who'd loved them. "This isn't John's Creek," I said. "Hundreds of men saw the Wicked God die. Our home *is* safe. And it's *ours*."

Pitts's eyes slitted. "Young lady, I have a whole town to think of: the barricades, the harvests, if our sewers will last. It is irresponsible to stay on that farm, and downright child-ish to ask for help and then quibble over everything this town offers you."

My fists curled. "We weren't asking for your help."

Pitts looked down at me, and his mouth twisted with sad disdain.

The rage in my belly exploded.

"We'd *never* ask for your help," I snapped. "You've been try-ing to take my inheritance since the day Papa died. I only even *came* here because James Blakely said telling you was neigh-borly, and we couldn't *not* warn you. We're not —" I grasped, drowning, for words. "We're not *monsters*."

Pitts stared for a long moment and then leaned back, all sad understanding. "I know you probably hate me," he said, "but I stand by it. It wasn't responsible to leave a young woman and a child out there on that much acreage, alone."

I shoved my hands in my skirt's deep pockets and crum-pled their fabric 'til it tore.

"They aren't alone," Tyler cut in, in that hard voice that reminded me of his father, "and don't you ever say that again." He turned, sideways, stumbling, and held open the door of the mayor's parlor. "C'mon, Hal. Let's go."

I glanced between Alonso Pitts's hard, pitying face and the door Tyler had flung open. And then I walked through it, and slammed that expensive door hard enough to shake the frame.

Tyler paced a circle in the hallway, stiff with rage. "I'm sorry," he said, and looked me in the eye for the first time since we'd set foot in the Pitts household. "I wish I could — *ugh*."

"I — no." I pressed my hands to my cheeks. My face was still hot: wrath and fear and shame, all mixed up. "I should have known. I should have remembered why we don't talk to him. Of course he'd find a way to make a simple question into a trap."

Tyler glanced at the door worriedly and shifted farther down the hall. I followed him — and stopped, not sure anymore how close was too close. Discomfort bloomed between us. He edged one step farther along, and my heart wilted. Windstown was crammed with people all the time. There was no private space to ask Tyler if he was all right — *no, if* we're *all right* — until we were back across the river.

I wrapped my mother's shawl tightly around me and tried not to feel utterly lost.

"What do you want to do?" he asked.

I bit back ruined humiliation. "Go home."

Tyler nodded gravely, once. "Then let's go."

We gained the front hall side by side, palpably and uncomfortably apart. Mrs. Pitts held the front door for us, as courtesy demanded. She looked at the wall and did not say a word.

"Thank you," Tyler told her as he stepped into the sunshine.

She hesitated, and then her chin came up. "Halfrida. Do give my greetings to your sister."

I clenched my jaw and just stared.

Mrs. Pitts bowed her head a little. "He's afraid of a panic," she said, her voice strained. "It's only been a month since the fear here's settled down. There hasn't been a sighting since September, but the Masons and Sumners still slaughtered three feral dog packs and burned a whole Bellisle orchard five weeks ago on nothing more than a rumor. I don't know what the town would do if the gossip woke."

"It doesn't need to. *He's* already panicking," I said gracelessly.

"Yes, he is," Mrs. Pitts replied. "Whatever you think being mayor means, he's just a man. And no man should be forced to defend against gods."

For anyone else I might have felt a twinge of pity. But Alonso Pitts's disdain was too fresh to let it through. "Thank you for the tea," I said, civil and formal, and saw myself down their front steps, head held high, still half owner of Roadstead Farm.

. . .

Mackenzie Green's General Supply was as cozy as a holiday kitchen, packed floor to ceiling with grain sacks and the smell of new wool and cider. The shelves were half empty for the first time I could remember; usually they teemed with things we couldn't afford. I stepped inside, too aware of Tyler's silence, of the distance between us—certain that all of Main Street was whispering behind our backs.

Mackenzie lorded over the narrow counter, a woman cut even narrower and just as precisely. Her face split into a wrinkled smile. "There's my Hallie," she said, and pecked me on both cheeks. "I sent your things and your hired man down to the docks. He looked like a man in need of making himself useful. Now, I heard you were up to see Pitts this morning."

It was true what they said about keeping a secret in Windstown: the only sure way to do it was to promptly drop dead. In the back aisle, a company of Chandlers lowered their voices, hands on their rucksacks of precious old-cities salvage. One of the older ones—Rami, his black beard half gray—shot me a look of profound sympathy.

"We were," I grudged. I tangled my fingers in Mami's shawl and wished I were in my barley fields, brown-gray and endless, silent, safe. Empty of everyone's gossipy, grasping *opinions*.

"We saw a Twisted Thing on the property," I said reluctantly, and Mackenzie quirked one black-silver brow at the Chandlers, who took the hint and dutifully filed out.

Mackenzie knew everything that happened in Windstown. Telling her—confiding in her—was worth the chance she'd confide back. "We came to find out if they've been back here in town, too. And in one breath Pitts was sending us off the farm, bringing in generals to rip up our winter plantings, and—I have to get home."

"Pitts," Mackenzie said, and sighed. "Well, he won't be mayor forever. I'll keep an eye out for your Twisted Things, child, and speak with Darnell Prickett. All the news comes through his doors that doesn't come through mine."

"Thank you," I said, overwhelmed. Not everyone in Windstown was Alonso Pitts. There were still people who cared for us, and who we cared for in return. "I don't know how we can repay you—"

Mackenzie's lips pursed. "Down to the docks, now. Don't lose the light."

I flushed. I'd offended her, and I didn't even know how. "Thank you," I stammered again, and we crept out into the afternoon.

The air on the riverfront was cooling fast. Crates and dry sacks scattered over the pier, stowed inexpertly about our riverboat—which had been packed with a total unfamiliarity with how the boat took weight. "Oh, Heron," I sighed, and looked around for him.

He stood on the garden walk beneath a leafless peach tree, in quiet conversation with Rami Chandler while the Chandler cousins loaded their boat. I glanced over my shoulder at Tyler—already shifting packages from bow to stern to bulwarks—and drifted to join them.

"Halfrida," Rami said, with a tip of his broad chin.

"Rami." I nodded back.

Heron glanced at me, surprised.

"My given name's perfectly all right. We're neighbors here," Rami explained, and reached into a pocket for an awkward, cloth-wrapped bundle. "I heard mention of the Twisted Thing on your property up at Green's. We thought you should know: we've had a sighting too."

He unwrapped the cloth—his spare keffiyeh, creased and clean—and produced a thick glass jar with *something* floating inside. I shaded the jar with one hand. Inside was the corpse of a lizard, no larger than my palm, curled in some viscous fluid.

I swallowed past a throat gone dry. The lizard's limbs bent in a way I couldn't understand: backwards, like a horse's hocks, but three times, a zigzag of joints. Its ruff was green and scaly, touched with purpling dots. And its ears, floating limp and free, were the red-tufted points of a fox.

It wasn't a fluke. There were still Twisted Things in the lakelands. I couldn't even begin to figure out what that meant.

"Be careful," Rami warned as I took the jar. "It's still throwing heat." The glass warmed my hands like a fresh mug of soup, even through Nat's fine blue gloves.

"When did you find this?" I asked.

"Two days ago. Ada found the nest," Rami said, and waved her over from the knot of busy Chandlers. I startled. I hadn't seen Ada Chandler in years, since the days when we still paid calls in Windstown and our neighbors' hospitality was good. She'd grown from a narrow, quiet kid into a woman taller than me, her dark arms hard with muscle and her black hair close cut in tight, dense curls.

"Ada," I said awkwardly. She anatomized me with a look; cataloged my own changes in seconds. The practical nod that was her verdict was Ada to the core: identify, recognize, and dismiss everything that didn't interest her.

"You've got a Twisted Thing, then?" she said, and leaned in with an intensity I remembered all too well.

"Yeah," I blurted. Not being sure what to do with Ada Chandler was a familiar, comforting feeling. "Yesterday. Just one."

Ada nodded, sharp as a rice merchant. "That fits. The nest we found yesterday was a new one — none of the specimens we caught this summer lived past two weeks. Their burns killed them off, and they disintegrated after, but this little guy's still nice and fresh."

"Caught?" I said, scandalized. "You kept them?"

Ada's bright eyes narrowed. "Of course we kept them. There's no way to fight something you don't *understand*."

A horrid image flashed across my mind's eye: twisted birds and lizards, centipedes as long as my arm, twined and floating in jars like Marthe's canned carrots. I pushed the jar back at Ada. The lizard bumped against the glass, and Ada took it like I'd cradle a sick goat.

"You're taking an awful risk," I said softly. There were punishments for harboring now, ever since Asphodel Jones, the Wicked God's general and living prophet, and his irregulars scattered into the hills above John's Creek. The Great Army found those who harbored Jones's men or failed to rid their lands of Twisted Things, and hanging was just the favorite death. There were dim rumors of others, less kind and uglier still. Stories had reached even our lonely farm of the swift blade of a regimental trial.

"Well, you can't harbor dead things," Ada said with a practical shrug. "Think of it as part of the war effort."

Heron's brown face took on a sickly tinge. "How long since you last saw a nest, before yesterday?"

Ada settled thoughtfully onto her heels. "They were gone for weeks. Since August, maybe; they died out, the first time, when the soldiers came home. This little mischief arrived yesterday."

The courteous light in Heron's eyes snuffed out. "Miss, I'll help settle the cargo," he said, and strode back down the pier.

"What's wrong with him?" Ada asked, much too keen.

"I don't know," I said before it caught up to me: I'd watched Heron arrive on the black-paved high road. The road that came from the old city, where the Chandlers studied its ruins.

He'd been there, and he'd been running. Bearing John Balsam's knife, the relic that saved the world. The relic nobody wanted on their land.

"Tell us if you find any more of them?" I asked, stuttery and distracted.

"Of course," Rami said, and shook my hand. I hurried down to the rowboat. It rode lower in the water with the weight of our supplies, its floor strewn with packages tangled in sacking.

"We're ready?" I asked nobody. Tyler avoided my eyes. He tucked his bad leg in and nodded.

We cast off into the river under a cold sun, slipping mockingly behind the burnt-out ruins of skyscrapers. "Row fast," I said once we were away from the shoreline, Windstown receding into smears and dots behind us.

Heron bent over his oars, wooden, hidden.

You and I, I resolved grimly, *are going to talk.*

NINE

WE REACHED THE RIVERBANK AT TWILIGHT.
The dock loomed out of the evening, looking half abandoned after the bright glass and gardens of Windstown. I fumbled the mooring rope around the post. The world was already doused in evening gray, too dark to see our chimney smoke across the distant fields.

"Strike a light?" I asked, and took the dockside lantern off its hook. "I'll get the wheelbarrow; you unload the boat."

"Miss," Heron muttered. He'd been withdrawn since we'd set sail. I shoved the lantern into his hands and hurried down the dock to the orchard, away from Tyler and Heron's moods, into delicious privacy.

Roadstead Farm's paths were written in the folds of my skin; they were memorized in my tendons and bones. I picked my way up the orchard track, dodging roots and stones by memory, through sleeping apple trees that loomed like starless gulps of night. I closed my eyes and drank in the rustle of wind on branches, the smell of chilled soil in the fields. *Home,* I thought gratefully; aimed it defiantly across the river at the ponderous Pitts house. *Home.* My stomach flooded with sick tension at even the memory of Pitts glaring down his nose at us, so effortlessly ready to swat our whole lives away.

The nausea curled around a new thought: *that knife.* Heron had said it was just steel and leather, unmagical, inert. *Steel and leather he doesn't want me—or anyone—to touch.* There was something wrong between that knife and Heron, something that didn't sum to whole numbers. A secret.

I was already full into the argument with him in my head when my foot landed on something round and *wrong.*

I went down with a shriek in the cold dirt path. *Twisted Thing,* I thought, blind and frightened, and scrambled backward. The night before me stayed silent. Behind me, it exploded with footsteps. "Hallie?" Tyler called, his voice muffled against nothing at all.

I listened hard for motion—the flap of wings or the stalk of feral dogs—but all I heard was the river, hushed with distance even though I knew it was just over the rise. I drew in a breath to shout back, call for Tyler, and I choked. The air was as thin as flour.

The coughs clawed at my throat, racking, grating. *But the feather came out of my hand,* I thought, and wrapped both arms around my belly. It couldn't be another Twisted Thing, or a fragment: no part of me *hurt* that much. Tyler shouted again, and then Heron.

Heron had grabbed my arms, before, and pulled me *back.*

I clawed backward, coughing, over roots and hillocks: back out of the airlessness where I'd fallen. My hand closed on something cold and solid as I scrambled back down toward the beach—a round river stone, still damp from the water, trailing slimy water weed. And then another, and another.

Marthe, I thought with a thrill of fear—and joy. *She left a note.* Marthe and I had written notes in twigs or pebbles when we were younger, when there was danger. We'd left warnings for each other when we couldn't speak aloud. She was talking to me again.

I looked up toward the chimney. In the distance, the house was dark.

Something is wrong.

I let the stone go, and it clacked against another rock, the flat kind Thom had taught me to skip as a child. River water seeped through Nat's gloves as I ran my fingers over heaps and piles of stones, disgorged wetly all around me, trying to read their jagged message.

Sparks lit the night: *the lantern.* It wobbled wildly along the beach, Heron and Tyler's footsteps slamming across the sand behind it. Heron shoved into the road, his fists clenched around a piece of driftwood. Tyler stumbled up beside him. The dockside lantern swung crazily in his hand, and its light smeared the dark trees gray, finally lighting the ground under my hands. "Hallie, what—" Tyler started, and confused horror spread across his face.

"Oh," Heron said, small and fearstruck.

I pushed to my feet and looked down.

The path to the farmstead was choked with drowned stones. I'd been sitting sprawled between them, inside a giant stone-hewn scream. The rocks I'd touched, the rocks I'd thrown formed the curve of a message written too large: WE'RE STUCK HERE. WE'RE DYING. HELP. PLEASE.

"Marthe," I gasped, and ran.

The house stood lightless and lifeless on the hilltop, its windows flung open wide. "Marthe?" I called as I burst into the kitchen. No one answered. The hearth was a mess of ashy coals, the fire hours dead. Flour spilled across Marthe's wood-block table in a shocked arc. "Marthe?" I rushed up the stairs. Our bedrooms, our washroom were all empty.

I crashed out the door, down the path, and past the goat pen. The goats were stirred up, wide awake and bleating. Blood pounded in my ears. She'd shut the kitchen door. She'd done that. She had to be unharmed still, and hiding from whatever had driven her from the house. I leaned my head, desperate, into my hands. *Where would you go?* I asked, my heartbeat wild, *if you were alone and afraid?*

The smokehouse, I thought, but that was my place, the place *I* would go. And then: *the hayloft. The barn.*

I took off for the barn on shaking legs. The door squealed wide under my frantic fingers and sent something scurrying for the corner, cats or voles or monstrosities in the dark. I bunched up my courage and burst inside, shouting, "Marthe? *Marthe?*"

The building held its breath, and then "Hallie?" floated down from the rafters.

I looked up and saw my sister, disheveled and ferocious in the rising moonlight, crouched in the hayloft with our pitchfork held high — and three scared marmalade cats at her ankles.

"Oh, Marthe," I breathed, and she dropped the fork, eyes wild. She was in just her housedress. Her hands were shaking with cold. I scrabbled up the ladder and threw Mami's shawl about her, rubbed blood frantically into her arms. "Marthe, how long have you been up here? What happened?"

She lifted one arm from her straining belly and tentatively touched my cheek. "I think I saw his ghost," Marthe said, all wonderment, and then my brave, cool sister crumpled into tears.

"Oh, no, Marthe," I blurted, and flung my arms around her: willed my heat and nerve and stubbornness straight into her heart. "You're okay," I begged, and chafed her cold hands. "We found your message. It's okay, I swear."

"What message —" she started, and my stomach knotted.

"The stones in the orchard road," I managed before the effort of pretending became too much. We looked down the hayloft ladder. Into the uncharted dark.

"A ghost?" I asked softly.

Her smile ached. "I miss him so much. But his eyes—his eyes were terrible."

She wrapped her arms around me, and we stayed there shaking, tear tracks on our cheeks, until Heron and Tyler brought the light in.

One of Mackenzie Green's burlap sacks was full of southlands tea: the last prewar batch from the Carolinas. There was enough of it to brew strong, dark cups for all of us while Heron ran to Lakewood Farm for the Blakelys.

Marthe checked all the windows, locked the doors, and pulled the blinds. Her eyes were red and haunted. They scanned the walls restlessly, marked every shadow's fall. I set milk and honey on the table and tried to forget her shaken touch on my cheek. She'd already pulled back into her fortress of reserve. I couldn't see a hint of her behind those deliberate walls.

"Town," she said, a dare to break the spell of normality she'd thrown together: tea brewing and the smell of sweet candle wax in the air. "How did it go?"

I bowed my head and handed back the accounts book. "That's a good price on salt," Marthe said after a moment.

"Heron did that. I was talking to Pitts," I said low, and Tyler excused himself to the parlor. I wasn't the only one who could feel Marthe's temperamental weather.

"And what did *he* have to say?" Marthe asked bitterly.

My jaw clenched into a snarl. "Pitts wants to pack us off

to Prickett's and quarantine the whole farm. And I told him where to shove his militia, his grudge, and his presumption."

Marthe's grim face flickered, and she scrubbed a hand across her eyes. "Good girl."

I flushed, and looked away. "He said there aren't Twisted Things in Windstown. But the Chandlers found one. It was all —" I shook my head. I couldn't inflict that pickled, floating corpse on Marthe.

My sister's face went still. "We'll just have to handle it, then."

"How?" I said, small, into the ghost-filled night.

Her jaw set, stone hard. "By ourselves, Hal," she said. "The same way we always have," and then the kitchen door opened and the Blakelys poured in.

Cal Blakely looked smaller and tireder already: a month older in the past day. He went straight into the parlor and touched Tyler's head softly. "You all right, kid?"

Strain etched lines around Tyler's white eyes. "Enough to keep walking."

"Good man," Cal said, and patted his shoulder. There were ghosts in his eyes too; ghosts snagged everywhere. "Nat and James brought the dogs. If whatever you saw was someone prowling about trying to scare you, we'll find them on the double."

"It wasn't," Marthe muttered, so low I barely heard.

I peeked out the drawn curtains. I could barely see Nat

and James in silhouette: two bodies, lantern-lit, in our cold barley fields.

"Who's at Lakewood Farm with Eglantine?" Marthe asked.

"Eglantine is the last person anyone wants to pick a fight with," Cal replied. "Come on. Let's see your stone letters."

Heron was out front with the water bucket, drinking in great gulps straight from the brim. We marched in a ragged line toward the river dock, each one of us head down, watching the grass. The path turned, and there we were: atop the shuddering plea written in the road.

Marthe read the stones and went pale as bleached cotton.

"Steady," Cal murmured. "You don't want to stress the child."

"That's an old wives' tale, and you know it," Marthe snapped.

"I'm sorry, sir," Heron cut in smoothly, and inserted himself between them. "We've likely obliterated any footprints."

"Can't be helped," Cal said with a sigh — Cal, who tracked like a fox. "Tyler, give me light?"

Tyler raised his lantern high, and Cal Blakely got to work.

He paced pathways around the muddy stones, circling silently. The lamp in Tyler's hand cast strange shadows. They made him look melancholy, bruise-eyed with age. We scoured the hard, muddy path together, down to where the sand and the river wiped every trace clean. "Anything?" I asked.

"There's water," Cal said quietly, and traced an imperceptible line on the rocks, away from the pathway and away from the docks. "Water falling from river stones, I'd think. But I don't think this was a prank or a prowler. Nothing with feet passed through here."

Marthe didn't react. She'd composed herself somehow since that first sight of the stones. Her face was utterly still, her eyes shuttered again. *She said,* I realized with a chill, *she saw a ghost.* Nobody knew about the stone messages of our childhood: nobody but me, Thom, and Marthe. I couldn't conceive of doubting Marthe: her keen eyes, her ruthless practicality, the way she always knew what to do. But there was no such thing as ghosts.

The knife that killed a god is hidden in your smokehouse, I thought. *Don't crack too wise about no such thing.* And suddenly the familiar night was full of monsters. I shuddered hard.

Cal Blakely lifted a gentle eyebrow. "There's nothing, Hal," he said, and led us back to the abandoned stones.

There was a new light there, around the corner that led to our dead, shorn fields. "We can't find your prowler, Marthe," James Blakely called from behind it. He and Nat came into view, the dogs slinking wary at their heels. "Flushed another Twisted Thing up the shore, though. We need to lay a fire. This doesn't look good."

"If there are Twisted Things about, we should clear off," Cal said.

"The air's back to normal," Tyler murmured. "It's fine."

"Wait," I said. "You felt that too?"

James's eyebrows rose.

"I couldn't breathe. Yesterday, when we found the Twisted Thing," I admitted, and James Blakely's face went slack. "And again, tonight. My chest hurt. I couldn't hear. I backed away, and it stopped."

"A fuzz in your ears," Heron asked quietly, "as if everything were very far away?"

The back of my neck prickled. The four men exchanged a long and terrible look.

"You know what this is," Marthe said.

Heron nodded reluctantly. "It happened in the war, ma'am. Spots where the air was bad. Where sounds changed."

"It was how you knew a Twisted Thing was coming," Tyler added. "And then you ran like hell."

Once, Ty's uncles would have chastised him for bad language. Neither did. They edged close together, and Cal held James's hand like a lifeboat.

"You ran because sometimes it got into a man," Heron explained. "And they'd cough. You heard them through the night: fit, healthy farmers choking like their air had turned to water. It's why the war went so hard," he said, despite Cal's glare. "We held our breath every time we charged."

"We didn't fight at John's Creek so we could scare half-grown girls with it," Cal said lightly. The edge on his voice would've cut brick.

Heron loosened his shoulders fractionally and stared holes into Cal's eyes. "We didn't fight to lie about it either."

"C'mon now," James said quietly, and squeezed his husband's hand. "We fought so this wouldn't swallow up our homes. Which means we use everything we know, *right now.*"

"Of course I married an optimist," Cal said, disgusted, and tromped up the path to the river.

Nat watched him go, the lantern flashing her pupils wide. "So it's the Wicked God."

James exhaled in the rumpled dark. "Some Twisted Things left over from the Wicked God, maybe — the shreds the Great Army's still hunting. The Wicked God is dead."

"What Twisted Thing learns how to spell?" Nat said dryly.

"I don't know," James said, and ran both hands through his hair. "Nasturtium, I am only human."

Silence pooled through the trees. Joy whined impatiently and snuffled Nat's hand.

"We have to clear this away," Heron said into the awkward hush. "Your flour and salt are still on the dock, ma'am."

Marthe stared at the stone letters for a long moment. "Fine," she said too lightly, and I reluctantly lifted the first stone. It felt wrong, like unmarking a grave. We obliterated the wet bones of that call for help and trailed back to the house in silence.

Marthe stopped at the porch steps, her arms still crossed above her stomach. "We'll be fine now, thank you," she said hollowly.

James gave her a long look. "We're not done yet. We have a Twisted Thing to burn."

"It's fine."

"Christ, Marthe," he said, ragged-edged, "stop being your father."

I flinched.

Marthe went pale. "That was low, Jim."

"I'm sorry," he said, and held out his weary hands. "But we're neighbors, and—"

"—we have to look out for each other," Marthe finished, her teeth still gritted. That was the *second*-longest argument in the world, repeated over and over with the Blakely adults from the time our Papa died. "Then look out for us instead of calling me *that*." The fire in her voice was weirdly soothing: this was the sister I knew, who took no nonsense, anywhere.

James nodded gravely, and I wondered if he'd done it on purpose—to kick her out of that awful, broken calm. "We'll loan you Sadie for a guard dog," he said, and Tyler blinked with surprise. "She's going into heat, and we can't feed puppies this year."

"We can't take your dog," I said, truly flabbergasted. The Blakelys' sheepdogs were family. To send one away, even in a lean year, was—staggering.

Cal glanced at his husband from the corner of his eye. "Actually, I've a better idea. Give us winter grazing rights in your barley fields. It'd be a good thing, this year, to not take the flock all the way to River Rouge."

It didn't take a breath for James to catch on. "That's a

thought. It'll put more eyes on the land and save everyone trouble." His smile stayed fixed easy on Marthe, but that's not where Cal was watching. Cal was watching Tyler.

Wicked, I thought. The Blakelys would have cheap winter grazing and the chance to keep an eye on us without ruffling our pride. And Tyler's wounded leg, around which so much revolved, would be inexorably kept safe, close to home. *God, what a plot,* I thought, infuriated and relieved.

"Fine, James. Do whatever you want," Marthe snapped. She turned on her heel, stripped of all manners, and went into the house.

"Well, that went well," Cal muttered dryly, and I scowled.

"I'm right here."

Cal's face stayed impassive; it was Tyler who flushed. "Yes," Cal said laconically. "You are."

I got behind him and started walking him, as stubborn as a sheepdog, toward their cart. "Not too happy with me, are you?" Cal said mildly as he backed down the path before me; as James, Nat, and Tyler rounded the turn.

"Nope," Nat said before I could. Cal cast her a startled glance.

"I'll get over it," I said through gritted teeth. "Just . . . get lost. Go home."

Tyler fell back next to me as his uncles readied the cart. My stomach seized, and I forced myself to meet his eye.

"Hallie, I—"

That ugly red color was back in his face. "What?" I asked, and bit my lip.

He took the measure of me, and looked down. Shook his head.

He didn't look at me again. Not once as they mounted the cart and drove, jingling, into the violent night.

TEN

MARTHE WAS LATE TO BED. SHE BALANCED THE ACCOUNT books, fussed in the root cellar, and swept the kitchen twice before finally coming upstairs. I held my breath for ten minutes after her door shut, and fought the temptation to knock on it. To break my sworn word, curl up in her quilt, and tell her every last scrap of the humiliation Pitts had served me; describe Heron's torn-up face when he looked upon that knife. To ask my big sister, who always knew, what to do.

"You're not six anymore," I whispered, the old refrain. And without Thom here to mend our squabbles, without the threat of Papa cleaving us together, united, Marthe wasn't *Marthe* anymore: she wouldn't dry my tears, tell a bad joke, and reassure me that everything would be all right. She'd look down at me, as cold-eyed as Alonso Pitts, and send me out into the fields again; send Heron onto the winter roads. Send anything that was a problem as far away as possible.

The world changed. Families changed. I'd known that since I was eight years old. What hurt was how I still couldn't stop myself from *wanting* those impossible things: the quiet touch, on nightmare mornings, of her hand on my hair.

I swallowed, and forced my head up high. "You are half owner of Roadstead Farm, Hallie Hoffmann. Take care of it." How we always had: alone.

I slipped out of my bedroom and closed the door behind me; tiptoed past Marthe's shut door into the night. My breath plumed: a real frost was coming on. I snagged our icy shovel from the barn and carried it with me to the smokehouse. There was a light in there, one lone, smoky lantern fighting the unwelcoming moon. I tapped on the door, quick and quiet, and Heron opened it warily.

He'd not yet prepared for bed. He was still in his shirt-sleeves, face wet and stubble dripping, his socks more darns than wool. He took me in with an ugly trepidation. "Miss Hallie," he started.

I didn't want to hear how that sentence ended. I thrust the shovel between our bodies like a wall. "Did the Twisted Things follow you here? Is that why nobody from John's Creek to the river wanted you on their land?"

The fear that had ridden his shoulders all the way from the Windstown docks flared, and then he tucked his head. "I don't know," he said softly. "There were incidents on the road back from John's Creek. But that was the war. Things . . . happened."

"Things?"

Heron's smile came thin as lantern smoke. "The last town

I stayed in proper was Caryville. We were there a week before a cloud came from the south and every bit of wood in the township scorched to cinders. They didn't have a tree or doorway left. The whole town stank of lye and burnt houses." He paused. "I was traveling with a quarter regiment, and the town hung half those men off the water tower—it was old-cities metal and it was still there. Their town was gone. They needed someone to blame."

I stared, my eyes full of rope and Thom's good boots dangling, and tried to find my voice.

"Things happened," he said, and met my eye, almost pleading. "So much of it had nothing to do with me."

"But some of it did," I finished. Some of it did.

Heron winced, but his face was unguarded again. "Are you sending me away?"

I recoiled, incredulous. "No."

His eyebrows rose—and then narrowed into an appraising stare. "Why in hell not?"

"Because it's winter," I stammered, and his frank gaze didn't falter. "You'll freeze if I turn you out."

"So?" he pressed brutally. "I'm a stranger. Your sister's pregnant. I can't say for certain those Twisted Things aren't flocking to John Balsam's knife, and I've already left a handful of towns to the tender mercies of regimental justice. I might just wreck your little farm."

"I don't *hurt* people!" I burst out—and covered my mouth with both hands. "I don't do that. Not to someone who's bringing a veteran's family his things. Not to someone who's trying to help save my farm."

"You don't do that in the lakelands," Heron said. Weighed me in his gaze, like a bar of soap in Uncle Matthias's considering palm.

My red cheeks ached against the midnight cold. "*I* don't do that," I said harshly. "We don't do that on Roadstead Farm."

Heron looked down at me, indecipherable, all fathoms. "All right," he said softly. "What's the shovel for?"

"I know you said it's not magic," I said, and set the shovel down. "But before the ground freezes, we're burying that knife. Away from us."

"I'll get my boots," he said, and disappeared into the smokehouse.

He came out with the knife shoved in his belt loop, swaddled in its leather wrappings; his face wholly unconcerned about what godlike powers it might stain on his skin. *So small,* I thought. *Such a nothing of a thing.* "Where do we put it?" he asked, tense.

"As far as we can get," I said, and we set off across the fields.

Roadstead Farm was large, larger than we could manage even when Thom had worked the land beside me. Whole acres were left to weeds and wilderness, to a vague *well, someday.* We followed those overgrown paths from the river, past our burying ground and the rough stones inside it: the graves of our parents, our grandparents, a smattering of great-aunts and -uncles who'd died young, or lived long lives without leaving. *We'll have to make Thom a stone,* I realized, and fought the lump in my throat. Marthe and I needed somewhere to visit. Her child would, when it was born.

The path wandered through scrub trees and dead dandelions and trickled out in an ocean of brush. "Here," I said, and hefted the lantern. "It's empty. No one ever comes."

Heron stopped where the path turned to weeds. "Whose land is this?"

"Ours," I said, and pushed a waist-tall sapling aside. "There are three generations of Hoffmanns back up the road who couldn't find the time to clear it."

I held the young tree aside for Heron. He ducked past it, and we waded into the scrub together, around broken bricks and the soft humps of rabbit burrows. Heron picked at the ground with the shovel, indecisive, and then sank it between the roots of a hawthorn. "Here," he said. "So I can find it in the spring."

I nodded. He dug, and I held the light.

The shadows twirled drunkenly around the tree trunk. My arms were tired. My *everything* was tired. I pretended that darkness was a burn mark, spreading slowly across the hawthorn like a Twisted Thing's footprints. I lowered the lamp and — there, it was gone. Like the town of Caryville. Like Coal Mountain. John's Creek.

"Tell me about it?" I asked Heron.

He didn't bother pretending not to know what I meant: John Balsam. John's Creek. The war against the Wicked God Southward. "That's a personal thing you're asking."

"Personal between every grown man between here and the southlands."

"I mean it," he said sharply. "You *do not* want to know."

I dropped the lantern to my side. "I just told you I did. God, you're just like Cal Blakely after all. If I'm harboring you, at least tell me what *against*."

Heron stiffened. "I thought the price for that was a winter's honest labor."

He'd forgot, for the first time, to call me *miss*.

"It's not a *price*," I pressed on. "You and Cal and James and Tyler, you all act like you can protect us from ever *knowing* there was a war, or Twisted Things." I gestured wide, at the burn marks in the brush he couldn't see. "I'm trying to help you. Don't insult me by pretending I shouldn't know what that might cost."

I yanked the light up—and stopped cold. That wooden look on his face wasn't anger. It was a dam, and behind it was grief.

My voice caught and unraveled. "Tell me about it," I begged, and he turned away, half in shadow. I leaned forward, farther into his space than a young woman should to any man but her suitor. "I want to know what he knew," I said, crisp and low. "I want to know what he saw and felt, and what it was like when—"

Heron looked up, looked at me, and his changeable gray eyes were suddenly, rawly young, as wide as Tyler Blakely's and wholly uncertain. "A man a few inches shorter than me, dark skin, brown eyes."

Angry tears scratched at the back of my nose. "Marthe's husband. He's my *brother*," and then my voice truly failed.

Heron shifted his weight, one leg to the other, through the thousand small choices that lay around us like snares. "How long since you stopped waiting for him?" he asked, and my heart froze.

"Just last week. Just when you came." I shook my head and clamped my jaw tight. My eyes weren't damp. They *weren't*.

That awful look, that studying look on Heron's face only deepened. "Miss," he said, differently deferent, "don't be so hard on yourself. It's only been a week and a half."

The sob shook out of me, and everything broke around it. I folded in on myself, against the hawthorn, and let out an ugly wail.

Our Thom was dead. My brother, who was going to fix up the smokehouse, who always got Marthe and me laughing instead of fighting, who I'd never even thought would fail to make it home. And finally, I could see the future roll out before me: I'd pull in the next harvest without him. I'd marry one day, and the place where I'd just assumed he'd be standing, broad and smiling, would be empty air. He would never meet my children. He'd never meet his own.

The emptiness grew, and split, and ate the whole world in its wake. It was never going to be all right again.

I heard—didn't see—Heron plant the shovel in the dirt. And then he disentangled the lantern from my fingers and wrapped his stranger's arms gingerly around my shoulders.

A shock traveled between us: *I'm not*—and he shook his head, once, definitive. *No, this is not.* He patted my back awkwardly, unromantically, and then I understood what the offer was: everything that had been missing since the war ended and the men came back with their hearts stranded miles away; since Marthe went behind her fortress of reserve and temper so she could hold herself up with its walls. Since she left me alone, on the outside, stranded.

Simple, human comfort for all the stupid things we'd lost.

I drooped against him and wept, but it was tempered now, grief mixed with awful, sagging relief. That brave face of mine had been so exhausting. It wasn't meant to stay up—to be held up—all alone.

The grief worked out of me slowly, like a splinter, and I finally leaned back, wiping my face against my sleeve. "I'm sorry," I managed, and hugged myself with both arms. The lantern guttered low beside us. I felt scraped clean under the skin. Lightheaded, hollowed. Gone.

"You don't have to be sorry," Heron said, and he stepped away, his hands closed empty at his sides.

"You don't have to talk about it," I started.

Heron shook his head hard. "It's all right," he said. "I will."

"The recruiter showed up on a Thursday," he said in the lantern's shadow, behind the hawthorn, in the dark. "He was half dead with hunger; he begged us to save John's Creek. So we talked among ourselves, and most of us decided it was too important. We were going."

The shovel set the rhythm: *crunch*, heft, *crunch*; behind it was the sift of falling earth. I knew this part well, like an old bedtime story. A recruiter had lighted in Windstown too, saying *There's a Dark God in the southlands. He's turning the rivers to rock, making desert of our green fields. You have to help us.*

Please.

"So we went," he said, and shrugged lightly in the breeze. "My cousins and I packed anything that'd shed blood: deer knives, wood axes. We went. I'd never been south in my whole life, and I'd never hit a man with more than my fist. We were woodsmen and farm boys, and we thought we'd be home before the leaves turned. We thought we'd come home heroes."

"But they told you about the Twisted Things," I protested, from the dark. "They'd told *us* about the Twisted Things, but we—"

"Didn't understand." Heron smirked. "Lizards, drought? We'd seen those things—or so we thought. We had no notion of *gods*. I grew up with Jehovah, Allah, Jesus, and Vishnu, and you can't touch them with your own two hands. We didn't know how real It would be, how Its voice scraped your eardrums raw."

I swallowed, even though I was leaning across my own knees for every syllable. This was unbearably intimate. This was private pain.

"We found a regiment at Aylmer, and then mostly we walked, marching in rows like real fighting men all the way down south. We tried not to gawk at the strange trees or the mountains. I'd never seen mountains before. It was still an adventure, you see. People lined up along the roadsides. We did drills for them, like a parade. And they lined up and blessed us for saving their families, even though we hadn't even reached John's Creek."

He leaned on the shovel, far away on that long walk. "It wasn't even a town when we got there. Folks said there'd been a town there six whole weeks before, but there wasn't one brick, one bone of it left. John's Creek was blind, dead desert, where the wind blew all night and whipped up the sand. Everyone who'd lived there had vanished in the storms or run so far they were past hope for finding. You couldn't blame them," he said simply. "John's Creek was the end of the world.

"The sand was brown, and the sky was brown. The air tasted like stale campfires and latrines. The dust got in your sleeves and burned you, speck by speck. The sun was a memory. And the wind—" He stopped and turned to me. "In the wind you heard the Wicked God screaming, and the wind never, ever stopped.

"I still dream about it," he added, almost offhand. "Its sounds were so very close to words that you stayed up all night long, listening. None of it ever came clear. It never made sense, up to the day It died. But I remember every syllable."

The shovel dug automatically, as steady as a man who never planned to stop walking. The lamplight drowned between the gnarled hawthorn roots.

"And the problem was, it wasn't really a war. We were exterminators for the birds and lizards that poured out of the desert every day. Asphodel Jones and his irregulars didn't line up and charge us, and we weren't a proper army: just a few thousand men used to their towns and making their own decisions, thrown together in a heap. Everyone had come to save the southlands, and we each had our own idea how—or where to strike camp, or for a better place to dig the cook-pits. You couldn't keep track of the disagreements; no leader lasted more than three days. It was chaos, and the desert just stretched toward us, closer every night. Every morning it crept closer, and another friend had stepped on a Twisted Thing and lost a foot. There was no one to really fight at John's Creek but each other."

"But what about Asphodel Jones?" I asked.

I'd heard the name only in whispers, the kind quickly put away. The Wicked God's prophet, Asphodel Jones: the first man to turn his back on John's Creek — on *people* — and act as mouthpiece to a monstrous god. The dark man, with a dark walk, who'd fought to bring the Great Dust to the whole world.

Heron scowled. "Jones had men — not many, but enough to give us merry hell. They slit a few throats every night. They set a few tents on fire, nibbled at our edges until we were ragged. It was Jones that got us going at last," he said, and his smile twisted into knots. "The countryside was empty. The foragers had to go farther and farther for food, and we'd slaughtered all the livestock whole weeks past. We were starving, and we couldn't fight the Wicked God. But we could tear apart Asphodel Jones."

I leaned back. There was bloodlust in those changeable gray eyes. Heron blinked, and looked down, and gave another resigned shrug. "Everyone was so angry," he said, still surprise-struck. "We were useless. So when de Guzman and Achebe said *Let's go kill Asphodel Jones,* nobody argued that they shouldn't be generals. All these beaten men came together, faced the Great Dust, and just . . . went in."

He paused, and in the chilled plume of his breath I saw row after row of tattered, dirty farm boys disappear into the blowing sand.

"And we killed things," he said simply. "The Twisted Things were thick as flies inside the Great Dust, and we stood there and killed them. You couldn't breathe or see past your elbow, so we just swung our weapons and hoped they cut the right flesh. Men lost their legs wading through the blood we spilled. Men burned to skeletons. My cousin Dudley died, and then my cousin Pierre. And before I ran out of cousins, General de Guzman's regiment signaled that they'd found Asphodel Jones.

"Jones and his irregulars had a stockade." Heron's smile curved, faint and pained. "It should have been ridiculous. This mad, stubble-chinned man with a god in his pocket, and he'd built It a pasture fence to keep It from grazing at the neighbors'. But it wasn't ridiculous," he said softly. "I hated him like I've never hated anything in my life.

"Everybody ran at him, every soldier left in the Great Army. All the weeks of death and waiting popped loose like a cork, and Jones's men met us, fighting just as vicious. It was their god they were defending; their wild, fenced-in god.

"Only a few thought to run *past* Asphodel Jones. Because they were thinking. Or cowards. Or"—a shadow crossed his face—"no knowing, now. But they ran around the barricade, through the ghost-flowers and sand, and we found the Wicked God."

"It was in the storm?" I asked, breathless.

"No." He sighed. "It *was* the storm. A million grains of sand and a hot wind, and miles of rage. Eating the goodness out of the land to feed itself, and howling for more all day and night."

"How—" I started, and Heron shook his head. *How do you cut the heart from a storm?* He didn't understand it either. He had no idea how the war, this sham of a war, was won.

Heron traced the lines of the leather-wrapped knife, traced its tornado twists and curls. "There was a calm at the heart of it: the eye of a tornado. A few inches of peace and quiet. And the knife went in, and cut, and—

"And it stopped," he finished, almost bewildered. "The wind died for the first time in months at John's Creek. Tons of sand rained out of a clear sky. The Great Dust just stopped."

"And the God died," I whispered. "And you turned your face away."

His dreamy, aching expression stuttered, and his eyes focused for the first time in what felt like hours. "Yes," he said, almost uncertain. "The God died. Jones vanished from the battlefield. And then the war was over."

My heart beat hard in my chest. This wasn't the story I'd thought to hear. I'd been ready for terrible battles, for the terrible cost of victory. This wasn't it at all. "What about John Balsam?"

Heron's eyes narrowed. "John Balsam was nobody. He was no one when he came to John's Creek, and he was no one when he left."

"But he killed the Wicked God," I said, shocked now, really and truly.

"By himself," Heron said, calm with contempt. "He killed the God alone and left the whole mess behind him. He led nobody; he knew *nothing* about gods or people." I saw it then: the ghost in his eyes. Whispering obscenities in his ear. "If he'd been someone men could follow, they wouldn't be sending his likeness to every town from John's Creek to the ocean, because someone, somewhere, would *care* enough to recognize his face."

I stepped back. "But you have his knife. You're taking his knife home."

The shovel landed with a vicious *thunk*. "Every nobody has a home," he said. Dirt flew onto the heap beside him, blotting out the stars. "Every nobody leaves something behind."

Something like me. Like Marthe and the child. I squeezed my eyelids shut, but there were no tears left. Heron's brown desert had drained them dry.

"It's deep enough," I told him, hoarse. "It's done. You can stop."

Heron blinked and looked down at the tomb he'd made. It burrowed past the hawthorn roots, past rusted old-cities garbage: a jagged gash in the crumbling earth. He flung the shovel away from him, back into the deep brush. There was dust and dying in his gray eyes, and his hands clutched, reluctant, at John Balsam's knife.

I eased carefully toward him and looked down into the hole. The hawthorn roots pierced its walls like fingers. "They don't talk about the war because it wasn't a war like in stories."

"They don't talk about the war," Heron corrected, defeat-bitter, "because we were animals, and we are ashamed."

And I finally, finally got it. They'd left home to do right, to stand valiantly up for the downtrodden and dispossessed. And come home stained with bickering, and powerlessness, and the taste of endless dust. All summer long I'd lain awake, wrestling with the failure I'd made of Roadstead Farm. I'd thought I understood failure. But compared to Heron, I hadn't a clue.

Heron drew John Balsam's knife from his belt and balanced it with all the care he'd withheld from my field shovel. "It'll be safe," I told him softly. "I promise."

He squeezed the wrappings tight and laid it crooked in the grave.

The hole filled in quicker than it had been dug. Heron tamped the earth down flat when he finished, and covered it with a stone and a scattering of brown leaves. An offering for John Balsam's knife and Heron's war, Heron's secrets.

"Thank you," I said, sore-throated.

He inclined his head gently. Here was the man I'd come to recognize again: the one I'd taken on because he'd seen in me something to call kind. Because I thought I couldn't hurt him, no matter what I did. His mannerly walls creaked back into place: another selfless, determined soldier walking his lonely roads. But I saw it, now. I'd seen it.

He was so weary it could break your heart.

I took the shovel from him and hefted it through the scrub. He followed me silently to the path, to where untracked wilderness became a field, a farm, a road. Heron looked back over his shoulder.

"It'll be safe," I repeated.

He picked a dead nettle out of his pantleg. "I'll at least cut the firewood here." He forced his head forward, away from his charge — the one thing he had to make himself someone's hero after all.

"We should sleep," I said, quieter.

"In the morning, then, miss," he answered, soft and formal, and set off across the broken barley.

I trudged, alone, back to the silent house: past the pen where the goats slept heaped and loving and the chickens called sporadically in dreams. My boots crunched gravel. Every sound hushed and echoed, wrapping around the emptiness we'd spilled and left behind us; abandoned, like soldiers and skyscrapers, to fall to quiet ruin.

The fields lay quiet. I snuffed the lantern at the porch step. Overhead, the broken stars burned.

WINTER

ELEVEN

THE KITCHEN DOOR HAD A NEW GOUGE ON IT WHERE Marthe had flung it shut the morning I left for Windstown. *Just last week,* I thought. *Not even eight days ago.* Old wood peeked through years of varnish, clean-looking in the afternoon light. That fight already felt a lifetime old. Everything did, except the dull ache in my chest where Thom's love used to live.

I'd slept badly for days. I never saw him in my dreams: just his boots, creased with work and age, walking slowly away from me through the brown sand, into the storm. In the mornings, there were chores: malting and mucking out with antsy Heron, who was still perpetually looking over his shoulder to where John Balsam's knife slept.

In the afternoons we burned Twisted Things. Marthe found them in the vegetable garden, one every day or two, scattered like acorns. Steadily, screaming, in drips and bursts they came up the path between our house and the river shore. They died and died, and we burned them in the yard and marked their deaths on a makeshift map Marthe drew of the farmstead. There were Twisted Things on Roadstead Farm, and none of them went near the grave of John Balsam's knife. Heron studied the map after supper by the light of his one lantern. "This makes no damn sense," he muttered, and it didn't. It made no sense.

It was already habit to leave the windows shut, to check our boots before we stepped into the house.

I wiped mine twice before I opened the kitchen door, and managed, "Butcher's here, Marthe," with hearty, fake good cheer. "Hang and Cua need you to sort the goats."

Marthe nodded, setting the lid on something rich with fresh game meat and onions. I looked down at the floor tiles and swallowed hard. The woodenness had worn off her, slow and trickling, but Marthe had not been the same since we'd found that stone message; since the night I found her in the hay barn speaking of ghosts. She moved like a foggy morning these days. She spoke like a woman underwater.

"I don't know which goats you want to keep—" I trailed off. The false smile was starting to hurt. "What should I tell them?"

Marthe wiped her hands on the dishrag. "I'm coming," she said dully, and tried a stretched-out smile. I flinched. You could see the shattered pieces of her trailing along the floor.

"What can I do?" I asked around the glass in my throat.

She focused, for a moment, and dipped a mug in the big soup pot. "Take this out to Tyler Blakely," she said. "I told Eglantine I'd give him lunch."

"Right," I said faintly. My stomach flipped with nerves.

Tyler. He'd been grazing the Blakely sheep in our fields for a week, and no matter how small fifty acres could sometimes be, we'd managed to tidily avoid each other. The thought of breaking that distance made my stomach seize. *I hate everything*, I thought dimly, and hugged the soup mug to my shirt.

Marthe fumbled her boots on. She looked up at me, waiting, and her eyes were a heart-dead mask.

I fled.

Sadie, her black coat smudged with dirt, was waiting outside at the porch rail. Her tail thumped cautiously against the old boards as I shut the door. "Hi, doggy," I whispered. She was too well trained to jump, but she butted my knee worriedly; she'd taken a bit too well to her new job as Roadstead Farm's guard. I ran a calming hand down her back. "Come on. We're going to find your brother."

She shook with delight and romped ahead of me, her nose fixed to the ground. We almost reached the highway before I saw him: Tyler Blakely, stretching his bad leg in a bitten-down barley field, surrounded by his peaceful, grazing sheep. I caught my breath, and Sadie plowed right past me, barking merrily away.

He startled and straightened awkwardly, an ugly red stain on his cheeks. Sadie plunged toward him; the sheep frayed against the pressure of her sleek black body. "Lunch," I said hesitantly, and nudged through in her wake.

"Thanks," he muttered. It took me a moment to translate the word. Before the war — before last week — I'd have had some witty comment about boys who mumble, or at least an elbow straight to the ribs. But I'd lost Thom. I was losing Marthe. And now Tyler's eyes were fixed away from me, his hands an arm's length away. Suddenly, nothing was the right thing to say.

"You here all afternoon?" I asked. *Stupid small talk* —

"Until supper," he answered and buried his face in Marthe's mug. Pain sparked between my ribs: there might have been a *miss* on that, for all the friendliness it held. *He doesn't want you,* the snarl in my head pronounced. *Go home.*

I bit my lip, hard. "Tyler," I managed. He lifted an eyebrow at the grass. I forced out, "Spite or pride?"

His face went awful with anger — no, with shame. And then he looked up at me, for the first time in an age, and smiled tightly. "This one's all pride."

That smile hit like a slap. "Ty, talk to me?"

"I've embarrassed myself enough," he muttered. "Just leave me *alone.*"

I shoved my hands into my pockets, stomach-sick. *It's over.* The boy who'd walked with me when we trailed behind Nat was just another bridge breaking; who'd —

"Remember that time you shoved a toad down the back of my shirt when I was seven?" I blurted.

He stared at me, suspicious, uncomprehending.

"I got Nat to help get you back. She stole every single pair of your skivvies out of the laundry, and we hung them on the big hawthorn at the head of the drive."

He remembered. I could see it in the way his flat, hard mouth softened. Remembered that I was *me:* the lean little girl in ribbonless braids who knew where his laundry basket was.

"You just sauntered out here, cool as you please," I said, and shook my head with broken wonderment. "Looked up at the tree, and went, 'Guess I'm swimming in my birthday suit.'"

Tyler's mouth quirked. "Please tell me I didn't reach for my pants."

I tucked my chin to hide the watery smile. "You didn't have to. We were so grossed out we went back *up* the tree and got them down ourselves."

"And threw them in the mud for me to pick up."

"Boy underpants are gross," I said lightly.

"Uh-huh. You two were awful little kids sometimes," he said. But he was talking. He wasn't turned away from me.

"I know," I said, a little ashamed myself now. "But if you weren't embarrassed about *that*"—and my voice went thin and frantic—"there is nothing on earth embarrassing enough to never speak like friends again."

He looked up at me, and the shame was gone, leaving behind it eyes like bleak white snow. "You have no idea, Hal," he pronounced softly.

"At least tell me *why*."

"How can you not know why?" he snapped. "You said it was just talk. You don't want me. So, fine; I'll stay out of your way. Fair enough. But now you're picking at this, and I don't know what you *want* from me."

I stared. A clear, staticky anger rose inside my ears. "Tyler—"

"I know everyone says you should be able to stay friends, but I can't pretend everything's normal, okay? You still don't want me, and that's—I can't just go back to normal. I need some *room*. I need time where we're not *poking* at it."

He slumped against his staff, planted in the dead dirt. I didn't know whether to laugh or to let loose like Marthe on a tear. "Tyler," I said, slow and clear. "I didn't say *any* of that."

His head whipped up. "You did. In the mayor's parlor, you said it was nothing but talk. If it's all talk to you, just me being puffed-up and vain and *stupid*, well . . . *fine*. But don't *lie* about it—"

"God, *stop!*" I burst out. He leaned back, wide-eyed. "Just stop talking and *listen*."

Quiet sank into the turf between us: the mutters of sheep, a scandalized bird. Dead leaves underfoot.

"Look, I was surprised, okay? I *am* surprised," I started.

Tyler looked down bitterly at his blunt fingernails. "And here I thought I was the most obvious fool in the world."

"Listening, right?" I snapped, and he pulled a face. "You put a toad down my shirt when I was seven years old. I've known you *forever*. Nobody expects someone who saw them burping and waddling around in diapers to look at them like—something *romantic*."

"Now who's embarrassed?" he said slyly.

"What?"

"So what if you said stupid things when you were two? I was *four*," he said, and his thin face firmed. "And who says that means someone can't like you?"

"That's not how it works," I answered weakly. The sheep edged away from us, smelling the fight.

"Who says," Tyler pressed softly, "how it *works*?"

The static in my ears dropped clean out. "Everybody," I said. The adults in Windstown, in every approving smile or shake of a disappointed head. Nat's suitors, stiffly formal, coming down the path in their best boots and most terrified faces. Janelle Prickett, when she gave us the gossip about who'd dared show a little too much of themselves to whom, and was turned away.

And . . . none of them were here. Nobody was here except Tyler and me, and the sheep, and the dogs, and the trees.

"You like *me*," I said distinctly. "Even though I put your skivvies up the hawthorn tree."

I saw his Adam's apple bob. "I like you. No *even though*."

"Oh," I said stupidly. The mown barley rustled around us, under the sound of nervous sheep. Joy finally intervened on their behalf: she leaned against my legs and pushed to drive Tyler and me apart. "Your dog wants us to stop fighting," I managed.

Tyler looked down at Joy. She shot him a dirty look and let out a herder's bark. "So she does," he murmured.

I gave up and let her push me into the milling flock. The gentle heat of their bodies licked my poor, frozen knees. I hadn't even noticed the cold.

Tyler closed the distance between us with a sheepherder's careful grace, and the air changed into something breath-caught and bright. My friend wasn't leaving me. He cared about me. He was *still here.*

"I didn't want you to be embarrassed," I said finally. "You looked so miserable, and I was so nervous about Pitts, and . . . sometimes I still say stupid things."

"You didn't want me to be—" Tyler started. His mouth worked and landed gracelessly on, "Oh. Shit."

I laughed. I couldn't help it; we were just too ridiculous.

He stared at me a moment and then let out a rueful chuckle. "My life has a terrible sense of humor, you know? I was proud of that speech." His cheeks were still ugly crimson. "I practiced it all week long to my bedroom ceiling."

"Did it have any good suggestions?"

"It said to definitely go with the wounded dignity. Very manly, super-tragic. I'm never asking it for anything again."

"The ceiling *or* Mrs. Pitts," I said dryly.

"God," Tyler said feelingly. "The Pittses. They ruin *everything.*"

I laughed unexpectedly, bright as a bell. Tyler shot me a sudden warm look and pressed on: "You want to go swimming, they'll drain the river."

"You make a batch of ice cream, they *turn up the sun.*"

He glanced at me sidelong, with that mischievous face. I grinned back, and the sunshine in him faltered.

"So," I asked, "what do we do?"

I'd heard a lot about Nat's ill-fated courtship with Vijay Chaudhry, and nobody had forgotten the spring where Will Sumner just wouldn't leave either of us alone, but I didn't know what courting looked like when it worked. When both people already knew and liked each other; when they were friends.

"That depends on—well. How you feel about it," he said. His broken eyes looked down at me, flicked away, crept back. Filled with nerves and—hope.

"I don't know," I said, breathless. "No, really, I don't. It's been just me here all summer. We barely sleep, and Marthe won't *talk;* she's gone somewhere in the back of her head where I can't get her. And all I've been telling myself is that I just have to make it until Thom gets home, but—"

The emptiness boiled up. It ate the light. It ate the world. "Ty," I said faintly, took a breath, and laid it recklessly bare: "I don't know how I feel about anything. I'm ... not okay right now."

He didn't laugh in my face. He didn't pull back, pull away. He knotted his hands around his walking stick, planted like a regimental flag, and said, "I don't know what to say." We stared unhappily, watching the dust of two private wars blow through each other's eyes.

"This isn't fair," I muttered, and he lifted a sharp eyebrow.

"No, not you. I wish it was next summer. All I want is some time to figure everything out."

Tyler paused like a man on a precipice. "We could, you know," he said slowly.

"We could what?"

"Take all the time we need."

I glared at him. "Don't you say you'll wait for me or something awful like that."

"I'm not *waiting*," he said, and drew up firm. "Just that we could, both of us. Take it slow. Take our time."

Who says how it works? rang and echoed through my head. I looked up at him — tilted head, considering eyes — and pictured it: No formal walking-out together; no talking to our families. No having him ask all the questions — would I dance, would I do more, would I permit him to court me and sneak up to the loft together — and hanging everything, forever, on my instant yes or no.

Just me and Tyler, and time to figure out what we had both become.

"Is that weird?" I asked. "Can we do that?"

"It's probably weird." Tyler cracked a nervous smile. "But maybe that's what courting *is*. Two people spending time, and finding out how they feel about it."

I nodded. The squirming nerves in my stomach still wouldn't settle down. "You're not going to stop being my friend if the answer's no?"

Tyler shook his head, fierce. "Never. Not on my life."

"You were ready to throw the whole thing away ten minutes ago."

"That was the stupid me," he replied, eyes glinting. "He's dead now. I put a hatchet in his face."

I watched him steadily until his broken eyes flicked to the ground. "I'm sorry," he said. "I was scared and just assumed everything, and it was . . . really stupid. I swear I won't do that again."

I swallowed. Reached out for his hand and tentatively took it. "I swear I won't let it stew for a whole week again," I whispered, and he nodded: *Thanks.* His fingers were rough-callused and thin under his gloves. I squeezed them experimentally; it had a whole new meaning now.

"Hal?"

"Yeah?"

He hesitated. "Can I kiss you?"

I stopped. Was this taking our time? *You can say no,* I reminded myself. *It doesn't have to mean never.*

I thought for a fleeting second what Tyler's cold-chapped lips might taste like. He smelled warm, like soap, clean sweat, lanolin. I'd never kissed someone before.

You can say yes, and it won't mean always.

"Okay," I said faintly, and shooed a lazy ewe out of the way. Tyler stepped close and looked down at me, serious as a church vow. I breathed in shallowly, terrified by his nearness: Tyler Blakely, tall and waiting as a guitar string.

His nose brushed mine, butted gently past, and then he

placed both hands lightly on my cheeks and leaned down to my mouth.

Janelle Prickett had called her first kiss summer exploding into midnight. I didn't see it. Tyler's mouth was on mine and it was too light, too hesitant for summer. The world was not ending. The earth had not gone standstill bright, or warm, or golden.

Tyler's lips moved, weird and living, against mine; small, infinitesimal spaces meeting and parting. His fingers leafed lightly along my cheek, warm in their knit woolen gloves. I fought the sudden urge to lean against them; fought an equal urge to pull away and run. My mouth flooded with the taste of him: soup-sweet and faintly metallic with fear.

The world shrank to fingertip details, and then he broke and stepped away from me.

I leaned back. The air was doubly cold on my mouth where his lips, that soup-taste lingered on. I resisted the impulse to wipe it away — or maybe to hold it, warm and private, in my palm. The sun streaked across his face — the sheer peace on his face. The rustle and *whuff* of the flock layered our silence into something softer.

I tipped my head back and let the afternoon sun glow through my closed eyes. All the frantic voices had gone out of my head. I couldn't remember the last time everything had been so . . . calm.

When I opened them, Tyler had dropped his hands to his staff and was watching me, rapt and anxious, his eyes bright in the hazel shreds still left to them. I opened my mouth; shut it again. I didn't know what you said after a boy—*a man and a soldier*—kissed you. I didn't know what you did. I wasn't sure I felt how you were supposed to feel.

"Was that okay?" I managed, and nearly smacked my own head sideways.

Ty barked a quick laugh. He grinned at me, wild and merry. "Like I'd know anything about it."

I snorted, and my own smile formed from nothing to meet his. "Fine, then," I said softly.

"Well, fine," he replied. We could go on like this for hours. We *had* gone on like this for hours, back in the days when we were small and annoying and Tyler Blakely was not somebody I had kissed.

"Fine—" Tyler started. And stopped.

I turned and saw a figure striding long across the highway, his hat low on his head against the chill-bright wintry sky. Tyler went pale around his chapped lips: the awful, helpless look he'd had when we found the stones strewn across the river path.

"It's just Thao Hang," I said, even as the creeping wrongness spread. Our goat pen was the other way; Hang's cart was still parked in the drive. I peered closer, and the figure stopped and turned in our direction.

"It's not," Tyler said, and picked up his knotty staff.

He limped across the field to the roadside, Joy and Sadie and the confused sheep in his wake. The figure on the road caught our motion and waved us over. There was a second man behind him, and a third. They moved to meet us: unshaven, sunburned, broad; pearly buttons at their wrists.

"Veterans," I said softly.

"No," Tyler said. "Soldiers."

"What d'you mean, soldiers?" I asked with a chill.

Tyler glared down the road. "The ones who stayed after John's Creek to burn every last Twisted Thing and hang Jones's irregulars. And find John Balsam. Find John Balsam, most of all."

My eyes widened: *the knife.* "We have to warn Heron."

Tyler wheeled on the path, but it was too late. The three men, armed and buttoned, had caught up to us. "Good afternoon, miss," the leader said in a rich voice. "We're looking for Roadstead Farm."

TWELVE

THERE WAS NO POINT DENYING IT; NO PURCHASE IN TRYING to lie. "That's us," I croaked. Tyler glanced at me uneasily. "How can we help you?"

The lead man doffed his cap. "Lieutenant Jackson, from General de Guzman's regiment." His accent was pure southlands: the round sound of rolling hills spread long into the sunset. A reassuring smile crinkled his brown face. "We were summoned here by the mayor in these parts."

My panic frothed into wrath. "Pitts."

"That's the man," the lieutenant said, a little more warily now. "Don't you worry, miss; we got here on the double. Now, where did you find the bogey?"

I blinked.

"The Twisted Thing," Tyler murmured. "We named them different in the war."

All three looked him over, taking in his hip, his splintered eyes. The fixed cheer slid off the lieutenant's face and left something sincere, and warmer. "What regiment?"

"Lakelands, out of Toledo," Tyler answered, and they dissolved into a circle of handshakes and half-remembered townships. I stood forgotten outside that wall of turned backs, torn between wrath and relief: *They don't know about the knife.* I bit back the urge to fly across the river and wrap my fingers around Alonso Pitts's throat. I'd said no, and he still sent them to put us under quarantine.

Years later, beyond all reason, he still wanted to push us off this farm.

I'll show you, I thought viciously. We'd send these soldiers back to him bowled over with how well we'd done. Full of nothing but praise for how the Hoffmann girls handled Roadstead Farm.

I straightened tall, and smiled.

"I'll show you where the Twisted Things fell," I said when the *do-you-know*s and *were-you-there*s died down. "We've had eight since: all small ones. Birds, most. One with cockroach legs that looked more like a field mouse."

Behind Lieutenant Jackson, the youngest soldier hissed out a breath. "That's a lot, Andre," said the third, a muscled, graying Chinese soldier who'd called himself Sergeant Zhang. "How'd they get this far out in the sticks?"

Tyler stiffened visibly beside me. I hadn't been talking to him through the last long, torturous week — but obviously Heron had. *Act natural,* I thought at him. It might as well have been written in lipstick on his forehead: *Hello, we have John Balsam's knife.*

"We've had the dogs out," he managed, too high and *much*

too fast. "They're good with tracking. But Twisted Things don't leave scent trails the same way."

You would never know that Tyler Blakely and his sister were related, sometimes. He couldn't have faked his way into a root cellar if his name was Potato.

"I'll show you. Right this way," I said quickly, and their masks came up again: polite and determined not to scare the children. *I will show you and Mayor Presumption,* I thought as we turned down the gravel path to the outbuildings and left Tyler snarled in his sheep. *I'll show you how to fight a war.*

Marthe and Thao Hang were in our tiny slaughterhouse, butchering the luckless among this summer's goats. Hang's sister Cua worked out back, at the slaughter: stunning the animals and then bleeding them out, all her attention on the knife. The youngest soldier, Corporal Muhammad—short and dark-browed like Rami Chandler—covered his nose, a little sick.

"Marthe," I said with the tight cheer she used for unwelcome company. "There are soldiers from the Great Southern Army visiting."

Marthe came to the door. "Soldiers?" she echoed blankly.

"Mayor Pitts," I said deliberately, "sent them to look for Twisted Things."

Cua's hand hesitated on the knife.

Now there might be a panic in Windstown, I thought with fleeting guilt. Mackenzie I could trust to keep discretion, but Cua and Hang had friends, and those friends had friends, and the gossip would spiral around town by sunset. *Pitts sent for the army,* I told myself fiercely. *He started it.*

"I see," Marthe said, and from whatever depths she'd been lost in for days, she finally surfaced: suspicion first, and the Hoffmann temper quick on its heels. She wiped her salt-pruned hands and stepped over the threshold. "You're aware that Alonso Pitts isn't mayor on this farm? His word stops at the river. He can't send anyone here for anything."

"Ma'am, we wouldn't presume," Lieutenant Jackson said. "We didn't come here just for Mr. Pitts. We've been tracking bogey reports, reports of—"

"Twisted Things," I supplied.

"—Twisted Things, moving northward for months now. General de Guzman sent us to locate their source."

"But the Wicked God is dead," Hang said warily from the doorway, and Marthe gave him a look that could scorch paint.

"Forgive me," she said, razor-edged. "Thao Hang and Thao Cua, from the butchery in Windstown. They don't speak for this farm either."

Cua set her knife down on the butchery block. Hang drew a patient breath and shook his head. *Oh, great,* I thought, exhausted. *Another ally lost across the river.*

"The Wicked God is dead," Lieutenant Jackson said firmly, and met Hang's eye. "And we won't rest until all His bogeys and His army of traitors are gone too."

Hang nodded slowly. He didn't look reassured. "We won't

keep you, then," he said, and gave his knives a swift wipe. Cua took the last carcass into the slaughterhouse and set off down the pathway to her cart, watching her boots before every step. *Looking,* I realized, *for Twisted Things.*

I started after her — and stopped. God knew what Marthe might see: me siding with a Windstown tradeswoman over her. God knew how a fight over loyalty would end right now, in front of three Great Army soldiers I'd hoped to send away utterly charmed. "Marthe," I pleaded, "can you show the lieutenant where the Twisted Things fell? That's all. Just that, and then they'll go."

The silence lengthened. Marthe blinked, focused on me, then on the empty slaughterhouse yard. The rage drained slowly out of her eyes and left a scum of appalled shame. "I'll just clean up," she muttered, and shut the door behind her.

I could feel the soldiers' eyes. Feel them like I was in the wide streets of Windstown, except that this was my family, my life, my homestead being judged, and not just my stupid hair.

"She's not always like this," I said, low. The normal, easy smile was getting harder and harder to wear. Sergeant Zhang and Lieutenant Jackson exchanged an embarrassed glance. I bit back the urge to scream, to call them every horrible thing I knew for daring to think my sister was irrational and mean.

"My brother-in-law didn't come back from John's Creek," I said, breaking the stem off every word. "Their child's coming soon."

Lieutenant Jackson looked at the closed door, at me, at the

grass dying cold between us. "Don't worry," Corporal Muham-mad said awkwardly. "You're not — we've seen a lot."

The sergeant silenced him with a frown. "We won't intrude on your personal affairs, young miss. Once we've located those bogeys, we'll be on our way."

My heart sank. He wasn't looking at me. He looked past me, to the horizon, for anything that moved. *It was never going to matter if you were charming,* I realized bitterly. We were just another chore to be done; another stop on the lonely road home from the war.

Marthe came out of the slaughterhouse with her hands clean and her knives wrapped up tight. "I'll show you the burns," she said, short and clipped, and strode off, head down, toward the house. The soldiers trotted after: dogs at the hunt, and I couldn't tell yet if they were feral.

I clenched my fists in my pockets and caught the lingering Hang, his butchery tools bundled beneath one arm. "Please don't hold it against Marthe —"

He shook his head. "It's a family matter," he said awk-wardly. Windstown gossiped. It wasn't going to be a family matter at all. "Your sister agreed to one goat, for our services?"

"That's fine," I muttered, relieved and disappointed and absolutely alone. "Just . . . tell Cua, please. That I'm sorry."

He shouldered a yearling carcass and made his way up the path, scanning the haunted horizon. I waited until he was a mote in the distance and then shut the slaughterhouse door. I'd left Heron in the henhouse, mucking out straw with a rake and pail. If he hadn't dropped to his knees yet and drawn them a map to John Balsam's knife, we might get through the afternoon after all.

Heron was still in the henhouse when I made it inside, cold and out of breath. "Almost done," he said distractedly, and picked at a tough-stuck spot. The smudges under his eyes were compost-dark; he'd probably not slept. He said he was watching for Twisted Things on the long night walks he took, but he'd yet to bring back a single body. Instead, the weeds were tramped flat on the path to our brush field and around the young hawthorn tree. I hadn't said anything. It hadn't been worth it until now.

I eased inside and shut the door slowly, breathing the warm, feathery must of hens and new-laid straw. Inside, the bright afternoon broke into dimness, shot with board-crack threads of light. "Three soldiers from the Great Army are on the other side of the house," I said, and picked up my own rake. "Can you stay out of the back field for at least a night or two?"

I expected to embarrass him. I didn't expect him to straighten so sharply he almost put the rake through the wall. "What do they want?" he asked, then shook his head jerkily. "No, I know what they want. What did they *say*?"

I fought the urge to take his shoulders and just hold him down to earth. "It's not the knife," I said, and Heron winced even at the word. "Oh, stop it," I hissed, and put my rake down. "The chickens aren't listening in."

He pressed his lips together, ducked his head. Was silent.

"They're looking for Twisted Things," I said, less comfortably now. "Pitts set them on us. He's been after this farm for years, and if he won't have it, he's not above manipulating a whole army to prove the council should have vetoed my father's will."

Heron quirked a humorless eyebrow. "Why?"

"What?"

"Why does this man want your farm so much?"

I opened my mouth, shut it. *I don't know,* I thought, brimming with stale rage. We only had theories: guesswork from the hairs and specks of evidence he'd left that we still picked over, scavengers, in the long winter nights. "He just hates us, and hated my father. He and Papa spent more time hating each other than most people spend eating or sleeping," I said. "They both had to know better; they were both just so big on being *right*. Papa said black, so Pitts says white. Papa left the farm to both of us, even though I was only ten years old, so Pitts said we couldn't handle it and tried to shove in an overseer. What happened to *us* never mattered to him. It's all about their stupid fight."

And that will was the one useful thing Papa ever did. I didn't say it. Some things were personal, even when you'd cried together. Some things you just didn't speak.

Heron sighed out a long breath. "Did Pitts serve?"

I shook my head. He was too old. All the older men

had stayed behind, pleading their knees or their thriving businesses.

"Then he doesn't know. He has no idea what he's called down on his little two-horse town." Heron's eyes glittered in the henhouse gloom. "Hallie, do you know what harboring is?"

The air leaking through the split boards was suddenly very cold. "We're not harboring. It's just the knife, not—" I stopped dead, mouth open.

Heron grinned, sickly tight. "No, I am not one of Asphodel Jones's irregulars."

"That's exactly what an irregular would say," I muttered.

"I told you," he went on softly. "I'm nobody. But that won't be enough for them if they find that knife. They want John Balsam." He paced an endless circle, round and round like a trapped fox. "They want their hero, and if I don't deliver him they'll tear me apart."

"They don't know," I pressed. "I won't tell them. Ty and Nat won't tell them a thing."

"I can't risk it." Heron's deep voice went thin. He peered out the crack where the door mismatched its frame. "I'll be off the land by sundown. Just say I went north. Went home."

My stomach squeezed into a ball of ice. "Heron, what are you doing? They're only staying for a day."

"That's how it starts out, yes," he said wildly. He wasn't seeing me; he was seeing something endless, beyond the slatted walls.

"God," I burst out. "The knife's cursed, isn't it? It's cursed to make you obsessive and insane. You'll freeze out there. You don't even have a coat."

"I *can't stay*," he pleaded. He focused on me, and his fear spilled, sharp. I could have named its every plane and corner. I swallowed. For an instant I felt the clawing fear that I'd lived with, forced down every time Papa's shouting stopped and his heavy tread came clumping up the stairs. It wasn't the knife sending Heron out to the winter countryside to starve or freeze or falter.

None of that mattered when you needed to *get away*.

I don't hurt people, I told myself. *I keep them safe. That is who I am.* Remembered Marthe's voice, soft and grim: *Go upstairs. Shut the door. I'll deal with it, baby.*

"We'll hide you," I said desperately, forcing my voice to come out calm. "Somewhere away from the smokehouse; somewhere they won't think to look. In the hayloft, or—no. Everyone always hides in the hayloft."

He grabbed for it like a drowning man. "The hayloft. Fine. Above the barn."

"I'll deal with it," I promised. "I'll get you when they're gone."

Heron nodded. And then he was already out the door, running across our wintering fields. Running faster than I thought Heron would ever move, like someone who had something, after all, to fear or love.

I shut the henhouse door and went the other way: to our

house, with its bird-burn, its old brick, its stale fear; its pall of fierce, complicated sadness that no one else understood. You could feel that sadness sometimes, a wall of words and crooked habits that kept Marthe and me both from being truly understood by our neighbors. Kept us from the open smiles and handshakes of the rest of the world.

Marthe was still with the soldiers, in the yard by the fire where we burned the Twisted dead. They came to a stiff attention before me. "Your sister says you've a hired man," Lieutenant Jackson said.

I thought of my father's crockery broken on the kitchen floor, my father's rages, my father's fist. Of Marthe's hands stroking my hair, deflecting his anger away from me. And said with my most plain and innocent face, "He's left for his homeland. He's gone."

THIRTEEN

THE SOLDIERS WENT OVER OUR FARM LIKE LAND BUYERS. They searched every corner, every cranny of the fields, and took notes in their leather-bound book. It left them worse-tempered than they'd started: you could see the rumble on Sergeant Zhang's face, the chagrin in Corporal Muhammad's step. Lieutenant Jackson kept an eye on the old-city road as they lined up outside our porch and said, "We'd be obliged for a bite of supper."

"We'll repay you in good coin," the corporal added, with a guilty glance at me.

"Fine," Marthe said, hard and tired, but not awful. I shoved my hands into my pockets, and we led the soldiers inside.

Marthe's game stew had burned at the edges. She ladled it out, rich with onions and sweet thyme, in portions stingy enough for five. "That's excellent, ma'am," Lieutenant Jackson said politely. "Can I ask what it is?"

"Rabbit," Marthe replied. "That hired man caught it fresh this morning." I looked down and bit my lip. There it was, that edge of betrayal in Marthe's voice—for another person who'd, without warning, left us and disappeared. *I'm going to have so much explaining to do,* I thought miserably. And so much of it wrapped up in things I never spoke aloud.

Lieutenant Jackson quirked an eyebrow at Corporal Muhammad, who waved it off. "It's fine. Rabbit's halal."

Sergeant Zhang was sharper. "Your hired man left just this morning?"

"He's got a family to go home to," I blurted, spotlighted in Zhang's dark eyes. "There's no crossing the river once it freezes. Winter's here." I wasn't good at insinuating, like Marthe or Nat. The *go home to your families* sailed right over their heads.

"So, not a local man," Sergeant Zhang said, hot on my heels. "What regiment?"

"Aylmer, I think."

Lieutenant Jackson leaned closer. "There's no regiment called Aylmer."

I fought the urge to flinch. "He had the buttons. He said he joined up in Aylmer. I don't know what regiment that means."

All three of them exchanged a grim look, ripe with need. Lieutenant Jackson took a spoonful of stew. "You've a strange pattern here, the way the bogeys landed. We're hoping we can keep investigating tomorrow."

I swallowed. It sounded like a change of subject. Sergeant Zhang and Corporal Muhammad's too-bland faces told me it was not. The Great Army's soldiers had heard something they didn't like.

Marthe looked between us and shrugged. "As long as you aren't in our way."

"I assure you, ma'am—" the lieutenant started, and it all faded into noise and every vivid tale I'd heard of regimental justice: hangings, confiscations, farms burned to the roots. *One day is how it starts,* Heron had said, so darkly certain—and trapped in that hayloft now for another day. He'd need supper. He'd need a blanket so he didn't freeze.

"Hallie," Marthe said, with an edge that said it was the second or third time. *"Halfrida."*

I startled. "Hmm?"

Marthe cocked an eyebrow at me. The table was dead silent. "I said, will you help me with the tea downstairs?"

I pushed out my chair. I'd entirely lost track of the conversation. "Yes, Marthe," I said nervously, and followed her down to the cold cellar.

The cellar was dim. The outlines of pickle jars, beets, and flour sacks sprawled across the shelves our Opa had bolted, half a century ago, to the walls. Marthe hefted a jar of amber honey, placed it in my hands, and picked up a hand-sewn sack of tea. "Hal," she said quietly, "what are you doing?"

My skin chilled. "Holding the honey?"

"That's not what I mean." There was threat in my sister's voice: plain, unsheathed. "What went on between you and Heron?"

Oh. I hugged the honey to my shirt, my brain gone

snow-blank. I'd never been a bad sister. It wasn't my temperament, and even after Papa's will came to light, I couldn't afford that kind of rebellion.

"I can't tell you," I blurted, and that fire I hated so much blossomed in her eyes. Both her eyebrows rose and hung in a half-moon across her brow.

"What do you mean you can't tell me?"

I swallowed a childish urge to run for the smokehouse. "It's someone else's secret," I managed. "I gave him my word that I wouldn't tell anyone."

Marthe stepped back and studied me afresh. "Hallie," she said, her voice edged with precision. "Are you in trouble?"

I looked down at my socks. Then back at Marthe's eyes, hot with the kind of fury that could bide its time for years. *She's mad at* him, *not me,* I realized abruptly. *She thinks he did something, and she's ready to wring his neck.*

"No," I said, shocked. "Nothing like that, no *trouble.* No."

Something in her loosened, something still human and soft. "Your word or not," she said grimly, and took me by the shoulders as if I was very small, "if you're in trouble, you tell me. Promise me you will."

I nodded wordlessly, and she released me almost unwillingly. Marthe glanced over her shoulder, then trod heavily up the stairs. I stood there breathing hard for a moment before I followed her.

The kitchen was fuller when I climbed the last step: Nat

Blakely stood on our doormat, wiping her boots, with her uncle James right behind her. "Marthe, Hallie," he greeted us, as straight-backed as a funeral, every inch of him a scarred and narrow efficiency. "Tyler mentioned that a detachment from the army was here. I thought I'd come and compare notes."

There was a rebuke in his eyes. Marthe lifted a weary eyebrow to meet it.

"You mean the young man with the sheep," Lieutenant Jackson said tactfully. *The young man with the limp.*

"My late brother's son," James said, and a tight look passed over his face. How Mr. Blakely died didn't even need to be said. "Sergeant Blakely, Lakelands Regiment. I'm the ranking officer in these parts."

I didn't know that anyone had ever thought about who outranked who in the lakelands, but the soldiers' guard came down like a bad fence. "Sergeant," the lieutenant breathed, and offered a relieved salute. "We'd be happy to discuss intelligence."

James nodded. "If we can borrow your parlor, Marthe?"

Marthe and James were good at understanding each other. She gave him a six-fathom look and said, "Fine, let's move this over." James gestured, and Marthe and the soldiers followed him into the parlor on the trail of his confident smile.

Nat waited until they were well and truly gone to slump into an abandoned chair.

"What was that about?" I asked her.

She flashed a weary smile. "Uncle James proving Marthe wrong on some obscure point about teamwork."

I threw up my hands. The pair of them had always gotten along. They liked the same orderly lines in things. But they argued like it was a scavenger hunt, complete with prizes.

Nat picked at the scraps left on Marthe's plate. "Rabbit, huh?"

"Heron was feeling enterprising this morning," I said, and then, "No, wait. Don't touch that." I grabbed an end of bread off the sideboard and opened a clean Mason jar. Heron needed supper, and now was my chance.

There wasn't much left over after the army had been through, but I scraped stewed rabbit and winter vegetables into the jar and tucked it into my pocket. I glanced down the hall, heard the steady murmur of voices, and grabbed the lantern by the door. "Come out with me? I've got something to do."

Nat lifted her head, and her thick eyebrows with it. "Right," she said. "Something?"

"Adventure, Nat," I said, and ducked outside.

The night was edged, and glitteringly clear. Everything sparkled to a knifepoint: the stars, the frost, our puffed breath under the pale half-moon. I held the jar of stew scraps in my pocket and crunched across the hardening fields. Somewhere on Bellisle, in the distance, a light burned.

"Where are we going?" Nat asked eagerly.

"The hay barn," I answered, and glanced over my shoulder. "Heron panicked when he heard about the soldiers. I couldn't convince him they weren't here for the knife. So he's hiding in the hayloft, and Marthe, the soldiers—everyone—thinks he left this morning. I have to bring him something for supper."

Nat squinted, critical. "You know everyone always hides in haylofts."

"I *know*," I said. *"Shut up."*

"Still." She shot me a speculative look. "Not bad. I didn't think you had it in you."

I crunched ahead faster. "Thanks."

"Oh, c'mon. You know what I mean."

I puffed out a breath. *That it's Nat's job to be sneaky*, I thought. *That it's my job to be good.*

"So what's the story there?" she asked as we rounded the pens.

I gave her a blank look. Her eyes were troubled in the dim glow of the shielded lantern. "Stranger arrives at your door not even three weeks ago with no past, no name, and John Balsam's knife."

I stiffened. "He's got a name."

"It's not Heron," she countered. "No one saw that man and thought *bird*."

I snorted, despite myself, and Nat's smile quirked. "What I'm asking," she said, "is what's going on between you two."

I stopped dead on the frost-hard ground. "You're the second person to ask that tonight."

Nat faced me, grave. "Because I'm worried, Hal. Because you're not acting like *you*."

The blood came up in my cheeks. "What's *me?*"

"Sensible," Nat said pointedly. "Grown up. Smart."

"Boring and scared?" I snapped.

The trees rustled in the distance, naked-limbed. Nat scowled. "I didn't say that."

"I did."

"And you're changing the subject." Nat glared at me, but her heart wasn't in it. There was a loose-leashed fear in her eyes.

So I'm not the same me after all, I thought, wistful—and weirdly glad. Sensible and scared wasn't all I wanted to be. "Nothing's going on with Heron—no, Nat, I swear," I said, and she closed her mouth. "He's almost Marthe's age. That's disgusting, thanks."

"Doesn't stop some people," she muttered, and I huffed.

"I'm grown up and sensible, right? Pretend I've got some sense. Besides—" I stopped abruptly. The memory of that long, warm kiss stung my lips.

Nat and I told each other nearly everything: our family squabbles, our fears, our crushes. But I wasn't sure I could tell her yet about that kiss.

She crossed her arms. "There's someone else," she crowed.

"No!"

"Yes," she pressed, and her cold cheeks bloomed into a grin. "You're blushing."

"It's cold," I muttered, defeated. I was certainly blushing *now*.

"Tell me it's not one of the Sumner boys. I'll hang you by your toes until your brain works again."

"Nat," I pleaded, and pressed my palms to my bright face. "I don't even know if it's something yet. It's too early to tell."

"So it's half something."

"God, *stop*," I begged. But I was smiling, smiling down to my toes. "Half something," I admitted. "Maybe. Let me figure it out?"

"All right," she said, and huddled into her coat. "You know I just want you to be happy."

"I do." I did. Suddenly I didn't feel the cold at all. We crunched, together, through the gathering snow.

There was no noise from the hay barn, not even a whisper. I lifted the latch, and we slipped in through a finger's-width of space. The scent of sweet, faded summer green drifted into my nose, little more than dust now, and more memory than smell. I unshielded the lantern carefully, and it threw shadows across the bales and rafters, a swaying fiddle reel of light.

"Heron?" I whispered, and caught sight of him by accident: the curve of a man's head and shoulder against the hayloft wall. "You can come out now. They're in the house."

Heron's voice floated from the high loft. "You're alone?"

"Nat's here," I said, and the silence stretched.

She snorted, and climbed the ladder to the loft. "Oh, come on. We can't *all* be army spies."

"We brought supper," I added, and climbed up after her.

Heron huddled, wrapped in three shirts and a tattered horse blanket, rock-still among the lean bales of hay. I lifted the lantern—and forgot how I could have cast him, even fleetingly, as one of Jones's irregulars. His legs were knit into a cradle, and in the center lay an orange cat, its tail limp on the floor.

"What's wrong?" I whispered. Heron stared at us hollowly, and wordlessly turned the cat over. The fur around his mouth was a strange, colorless shade: a splash of transparent wire in the mottled orange and black. His nose was bleached white, an acid splash in his bristling fur.

"Gussy?" I whispered, my palm hovering over his back. Our cats were all Gus—a joke of Marthe's that she'd never got around to explaining. It wasn't like they answered. They hated company, hated to be touched. You could pet them for a minute and then they'd be off into the haystacks, hissing. "What happened to him?"

"Oh, damn," Nat said quietly, and pulled my hand away.

The cat's eyes were gone. The sockets swelled with thin pink flesh, scar-torn and sickly. I could smell them, still burning, acrid against the sweet, soft dust.

"I found him this way," Heron said tonelessly. There were tears running, silent, down his windburned cheeks. "He could still see, a little bit, before sunset. He died before dark. I couldn't just get the hammer and—" He shook his head. A whole universe of inability rushed into that silence. Heron's hand moved soothingly across the cat's back, as if it couldn't stop.

"Cat, what did you do?" I whispered, as if I didn't already know. Most of our Twisted Things had been found in the garden, but there had still been that first one: that smear of burning wings cairn-buried at the riverside. One curious cat, prowling for morning prey, had lifted it there for breakfast, and its poison touch ate him slowly from the places they'd touched.

"Twisted Thing," Nat said grimly, and shook her head. "I'll go light the fire."

"No—" Heron snapped, a child's outrage.

"Yes," I said. "He's poisoned by a Twisted Thing. He's dead, Heron."

"There's got to be something—" His voice trickled out.

"You're not a farm kid, are you?" Nat asked gently.

Heron held Gus tighter and shook his head. "My mother and I make cheese. In a little woods town three hours outside Black Creek." The long muscles of his back shook once, twice, with hiccupping sobs.

"You're a cheesemaker," I said quietly.

He nodded, every mile and inch of highway written across his face. "I never should have left home."

"You have to let him go now," I said, and hated myself

for it. Heron lifted the cat from his lap as if his heart was breaking.

I took the cat's stiff body and stroked it mindlessly. Orange fur clumped on my blue gloves and floated into the hay bales. Heron's eyes were red and freely crying, his breath hitched. I took his hand and squeezed it; felt Nat pat my back and almost choked.

"I can't tell Marthe about this. Not now," I said. "She fed these cats from the bottle."

"We burn it out back, then," Nat said grimly, and pulled me to my feet.

Heron swung his legs over the hayloft ladder like a man long bedridden. I wrapped Gussy gently in the tattered blanket. "Take the lamp?" I asked Nat, and clambered down the ladder.

"If Marthe asks, where were we?" Nat asked from above.

"The smokehouse. No—looking for Twisted Things. I don't know," I said, and huffed out a breath. *I am already tired of secrets,* I thought, and opened the barn door.

On the other side of it, shadowed against the night sky, someone yelped.

FOURTEEN

HERON SWORE. I JUMPED BACK, THE CAT'S CORPSE IN MY arms. The shadow took a step forward. "Hallie?" Tyler's voice.

"Ty," I breathed, and sat down hard on a hay bale. Tyler scrambled into the barn and leaned hard against the wall.

"What are you doing here?" Nat hissed, pale in the lamp-light. "Mum said you need to rest."

The glare he shot her was fierce. "Right. And what are *you* doing?"

"Look," I said, between them, and held up Gus's body, shrunken and stinking, the orange gone to white.

"Oh," Tyler managed, the fight punched right out of him. He hesitated, and then wrapped a clumsy arm around my shoulders. I stiffened: You didn't just *touch* like that in front of people. Not before your family knew you were courting, and approved.

Good thing we're not courting, then, I thought fleetingly. My heart felt bruised and my head spun with nerves, and if Heron or Nat could offer me comfort without it *meaning* things, well —

It was pointless, the kiss and our promise to do things *our* way, if we couldn't even hold each other up.

I leaned into Tyler's strange-familiar warmth, wiped my eyes on his flannel shirt. His arm tightened around my back: awkward, new. Defiant.

Nat looked at me, looked at her big brother, and her mouth shaped a perfect, astonished *O*.

"What *are* you doing?" Tyler asked again, closer to my ear.

"Heron's hiding," I said thickly. "We're going out to burn Gus's body."

"I'm sorry," Heron said awkwardly. "But those soldiers will ask about a dead barn cat. They'll want to search in here. Every inch."

I swallowed the scent of Tyler's shirt. "They're going to search it anyway. They're staying the night to look around for Twisted Things tomorrow."

Heron turned the color of dirty tea.

"Look," Nat said, off balance, unsure where to look between a hired man playing fugitive and her best friend in her brother's arms. "That's easy. I can get them out of here long enough for Heron to move."

Tyler's chin shifted on my shoulder. "What are you plotting *now?*"

Her lip curled. "I will go back to your kitchen," she said loftily, over Tyler's head, "and offer them the bunkhouse at Lakewood Farm."

Tyler eased back. "That could really work."

"Of course it'll work," Nat said bitingly. "They looked at Uncle James like he was John Balsam himself." She put down the lamp and fixed Heron with a sharp eye. "Is tonight enough to get your things and get yourself to ground?"

He nodded, his face ravaged.

"Good," she said, absolutely in control once again. She might be leaner, and taller, and half strange with absence, but she was still the same Nasturtium Blakely who'd run all our games as a child, forever frustrated that we were catching her imaginary trout *wrong.* "I'll take them over the high road. Don't go anywhere 'til we're gone. And you," Nat added, and pointed a finger at her brother.

"Me," Ty agreed coolly.

"Don't let Uncle James see you out of bed or he'll stripe your hide," she said, and stomped out into the frost.

"No, he won't," Tyler added, unnecessarily, once she was gone.

Heron sank, exhausted, to the barn floor. I detached myself from Tyler's arms. "Will you be all right in here a little longer?"

Heron nodded curtly. "I'll get my things from your smokehouse. I stuffed them down in back." He seemed to have run out of feelings to feel.

I swallowed a clawing worry. "Eat. Here," I said, and pressed the scraps jar into his hands. We waited for Nat's steps to fade before I hefted Gus's body, and then we walked, Tyler and I, to the back fields to burn our dead.

. . .

We lit Gus's pyre on the other side of the hawthorn tree, between John Balsam's knife and the river. It took too long to build the fire: the ground was frozen now, the wood wet, and my gloved hands kept slipping on the striker. Tyler held the lamp high, and I blew endlessly on the curling tinder to grow our meager sparks. We didn't speak.

Tyler set the cat's limp body into the flames when they caught, solid and bright. I stared off across the river, at the choppy winter waves. I was starting to hate this field. When this was all over, I would level every weed inside it and drown it in river water.

"The gloves too. They touched the body," Tyler said, and I peeled off Nat's fine blue gloves regretfully.

"She'll be so upset."

He found my good hand and squeezed it. "She won't. They're just *things*."

They curled like crackling paper in the low orange flames. A wild dog called, lonely, up the river, and its cry sank into the snap of dying logs.

"Do you want its ashes?" Tyler asked. I stifled a bitter laugh: what a mockery that would be. A cat's ashes in that venerated place on our mantel while Thom stayed unburied, missing, gone.

"No," I said, and kicked the cold dirt. Another loss on Roadstead Farm, half-funeraled, done in secret. Another piece of mourning we couldn't finish and move on from.

When the fire cindered, we walked single file through the broken brush to where our fields started, to where everything still tenuously made sense. "Walk with me a bit farther?" I asked Tyler after a moment. Our house was a dark cloud atop the hill, and I couldn't face it yet with the feel of that orange fur on my hands.

"It'll be more of a meander," he said dryly.

"I don't care."

"Yeah. Okay," he said, and we changed course: down the frosty field road, toward the orchard and the cold riverbank. He took my arm after a moment, and it wasn't to hold me upright or to ask me to keep him from falling.

"This is still weird," I said into the silent fields.

"Yeah. Um—" Tyler started. "Thank you for saying that. It's weird."

I couldn't tell why it felt less okay when it was him who said it.

"Bad weird?" he asked as we approached the glittering orchard trees. The apple branches loomed, frosted into false stars.

"Not bad weird," I said, and slid my hand down his arm. Took his hand.

His lips pressed to mine, gentler now, steam-warm against the night. I pulled back, drew breath, and bumped into his frozen nose. "Right," he said. "No, your *other* right," and I laughed, a nervous giggle that bloomed into an all-out grin.

Tyler looked down at me, his frost-pinched face weirdly fond. "I missed your laugh."

I wiped my eyes with gloveless fingers. "I do too," I said when I could breathe again. "I just . . . I've had about a hundred feelings since I woke up this morning, Ty. It's too much. It's exhausting."

His shard-bright eyes shuttered. "I'm sorry. I didn't mean you should do it for *me*, or—" He ran a hand through his hair. "God, I'm bad at this."

"I'm an expert," I proclaimed brightly. He stared at me for a second, and then deliberately poked one finger into my gut.

I laughed again, helpless, ticklish gasps, and his face went less grim. "I like when you're happy too," I said, and wrapped my cold hand around his finger. "Just . . . take it slow. Give me time. I need—I need to breathe."

"Right," he said softly, and turned his caught hand to take mine. "C'mon. I'll walk you home."

We set off up the frozen path, slow enough that I could think about that hand in mine and what it meant. Ice popped sharply beneath our boots. We gained the orchard path, and Ty's arms moved like shadows flecked with dim starlight. His bad leg lagged through the hardened dirt: *crunch, crunch—clink.*

"What the hell—" he started softly, and stepped back. "Not again."

Right, he swears now, I reminded myself, and tugged my hand free to unshield the lantern.

A river stone. Five river stones. And then a whole pathway of them, icy wet, small, and graying. They'd come back in the night: a long howl written dot by dot across the frozen mud.

"Oh —" I said, and my stomach dropped. I knew the way those stones clustered together. The same hard corners and tight curves had told me for two silent years, two terrified years of living with Papa after Uncle Matthias was gone: STAY CLEAR TONIGHT. LEFT YOUR SUPPER IN THE HAY BARN. BE STRONG. I LOVE YOU MOST. "Marthe wrote this. She's writing *back*," I said, and in the lamplight, Tyler went still.

"TELL ME HOW TO HELP," Tyler read, barely above a whisper. "I DON'T KNOW HOW TO FIND YOU. LOVE," and his voice stumbled. "I NEED YOU SO MUCH I CAN'T EVEN BREATHE."

"Marthe said she saw a ghost the night the first message appeared," I said, and the words burned my throat to the tongue-roots. "She saw Thom. She thinks it's *Thom* asking for help."

The last line glimmered at the lantern's edge: I NEVER SHOULD HAVE LET YOU LEAVE HOME.

I reached for Tyler's hand, and it fell limp between my fingers. The stars glowed, gap-toothed, and between them I also burned with unruly embarrassment, with fear. Marthe had to be hallucinating: wishing for magic, wishing for a miracle so hard she'd fabricated one whole. She *had* to. I'd worked so hard to stop waiting. I'd just finally learned to let Thom Clarlund go.

The ember of hope Marthe's letters woke inside me burned. It *hurt*.

Tyler's hand tightened on mine. "Hal, we should go up to the house."

I tossed him a confused glance. He stared straight down the path, his white eyes gleaming. "There's something down the road right now," he said in a too-calm voice. "On the beach. And I think it just *saw* us."

My heart stuttered awake. "A Twisted Thing? We'll get the soldiers—"

"No," he said, and squeezed my hand until it hurt. "Not a Twisted Thing. A man."

"Marthe said she saw a ghost," I repeated with a seizing terror, even though I didn't, not for real, believe in ghosts. Tyler pulled me backwards slowly, step by inching step, and I backed away with him and hated the weakness in my knees.

"It's not a ghost," he said softly. "It's walking toward us. And it's real."

I dug my nails into my palms. "I can't see it. How are you seeing this?"

Tyler's Adam's apple bobbed. "I saw the Wicked God die, Hal," he said softly. "And now I see Twisted Things. I see *everything*."

I opened my mouth, soundless, and stared at his pale, thin face. "I . . . how?"

He grimaced, dark, in profile, his eyes still fixed on that advancing threat. "We were on the front line when John

Balsam killed the God. It was like the world exploded, but *inward:* the Great Dust swirled into the hole Balsam cut in the God's heart, like water down an outhouse drain. And suddenly there were trees, and—" He shook his head, still ashen, still backing out of the orchard trees. "I've never told anyone this. It's insane. I don't want you to think I'm insane."

A feverish memory surfaced: Nat chasing a terrified Tyler down on the beach where Gus had dropped that first Twisted Thing, asking *Do you have to act so insane?* "Tell me," I said, and gripped his hand tight. "Please."

"Inside Him, somehow," he said, confused and, more confusingly, *yearning,* "there was this whole other world. There was a forest in the Wicked God's heart: droopy, pointed leaves, blossoms falling free in the rain, warm and wet. Just the colors were—" He let out a shaken breath. "That's what broke my eyes when the Wicked God died: I watched all the Twisted Things scatter into that world, running from the desert. But now," he said, and shook his head like a stunned man, "I can't *stop* seeing it."

"Seeing it where?" I whispered.

"Everywhere," he answered, and waved his arm wide across the night sky. "It's laid over our own world like a veil. There's a lizard-fox nest right in front of us, against that tree. The webspinner birds are on a branch two feet higher, feeding their chicks something dead. But it's not here; it's *there;* it's in the Wicked God's world. They couldn't see us if they tried."

We backed out of the orchard, into the plain, empty fields,

into the plain, empty, mundane night. "It wasn't just that bird you saw on the beach last week," I breathed. "I knew it. I knew you lied."

Tyler's eyes flattened. "A figure. A man, standing at the riverbank. How was I supposed to tell you I saw someone in another *world?*"

I risked a glance behind us at the goat pen and the house on the hill. Our feet moved in concert; our hands were fused together. "You're telling me now."

Tyler flushed, and nodded slow. "I see Gods in the lakelands. I see monsters. They crawl across the sky and through the walls at night. But all the way from John's Creek to Windstown, I've only seen monsters. This is the first time I've ever seen a *man* there."

We backed painfully up the hill, the lamp swinging wild. The porch loomed, and Sadie leaped up from it, from the night-darkened house. She whimpered, confused by the smoke-stink on us and the palpable taste of our fear.

"Is he still there?" I asked. The world was tipping like thin china, headed for the floor.

The wind curled through Tyler's shaggy hair. I lifted the lamp against the darkness, against something I couldn't see. "He's going up the hill," Tyler whispered, and traced a path with a pointed finger. "Down the other side."

His finger dropped. *Gone.*

"God, I'm tired," Tyler muttered, despairing, and buried his face in his hands.

Sadie whined and snuffled Tyler's knees. I looked at them both, set the lamp down, and placed a hand on his shoulder. "Ty."

He took it, enveloped it in his mittened palms. "That was the same man I saw on the beach, Hal. That man, whoever he is. And *he saw me back*. He saw us. If Marthe left that message, *she* saw him too, somehow. The Wicked God's world and ours have never *touched:* not since John's Creek. Not since the war. And I — Hallie, what do we do?"

You're asking me? I thought wildly, and swallowed the thought back. He needed me. To be smart, and brave, and strong.

I squared my shoulders and curled my fingers around his. "Marthe left a message," I said haltingly. "We wait for him to answer."

FIFTEEN

DAWN SMOKED CLOUDY ON THE HORIZON WHEN I WOKE, rumpled and still dressed, in my unkempt bed. Marthe clanked about downstairs, every piece of her steady routine stubbornly unchanged: the ring of the kettle on the stove, then the thunk of stacked wood to feed the fire. *We are living amidst gods and monsters,* I thought, and shivered in my quilt.

She'd left Tyler's shadow man a message. An answer might have come.

There was one bun, one teacup on the table this morning, and my sister's basket was full of washed milk bottles. "Good morning," I said cautiously, and Marthe leveled her infamous stare.

"I found Tyler Blakely on the sofa this morning."

My cheeks kindled. Of course she had. It had been much too dark to walk through the icy fields alone, and he and Nat both knew where our spare blankets were. "He, ah—" I started.

"Let me guess," she said dryly. "You can't tell me."

The part of my head that could make up stories failed. "I'll go get the eggs," I blurted, and hightailed it out the door.

The farm was eerily silent without Tyler's sheep out; with Heron gone to ground. I crept, tiptoe to match it, down the orchard path to the river.

Marthe's letter had been disturbed in the night: the smooth gray letters duller by daylight, broken off mid-word. Robbed of the mystery of the night air, they looked absolutely crazy. I caught the edge of voices farther down the path — Heron's low baritone, Tyler's tenor — and hurried along the scree to find them, their heads bent over the shoreline.

"What're you doing?" I asked, and they jumped apart like guilty children.

"Figuring out if we have enough firewood," Heron said, and pointed down.

The shoreline was rotten with Twisted Things: dead, stinking, crumbling. A pile of them lay soot-smeared and burning at Heron's feet.

"What—" I started, my eyes caught on whiskers, on ears like leaves. There were at least two dozen of them — a whole heaped massacre, drifting in and out with the current.

"We found them," Heron said numbly. "We came down to pick up those stones."

"You're not even supposed to be outside," I muttered. Heron looked awful: stubble-faced, blue-lipped, utterly exhausted. A Twisted Thing crawled from the beach toward us, smoke rising behind its lizard legs, and Tyler crushed it with his stick.

"Where are they *coming* from?" I asked, and paced alongside the Twisted Thing's trail. The rock had crumbled in its wake, turned into ash and the stink of burnt lizardflesh. I covered my nose and traced the blackened, glassy footprints down a small hillock and around the riverbend. The air shimmered. That same thinness I'd felt before scored my throat, made me cough. There was a circle of sand here, scorched smooth and entirely black. Its edges bled messily out across the beach, a burn licked into paper.

"This is where we found that bird," Heron said. His voice echoed weirdly in my ears. They felt full of water.

Tyler walked a jittery circle around the stain, his white eyes sharply focused.

"Tyler—" I started, and he wrapped an arm across my shoulders and yanked me back *hard*.

"Hey, what gives—!" I managed, falling against him, stumbling together.

The Twisted Thing materialized out of nowhere and flew, squawking, right past our noses.

I let out a squeak. Heron yelped and flung a rock at the fluttering sparrow wings. It missed by whole yards and splashed into the river. The bird cawed and sped away, wild, into the clouds.

"No way," I managed, and shook myself free. "They can't just come from *nowhere*."

"They aren't," Tyler said, his eyes squinted against a light that wasn't there. He poked his shepherd's crook into the air, waving it like a dowser through that shimmer of heat. It wandered through the patch of sky just in front of us—

—and the knobbed wood smoked and vanished, inch by inch, into empty air.

"What the—" Heron muttered.

Tyler pulled the crook back, and it was six feet long again, the last foot a browned, sparking mess. "That's how he saw us last night, Hallie. Now it makes sense."

"No, it doesn't," I said, and my voice cracked. "What *is* that?"

"It's where the Twisted Things are coming from," he said, struck with awe and terror. "It's a hole into the Wicked God's world."

It was warmer in the smokehouse. Tyler held the door and scanned the empty fields as we scurried inside. "I'll find Nat. She needs to know about this," he said. "Don't open up for anyone else."

"Of course," I answered irritably, and he shut Heron and me into the dark. I wedged the shovel across the jamb and rubbed my cold fingers together. The smokehouse didn't look familiar anymore; all its shapes had shifted in the weeks since Heron came. It was a wilderness of history—someone else's now, not mine.

Heron lit a twig off his battered striker and eased it into his cookpot. He fed the spark wood scraps until it smoked and glowed, until it flung the shadows of hand-carved cradles onto the walls. "God, I'm tired," he said softly, as haggard as Tyler had been the night before.

"I brought you breakfast," I said, useless, and fished the other half of Marthe's bean bun out of my pocket.

Nat and Tyler tapped on the door half an hour later, flushed with running, Nat's cheeks two bright round spots. "Did he tell you what happened?" I asked, and she fixed me with a furious glare.

"Yes," she said, "which is good, because I spent all night looking through ditches for my brother's stupid corpse."

I flinched. "I'm sorry."

"You should be," she shot back. "I can't *pretend* you came home last night, Ty. That was the worst thing you could've done to Mum, the absolute worst, and I wish to God anyone was trying to make this family work but me."

Tyler looked up, suddenly dangerous. "You mean by trying to keep Mum off my back because I act *so insane*."

Nat colored helplessly. "Tyler—"

"That was shit, Nat," he said. "That was really shit."

"Children," Heron said with a hard intensity. "We just pushed a foot of wood into thin air. *Not now.*"

Tyler ducked his head. "Sir," he said meekly. But his eyes found Nat's and promised: *This isn't over.*

Heron crouched in the smokehouse corner, his dirty hands over his cookpot fire. "That's the second time you've used that good eye of yours, Private. Is there anything we should know?"

Tyler slumped against the wall. And then his head came up, slow.

"Go on," I said softly, and he cast me a bleak smile.

"I see things," he said, defiant, and held up a hand to forestall whatever Nat might have said. "Since the battle. Since the God died and my eyes went all—" He shrugged. "I see Twisted Things and the world that opened up when John Balsam cut the Wicked God's heart."

"What do you mean?" Nat asked, too fast.

Tyler flashed a sour grin. "As in: Am I acting *so insane* again?"

"Ty," I said, awkward. The awful smile dropped off his face.

Heron watched Tyler with a naked, yearning fear. "You saw it. When the God went down: You saw the place on the other side of that knife cut. You saw the rain."

Tyler blinked. "How close were you?"

The ghosts settled on Heron's face. "Close enough."

"I saw it," Tyler said, and looked down at his scraped hands. "I'm still seeing it. Those vines crawl across my ceiling every night."

"Allah, Buddha, and Jesus," Heron said softly, and I startled. I'd never, ever heard him swear.

The red spots were blanched clean from Nat's face. "Tyler—" she stammered, and rubbed her face with both hands. "That can't be. You can't be seeing another *world*."

"Ask the uncles," he said with a hard glitter in his eye. "Ask them about the time I stopped, three days out of John's Creek, and pointed to a Twisted Thing as tall as an oak tree, a growing, walking tree made out of dead deer horn. They'll tell you

I was feverish. They couldn't see it. They still can't. We drove right through the thing, Nat. I thought it was going to touch me. I thought I was dead."

He shuddered, and his smile—his smile could break hearts. "I saw its insides when we went through, you know. Its heart was an acorn, seeping blood. Its guts moved like grass snakes. It sat five feet behind us, poking its bone-roots into the ground and popping grubs into its awful white mouth."

"That's real," Heron whispered, a thousand miles away. "I saw one of those at John's Creek."

"It's real," Tyler said. "For weeks and weeks I thought I'd gone crazy, and then that Twisted Thing came through on the beach, and I figured it out: I see them, but they're not quite *here*." He shrugged. "No one else sees them. No one else has *these eyes*. So I kept it to myself. So nobody else calls me *insane*, Nasturtium."

Nat's mouth was open. Her hand crept out toward mine and caught it, all her rage forgotten. "I'm sorry. Tyler—oh, damn. I'm such an absolute shit."

Tyler's eyes caught the place where my hand squeezed Nat's tight. "Apology accepted," he said grimly. "And don't you *dare* tell Mum any of this."

Nat's eyes went impossibly wide. "God, Tyler. I would never."

"But you're saying," Heron pushed on, "the place with the rain is real *too*."

Tyler sagged against the wall and nodded. "It's where the

Twisted Things live. It's their world, their home. It's just a little *off* from ours, I think, like a pair of shears that don't quite close. But they're closing now. I saw that spinner bird, this morning, *there,*" he said, and shaped its wing with his hands, "before it appeared on the beach, here. It came from that world to ours."

"Through a hole," Heron said hollowly. "Through that thin spot on the river."

"Something's changed," Tyler said, and turned his burnt walking stick end over end. "Something broke that hole between us and their home."

Something, I thought, and my whole body went cold. "Tyler. The man you saw. Marthe's ghost."

"What man?" Nat snapped.

Tyler squinched his eyes shut. "Right. There's that too."

"Tyler," Nat said dangerously, and my patience for their sibling swordplay snapped.

"There's a man on the other side of the—whatever," I said, and Tyler shot me a reproachful look. "Tyler saw him walk up the orchard road and over our hilltop last night. Right where we found the stone letters. And from what Ty said, he saw us *back.*"

"What?" Nat managed.

"Marthe's ghost could be real," I shoved out. "Whoever he is, *he* left us that message. And after what Marthe did, there'll be a reply."

Heron leaned in, wildly intent. "What'd he look like?"

"Tall," Tyler said reluctantly. "Thin as a corpse. The sleeves of his coat were all tattered, and his hat had a bowed brim." He swallowed. "He looked lonely. He looked mad as hell."

He looked like a veteran, I filled in, sketching about the edges. Like a ripped-up scarecrow thing put hastily back together.

Tyler's eyes were abruptly young again: the Tyler Blakely who'd sucked in a breath to steady his nerves before he kissed me. "I stayed on your parlor couch all night in case he came back. I had this hope I'd get a good look at his face."

"About that," I said quietly. "My sister noticed."

"Oh, great."

Nat sagged against the cedar chest. "*Mum* noticed. I have no idea what to tell her."

"And I have no idea what to tell Lieutenant Jackson," I added. "They're looking around the property. They'll find that pile of bodies on the shore."

We lapsed into silence: ceded the room to the twig-fire, the squeak of my stool, Heron's labored breath, to imagining army camps in the broken barley.

"How do we fix this?" I asked Heron. "We got the knife away. The Twisted Things aren't even *interested* in that knife. So how do we make this all *stop*?"

Heron knotted his hands in his long, dark hair. "I *don't know,* all right?" he said, and his fists tightened. "Why does everyone think I have all the answers?"

"You're the man with John Balsam's knife," Nat said.

"So what? I'm not a *god,*" he snarled. He scrubbed his eyes;

scratched his arms with the bitten-down nails of that broken hand. "I don't know how this works. I've dodged Twisted Things everywhere I've gone since John's Creek. So fine, they don't want the knife; they don't go near it. They want *something*. They fall out of the sky after me, and I *don't know how to make it stop*."

Nat quirked an eyebrow mildly. "Get over yourself."

Heron's chin jerked up.

"They're not after *you*," she said, January-cold. "Tyler told me Ada Chandler's pet lizards turned to dust inside two weeks' time. If the Wicked God's minions were picking holes in reality just to find *you*, they'd be everywhere from here to John's Creek. You'd be dead already. Quit pouting and work on a *solution*."

Heron's mouth opened and then hung. *Harsh*, I thought, with a dark satisfaction. This wasn't even Heron's farm. He wasn't even the one with the most to lose.

"If anyone knows how to fix this," Tyler offered, tentative, "it might *be* Ada Chandler."

Nat's eyebrows skyrocketed.

"She's studying Twisted Things," he said, speculative, "just like the Chandlers study the ruins. Ada probably knows more about Twisted Things by now than anyone. If anyone in fifty miles knows about their world and how to close up that hole, it'll be her."

"Even if she doesn't," Nat said — Nat, who'd never really even *liked* Ada Chandler — "you're right, she'll go find out. She never wants to do anything except pin bugs to boards or pick through old-cities houses for salvage. Ada *hates* not knowing things."

"All right," I said, curling my fists around my shirt hem just to feel like I had hold of *something.* "We get Ada. We tell her everything. And we hope to God she can use it to figure out how to close that hole and lock the Twisted Things on the other side."

Heron looked anxiously at the shovel barring the door. "You said you'd keep my secret."

I stood and faced him full. "There are Twisted Things pouring onto my riverbank, soldiers touching every inch of my farm, and my sister thinks you betrayed us and skipped town northward. Telling Ada Chandler about that knife is the *last* thing likely to get you killed right now."

Heron bowed his head. I could see it running through him: *I should have never left home.*

"Well, you did, and now we've got to deal with it," I said softly, and the gaze he turned up at me was hooded with regret.

"I'll go to the Chandlers, then," Tyler said. "Now. We can't afford to wait."

Heron's eyes shut, exhausted. "Where do I stay?" Now I knew what he was picturing when he closed his eyes: a cheesemaker's shop in a small town in the woods, where everyone spoke with his short and lilting grace.

"Not the hayloft," Nat put in, and I gave her a filthy look.

I looked around at old desks and cradles, the shattered settee. "Here," I said. "They've already been through the place, and everything here's broken. Nobody really *looks* for anything in here."

Heron examined the endlessly branching trails I'd made when I was a child. "I'll find a spot," he said softly, and wove into the ruins.

Nat cautiously unbarred the door, and we followed her like ducklings into the cloudy morning. The bar scraped back into place the moment the door shut.

"What do I tell Mum?" Nat asked.

Tyler huffed a cloudy breath. "Don't. I'll deal with it myself."

Nat's baleful stare turned wounded for just a moment. "I'll find the lieutenant, then," she said, and stomped toward the fenceline.

"She's mad at us," I said when she was far enough away. "I didn't think she'd be mad."

I rubbed my bad hand fretfully. Ty snorted, and folded it into his; tucked them both into his warmly lined pocket. "Nat's had a bad summer."

Carrying Lakewood Farm. Tyler's leg. Her uncles. Her father. None of us had had a good summer at all.

"You okay?" Tyler asked. *No,* I thought. *Yes. No.* I shook my head, once. I was not okay.

Tyler drew back, confused. "What'd I do wrong?"

"Nothing," I said, and took a shuddering breath. "Nothing.

You did everything right." I let myself lean into him for one more moment and then stood, cold, on my own two feet. "You have to go get the Chandlers. And I have to gather the eggs. I told Marthe I'd do them over an hour ago."

"Right," Tyler said wistfully, and pecked me on the cheek. It was strange how quickly a thing became normal. Bonfires of dead birds and lizards, your brother's absence, the texture of lips upon your cheek.

"Be careful," I said, uncomfortably like Marthe, and he chuckled.

"Wear a warm scarf and hat, and do up your jacket."

I socked him in the shoulder.

"Right," he replied, and quirked a grin. "Be back soon."

I watched him limp to the highway, a shuffling dot of warmth, before I ducked into the poultry barn to gather the day's eggs. Marthe had moved on to making sausage when I got in, and the look she shot me should have withered my bones: *Shiftless, lazy, irresponsible, childish Hallie.*

"Eggs," I said, and set them on the counter.

"At ten minutes per hen?" she said acidly. My child's fears wriggled, but I ignored them. *I am doing something important,* I realized for the first time. *She doesn't even know it, but for once, I'm taking the weight off her. For once, I'm taking care of* Marthe.

"Eggs," I repeated, and slipped outside. The fresh, cold air prickled my face and stung my eyes. There was a fire to lay, down by the river. I put my mitts on and brought the wood down, ready to burn.

SIXTEEN

IT WAS A TENSE AND SILENT AFTERNOON. I TAPPED A DOUBLE dozen shingles onto the poultry barn, filled the lye barrel with ash and snowmelt so we could finally make soap, burned twenty-seven Twisted Things to dust down by the river dock, and Tyler still didn't return. I worked like a proper farm girl, from light 'til dusk, and it still didn't block the quiet out of my ears.

A way of life becomes normal so quickly. I'd forgotten how lonely the farm was without Tyler here; without Heron just around the corner, whistling low. Fifty acres was a lot of land, much too much for just two people to live on. Much too desolate and cold.

Supper was even tenser. Marthe was angry—real anger, for the first time since the soldiers arrived—and her rage splashed out across the kitchen, into the air. The goat sausage drying on the rafters had a squeezed and vicious look, and she pushed pickled beets across her plate in short, sharp shoves. I kept quiet, kept from calling her rage my way, snuck glances at the windowpanes and listened for Tyler's step. Marthe gave up on the beets and shoved her plate away. I glanced at it, awkward. There was nothing to say.

I took my empty plate to the basin, dropped it in. "I'm going to check for Twisted Things," I said, and lifted my coat off the hook.

Her eyes veiled with suspicion: hard, mean, and hurt. "I swear," I added, small. "Just to the poultry barn and the river. No secrets."

"You still haven't told me why Heron left," she said. I swallowed, but she just waited: a fisherman's sort of patience, the kind with a hook pushed through your lip.

"Please don't make me make things up," I blurted desperately.

"Nobody *makes* you," my sister said, flat and even. "You tell people the truth or you don't."

I bit my lip. Marthe winced behind her long bangs and put a hand on her belly.

"You okay?" I asked immediately.

"It's just the baby kicking," she said, and lifted a baleful brow. "You can't change the subject like that."

My stomach knotted. "Do you need me to get something, or—"

She stared at me skeptically. "I'm pregnant, Hallie. Not dead."

You either tell the truth or you don't, I thought, and sucked in a breath. I didn't even know where I'd begin anymore; I *couldn't* begin. I could see only one way out of Marthe's carefully laid trap, and it was the worst thing I'd ever done, ever.

I looked straight at Marthe's belly and—deliberately—flinched.

Her eyes opened wider—all the way. "Hallie, *talk to me.*"

"What Cal Blakely said," I said, and took care to make my voice stumble. Her eyebrows rose. "About the baby. About upsetting it, and—"

Marthe darkened like a storm cloud. "That is an absolute stupid fairy tale," she said. "Uroma was pregnant with Opa while the old cities were falling, and she spent all day building the house and all night chasing bandits off our land. It takes more to lose a baby than *this.*"

I let out a breath. The steely grit was gone from Marthe's eyes. "Is that why you won't tell me anything anymore?" she said, quieter.

It worked. I looked down at the table and shrugged. She'd take it as a yes.

I am horrible.

"The baby's fine," she said, just handing me the comfort I'd worked so hard to steal. "Here." And she placed my hand on her belly.

My fingers spread over her stomach: two thin layers of fabric between them and her tight, stretching skin. I sat there awkwardly; this was almost unbearably close for us. We never hugged or touched the way the Pricketts or Chaudhrys did, light and laughing, like it meant nothing at all. I started to pull away, and then I felt it.

So small I could have imagined it: an insistent little push. Something touching me through skin and Marthe's cotton dress. I jumped, and Marthe's mouth twitched with the ghost of a smile.

"Your niece. Or nephew." Her bleak eyes met mine, and hidden in them was a flush, a rush of pride.

I beamed back, not lying now; unexpectedly euphoric. "It's a real baby."

She nodded, and edged back enough to let my hand drift off her belly. My palm still felt warm, the ghost of stubborn life whispering across it. I closed my fingers on that feeling to keep it from wisping away. She'd just given me something: a gift. Something special I should have earned, not taken by stealth to deflect her.

The worst part about learning to lie was the way you lied to yourself. How the lies seeped into, and tainted, everything true.

"I made you some lye," I said. I had nothing else to offer. I wanted so desperately to have something to offer her.

Marthe swallowed. "Thank you," she said, strained again, and took her own plate to the basin. "Just to the river."

I slipped out the door, coat in hand, and shrugged it on halfway down the slick porch steps. I would have something to offer if Ada could give us answers: safety for our farm; proof that I could be the one who took the weight, faced down the terrors; proof, once and for all, how much I loved my sister. I dutifully checked the sleeping hens and then skirted the path down to the orchard, to where Marthe's stones lay. To where we might already have an answer written out.

My heart hammered behind my ribs as I struck a spark, flared tinder. *Please,* I thought. *Please answer us.* I lit the lamp and held it high.

The ground was disturbed where Marthe had written her message, the rocks rolled painfully into new letters and words. I caught my breath, hard, and squinted at their curves. YOU HAVE TO OPEN—they said in the same long, shaky hand that had cried silently out for help.

The crunch of footsteps echoed softly against the shore: a thick boot's tread, slow and deliberate. Setting pace for a road that would never, ever stop.

"Heron?" I whispered, terrified, as alone in the dark as I'd ever been in my father's house, unprotected by the thin wooden walls. "Tyler?"

There was fear in my mouth. I could taste its bloody tang. My legs cramped from the desire to run to the smokehouse, lock its door. The ghostly pacing faded down toward the river, and I narrowed my eyes. How dared I tell myself a lie that big—that all my inability to even *find* a way to put this mountain of made-up stories right was somehow bravely facing down monsters for Marthe. "Look at you," I whispered, hissed through my clenched teeth. *"Look."*

I lifted my lamp. If I couldn't tell the truth, I would damned well face *something* down.

I strode, back tall, down the path to the river shore.

I wasn't surprised to see nothing there: the lonely strand, the moon-stained waves. The creak and shatter of melted sand sounded against the current and a curious absence of bird-calls. I set my jaw and lifted the lantern high.

There was a bootprint in the round, glassed patch of sand, burned deep as a cattle brand.

"Who's there?" I said, and it came out in a squeak. Glass broke with a soft *pop* at the shoreline. Ash scattered into the still air. The new print formed right before my eyes, under the weight of nothing. The steps of ghosts: the steps of something leaking through from another world.

I shivered — and shook it off. Tyler had sat up all night to try to see its face. I couldn't run now. I couldn't.

I stalked behind it, step by step, to the freezing shallows.

Loose bubbles flecked the river chop: trout below, or buried crabs. The flame of my lantern danced in the dark water, distorted, a swirled reflection. If I squinted, I could almost see another figure beside me, folded weirdly at the torso, its coat pure dark.

My skin prickled. I backed up. "He can't touch me. He's in another world," I whispered — I prayed, throat icy dry. "He can't touch me."

The reflection wavered, then blurred into a new shape on the running river: tall, long, stretched full upright. It edged closer, turning into arms and shoulders and the whites of human eyes. I shuddered in the stagnant air and leaned forward, over the river. Into the ghost's clearing face.

"He can't touch me," I whispered, heartbroken. And suddenly I couldn't breathe for the grief, the need, the *hope*.

Thom Clarlund's hand reached toward me — and through me. Thom Clarlund's face, distorted by war and waves and the walls between worlds, peered at me through the current and burst into tears.

I reached the smokehouse sobbing, choking with grief. "Heron?" I hiccupped, half blind, my face smeared. "Heron, please —"

Heron rose from a warren halfway through the maze of junk, one hand on his belt, his hair a black cloud. "Hallie? What's wrong?"

I was at him in an instant, my hands tangled in his shirt-sleeves. "It's Thom," I sobbed, heaving tears like I hadn't since I was tiny. "Marthe's ghost. I saw him. I saw Thom in the river."

Heron's hands found my shaking shoulders, grasped them almost too tight. "Hallie," he said. "What do you mean — slow down."

The story came out in pieces, shattered like the moonlight, like my splintered nerves. I gasped it into Heron's sleeve by lamplight, leaned up against the table I'd hid beneath on the night my uncle left.

"We have to get him out of there." The tears would not stop coming. They stung where their cold trails had chapped my face raw. "Heron, I will *do anything*."

He squeezed his eyes shut. His brow furrowed, hard. "Don't say that."

"I would—"

"Don't *say* that," he said sharply, and crouched on the flagstone floor. "We'll get him out. I promise you. We'll bring your brother home."

I picked a cobweb out of his ponytail. He winced, and I dropped my hand. We leaned together: cold, exhausted. Breathing.

"We have to tell Nat and Tyler, and Ada," I said abruptly, and leaned back. "This changes—this changes everything." I cast about in my coat's fifteen pockets for a pair of warm gloves. Heron's hand patted my back: regular, warm, human comfort. So new that I couldn't find words to explain that there was such a thing as the one human whose comfort I wanted.

I need Tyler, I realized. *I need the way he listens.*

I need to be held.

"I told Marthe I'd only go down to the river," I said hastily. "You have to help me think up something to say, something to tell her—"

"You're going to find them at this hour?"

"I *need* him," I said with an urgency that shook my bones.

"How suspicious," he asked quietly, "do you want your sister to be?"

"I—" My thoughts caught. I'd sworn to her I wouldn't go past the river. If she came looking in the smokehouse and found Heron here, there'd be no explaining what we'd done. "I'll think of something," I stammered, balancing the delicate scales of our need against Marthe's increasing, chilly rage.

"You will stay here," Heron said firmly, and I blinked with sheer surprise. It felt like years since landowner and hired man had fit our secretive allegiance, but he had never given me an order before. He'd never once thrown at me that he was older, or a veteran soldier; that he'd seen more of the world than one tiny lakelands farm.

"Hallie," he said. "Miss. You hired me to save this farm. And your farm will die if you and your sister completely break apart."

I caught my breath. How had he seen? *How*, I realized, *could he not see?* "But if I don't, we might not get Thom back—"

"So you'll save your brother," he answered. "And then the trust between all of you will be so far gone, you'll starve or break by midwinter."

For the first time ever, I hated those gray eyes. They saw me truly. They saw too damned much.

I swallowed humiliated fury. "What, then? I should just stay home and leave him there?"

Heron pulled on his too-thin flannel shirt. "Your sharp

little friend told me to get over myself," he said quietly. "I found a pair of old boots in one of those boxes. I'm going to put them on and tell Tyler and Nasturtium what's happened here. And then I'm going to treat with your Chandlers myself, like I should have from the beginning."

A perverse pain rose up in my throat — *Uncle Matthias's winter boots.*

"What are you asking me to do?" I whispered.

Heron looked down at me, down his broken, twisted nose. "Go home," he said, "to your family. You can't do this to them."

I swallowed. Hard.

"Keep the boots if they fit," I forced out, and he whuffed a grateful breath. "You'll need them in the spring."

He nodded sharply and pulled on the boots. "Anyone out there?"

I opened the smokehouse door and looked into a sudden dazzle of snowlight. "No," I said. And then, through a thick throat, "Go."

He eased out the door, cautious, and up the gravel path. I turned my foot sideways and wiped his bootmarks from the new snow, left alone between white ground and gray sky. My own boots made a solitary path back to the kitchen porch.

"I'm back," I called to Marthe as I banged through the door, hands blue with cold and worry. Eyes red from endless tears.

"Good," she said, laying bread dough for an overnight rise.

Simply, kindly: *Good.* I edged up the stairs, peeled my work clothes off, and eased into a clean nightdress. The mark of the burnt Twisted Thing stained my windowsill. I stared past it into the snow, into the fine space between two worlds.

Watching for a light. Waiting.

SEVENTEEN

I WOKE TO A TRACKLESS WONDERLAND OF SNOW, A WORLD turned sparkling white. The kind of day that, when I was young, was my favorite of all—a morning building snowmen with Marthe on the side of the hay barn and then the hot spiced cocoa Uncle Matthias made to welcome us home. The sun was high above the trees, and from the road to the river, the fields glittered and dreamed.

I overslept, I thought with a tinge of panic, and dug for a clean pair of work pants. Heron would be back; Tyler would be back. Thom was trapped in the Wicked God's world, waiting.

We didn't have a second more to lose.

I threw my hair into a ponytail on my way down the stairs, calling, "Marthe, what time is it?"—and stopped. Marthe sat at the table wearing a creased frown. And Lieutenant Jackson perched in Thom's usual chair, his elbows on the table.

"What's happened?" I managed.

"Nothing," Marthe said slowly. I swallowed hard, trying to look less like I was half jitters and half lies. "The lieutenant wants to hire our boat to row out to Beast Island."

"Sergeant Blakely requested the family's privacy this

morning," the lieutenant said. "Something to do with his young nephew arriving home ill. So we're off to investigate the river."

"Right," I said, and grabbed the banister to stay upright. They hadn't found Heron, or Thom's messages, or the knife. And Tyler—Tyler was ill, at home. *What does ill mean?* The alarms in my head shrilled. "Sure, take the boat," I said, and Marthe eyed me, bleak and tired. I looked away, at the lieutenant's pleased smile.

"Much obliged to the both of you," he said, and rubbed his short-cropped curls. "There was just one other thing I missed asking the other night." *I've got to go,* I thought fruitlessly as he reached into his coat pocket and pulled out a carefully folded bundle of paper tied with butcher's twine. He pulled the knot and dealt the pages like playing cards. "You wouldn't recognize any of these faces?"

Marthe took the first one. I came to the table and uncurled the second with my fidgety hands. They were wanted posters: pen-and-ink portraits of Asphodel Jones's irregulars, traitors every one of them, who had fought the army at John's Creek.

I didn't recognize any of them: a slight man with distant eyes and a crown that was softly balding; a thickset boy, younger than me, who could've been a Sanchez cousin; a woman, dark-eyed, round-faced, bob-haired, with a tilt to her eyes somewhere between Sergeant Zhang's and the Thaos'. They looked normal: shopkeeps or diligent shepherds. I let out a breath I hadn't even meant to hold.

Heron had army buttons. I hadn't thought him an irregular, truly. But the more he said *I'm nobody,* the less I could make it feel true.

There was another page beneath them, the most folded, the most loved. *They're sending John Balsam's likeness from John's Creek to the sea,* I remembered, and unfolded the worn sheet of cotton paper.

It had yellowed on the road. The ink-black image was stained by dust and sweat, and the creases worried at its thin, stern mouth. I flattened the likeness on the table and leaned close for a better look.

The face of John Balsam was sharp and lean, all harsh lines, as distant as the river. He had dark, straight hair, and his eyebrows were sketched in fine beneath it. The artist had made his cheekbones high and his jaw as square as a barn wall. He looked off the page, thoughtful, brooding over all our rescued tomorrows. He looked halfway familiar, and I squinted at the ink. *He looks,* I thought, wistful, *like a hero.*

"Well, miss," Lieutenant Jackson's too-hearty voice said. "That's our boy. John Balsam." He beamed, his eyes warm for real now: every inch the picture of soldierly pride.

"I'd only heard the name," I said. For all my thoughts of who might be waiting to receive that twisted knife home, I hadn't actually thought of John Balsam as a man, with a man's face.

"I saw him once," the lieutenant said, softer. "From a distance, in our camp once the Wicked God was slaughtered. He walked so tall. Even with everything we'd been through, he walked like a man who could find his way through hell. Made a man want to follow him; see how it's done. See if perhaps you could turn out like that yourself."

Marthe flicked the paper with a fingernail. "What changed to send you hunting him, then?" she said acerbically.

Lieutenant Jackson left the desert and drifted back to earth. "That one's not a Wanted, ma'am, it's a Missing. He's not been seen since after the battle; he just plain disappeared. We thought he was dead until the sightings began: a town outside the Great Dust; a farmstead by Ball Creek; on the old black road outside Ooltewah, cutting back brush for a campfire. Then it was people telling stories of John Balsam saving them from beasts and bogeys with his God-kill knife."

Liars, I thought, with not a little scorn. And then reconsidered it. Perhaps this was what Heron had meant: farmhands and soldiers wanting to see their hero so badly that they conjured him up for themselves. Passed around stories of such sighting or such passing by, because then that grace might touch them, too.

"Wherever he is, he headed north," the lieutenant said. "It's where they say his family's from: far away, in the winter wastes. And so all of us scouting north ask after John Balsam."

Marthe's lips pressed together in an edged smile. "And what'll you do with the man when he's found?"

"Give him his army, ma'am," the lieutenant answered,

ignoring Marthe's flippant eyebrow. "De Guzman is our provisional general, but John Balsam saved us all. We stand ready to march at his order, or establish his territory, the moment he's found."

Marthe lifted the other brow. "Poor man," she murmured. "All I have to run is a farm."

I stared down at that brave, strong jaw to hide the disbelief in my eyes — and finally understood Heron's wild-eyed fear. They'd never believe that he'd just found — or been gifted — John Balsam's God-kill knife. The Great Southern Army wanted their Godslayer. Bad enough to string any man who had a piece of him up high and name him John Balsam's killer.

"I hope he comes back to you," I said softly, tracing the stern mouth, the all-seeing eyes.

The lieutenant's discipline sagged just enough to speak of long miles and a hope wasting on wintering branches. "I'll ask you to show us the boat," he said.

I folded up his wanted posters and handed them across the table. "Right away," I said, and put on my boots. "Marthe, I'll visit at Lakewood Farm afterward?"

She looked out the window and nodded; there was precious little outdoor work one could do under all that snow once the chickens and goats had their feed. "Give Eglantine and James hello for me," she said, and it felt good. It felt good to go somewhere and not have to lie.

The lieutenant tied his posters lovingly back into their bundle. "We'll have it back to you by dusk," he promised, and let himself out the door.

I walked him down the orchard path, across the blank white sheet of the riverbank. *No bootprints this morning,* I thought as he shipped the oars. *No Heron, no Ada, no ghosts.* Sergeant Zhang and Corporal Muhammad stood shivering by the dock, muffled in caps and gloves, miserable with cold. "Good luck," I told them.

Corporal Muhammad beamed. "Thanks!"

Stay away all day, I thought, and waited for the boat to disappear before I brushed the thick snow off the orchard path.

The stones had been scattered by the snow and by my hasty, light excavation. YOU HAVE TO OPEN—I read, and halfway guessed—THE HOLE WIDER. WE ARE TRAPPED. HELP US FREE. And then in a scatter of barely legible rock: HURRY.

My hands shook like dead leaves. *Open the hole wider.* Spill all hell itself into the river, into Roadstead Farm.

We couldn't. There had to be another way.

"Thom, that is crazy," I murmured bitterly, and wiped the stones away.

GETTING CHANDLERS' AID, I spelled out, and then helplessly: WE LOVE YOU, in the message's broken ruins. And strode across the empty fields to Lakewood Farm.

The walk to Nat and Tyler's was achingly familiar: over the wood-and-wire fence, and then a shortcut through the soft-hilled pastures that paralleled the black road and took the river to its mouth. Even in the morning light it felt warm with habit: just another snow day, chores suspended, where I went over for Mrs. Blakely's honeyed churros and endless talk with Nat by the fire. Except for the worry that gnawed, ratlike, at my guts. *Thom,* ran round and round my head. *Walk faster.* I put my head down and clambered through the fields.

The curtains were open at the Blakely house, bright and welcoming to all. I took the steps up to their door two at a time and knocked. James Blakely answered it with a hint of surprise. "Hallie," he said, and flung the door wide. "What's wrong?"

It would take too long to list all the real answers. "Nothing," I said instead. "I just heard Tyler wasn't well."

He nodded, his face grave. "Come in," he said, and I ducked inside after him.

Lakewood Farm was everything I remembered — everything I'd always wanted our own house to be. Bright lamps burned in the cushioned parlor room. The air smelled of sweet tea and posole and fresh baking, and even black-clad, even in mourning, the house had a spirit, a *life.* Mrs. Blakely sat on the patched sofa, spinning new yarn from a basket of autumn wool. Nat and James were carding, sleeves rolled up, for the spinning basket. Cal's voice moved steady above them all, reading about a boy and a quest and a stone from a fat old-cities book.

On the mantel, above the fire, the vial of John's Creek

ashes that Tyler's regiment had borne home stood watch over the whole family. A memorial to Nat and Tyler's father, who was gone; an honored and beloved grave.

Tyler was in his father's chair, the one with the footstool attached to its end, with his leg up at a splayed angle as he moodily darned a sock. I let out a breath. He wasn't dying. He was right there.

"Hallie," he said, and struggled upward. His uncle Cal gave him a torn-up look and boosted him upright with one silent hand. "Please, sit," Tyler said. "No, never mind—let me get you some tea first. You're frozen."

James and Callum glanced at each other, knowing, and my face flamed painfully bright.

"Can we sit in the kitchen?" I asked, and wrung my ponytail out. "I'll get snow all over your rugs."

"That's all right, Hal—" James started, lazily, until Eglantine of all people halted him with a hand.

"That's very thoughtful, dear," she said, and for the first time in a long, long time she actually smiled. "Why don't you two have a snack?"

James looked at her, then looked at us. Sat back down and shut his mouth.

Nat stifled a snort. My face flamed hotter. *Don't argue,* I told myself, and picked my way to the stove, my hair dripping rivulets of snowmelt.

Ty followed me slowly. His shuffle was worse than usual today, a halting, sliding rhythm that bumped all the wrong ways. "I'll get the kettle," I said when he gained the kitchen door.

"Hal—"

I quirked an eyebrow: *Spite or pride?* We didn't even need to say it anymore. He sighed and sank into a kitchen chair, his bad leg stretched achingly wide.

I sank the dipper into the Blakelys' rain barrel and filled their copper kettle high. "How much did Heron tell you?" I asked, and he squinted.

"Heron?"

My stomach iced over. "Heron left last night, to find you. He was going to tell you about Thom."

Tyler struggled upright in his chair. "*What* about Thom?"

The tears started in my eyes again: involuntary, evil things. "It's him, Ty," I said, as low as I could. "I saw the ghost, and he's not a ghost. It's Thom. I saw his face in the river. He reached out to me. He's stuck on the other side—"

Tyler ran a hand through his messy hair. "Oh, damn."

The tears seeped into the corners of my mouth. "I should've come myself last night. I just *needed* you," I said, and sank to my knees before his chair. "I need—" The words choked dry.

Tyler's hand shook at my cheek; brushed away a tear. "Damn," he repeated, his brow furrowed into one thin line. "I'm sorry, Hal. I'm so damned sorry."

"Don't be sorry," I whispered, and leaned against his hand. "Just tell me what Ada said."

He flushed beetroot red. "I never made it," he said simply.

"I pushed the leg too hard, and on the way to the Chandlers' there was a patch of ice and I fell. Cal and the dogs found me two hours later, crawling home. In the ditch."

"Oh, Tyler—" I breathed, and he held up a hand.

"This is what you'll get, you know," he said numbly. "A man who can't walk down the road on a clear day. Who won't be there when you're hurting. I should be sorry. I'm going to disappoint you."

My hands dropped to my sides. "Tyler." He didn't look up. "Did you practice this to your bedroom ceiling too?"

Ty sucked in a breath. "That was cruel," he said.

"Well," I answered weakly, "this *hurts*."

He looked up, and his eyes were rimmed with red.

"Are you leaving me?" I asked, surprisingly small.

His throat bobbed. "I wasn't sure we were doing anything we could leave."

"Apparently so," I answered past the lump in my own throat. We stared at each other, trapped; no way to back out now. The kettle whistled, and I took it off the stove and ignored it. "Please say something."

He looked away, blinking fast. "I just . . . I don't want to hurt you, okay?" he said. "And no matter what I say next, it'll hurt you. I can't win here."

A dull ache spread beneath my ribs. "So," I managed, and cracked a grim smile at the irony, "say what's true."

He hesitated and then looked up, the hazel shreds of his

eyes ablaze. "I want to kiss you. I—forget I said that: I just want you around. To talk with, to help each other. To be there. But then there's *this*." He thumped, bitterly, his bad leg. "And I know I can't take you walking, or dance worth a damn any-more, or even make it a few miles up the road to keep my word to you when it means—oh, God. When it means Thom's life. I can't make it so we're partners. I can't make it equal. And I wonder who I even think I'm fooling, because sooner or later a guy who can *walk* will come along."

I swallowed hard. The very air felt too close, and not from the presence of Twisted Things. "We don't have to dance, then," I said thickly.

"But—"

"Nope," I said, my voice hitching. "My turn. We'll go for shorter walks. We'll do other things. You'll be there. You've already been there. My list of perfect dreamy things in a suitor never had *must walk without a limp*."

"Don't mock me," he snapped.

"I'm not," I said, just as hard. "Y'know, this guy I know told me once that there was no right way or rules to this. I for-get his name: Ty? Tyrone?"

"Tiger," he said with a shard of a smile, and wiped his eyes. "You twist my words."

"Uh-huh," I answered, the knot in my chest untangling slowly. I rubbed a hand across my face. "I needed you. You need me too, sometimes, when I'm not there. That doesn't mean we're not equals, or I'm disappointed, or I'm going to run off with Will Sumner because he has a leg, because believe me, he has *nothing else.*"

Tyler snorted.

"It means I want you when I'm sad. Because I—" The words tangled. I flushed hard. "That's all."

Tyler's gaze had steadied. It was faintly ashamed. "Maybe I'm not really okay either, Hal."

"S'all right," I managed, and reached out for his hand. He took mine, his skin breath-shakingly warm. "We've got time."

Footsteps clattered, nice and loud, down the hallway, and Nat eased into the kitchen. "Well, you're getting better at cover stories," she told me as she pulled out a chair. "Next time pick something that doesn't make me have to convince Mum I'm interrupting her future grandchildren."

"*Nat!*" Tyler hissed.

I closed my eyes. She meant it well; she did. It wasn't her fault she was all edges, always.

She leaned in with bright intensity. "You two all right?"

I nodded, then let out a breath when Ty did too.

"You don't look all right," she said critically, and I bit my lip. And told her, in brief pieces, about Thom.

"Heron never showed up," she said at the end with a shred of leftover disdain.

"He never came back," I said softly, and stood up. "I'm going to the Chandlers'. If he didn't make it there"—the lump rose in my throat—"they'll know better where to search."

Tyler winced. "I can't." His face grew sour, and Nat sighed. "Mum isn't too happy with me about the other day."

"Not just Mum," Nat muttered, and her mouth crimped tight.

"Fine, everybody," he retorted. "And I'm not allowed off the property for a while."

"Oh. Damn," I said feelingly, and Nat snorted into her hands.

Tyler gave her a dirty look, such a normal, familiar dirty look I almost giggled — or sobbed. Nat banged her head lightly on the table. "Right, Hallie. Let's go. You and me, to the ruins to rescue your scarecrow hired man. Adventure."

I looked over my shoulder, down the dim hallway. The murmur of Cal Blakely's reading moved on, uninterrupted. "Right," I said. "What do we tell them?"

Tyler snagged my fingers, twined his between them. "I don't know," he said. "I'm blood relations with *that*. Trust me to make up a ridiculous story."

Nat stared at the hinge where Tyler's fingers slipped through mine. "You know," she said mildly, "if either of you hurt the other, I will kill you."

"Which one?" Tyler asked.

"I can't decide. Neither. Both." She shook her head. "I'll call it even and you'll both just die."

She wasn't joking. There was a tremble underneath the flippant smile.

"I understand that we will both be dead," I said solemnly,

and took her hand with my free one. "And I will not hurt your brother unless he acts like a complete and total jackass."

"Hey," Tyler said.

A smile ghosted over Nat's face. "Right," she said, and squeezed my hand back. "Go pretend we're out behind the barn," she told Tyler, "gossiping about how goopily you probably kiss."

Tyler's face could not have gotten redder. "I hate you, and you will pay," he said, and limped gently through the kitchen door. Nat grabbed her jacket, and we crunched across the lawn to the road that ran up to the ruins.

"I really will," she said after twenty minutes of the ruined old city growing larger against the sky. "Kill you both. Don't make me hang for murder."

"I know," I said peaceably, and we trudged toward the gates of the ancient abandoned towers; down the pathway to the dead city where the Chandlers toiled among the graves.

"Adventure, Hal," Nat said, and pulled me forward into the maze of concrete ghosts.

EIGHTEEN

IT WAS TOO QUIET AT THE CHANDLERS' HOMESTEAD: A CIRCLE OF whitewashed houses tucked between the moldering sky-scrapers, their gardens and cattle pens under straw for the winter. The Chandlers' cooperative of my memory was a noisy, bright-painted place full of the sound of hammers and chatter, blooming among the dead ruins. But today the bright shutters were locked tight, the flower beds heaped with piles of old-cities junk. Nat turned a circle beside me, scanning the desolation. "Hello the camp?" I called. "Anybody here?"

A body shifted behind a doorway. "Hello?" I said, softer.

A slight, dark young girl edged over the threshold, dressed in a dust-smeared coat and leather work boots. "Stop," she said in a piping, tough voice. She lifted a metal contraption with both hands and pointed it straight at us. "Stop or I'll shoot."

Nat raised an eyebrow. I stopped cold, sorting the face from the passels of Chandlers we saw, so fleetingly, on town days. *Ada's cousin,* my memory supplied: an image of short braids and a big, thoughtful smile. *Her name's June.*

"Junie?" I tried, and her eyebrows drew in.

Nat leaned against a fence post. "That's a pretty tough—whatsit you've got there, Junie."

The girl's rigid arms faltered. "You'd better not be soldiers," she said nervously.

Nat whuffed out a breath. "We're not soldiers, hon. You know us: Nat Blakely, from down the road at Lakewood Farm, and Hallie Hoffmann from over at Roadstead. Where is everyone?"

The recognition came slowly. She dropped the device loosely to her side. "Hi, Nat," she said seriously, and her face was a ten-year-old's again. "I just had to make sure you weren't soldiers after all."

"That's a good idea," Nat said soothingly—Nat, who understood young kids, whose Sanchez cousins followed her like ducklings around Windstown. "Do you know where your cousin Ada is? We came to visit with her."

June nodded hesitantly. "She's in her lab. But we're not supposed to bother her there. She'll yell if you do."

"It's very important," Nat cajoled. "We won't bother her long."

June's face squinched up. "Cross your heart?"

"Hope to die," I said.

"Okay. C'mon," she said reluctantly, and led us into the ruins.

I had never spent much time at the Chandlers': as unpopular as Marthe and I were, they were outright ostracized, tolerated for their relics and nothing else. They were a clan built on drifters and runaways, and they and Windstown had existed uneasily together as long as I'd been alive — ever since Rami Haddad left home, moved down the highway, and changed his name to Chandler, and his new brothers outright refused to make him go back.

I could go there, I'd thought time and again, on days when Papa was worse, or late at night, when Marthe and I argued especially hard. No need for a lonely road south, into the unknown, when I could run away and live free as Hallie Chandler. It hadn't taken long for me to realize that the Chandlers, every one of them, were *smart.* There was no place for a maker of malt and a keeper of goats among their sharper minds.

I enviously drank in their houses as June led us through the compound: houses sealed tight against feral dogs and ruin rats, built by people who had, even when they'd lost families, found a family waiting down the black road. June ducked between rusted siding and old concrete thoughtlessly, humming a skipping song, and rapped on a burn-scarred brown oak door. "Ada?" she said, and pushed inside. "It's not soldiers."

Ada Chandler turned, in a thin sliver of winter light, and I let out a breath. The door was ancient and battered, but the room inside was an old-cities dream. Shelves of precious board-bound books spilled over each other, the gilt lettering of their titles flaked off and rubbed dry. Her butcher-block counters bristled with relics I didn't even understand: metal and glass, and trays of sun-bleached shards with wires twining out. Ada put down an ancient book, took off her leather gloves, and said, "Oh, great. There's more."

Perched beside her on a tall stool, looking utterly exhausted, was Heron.

"There you are," I burst out, and Junie's hands went to her metal contraption, suddenly unsure.

"I've told you fifteen times not to play with that thing," Ada said, infinitely tolerant, and plucked it out of June's small hands. "I'm not playing," June protested.

"What is it?" Nat asked.

"Gun," Ada said, and tucked it on a high shelf. "Old-city weapon. Don't worry; it's never loaded. Jerome was teaching her piston engineering and was stupid enough to tell her what the thing's really for when she started having nightmares about the soldiers in town. She's been playing Guardian of the Compound nonstop."

"Ada, you don't *understand*," June started up.

I barely even heard her. My eyes had snagged on that high shelf, and the five beneath it. They were packed with rows of floating bodies caught, loose-limbed, under glass. Stick-legged mice; lizards, hatchlings and adults; a bird or two, with soggy feathers. A whole farm's worth of Twisted Things, displayed in neatly labeled jars.

"Good God, Ada," Nat said softly. "Are you *trying* to get hanged?"

June's dark eyes went as round as saucers.

Ada cast Nat a dirty look and patted June's braids. "No

one's getting hanged, love. Go find your dad, hmm? I'm sure he's got some math for you to do."

June brightened, and skipped out into the snow. Ada turned and fixed Nat with a hard eye. "Where do you get off, saying that around a kid?"

Nat shrugged. "I'd say she's figured out the risks all by herself."

I edged around them to Heron's side. "Miss," he said quietly. "I thought we agreed you'd stay home." He looked cleaner, at least. Someone had got him a bath and a warm jacket.

"Don't even," I said. "You didn't come home. What were we supposed to do?"

"Travel out of the compound's restricted as of last night," Ada cut in impatiently. "There are still army scouts in the neighborhood. You shouldn't even be here."

"We know there are," Nat retorted. "Who do you think's been leading their wild-goose chase?"

I rolled my eyes. It had been long enough since someone put Nat and Ada in the same room that I'd forgotten why you just *didn't*.

"Look, they're not here now," I said, before they could get back to it. "They borrowed our rowboat. They're at Beast Island, all day. And—" I couldn't keep my eyes from filling. I swore, inward, at their constant treachery. "Thom's in danger. He wants us to open the hole."

"That's a stupid idea," Ada said promptly.

"I *know*," I overrode her, and then reined back my panic. "But we have to bring him home. There's got to be something you can do, Ada. Please."

Ada tore herself away from the serious task of glaring at Nat. "I'm not a miracle worker. I do research, not—extra-dimensional magic breakouts."

"I'll give you the run of our whole shore," I said impulsively. "You can set up research, do experiments, whatever you want—as long as you need it."

Ada clucked her tongue. She hadn't changed that much: the one thing she couldn't resist was her curiosity. "I'll ask Rami if we're clear to travel," she said, and leveled a finger at Nat. "Don't touch *anything*."

Nat put her hands innocently behind her back, and took them back out the second Ada vanished around the corner.

"Don't," Heron warned. "She's been showing me some of her research. I wouldn't lay a finger wrong in here if I were you."

Nat stuck her hands behind her back again, sobered. Her eyes roamed the half-lit jars. I shuddered.

Ada was back inside ten minutes, brisk with energy. "Right," she said, and swept up a handful of instruments from her desk. "You're very lucky people."

"Yes?" I said, my heart lifting fast.

"Yes," she said, and stuffed them into a satchel. "We have until sundown to see your spooky beach. Let's go."

• • •

There was no magic to it. Ada measured, hummed, poked stick after branch through thin air into the Wicked God's world, and then scraped up jars of the melted, ashy ice beneath it. Heron paced back and forth under the tree line, standing watch for our little rowboat on the horizon. Nat sat beside me on a driftwood log, and we watched.

"I'll come back tomorrow," Ada said when the sun stained the trampled snow orange. Frustration wriggled behind my rib cage; Ada looked as mild as a flower. "I'm going to need help with this one," she said. "You didn't even *begin* to cover how big a job this'll be."

"But you can get him out, right?" I asked through a dry throat.

Ada closed her pack. "I don't know, Hallie. There's a lot going on here. The composition of the air's really finicky, and I want to know everything we can about those chemical burns on the sand. I don't want to get it *wrong*, all right?"

I closed my hands into fists. I didn't understand half of what she'd said, except the unmistakable tinge of *no*. "Just . . . hurry, okay? Please. It's my brother in there."

"I'll walk you to the crossroads," Nat said dryly, and brushed snow off her hat.

Ada sized her up warily, and nodded: a sort of truce. "Fine," she said, and they set off up the path.

Heron eyed me for a moment in that old way, the one that

wouldn't meet my eye. *He's worried about me,* I realized. "Go on," I said after a moment. "I need to talk to him. To Thom. We need to talk."

Heron nodded silently and strode through the orchard trees, to another long, cold night in the smokehouse.

I watched him go. And then, hands shaking like dead leaves, I picked up a handful of Thom's river stones and wrote a letter about everything that'd happened this summer on Roadstead Farm.

It was dark when I followed Heron's mangled footprints up the orchard trail, to the crabbed warmth of the kitchen porch.

Our door opened before I could touch it: James Blakely, muffled in boots and coat, let himself out of our dim kitchen. "All done?" he asked, and I colored helplessly.

"I didn't know you had come by," I said, and he smiled, a humorless sliver. My gut turned over.

Something was very, very wrong.

"Clearly not. Walk with me?" he said, and steered me off the porch.

"Sure," I said, perplexed, and fell into step beside him. He'd brought a lamp. It cast soft marks onto the lane and over the sleeping hummocks of the fields.

We crunched silent through the snow for a few minutes. And then he asked, "What are you playing at with my niece and nephew?"

I went rock-still. His gaze was calm and steady, and I couldn't think of one good lie to tell.

"I changed diapers for all three of you, you know," he said, casually enough. "It's pretty plain when you all start sneaking. And if it's plain to me and your sister, you'll want to consider what General de Guzman's soldiers think."

I nearly stopped breathing. "What did they say?"

James stared down his scarred nose at me. "They spent an hour asking about your former hired man last night. It's too much of a coincidence: when he showed up, when he left. And how little you want to say about it."

I swallowed. His eyes burned holes through my brain. "I gave my word," I stuttered. "I can't tell anyone."

"Is that how you put your sister off?" he asked mildly.

I wanted to sink into the ground and die.

"Don't bother. I just spoke with her. I know it is," he continued. "She told me plenty about how you're haring off and dodging your chores. If your fields aren't ready for the springtime, you're not going to have a farm next summer. I'm not sure anymore that you're taking that seriously."

"We are," I burst out. "We're doing *everything*."

"Such as?"

There was nowhere to start: the ghosts in Tyler's eyes, Thom's stones, Ada's endless rows of jars. In the back field, slumbering, John Balsam's knife. James shook his head and started walking again, along the land that our family had held since the cities fell; since all the machines of the world went dark.

I'd thought I wanted to die of shame before. It would have been better, now, if I never existed.

"There's a hole between our world and the world behind the Wicked God's heart," I forced out. "On the beach, near the riverbend. That's where the Twisted Things are coming from; they're coming *out*. We were trying to fix it, but those stones in the pathway—" I stopped, swallowed hard. "James, it's Thom. He's stuck on the other side."

James Blakely stopped mid-step.

Keep Tyler's sight out of it, I told myself. *Keep Heron out.* "We went to the Chandlers. That's how Tyler got hurt. He was going for Ada, to find a way to bring Thom home. And she's working on it: she took measurements and samples, and there'll be a whole team with her tomorrow. But we can't let the soldiers find out that hole's there. They'll tell Pitts, and he'll force us off the farm. We'll lose Thom forever."

James's scarred face set into pale shock lines. "You've been creeping about under our noses, trying to solve what every fighting man in the country couldn't handle."

I nodded.

He shook his head. I couldn't tell if he was laughing or furious. "God," he said wonderingly. "I wish I was sixteen again: totally brave and utterly stupid. What on earth," he asked, and closed the distance between us, "made you think that you couldn't tell *us?*"

My careful lies swerved, halted, and crashed.

I didn't know. The road here had gotten so long. It was hard to even remember what I'd had, once, for reasons. *I wanted to protect Marthe; to show her I could do it. I wanted,* I thought, older and more selfish than I'd ever felt, *to save the farm.*

James tilted his scar-torn chin. "Halfrida. You have to tell your sister about this. Right away."

I shook my head wildly. "I can't —" My heart lurched to life under my ribs. "She'll kill me. She'll never speak to me again."

"Your sister," he said with a glance back to that dark house, "cares more about you than you realize."

"You don't understand. I can't tell her this. Not ever."

"Because you're afraid of her," he said quietly.

The sound of branches rattling in the distance was suddenly very clean and sharp. "She's my *sister.*"

"When she gets angry," he continued without mercy, "you shrug your shoulders down. You pull back into your head. You think about every single word before you speak, and your face goes flat like — there."

I fought to keep myself from doing exactly that, forcing my chin up even though my head buzzed with the need to run. "She's my sister," I whispered.

"Hallie, I know what happened inside that house," he said, and my whole soul froze solid.

"Your grandfather was a hard man," he said after a moment. "Your father did a little better, with your mother and with the both of you. Your sister does even better than they did, with some very hard choices in the mix and a lot of troubles I know she never wanted.

"Between the two of you," he said, very serious, "I have high hopes for how much that child of hers will be loved."

"Why are you saying this?" I said through a tight throat.

He shoved his hands into his deep coat pockets. "Because Marthe is my friend. My best friend. And you're old enough to take responsibility for your actions." He paced a small furrow in the field and looked up. "Every child has to carve out their own place in the world. But if Thom's caught on the other side of that—whatever it is—what's at stake is Marthe's husband. And keeping that from her is cruel."

I'd thought *childish* was a punch to the gut. It was nothing compared to this. I knew what cruel was: Papa's acid tongue, his elaborate punishments. They'd grown terrible once Uncle Matthias wasn't here to stop them. I closed my eyes, and the sound of his shouting rose up, always just a thought away: curse words shoving through the floor, around the corners, under the solid wood of my bedroom door.

Through Marthe's arms and Marthe's hands clamped stubbornly over my ears.

My sister. Not much older, then, than I was now. Telling me in an endless monotone that she'd keep me safe forever.

"I'm not like that," I burst out. "I'm not *him*."

"I'm glad you're not a fan of the idea," James said calmly. "But Marthe's seen you pull away from her. She's caught every lie you've told. She has years of reasons to be afraid right now."

"Marthe's not afraid of me," I protested. I couldn't even conceive of it. "She's *Marthe*. There's nothing I can do to her."

James looked down his nose at me sadly. "There's plenty our children can do, or be, that makes us afraid we've failed them."

"Failed?" As if Marthe could fail *me*: Marthe, who'd shielded me from Papa's temper through the long, lonely, hard years; who came home from Windstown with his will unproven and swore in the most frightening voice I'd ever heard that no one would tear this family apart.

I'd spent years trying to repay her, run myself dry trying to live up to her.

Marthe could never even *touch* the word *failure*.

I clamped my gloves over my mouth, and the sobs escaped anyway, wrenching slaps of grief that curled me around them like a beating. "Hey, hey—" James Blakely said, and reached out. I shrugged his arms off viciously. I couldn't be touched right now, couldn't be held. I had to keep myself from flying apart.

"I can't do it," I said, gulping, gasping. "All I do is disappoint her. I'll never be as good, as strong, as fast, and she'll send me away. There's a baby coming. She'll get tired of putting up with me, with pretending I *earned* my half share of Roadstead, and she'll push me off the farm."

"That's not true—"

"Don't *say that!*" I shouted. "Uncle Matthias told me the truth: she'll only let me stay here if I'm good to her. If I'm *good*. He was the younger son; I'm the youngest daughter, and Papa made Uncle Matthias go. Opa made Great-aunt Millie go. Nobody wanted me to inherit anyway — nobody wanted Papa's will. I've always known it was her or me, okay? So don't tell me *lies*."

James Blakely stood back in the snowlit field, his mouth wide open. "That is bullshit," he said darkly. "That is shit from start to finish."

"I *saw* Uncle Matthias go —"

"Because of his stupid pride," he snapped. "Pride's the Hoffmann failing. Not one person who worked this dirt has ever known when to just *apologize*." James shook his head. His face smoldered. "I hate them both right now, you know that? And I didn't think, when your father died, I could've hated him more. I hated him when we were children. I hated him every time I had to wipe your sister's eyes and make her go back to that house."

It shocked me right into breathing.

He smiled bitterly and dug a handkerchief out of his pocket.

I took it, crushed it small inside my fist. "I don't need your handkerchief," I whispered.

He smiled awfully at me. "You're Matthias to the bones, too. Never a second after he learned to talk that he wasn't saying 'I can do it myself.' I followed him around like a lost kitten when we were kids. I wanted to *be* him, and now I hate him too."

"Don't you dare," I managed. Uncle Matthias had been kind to us. He was the last kindness, until Thom came, that I'd had.

"You're old enough," James said almost gently. "And don't say I don't understand somehow. It was almost easier on me when Matthias left than when I realized he wasn't powerful and perfect." James Blakely smiled the crookedest smile I'd ever seen. "He left, Halfrida. He decided he could do it himself. He planted something that festered until it drove you and Marthe apart, and then he walked off down the south road, and hasn't been back in eight years.

"Don't be your father," James said softly. "But damn it all, *don't* be Matthias."

I stood there, hugging James Blakely's handkerchief, and felt my rib cage shatter and strew bone shards into my lungs, my heart.

"This appears to be my fence," James said.

It was. The posts Thom had cut, the wire I'd strung between them stretched through the dark not a handspan away. Our farm looked dark from the outskirts: something abandoned to the winter wastes.

"Keep the handkerchief," James said, and started across the empty fields to his bright home and his laughing husband. His family, full of love. "You can return it in the morning. I'll be there to talk about Thom, and our options. Together."

I held on to the kerchief, clinging, hating. I held on a long time. There was no mistaking it: That was a deadline. With or without me, Marthe was going to find out all the lies I'd spun her, tomorrow.

I turned around and walked home across the snowbound fields, the back ways and brush-clogged remnants of Roadstead Farm. Walked, and just kept walking, because there was nowhere to go. There was no bright house for me anywhere; there was no end to that road.

I turned a corner, tripped, stumbled—

—and almost walked right into a waiting shape in the darkness.

I jumped. "Hey—" and then its head came up, and I let out a breath. It was just Heron, crouched down by the hay barn wall, with our firewood ax in hand. Staring moodily into the bare brush field.

He sprang up to meet me. "We need firewood. There are Twisted Things down on the beach again. Can you keep your sister away if I burn them?" he said. I held up both hands to fend him off: his secrets, his plans. How thoroughly even this stranger knew that Marthe and I weren't *family* anymore. How we lived afraid, divided, and—*cruel*.

"I can't," I said, too high, and he stopped, surprise and offense battling on his face. "I just can't anymore," I choked, and pushed past him, clutching James Blakely's kerchief. Into my empty, ghost-ridden house.

NINETEEN

I TOSSED ALL NIGHT.

I practiced conversations that never ended in forgiveness, argued in my head, thought about running away forever as James Blakely's *Don't be Matthias* turned cartwheels in my gut. Couldn't sleep; couldn't dream for all the ghosts in the walls. When dawn crawled hand over hand through my cracked window, I still didn't have the words to explain any of this to Marthe: that I'd wanted to give her something the size of all she'd given me; to be her hero.

How that had somehow been eaten up in lies.

Marthe rapped three times on my door, harsh enough to rock it in the frame. "Breakfast, Hal," she said, unknowing, utterly unprepared. The sun spilled over the horizon filthy bright and *cruel, cruel, cruel* filled my ears. I could already see the look on her face when I loosed all the terrible secrets I'd kept. It wrenched my guts. *I can't do it,* I thought despairingly. *I can't.*

My bedroom door still locked from the inside. Marthe had installed the lock for me the week after Papa died, and told me

I could use it, that I shouldn't be afraid. I locked it and curled up under the quilt to wait for the world to end.

The knock came twice more, and then: "Hal, please. Damn it, why do you never just *talk?*" My door handle jiggled. I froze beneath the blankets and begged every god there was to just let me stop existing. Marthe'd said six years ago that nothing would tear this family apart, and nothing could. Nothing had, except ourselves.

I'd been a fool to think I could fix *us* by somehow saving Roadstead Farm.

The door's rattle fell silent. From the faraway place where I curled up, waiting for the blow to land, I heard her sniffle. And then her steps moved slow down the stairs. The kitchen door opened. The kitchen door shut.

You couldn't even tell her yourself, I thought bitterly: my final failure. James would tell Marthe how I'd lied to her, betrayed her, and she'd finally turn me out of the house. I would fill my half-packed bag, hidden in the smokehouse all these years, and wander like Heron, walk the lonely roads. After so many years of waiting, it was almost a relief.

All summer long, all fall and winter, the world I knew had fallen away under my feet, piece by piece. I wasn't Marthe's treasured sister anymore, wasn't a maker of malt and keeper of goats, half owner of Roadstead Farm. If I couldn't still be the girl Uncle Matthias stood up for, comforted, *loved*—I didn't know *who* I was anymore.

I didn't know what to hold on to, to keep from being utterly lost.

James's knock rang on our kitchen door slow minutes later, shaking the house on its ancient foundations. The murmur of voices drifted up through the floorboards: James's baritone rumble, Marthe's words curt and soft. Tears snuck like traitors into the corners of my mouth.

Then the voices drowned in footsteps, too quick and muddled to be Marthe. A tentative knock: "Hallie? Are you okay?"

Tyler's fear rent my heart in two all over again. I opened my mouth and closed it, scrambled for a word to slide under the door to him. The walls of Roadstead Farm were tumbling down inside me—the walls of love and family, the only ones that ever mattered—and there was nothing. My mouth was dust.

"Hal—" he started, and stopped again. "You don't have to come out. Just please, talk to us."

"You are scaring my brother," Nat said through the door.

I got up and let them in.

They both registered it at the same time: my messy hair, my sweaty nightdress, the blank pain vulturing on my shoulders. Tyler's hazel-shard eyes widened. "Well," Nat said, "you look like hell."

Tyler shot her a filthy look. He'd never quite understood Nat the way I did.

"You're supposed to be stuck in the house," I said dully.

Ty's mouth skewed, all out of tune. "Whatever you said to Uncle James last night, he came back in a fury. He sent the soldiers to the Masons' place and then gave us both hell for not telling him about Thom."

I looked away. Everybody knew now: everyone. "I didn't say a word about Heron," I mumbled. "And I didn't say a word about your eyes."

"I said more than a word about my eyes," Ty said bitterly, and put his hands on my hunched shoulders. "Hallie, what did he *say* to you?"

The truth, I thought distantly, and shuddered: that Uncle Matthias had abandoned us. That Marthe and I were just as afraid of each other as we'd been of Papa. That it was too late: We were ruined for loving people. We were ruined for being loved.

There were things you didn't speak aloud in this world: the twist of love-hate that still burned some nights when I thought of our Papa, because he was still our *Papa,* who bruised our hearts and bodies but made damned sure we kept our land. The fear that his ghost might sneak into Marthe's hands someday and speak out of her throat and eyes. I'd never even thought he would slip, instead, into mine.

There were no words to tell Tyler — kind, innocent, *loved* Tyler — about that fear, that taint. How much I would give to destroy it. And how much, deep down, I hoped he never would truly understand.

Tyler's eyebrows knitted painfully together. "Can we tell Marthe you're all right?"

Somewhere below, Marthe's voice rose in outrage. I caught a breath, and my face crumpled.

"She's not all right," Nat said shortly, and Marthe came scrambling up the stairs.

"Marthe, no—" James said behind her, but it was too late. She burst into my room, hair wild, arms wrapped tight around the child still stubbornly inside. I cringed under my bedquilt, my tongue tasting metal, my spine aching under the memory of Papa's belt, Papa's fists.

I looked up.

And I'd been wrong about it all along: I couldn't see Papa in her eyes. I saw myself: eight years old, shell-shocked, outraged at the world, screaming at the person she loved most: *Liar! You promised!*

Marthe looked down at me cowering in my nightclothes, tears choking her eyes. "You little monster," she said coolly, and then her voice split into a sob.

"Come on, Marthe," James said, thick with disappointment, and led her away from my door.

The sun had crested in the sky when I lifted my head out of the pillow. I'd slept. Somehow I'd slept, exhausted from the culmination of eight years of fear.

Nat was in the chair at my bedside, spinning yarn. Her

spindle whirled up, down, up again automatically: *chores.* All the daily, tiny bits of maintenance that kept a farm, a family, alive.

"You stayed," I said through a dry throat.

Nat's mouth firmed, and she lowered her spinning. "Awake now?"

I hesitated, and her mouth quirked thinly. "She's not here, Hal."

I nodded. The house was silent. I could hear the emptiness in the walls: no one singing, no clank of jars or baking smell coming through the old vents. I hadn't understood how much Marthe *was* this house, this farm, until she was suddenly gone.

The emptiness spread through my belly again—*you're just like Papa, and you drove her away*—and I clamped it brutally down.

"Where is she?" I managed.

"At the river with Uncle James, Tyler, and half of Ada's cousins. Ada showed up three hours ago with a pile of strange-looking machines." Nat wound up her spinning and tucked it in the basket by the chair. "We can go down if you want."

"No—" I said quickly. The thought of Marthe's hurt eyes, her wary step, made my stomach turn.

"Hallie," Nat said, utterly bereft of sarcasm, "I think you should get down to the river now."

"You're disappointed in me."

Nat stood and lifted my blanket off me. "I'm a little pissed off at all of you. I'll get over it eventually. We've got work to do. C'mon."

I worked myself out of the sheets. "Are — we still friends?" I asked weakly.

Nat tossed me a scornful glance. "Of course, you jackass. That's not how friendship *works*. This is why I get scared about you and my brother, you know. I don't know why you think messing up means lying about it or beating yourself with guilt or — just walking *away*. You messed up; *fix* it. You want forgiveness, get downstairs and start making some amends."

I swallowed. I felt beaten and bitten, cut utterly to the quick. But Nat was still here. She wasn't leaving. She loved me still.

That was something to stand on. A tiny piece of land, solid under my feet.

"I'll get up," I whispered, and went into the bathroom to wash.

Nat had not exaggerated: the riverbank swarmed with Chandlers. Through the break in the orchard trees the beach swam with bodies in homespun, scratched goggles on their faces and metal tools in their hands. Wooden stakes and string marked out a hard fence around the hole in the air.

The hole was scorched black into the riverside now, a jagged tear just as agonized as the mark of those first broken wings. Twisted Things seeped from the wound, hissing and screaming. James Blakely stood, his sleeves rolled up, at the perimeter and bludgeoned them into the dirt. Beside him, wearing fat gloves that bled dark brown smoke, Jerome Chandler scooped body after body into jars.

Tyler leaned against a scrubby tree beside them, squinting into the gap. "Lower," he said, and James repositioned his shovel. A thin spinner bird tumbled through a moment later, and the shovel fell with a crunch.

"Ty," Nat said, her voice pitched to carry. He caught our eyes and picked his way across the strand.

"Hallie, you're—" he started. He was fidgeting again, his fingers playing on his shirt hem as if he dreaded the answer. "Not okay?"

I felt Nat's eyes on me, on us, like a vise. I grimaced and looked away. "Not okay."

His hand crept into mine. "You well enough to keep walking?"

"You said that before. To your uncle."

Tyler looked away. "You didn't have to be okay to make it back from John's Creek. Nobody was okay. But you had to be well enough to get one more day closer to home."

I looked down the strand, forced myself to look until I found the familiar check of Marthe's work shirt, our mother's shawl draped over her shoulders. She sat to the side, on a driftwood log, her fingers tracing a haphazard line of river stones. I could not see the shape of those private words.

She looked up at me, her eyes burning with a cold, heart-broke light. I swallowed: *I'm so sorry.* It wouldn't come loose. My sister stared at me, incandescent with betrayal, and deliberately turned away.

I took a shaking breath. *Can you go another day like this?* Maybe. Eight years' fear had finally come to pass, and I was still walking and talking, and I could probably walk and talk another hour. I could bear it a bit longer, and that was what mattered now.

"Well enough, yeah," I said softly. Tyler smiled in shards and kissed my forehead.

James Blakely lifted an eyebrow at us over Ty's head. Hot blood rose in my cheeks, and then: *So what,* I thought with a new, peculiar lightness. All I had to do was last another hour, and we'd already done everything backwards anyway. Tyler's lips were dry on my brow. It soothed me, the way everything about him had slowly become calming: his quiet hands and dry jokes and everlastingly ridiculous grin.

I leaned my head on his shoulder, suddenly profoundly grateful it was there.

"I'm glad you came home," I said quietly.

He looked down at me, startled: a too-young man who'd suddenly found a shaft of sunlight in his hand. "I'm glad, too," he said, and buried his cold nose in my hair.

"Hey there," Ada said with a softer edge than she normally wielded. "Either of you kittens expecting anyone else?"

Nat's mouth opened halfway. "No," she said, and Ada pointed to the horizon.

There were silhouettes on the hillocks downriver, outlined against the sky. Grown men in formation, moving this way.

"Ada," Jerome said nervously, and she snapped to life.

"Pack up everything," she ordered. "Stow the instruments. I don't care where. *Go.*"

"But I'm getting something," Jerome started, and pushed a fat lizard corpse into the air around the burn. "Look. It blocks the portal wind. And it doesn't rot."

Ada rolled two jars into the underbrush. "Great. We'll take that back to the lab. Now *put it away.*"

The Chandlers flurried into motion. Sealed jars and tools and devices disappeared into burlap sacks. Jerome kicked dirty snow over the burn on the shore. "Too late," Nat muttered, and clutched my hand.

Marching over the rise, weapons drawn, were Lieutenant Jackson and his men.

All three surveyed us with flat, grim eyes. "Sergeant, not you too," the lieutenant said. James Blakely opened his mouth — for once, at a loss for words.

Nat yanked up a puzzled smile. "Lieutenant, good to see you. We're just doing some dredging —"

He cut her off with one scornful glance. "Miss, don't bother. We've spoken to your neighbors in Windstown. And we've seen your filthy hoard."

Sergeant Zhang pulled a dirty glass jar out from his coat. Ada startled. He rolled it down the hill, and it shuddered to a stop in the thick snow at her feet. When she looked up, her eyes burned. "You touched my lab."

Lieutenant Jackson crossed the beach to her implacably. "As is my duty as an officer of the Great Army, and under de Guzman's Law, I hereby detain you for treason and harboring."

"What?" Nat burst out.

"You *touched* all my hard work," Ada said, absolutely amazed.

"The penalty for failure to destroy bogeys is hanging," Sergeant Zhang said. "There are three witnesses, all sworn officers of the Great Army."

"Miss, just come quietly," said the lieutenant almost sadly.

"Wait a minute—" I broke in, and Ada Chandler's fist smacked into the lieutenant's face.

He reeled back, shocked, and then the Chandler cousins rushed in, howling with rage. Up on the hillock, Corporal Muhammad flinched, and then he and Sergeant Zhang were tumbling, war knives drawn, down into the melee of flesh and shouts and bodies.

Nat backed up, mouth agape, and dove in, tearing at arms, trying to pull someone, anyone, out of the fight. I caught a flash of hair here, an arm there. A Twisted Thing tumbled out of the hole on the beach, hissing, and skittered away.

Lieutenant Jackson had Ada in a bear hug from behind, fighting to pinion her squirming wrists. "Zhang, *help me*," he hollered, and she wriggled away.

"Do you even understand what you did?" she snarled, and dove for his knees.

He whirled and loomed over her, fist upraised, and a white-hot ember kindled in my brain. I flew between bodies, between fists, around driftwood, until I was right between them, my feet planted and braced for a punch. "Leave her alone!" I shouted at the top of my voice. "Get off my land and leave her alone!"

The blow never fell.

I looked up, and Lieutenant Jackson stood over me, horrified, his hands up in surrender. Not over me: over *us*. Marthe was right beside me, chin out, face hard, her round belly heaving with exertion and wrath, her elbow brushing my elbow. Unconquerable.

"Is that what you do?" she asked, monotone-quick, a too-familiar glint in her eye. "Beat up little girls? Travel around looking for someone to hit?"

"She's not a little girl," he said helplessly. "She's a traitor. Playing with bogeys almost destroyed the whole *world*."

"Touch that girl again," Marthe said softly, "and I'll slit your goddamned throat."

The lieutenant backed up one more step. "Ma'am. Miss," he said. "This is the last time I'll ask you to step aside."

I looked at Marthe. She looked at me —

— and behind us, a crack like towers falling split the sky.

Nat shrieked. I covered my ears and ducked along with everyone else: soldiers, Chandlers, Tyler sprawled on the river-bank. Ada ducked out from behind us and ran hard for her family. They caught her, heaving hard breaths, and walled her behind their bristling shovels and knives. Lieutenant Jackson swore, a vicious litany, and the clear sky cracked again behind us.

"That's *enough*," our hired man said.

Every head on the shore turned to watch Heron pick his way through the crowd: wild-haired, stick-thin, with days of new beard on his cheeks. In his hands, pointed up into the sky, was the black weapon June had trained on my heart. But this time it was loaded. This time it was armed.

Marthe stared. At Heron and his borrowed boots, the boots that were all Uncle Matthias had left us to remember him by. The look she turned on me stung like salt sown into our fields. "What in hell —" she started in a deadly level voice.

Heron lowered the old-city gun to the dirt. "I think it's time we all calmed down now."

"Who *is* this?" Lieutenant Jackson snapped, and my tongue wouldn't move. The lies were too snarled now, too tangled around each other.

Heron drew himself up with all the curious grace that had told me, once upon a time, that he'd take my failures kindly.

"I'm called Heron," he said, and held up his sleeves. The scratched buttons on them shimmered. "Northern regiment, out of Aylmer."

"The northern regiment was decimated," Sergeant Zhang said quietly.

He nodded, infinitesimal. "And I'm the hired man you're hunting."

Lieutenant Jackson's eyes narrowed to slits. "You told us he'd left town."

"I asked her to send you on," Heron said, and stepped closer. "It was my lie. And what you found in Miss Chandler's house is being done to save another fighting man."

Marthe's eyes went furiously wide. "*He* knew. You told *him*, and you didn't tell your own sister—"

"Growing Twisted Things?" the lieutenant said acidly.

"Don't be ridiculous," Ada snapped from well behind her kin. "Can you grow a dead bird? I'm *studying* them."

Corporal Muhammad looked at his superior officers, counted the restless crowd before him, and his jaw worked in sudden terror.

"Tell them what you found, Ada," I said, suddenly inspired. "Tell them how the Twisted Things die."

"They burn," she pronounced with a cold, intense satisfaction. "Every second after they show up here, 'til they die, they are burning. I've seen it under my glass: the air eating away their skin. That's why you burn if you touch them: from their heat. They're boiling inside, all the time."

I winced. Tyler reached blindly, took my hand.

"The smaller ones, the birds and lizard-foxes, last maybe two weeks. They're stronger when they grow large. The Beast out in the river might be there for years, boiling the Bellisle current, with the air eating its bones down to nubs."

Corporal Muhammad stared down at the spider-cracked jar in the snow. The thick liquid inside oozed. "You're keeping the air off their bodies."

Ada nodded, like one might to a particularly precocious child. "They don't break down so fast in the jelly. It gives me time to figure it out."

"Figure what out?" Sergeant Zhang asked.

She rounded on him. "What they are. Where they come from. What your whole war was actually *about*. And this week, how to get Thom Clarlund home in time to meet his child."

A shining lizard tumbled from midair into the stained snow, and James quietly crushed its skull.

Lieutenant Jackson's hand looped around his knife. "You're *all* in on this."

"Wherever those things are coming from, my brother's stuck there with them," I retorted. "There's a baby coming. I will move *hell* to bring him home."

"You're going to," the lieutenant said. "You're going to move it right here, and destroy the whole world."

"Use your eyes, man," Heron pressed. "There are Twisted Things coming through *absolutely nothing*. Hanging anyone who looks at it will *not* make our problems go away."

The silence crackled through the open air. Behind me, someone, nervous, giggled. "Oh, for the love of—" Ada spat, and ducked between the press of bodies. Snatched the jar from the snow.

"Stop!" Lieutenant Jackson shouted, too late. Ada twisted the jar open with a hiss and poured her lizard-fox on the ground.

The slime slid off its bumpy skin and sank into the thick snow. Corporal Muhammad jumped away from it, his pupils dark in his wide eyes, knife drawn and nowhere to use it. The liquid spread, glistening, and the lizard began to smoke. "Lieutenant," the corporal said as the body ignited, crackled.

The flame almost took his eyebrows off. It shot up like liquid light.

"Can you hang that?" Ada shouted from behind the fumes. "Look at it! Can you pretend we made *that* just to spite you?"

Another gout of flame burst out of the lizard's corpse. Its delicate, soft-eared skull caved in and disintegrated to ash.

"I've seen enough," Sergeant Zhang said quietly, and sheathed his knife. "It's time to bring in the authorities."

My eyes widened. "Pitts? You're going to let that—that slime take our land?"

He looked down his nose at me with mingled pity and disgust. "I don't care about your mayor. This is clearly a quarantine zone. And if you won't cooperate to isolate and burn whatever's wrong with this land, I'm calling in the regiment."

Heron sucked in a breath.

Zhang turned his back and walked over the hill, and Nat burst into tears.

TWENTY

I T WAS AN IDIOT RISK," MARTHE SAID, AND SLAMMED THE MUG onto the kitchen table. I huddled under the blanket wrapped around my shoulders and said nothing. The smell of salt-meat broth rose queasy to my nose. I wasn't hungry. I wasn't sure I'd ever be hungry again.

"Ma'am," Heron said from the kitchen corner. "I was the one who asked Miss Halfrida to keep me hidden. She was doing me a kindness. It was my fault."

Marthe rounded on him. "*Your* fault." Her voice cut. "You take our hospitality and then lie, hide, interfere with my sister—" She shook her head. "Actions have consequences. There is a regiment coming to burn our home to ashes. Sorry is *not enough.*"

This time James didn't stop her with a soft word, a light hand. He stood behind her, his arms crossed, his face as hard as stone.

"We didn't want trouble," I said faintly. "We just wanted to bring Thom home."

"Well," Marthe's voice quivered, "he's not coming home to me now—"

"Marthe," James interjected.

"You tell me how to solve what John's Creek couldn't before that army shows up. He's gone, James," she said bitterly. "My husband is dying. He's going to die."

Her hair hung loose and limp over angry cheeks. She wouldn't look at me. James would: over her shoulder his scarred face, ever kind, was an effigy of disappointment.

"Northman, I want you off my farm," Marthe said. "Gather your things up. Get on that highway. Never set foot here again."

Heron slumped into himself.

"Marthe, please—" I started.

"And *you*," she said, rounding on me, and I shrank back. "Get up to your room. And don't you *dare* come out."

I looked back at Heron, desperately. His eyes were hooded, his unshaven chin tucked low. *We've failed,* I thought. *We're doomed.*

"Hallie," Marthe snarled, *"go."*

My window was the best in the house our great-grandparents had built a century ago on a hilltop in the wreck of the fallen world. It opened out over the river and the fields, over the blanket of snow glittering on the orchard trees. I knotted the paisley curtains in my fist. I couldn't bear to watch Heron pace out to the smokehouse to pack his single bag.

I couldn't bear *not* to watch when they finally made him go.

Lamplight licked the mark the Twisted Thing's scorched

wings had left, forever, on my windowsill. I deliberately looked away, into the clear, cool sky. The gap-toothed stars stared back at me, suddenly impermanent. They'd be different somewhere else, on someone else's land, after the army had been and gone again. When everything I knew had crumbled into ash.

Stop being Uncle Matthias, my brain snarled. It had taken on an edge, unbidden, in just a day: *Abandoner. Quitter. Giver-up.* My soul ached. Even thinking about my uncle and how my love for him might spoil sent me dizzyingly close to that morning's despair. "You have Nat," I whispered, like a protection, like a prayer. "You have Tyler. They love you." It kept back the dark.

Don't bring Uncle Matthias into it, I corrected. *Just stop giving up. Somehow.*

Heron emerged from the smokehouse, pack in hand, silhouetted in the light of James Blakely's lamp. He was small against the horizon: a bent man with a bent back, treading slowly into the night. James herded him up the path at a crisp pace. Heron looked back, and James shooed him on: *Soldier, march.*

I watched until I couldn't, my hand on the windowpane. Just a silhouette framed inside it, one lonely lamp burning.

Marthe's evening sounds filtered through the vent in my floorboards: the clank of plates, the sigh of cloth, the click of the kitchen door's heavy brass lock. She came up the stairs, heavy tread and slow shuffle, and paused in front of my bedroom door.

"Put out that light, Hallie," she said. "Go to bed. You have chores."

We didn't have to discuss it. We knew where to meet.

I found Heron at the join where our path met the main road, freezing in his shirtsleeves, utterly undone. He looked up at me as if he'd doubted, deep inside, that he'd ever see a friendly soul again. "You shouldn't be here," he said, too relieved for me to believe he meant it.

"You can go to the Chandlers," I told him quickly. "They'll take you in. We'll get Thom back. We *have* to."

He looked down at me, haunted, and shook his head once. "It's done, kid. The army's coming. I'm—" He stopped. "I'm so damned sorry."

"We can't just give up," I argued, and he shook his head again. His tattered boots were pointed northward, up the river road, to the lake. They'd taken back Uncle Matthias's warm winter pair and left him to the snow and ice with only shreds. *Stop giving up!* I wailed inside, eight years old again, at two different men, one years and miles away. "If you're just giving up, why'd you even wait?"

"The knife. I couldn't get it. I didn't have a chance," he said, and paced a crazed line along the road. He looked up at me, desperate, and I knew what he wanted me to do.

"So they can raze our land for nothing," I said heavily.

"So you can wash your hands of me and everything I've brought on your heads," he snapped.

I let out a bitter laugh. "Heron, it's far too late for that."

He looked up at me, his mouth open, and I turned away to the empty snowfields. There had been so much, when he'd shown up, that I hadn't understood. I'd been a fool to think I could take on, could put my trust in a stranger, and that when it all went wrong, he'd stay a stranger and just disappear with no hurt or blame. I'd been a fool to think we couldn't break each other's hearts.

"I'll get your stupid knife," I said, and pulled my gloves from my pockets.

"You don't have to—" he started, but I knew he didn't mean it.

"Shut up," I said softly, and went to get the shovel.

The hawthorn in the back field was dying.

White stains roped around the sides of the tree, and where they spread, the wood buckled and fissured deep. There were strange flowers growing through those cracks: moon-bright, delicate white, their striped petals warm and glowing. They'd brought the tree into leaf out of season: a full head of brilliant green glittered on the branches, each leaf half uncurled when it had frozen solid. It was an incandescent nightmare, awful and beautiful, begging to be touched. Fishing for a brush of my hand just as Beast Island had lured fishers and shopkeeps to their doom.

I put my hands behind my back. *Magic,* I thought bitterly. *It's not just a knife; it's magic.*

And then I swallowed adrenaline, because it'd been in front of us all along: the one secret we'd actually managed to keep.

We had the knife that killed a god. Its edge, strange and magic, could cut *worlds*.

My heart flared desperately. I set the shovel between the roots and *pushed*.

The hawthorn trunk cracked as the iron went in at its roots. Its whitened bark shone with stress; wood creaked like a tortured scream. "Come *on*," I muttered, and wrenched the blade. That white bark bubbled angrily, like fine soap.

"Just — give it — up!" I hissed, and drove the shovel as hard as I could.

The ragged hawthorn tree shattered.

Branches flew through the night, landing hard in the snow, and the once-solid trunk rocked and split. Its two halves peeled, rotten, to the ground, and out of it came a miasma stench: the stink of blood and burnt land, of salt and shit and dead birds' bodies tangled in vines from another world. The ghost of the Wicked God's dark war rose and whispered through the night sky, traveled like rumors into the thick soil of my fields.

Two leaves, as bright as summer, smashed to splinters on the ground. Flared green, and were finally still.

I brushed dust and sweat off my forehead and hesitantly poked my ruined shovel into the roots. Like a splinter, like a spray of diseased feather, John Balsam's knife stood out of the gray dirt.

I caught the leather-bound hilt and twisted it. It came sharply free: the knife that cut the heart from the Wicked God Southward, clutched in my frozen hand. The soft wrapping caught in the dead hawthorn roots, and I let it fall to the dirt. Naked, the knife gleamed dead and dark in my palm, edges undulled by its time underground. They were still liable to take your finger off, if your finger could somehow navigate the twists and cliffs it had become.

This knife cut the heart from a god, I thought, and ran toward the crossroads.

It was hard to hold. The wound in the hilt had seen to that: a parody of clutched fingers, matched to one man's hand. *John Balsam's hand,* I thought wildly, pelting through the snow. *I'm holding it just where he did.*

And then I skidded to a halt in the snowy weeds. Remembered Heron's curled fingers around our good Windstown crockery, every one of them broken and reset in crooked lines.

His sad eyes. His evasions. *I'm nobody,* he'd said, and tried not to meet my eye.

Torn leather pricked my fingers on the twisted, grooved hilt. There was only one hand in the world like this, one hand that fit the swirls of a dying god's rages. And it had carried this knife all along, all the way to John's Creek — and back.

You sneak, I thought, awed. *You liar,* and I ran again, knife in hand, to the man waiting at the crossroads.

He hadn't waited quietly where our path met the high

road: he'd paced a damp circle on the asphalt to mirror the moon. His head flicked up at my footsteps. "You found it?"

I could see the face on that Missing poster in him now: wasted by hunger, too young, too sad; never that heroic after all. Lurking under the face of my friend, the man who had comforted and understood me: dark hair, light brows, cheekbones high and clear, square-jawed.

I marched up to him, nose to nose, and put the dagger in his right hand; closed his jagged fingers around it. They fit like destiny: the curled blade and his scars.

"Don't you tell me," I said, "that you're nobody."

Heron's mouth opened, flailed, and shut. He was so young. A young, scared, lying boy.

"John Balsam," I pronounced, and Heron, God-killer, world-saver, hid his face from me, eaten with shame.

"Yes," he said, hoarsely. "That's my name."

I swallowed around the lump in my throat. "Was anything you said true? The war, the towns, your mission —"

Heron's chin came up. "All of it. Every word."

"Except the part where you killed a *god*."

"Please let me explain."

"How can you explain? You *said* you didn't know where he'd gone."

Heron opened his free hand and grabbed onto thin air. "John Balsam's a cheesemaker," he said, cracking, breaking. "He lives in Kortright and feeds the cats, and reaches jars off the highest shelf for his mother. He's learning to play his grandpa's fiddle. His best friend works the logging camps, and when he's home, we go drink and tell stories about the road, all the places I'd never been and didn't dare go, Sunil's ten thousand girlfriends—"

"You *lied.*"

"I *don't know* where that man is," he burst out. "I have walked and hid and starved across more land than I ever thought existed, and *I do not know* where John Balsam has gone." He hugged himself like a lost child; like he wanted to dig off his skin. "I don't know anymore what that name means."

He is taking John Balsam's mother what is left of her son, I realized, and put my trembling hands behind my back. "Tell me the truth," I said unsteadily. "Tell me what *actually* happened."

"It was true," he said defiantly. "Every word. Except that we were the ones who slipped around Jones's barricade. Because . . . we were stupid. We got lost."

He smiled, a hard, sad wince. "There was dust everywhere, and we just kept moving. And then in front of us was this *place,* this blotch of rain and calm. It had been so long since we'd seen rain. So I stumbled into it for a drink of water, absolutely resigned, because I knew I was going to die. My cousins were dead. My friends were dead. At least I wasn't going to die thirsty.

"Except I looked behind me and something moved: The walls of the storm, pulling in like a heart. Pulling away from me; taking away my rain. And I was just so frustrated that I *stabbed* them, I cut—

"And the whole storm," he said, confused still, "exploded.

"It broke my nose. It threw me across the ground, back into the dust. And then the storm swirled in around me through the cut my knife had made. It bent the knife, broke my fingers. And the Wicked God Southward drained into that wound like water. And it was done. I was alive. The war was gone."

"There was a hole between worlds in the god's heart, and you cut it open," I breathed. A hole like the one festering on the river. My hands itched for that knife.

"I guess so," he said, and shook his head. "I cut a hole in *something,* and the god fell through. I was too afraid to look. I *didn't want to die,* Hallie. So I held my broken fingers and ran like hell.

"It was only after," he said, animal-stunned, "that I heard talk about John Balsam, the brave hero who slew a God. And I knew—I just knew—that the truth would break them: who I really was. I could never live up to that big a lie.

"So I ran," he finished softly. "I took my pack, and I ran as far and as fast as I could. I deserted the Great Southern Army. I left my name, my friends, my regiment—everything. And I have *no idea* how a living man kills gods."

I stared. "You've been running this whole time. You and your enchanted knife."

"It's just a knife," he said weakly. "My mother bought it when I was ten years old, from the blacksmith in Black Creek.

I used to cut my name into trees with it, slice turnips for our supper."

That hawthorn flitted across my memory, its trunk twined with glowing flowers rooted in another world. "Ask any veteran in the lakelands," I said softly. "It's not just a knife anymore."

His shoulders crumpled. I watched him, watched the strings and strands of the lies we told ourselves come spinnereting down. Because as long as John Balsam could say it was just a knife, he could tell himself equally that he was just a man. I could tell myself that a scrawny girl could save a fifty-acre farm. That if I did, my sister might love me again; that it would erase eight years of secret strain.

I could tell myself that if Roadstead Farm was going to, no matter what, be lost, I loved Windstown and its safety more than I loved my brother.

I reached out and took the knife that killed a god from Heron's hands.

"I am taking this," I said coolly. Finally honest; finally resolved. "And I am going to the river to get my brother back."

"No, wait—" Heron said, and I turned my back on him.

I balanced the knife's twist against my palms, like a shard of winter, and walked down to the hole in the world.

TWENTY-ONE

THE WEATHER HAD TURNED WORSE: IT WAS FREEZING COLD, and sleeting. Icy powder sifted into the tops of my boots, and I ignored it. I had John Balsam's knife. And maybe the farm would be obliterated by the army or the Twisted Things, and maybe Marthe would never love me again, but goddammit, I would save *something* I loved.

The shore was a mess of ash and scattered jars. Thom's stones jumbled into letters, half words, noise. The hole's scorched shadow had grown to the size of a bucket, and it had eaten the Chandlers' stakes and string to dust. All the normal winter sounds — the sluggish water and the calls of wild dogs — were gone, and the whole river stank of wet violets and lye. *This is what it'll be like,* I told myself. *This is what you might loose into the world tonight.*

The first twinge of doubt nibbled at my belly.

"I'm coming, Thom," I said, and plunged John Balsam's knife into the dead space in the sky.

I felt, smelled, tasted the cut rattling through the air; felt the sky rip like rotten cloth. Purple light arced through the night as universes streamed from the tip of John Balsam's twisted knife. I felt — no, heard, smelled — a small *pop*.

Magic, I thought.

And then everything imploded.

I flew forward along the beach and landed, rolling, bruising, in a drift of sodden snow. Sound gushed into the world, too loud, too bright: the calls of birds and a rising wind, sweetly humid and rich with life. I sat up, shivering against the chilly air, and a gust of warm wind shoved me back into the snow. That hot green wind Tyler and Heron had touched at John's Creek was still blowing: blowing, now, into *my* world through a shimmering tear in the sky the size of a barn door. *I did it*, I thought, and then heat lightning crackled through the sleeting sky.

I'd made a hole in the world, gashed bright, edges curling, and Twisted Things rained out of it like stars.

They took to the shore, stumbling, flapping, squawking their alarm calls. The rock beneath them crushed under their endless tracks; it melted and ran in the sucking, whistling storm. I wrapped my hand around John Balsam's twisted knife and whimpered as they pattered along the shoreline, past my knees, and took wing.

You've done it now, Papa's voice, ever-present, whispered in my ear. "You're dead," I told it, pulled painfully to my feet, and walked into that rip in the world.

I knew every step of Roadstead Farm, every blade of grass and tree hollow. But I didn't recognize the place where I drew my next breath, two steps down the riverbank. I stepped from snow, farm, river into a lush, bright valley painted in violent purple and rolling green. Rivulets of water ran from my frozen boots onto thick-thatched grass, vibrant with life. The flowers were in spring bloom, dozens of them, hundreds: white-petaled, red-stemmed, as luminescent as tiny stars.

I turned a circle, disoriented, in the sweet, humid air. Home shimmered behind me, a half dozen or a thousand steps away. Its warm lights and familiar corners felt farther away than the stars.

"Thom?" I called, and coughed lightly, then harder. Tyler and Heron had called it the sign of Twisted Things coming—that thin air that made it hard to hear, hard to breathe. It was more: it was the air of another world, a world where it was warm, and quiet, and always raining. Where exhausted soldiers might have found, for a few moments on the battlefield, some peace.

Nothing stirred in the grass or in the forest that stretched out before me, patched and thriving, its blooms wafting sour and sweet. "Thom?" I called again, and a lizard scuttled, terrified, away. I was alone in the Wicked God's strange paradise: entirely alone.

I pushed forward, the knife heavy in my hand, searching for flattened grass or footprints. The wind retreated. Nothing felt real anymore except the ground springing beneath my feet and the silence that muffled my hurrying steps.

I'd thought I understood aloneness, tending a farm that

didn't speak to its neighbors with a sister who didn't, sometimes, speak at all. But wherever this was, this untouched land, it was the loneliest place in the world. Here I could understand how Heron had lost John Balsam for good. Here I could face what it meant to feel my world crumbling: *I am losing Halfrida Hoffmann.*

I was so damned far from who I wanted to be: someone who wasn't aching with anger all the time. Who smiled, who looked at her neighbors with trust and not fear. Someone who loved her sister and knew how to do right. Nothing I'd done, said, *been* since Thom left home had truly felt like me. Except kissing Tyler Blakely and taking on a hired man because he had reminded me what it was to be kind.

I stumbled on the hummocked green, on the infinitesimal and unbridgeable ground between me and the clean sheets of home. I owed Heron, I realized, more than I could repay. He'd reached across all the polite distance I kept between myself and other people: the ones I loved, the ones I hated. He had called me kind. I owed Tyler and Nat, who had insisted that I open my closed bedroom door, who had lifted me up, who had *stayed*. In our desperation, we'd offered each other comfort, sheltered each other. Everyone in my universe was farther away than the stars tonight, but Heron and me, and Nat, and Tyler: we held fast like a constellation. We made each other less alone.

I had to stop lying to myself. I had to stop it for good. Because if I was brave—if I was honest, when I stepped out of this silent world onto the shores of the river I was born next to, into whatever destruction I'd just created—I wouldn't have to be alone at all.

I blew out the last of my dead air and said, "Keep on walking." Heron had cut the belly from a storm, alone. And I wasn't alone.

"Thom?" I called again, and stepped into the soft forest shade.

Long green leaves bent in streamers to touch the loamy carpet of veined white flowers. A spinner bird flitted from branch to branch, brown-winged, its talons crafting a web to trap crickets. The air drew a loving finger across my cheek, brought the scent of dampened earth. Through the branches I saw clouds forming for another round of quiet rain.

And through it, improbably, I caught a whiff of home fires.

"Thom!" I called, and followed the smell of cooking, of safety, of community, through the rain-whipped trees.

The source of the smoke was less a cave than a hummock, hollowed out painstakingly by stones and blistered hands. The low sound of human voices wisped out of it on the smoke: the most welcome thing I'd heard in hours or years. I peered into that crevice, ready for ghosts, men, gods—and a human face, battered and burnt, short hair matted with illness and road dust and pain, peered back.

"Hallie?" Thom Clarlund said.

"Thom," I whispered, and flung myself toward his scratched-up arms.

He backed up fast; far, far away from me. His seared face stretched into terrible lines. "This is another nightmare. This isn't real."

"It is," I insisted. "I came to get you. I'm here."

From behind him, another voice — a thick, deep, musical voice — said, "Are you talking to yourself again?"

The man at the campfire looked like the specter of death: a dark hat, tattered sleeves, a bloody bandage twined around his left knee. His boots were drying by the fire, or what was left of his boots: a pair of rot-soaked, beaten leather rags, reeking of mold and dirt. His grayed eyebrows rose to his hairline. "Who in God's name are *you*?"

"Hallie?" a voice called — howled — against the trees, and I whipped around. "Hallie, goddammit, where are you?"

"Heron!" I answered. Heron was here. Heron had walked through the worlds for me.

"Thom," I said urgently. I grabbed his hand, and he winced. "We've got to go. Marthe's waiting. There's soldiers coming — we've got *no time*."

Thom's hand spasmed on mine. His face was as gray as a burial cairn. "You're real."

I blinked away sweat, blood, hot tears, and nodded.

"Hallie," he said, dead urgent. "Go."

"I can't leave you behind," I said.

"We'll be right behind you," he said, and put both hands on my cheeks. *"Go."*

I crashed, desperate, back through the alien trees, John

Balsam's knife frozen to my hand. Branches whipped at my face and I ducked them, listening, listening for the sound of Thomas Clarlund behind me, coming home.

I broke into the clearing where the hole sprawled between the worlds, and Heron — pacing, coughing helplessly — looked up.

"Hallie, dammit," he said around a gasp — one that had nothing to do with the thin air floating about us. "Do you *know* where you are?"

"I've found Thom," I said joyously, tears starting in my eyes. "Heron, I did it. He's coming. He's safe."

"You absolute madwoman," he said, taking both my arms, and propelled me through the rent between worlds.

Sound snapped back into my ears. Sound *exploded*.

The riverbank I'd left was obliterated. Stones flew and rattled through tornado-force winds; the screams of Twisted Things rose shrieking against the winter chill; and everywhere, everywhere, I smelled burning.

Heron dove after me onto the shattered shore, materializing in pieces against that forest sun: a blistered hand, a leg flailing for solid ground, shirttails flapping in the breeze. And after him, through the rain of feathers and lightning, came Thom, bent down against the bloody purple light.

"I have to go back," he croaked, and collapsed on the sand. "There's another man in there."

"Where?" Heron asked, behind me, through the storm, and Thom's jaw dropped.

"You," he said. "Godslayer. You're the one with the knife."

"Yes," Heron snapped. "Where *is* he?"

Thom pointed. And Heron sprang into the stormwinds, through the rain of Twisted Things, into another world.

I dropped John Balsam's knife on the windblown, root-split stones. Wormed my arms under Thom's shoulders and dragged him desperately away from the hole. He shook me off weakly. "Wait."

"We *can't*—"

"Have to," he insisted, and then Heron emerged from the awful tear in the sky with a black-clad body, limp over his shoulder.

Thom stumbled to his feet. I took his hand: a twinned mess of scrapes and blisters and burns. We stumbled through the death-lit night, through the destruction, with all hell at our heels.

The orchard trees smoked under the rain of Twisted Things; we cleared their shadows just as the first flame licked free. We limped past the pens, rounded the corner to the house. "Marthe!" I shouted as we climbed the rise to the kitchen porch. "Marthe, it's Thom, *please!*"

She opened the kitchen door as the flames bloomed in our cherry trees, wild-haired, eyes full of reflected lightning. "What—" Marthe said, and stopped cold. Her arms unfolded from her chest and reached longingly. "Thomas?"

Thomas Clarlund staggered up the steps he'd left so many months ago, into my sister's arms.

"We found him," I gasped as I sagged onto the porch. A last bit of vanity. Before I put it away, became myself. Stopped telling stories that weren't true. "We did it. We brought him home."

Through the dirt, through the rough fabric of Marthe's nightdress, his voice choked out, "Baby, baby—"

She squeezed out a sob, her hands trembling, and then looked past me to Heron behind me and to the man he'd laid out like a carcass on the porch. "Hallie," she said, "who is that?"

Heron looked up—his mild eyes twisted with rage. "Yes, tell us who it is, Thomas."

"Heron—" I objected.

Thom wiped his eyes, his bleary, sick eyes, and said, "That's Asphodel Jones."

Behind me, rainbowing through the night, the smoke and screams and ash reached upward, and Roadstead Farm began to burn.

THE
QUIET
PLACE

TWENTY-TWO

"HEAVE!" HERON CALLED, AND WATER BUCKETED OVER THE burning trees.

Small green lizards, flushed by the smoke, squeaked and fled the orchard, and Joy and Sadie darted quick-limbed through the shadows and herded them into our knives. It was already a losing battle: thin tangles of web shone between our fence posts, growing thicker with every passing minute, and they were nothing to the monstrosities that stretched into the sky. Beyond the fields, Tyler's nightmare tree shambled across the lane on fat roots, the points of its knotted horns bobbing dark against the moon.

There were gods in the lakelands now, for real. There were monsters, and I had let them in.

In my head, everything was still silent and calm. *Bucket in the well, water to the upstairs basin,* I recited with a coolness I had never felt before. *Don't give up. Keep walking.*

I'd run out of fear. I'd run out of fury. They would spit on my name from Windstown all the way to the old battlefields, but I'd made my choice there, on that shattered riverbank. My brother was finally back from the war.

Now I just had to live with the consequences.

I hauled clean water up the stairs to Marthe's room, bucket after bucket, while the world burned.

Marthe perched on the edge of her bed, wiping dirt and blood from Thom's blistered face. She was crying silently, distractedly as he emerged: skull-thin, the twist of his mouth bitter, his dark brown skin ashy with illness. His good shirt hung loose on him, torn to shreds, half the buttons just stumps of brown thread. The rest glowed, scratched and dust-stained: a veteran's polished pearl. I recognized him less and less with every bucket of dirty water I emptied off the porch.

"What day is it?" he croaked, and shrugged off Marthe's dabbing cloth.

"It's the third of December," Marthe said. "Winter's come in."

There was no sound in the room but his distorted breathing. "Did I make it in time?"

A curious look came over Marthe's face, and she shuddered down to her toes. "Just in time," she said, like an afterthought. "Just."

Thom drew a harsh breath, let it out, and sank relieved into the nest of rucked-up sheets. I put down the bucket, mouth open. "Marthe—"

"I'm pregnant, not dead," she said, fainter now. "The contractions aren't even regular yet."

She pressed a hand to her dress, her wet-stained dress, and I finally realized it wasn't from spilled well water. There was fluid seeping through it onto the rug, down her calves. The baby was coming. The baby was *here*.

"Marthe—" I whispered, and ran down the hall to Papa's old room.

We hadn't used it since his passing—just closed the door and left it closed, as if we might board his ghost away. The room was a swim of fabric: moth-eaten dust sheets and a pile of bandages heaped high on the chestnut rocker Mama had nursed us in. Between them lay the Wicked God's prophet, half stripped and unconscious, on the ruins of my parents' bed.

James and Cal Blakely stood in the far corner, clinging tight to each other's hands. Mrs. Blakely paced past them, up and down the length of the bed. No one had cleaned Asphodel Jones's wounds. He seeped under the scrutiny of three shaken, fear-lined faces.

"Marthe's water broke," I whispered. Afraid to speak lest that man wake up.

Round, homey Eglantine Blakely's eyebrows shot up. "She's early."

I wrapped both arms around my rib cage. I didn't know what to say.

Mrs. Blakely took a deep breath and smoothed her dress. "All right. We'll do this in the washroom. I need boiled water, a cushion, and all the clean towels you have."

"Ma'am," I said automatically.

She strode to the dusty threshold, and hesitated. "Listen

here, the both of you," she said. "Don't you do the fool thing you're thinking once my back is turned."

"Eglantine—" James said, agonized.

"Don't make yourself a murderer, Jim Blakely. Not for *him*." James flushed, and his sister-in-law disappeared down the hallway and rapped hard on Marthe's door.

James and Callum looked at each other, and their fingers twined tight. "We need to set a guard," James said low. "He'll wake up. We have to know what to *do* when he does."

A Twisted Thing clattered against the window and smeared down the pane. Callum, his eyes dark-circled, pulled shut the blinds.

"Jim, I can't do this," he said simply.

James put his head in his hands. "I know."

The Wicked God's prophet bled onto Papa's sheets, and I fled.

Nat shoved through the door, wild-haired and soot-marked, just as I put the kettle on the stove. She took water straight from the dipper and drank it down, down, down.

"How's it look out there?" I asked her. The firelight made her face narrower, sharper: a study in fatigue and fear.

"They got one of the kid goats. I've moved your animals indoors. We couldn't save the orchard if we wanted to save the goats." She coughed and shook her head. "They're pouring into the brush now. The little monsters know I can't reach them there. Tyler's gone for the Chandlers, but they just keep *coming.*"

This is how it started at John's Creek, I realized. Slow, until it overran you. I met her bleak gaze. *It looks,* I read there, *bad.*

"Heron won't tell me what happened," she said.

The calm of that green, rain-soaked place peeled off me like a blister.

I don't know, bubbled up to my lips: the safe answer. The answer that would keep Nat's sympathy on my side, smooth it all out for the days to come. Three little words of pretend ignorance in the ways of a god a whole army couldn't understand.

It'd be another secret to carry—forever. A dead thing, rotten and feathered, poisoning the soil of my oldest friendship.

I shoved another stick into the stove and stirred the flame. *Stop lying to yourself,* I thought savagely. *You made your choice. Face the consequences.*

"Nat," I said—mumbled into the stove, and took a deep breath—"I couldn't wait."

I felt her silence. Felt her draw back from me. "What?"

"I couldn't wait," I said, and adjusted the kettle on the stove top. "Heron was leaving. The army's on its way. I dug up the knife and cut the hole open to get Thom back."

This was how the truth hung in the air: clean, like a falling glass, for a long moment before everything shattered.

"Good God, Hallie," Nat finally said. "How could you—*look* at me, dammit!"

I turned around, slowly, and met her appalled eyes.

I don't know what she saw in me, but her cheeks flushed even redder. "You let them in."

The first twinge of panic shook my chest. "I'm sorry, Nat—"

"No, you're not! Did you even *think?* Monsters don't stop at *fencelines,* Hallie. Did you think about us or the Masons or the Chandlers? Did you think about our sheep? About *any* of the people who haven't already decided they're going to walk away?"

"I didn't—"

"You did," she cut in. "You've had a bag packed for eight years, ready to blow out of here. *I know where it is.*"

The kettle boiled. I silenced its thin scream with a flip of the whistle spout. Nat's face was furious red; she looked as lost as a child. "This is just like you," she whispered. "Walk away, mope and sulk, do whatever you damn well please because you're convinced there's no winning anyway. It doesn't matter who it hurts. It's always you and just you."

I sucked in a breath. "Nat, no, I never—"

Nat put the dipper back in the barrel. "I'm not going to lie for you this time."

I shook my head, silently. *No.*

She pulled her hair back—one last, fruitless frustration—and stomped out through the kitchen door.

I stared after her until the kettle rattled from the sheer force of the steam. Picked it up and poured the hot water into my bucket. *The consequences are that you might lose your best friend's love.*

Tears squeezed out the corners of my eyes. "Turn around," I muttered savagely. "*Face* it. You made a choice."

Just a morning ago, a mere day, Nat had given me the key: *You want forgiveness, get downstairs and start making some amends.* Fix it. Mend it.

Turn around.

I swallowed, hard. Not for gratitude, and not to prove something to the world or Alonso Pitts or my sister; not to keep people from leaving me, or to strike a blow in the endless battle in my head over whether I got to leave or stay, I had to fix what I'd broken so horribly.

I had to close that hole on the riverside. I had to save Windstown, and the lakelands, and Roadstead Farm.

"Start with chores," I told myself: Marthe's voice in miniature. And carried water up the stairs, one step at a time.

TWENTY-THREE

SUN STAINED THE ROOFTOPS BY THE TIME THE CHANDLERS arrived: bright, watery daylight filtered through ash gray. I led them to the riverbank through a damaged, changed world.

Branches were down all over the orchard, seared into black charcoal. The fields were sickly spotted, stained with burns and churned mud; they rustled ominously as we passed. Past them, the hay barn sang its rattling hymns. Tin shingles clattered, leaflike, to the ground. I veered away from it and the river into the bare yard, looking for anything left unscathed.

Heron was replacing blackened shingles on the poultry barn. He'd tied Sadie's lead to an old post outside it, and she prowled back and forth, restless with the scent of Twisted Things. "She'll terrify the chickens," I said.

"Too late." He readied a nail. His fingernails were blackened with bruises and soot. "How's your sister?"

"Still pushing," I said fretfully. They'd sent me for water, for towels and cushions, for broth, for honey so James and Cal could treat Thom's burns. I'd brought it all, with Marthe's exhausted moans beating at my ears, and then Eglantine Blakely had tossed me, unceremoniously, outside.

I leaned, tired and beaten, against the barn wall. "You know there's no point in fixing that roof right now."

"Just let me do this for you," he said, and buried another nail deep. The chickens muttered on the other side of the wall, as normal as Marthe in the morning, putting fresh cream into my tea.

Sudden, grateful tears stung my smoke-red eyes. "Do something else for me then?" I asked around the lump in my throat. "Help me guard Asphodel Jones."

Heron's fingers hesitated in the nail pouch at his belt. "I *told* you I don't know how to fight gods and prophets—"

I held up a hand. "I'm not asking *John Balsam*," I said, and scrubbed my eyes. "Heron, I'm asking *you*. And besides, I know you still have June Chandler's gun."

Heron flushed. "Hallie, that's too much to ask." Beneath his three-days' beard, his Adam's apple rose and fell. "I have never hated anyone like I hate that man."

"I know," I said, remembering the flat death in his eyes as he'd dug the knife's thin grave. "But I don't want him near Marthe when he wakes up. I don't want him near *anyone,* and we can't let him loose. There has to be a trial, something, when the army comes."

John Balsam—God-killer, cheesemaker—tapped in another nail. "They'll hang him, most likely. If he's lucky. Drawing and quartering was also talked about."

I squirmed in my sopping boots. "As long as it's just. As long as it's done by law."

Heron squinted down at me. "As long as it's not by our hands, or as long as you're not your father?"

"Who told you that?" I snapped.

He shrugged. "You did. In all the corners of what you didn't say."

I looked away, down at the neat pattern of fresh shingles on the roof.

"Where are we taking him?" Heron asked, and put the hammer down.

My mouth curved, a grim sliver. "Where else? The smoke-house."

No one had dared, yet, to put a hand on the sleeping Aspho-del Jones. James and Callum lingered near the doorway, eyes averted, as Heron appraised the body of the prophet of the Wicked God.

Papa's old sheet had stuck to his blisters where they wept and seeped. Heron tugged the cloth gently and frowned. "We have to take it with us. I'm sorry."

"I'm not," I said, and rolled down my sleeves so my skin wouldn't touch his skin.

"Hold the door for us," James said neutrally, and Cal turned away as I took Jones's wrapped feet. James shouldered a torso so emaciated it made me want to cry. Heron cradled the prophet's head, lamb-fragile, breathing shallow, and we steered him awkwardly down the stairs, past the gruff sounds of Marthe's labor; past the rustle of bandage cotton held against Thom's wounds. The sheet trailed under him, a fluttering, living shroud, through the kitchen and out the porch door.

Jones shuddered as we pushed outside into the frost. Heron's tight expression tightened further. "Keep up the pace."

"I'm trying," I muttered, and we waddled to the abandoned smokehouse.

"I'll light a fire," Heron said once we'd laid Jones on the flagstones and James, disapproving and silent, had departed. The small stove had gone cold in the days Heron had spent hiding. He brushed ash out of the woodbox. "What do we do with him?"

I don't know, I thought, and sat back on my heels at Asphodel Jones's side. I didn't know what I'd been expecting from his face: dastardly eyes, a pointed chin, a classic villain out of Windstown summertime theater. Asphodel Jones was a plain, sickly man, his skin leathered rough from war and a lifetime in the sun; short brown hair threaded with gray over drooping, self-satisfied eyes. He looked more like a sleepy village cooper than a prophet — the kind of man who fed pigeons outside the Windstown coffee shops.

"He's normal," I said, surprised.

Heron snorted at the stove. "He slit a dozen throats a night and wiped out a whole town. There's nothing *normal* about that."

I rolled up the tattered sleeves of his coat. Here and there, an uneven button glinted in the foggy light. *Army buttons,* I realized. The knots were split and fumbling. Brown thread raveled beneath them, mismatched on a shirt that had once been deep green. I counted the buttons on my fingers, then counted the buttons we'd peeled off Thom's shredded shirt. *They're Thom's.*

I dropped his sleeve. "Why would Thom bring him here?"

Heron caught a spark in tinder. His dark look came clear in the thin flame. "That's a question I'm looking forward to asking your brother."

What do we do with him? circled behind my exhausted eyes — and came back with an answer. "Heron?" I asked softly. "How much do you think Jones *knows?*"

Heron's eyebrows went up, surprised — considering — and then Asphodel Jones's basset-hound face contracted, and he shivered. "Heron," I said, tremulous, and the Wicked God's prophet opened his bloodshot eyes and found, with them, my face.

"Don't try anything," I said.

The Wicked God's prophet coughed wetly against the stones my great-grandfather had laid. "What could I try?" he rasped. I looked away. It sounded foolish. He couldn't even walk.

"He needs water," Heron said grudgingly. "It's still murder if we let him die."

Shallow breath hissed out through Jones's broken teeth. "*You.*"

Heron pulled himself to his feet. "Asphodel Jones."

The look that passed between them was drowned song-birds, their feathers raggled with river water. There was something old and bad in that space; something soaked with the dust of the broken southlands, as wide as the bones of a killed god. Utterly unbelonging in the old stones of my smokehouse; in the ever-damp lakelands soil, where there had never been a war.

Jones twitched in his cotton shroud. "Look at me. You must be absolutely thrilled."

Heron looked down at him, hands shoved into his worn pants pockets. "No," he said evenly. "You're the worst thing that's ever happened to me."

The defiant lines around Jones's squint loosened with surprise. "Well, then. What do you want?" he asked after a moment.

Heron bowed his head. "That's up to her," and I startled against the smokehouse wall. "It's her farm."

Jones turned toward me slowly. His eyes flickered, uncertain, for a moment before he wiped them as blank as the grave. "Well?"

I wished I had another step to back up. Not from the

menace of a man who had brought down a town, but to get away from the calm despair of his gaze. I knew what to do with Asphodel Jones, and it was the biggest gamble I'd ever taken in my life. "I want your help," I stammered. "You know about the Wicked God's world, and I want to know all of it. Every last detail."

His face clouded over: a storm of loss, pain, and wistful grief. "Don't call Him wicked," he said simply. "He had a name. A good name."

My curiosity caught. "He did?"

Jones met my eye. "You're a heathen, young miss. That's sacred knowledge. I'm not telling you that."

I swallowed. I was not a general. I was not cut out for negotiating with prophets and killers.

"Don't change the subject. You talk—honestly, mind—about how the way to the God's world was opened, and how we can close it again, and you'll have food, water, the best medicine we have."

"But not my freedom," he said.

I shook my head. "The Great Army's coming. They want to quarantine our land. They'll be here inside two days with a full regiment."

Jones propped himself up on a weak elbow. "You're hoping to give them me instead."

"You did murder," Heron broke in, a little too fast and harsh. "You were never going to get away from them. If anyone put your head in the noose, it was you."

The Wicked God's prophet raised one grayed brow. "I suppose that's true," he said, and sized me up, frankly, from the flagstones. "I'll die by lynching if I cooperate. And if I don't?"

Papa's ghost laughed. I shrank back into the dark.

Heron shuffled closer, until he loomed above that scarecrow man. "I'll put you back," he rumbled.

Jones flinched. "You wouldn't go in there."

"I already did," Heron said quietly. "To bring you out."

Jones's eyes widened to the whites. "You?"

Heron shrugged. "Me."

Asphodel Jones, the Wicked God's dark prophet, closed his eyes on the smokehouse floor and barked a hollow laugh. "Of all the irony," he said softly. "Of all the nasty cosmic jokes." His chuckles bounced off the old stone walls. At the right angle, they sounded like sobs.

"You have a deal, John Balsam," he said when he could breathe again. "Food, water, medicine, and I'll give you my confession. I know my own price."

I let out a breath and nodded, weak with relief. "Deal."

"Deal," Heron rumbled quietly from where the stove had begun to burn. "Don't make trouble, or I'll bury you to the neck in that forest floor."

"I do not doubt it," Asphodel Jones said softly, and I dipped a rag in the water bucket to clean the most wanted man in the land's bloodied wounds.

. . .

There were three voices in the washroom when I came back into the house for provisions: Marthe's gritted one, Eglantine's, and something high and sharp and utterly new. I swallowed a rush of feeling: joy, and fear, and guilt. I couldn't go up there. My hands felt filthy with the skin of the Wicked God's prophet, and I had no excuse, nothing to *give*.

Shut up, I told myself. *Stop working up bribes to make people not turn you away.*

I took a deep breath, walked up the steps, and opened the door.

Marthe slumped against the claw-footed tub, wrapped in towels and blankets, hair lank with sweat. The water in the tub was red with blood; the room smelled meaty, thick. She looked up, and something *moved* against her chest.

Damp and tiny, wholly alive, my niece squalled in her arms.

"Hallie, close the door," Eglantine said from the basin — but she was smiling now, exhausted and smiling. "I'd like to keep the heat in."

I closed the door behind me and stared at the baby — her sparse black curls slicked to her delicate head, her compact hands, her red-brown skin hot with the strain of being born. "She doesn't look like him," Marthe said, faintly stunned. "Except the hair —"

Eglantine wiped her hands. "She'll get darker. All my cousins did." She paused. "And look at those eyes."

I swallowed. They were the Clarlund eyes I remembered:

soft-lidded and warm, taking in the world with a kind bemusement. "Hi, sweet girl," I whispered, and Eglantine cast me a smile.

The child stirred against Marthe's sweaty chest, groping for something she didn't even understand. Eglantine shifted Marthe's towels carefully.

"What's her name?" I asked.

Marthe looked down at the naked brown bundle, mouthing at air. "Hazel. Thom had a great-aunt called Hazel Mae."

"Here," Eglantine said, and arranged that tiny mouth carefully at my sister's breast. "Hand behind the head — like that. All the way in."

I watched them rearrange the small body against Marthe's chest; listened to the little coughs and cries. On the fourth try Hazel took the latch and nursed in great, desperate gulps: her first taste, her first swallow; for all she knew, it might never happen again. I watched it, absolutely ensorcelled by her tiny muscles, her breaths.

Marthe pressed the child to her shoulder after an endless minute. "I'm already exhausted," she said with a terrible laugh.

"Shh," Eglantine said quietly, firmly, and stroked Marthe's hair. "You're doing fine, *querida*. You're going to do just fine."

Marthe stared at the wriggling child: a battleground of love and pain and fear.

"Hallie," Eglantine said, "do you want to hold your niece so Marthe can wash and dress?"

Marthe lifted her head and regarded me, standing useless by the washroom door. "Is that okay?" I said tentatively.

Marthe blinked at me, overwhelmed, her arms still locked around that tiny girl. "Be careful," she said, and it held all the urgency in the world. Never raise my voice to her; bring her hot cocoa in the wintertime, when the farm was choked with snow; dry her tears, and never cause them; make her smile. Always be there.

Be careful.

"I promise," I said, and tentatively plucked the drowsing Hazel from her arms.

She was light, so light and delicate. A shiver ran through my arms and pooled in my spine: *little live thing.* So new and fragile, so amazingly, delicately made. I sat down carefully on the washroom floor. I could not drop this little girl. I could not let her fall.

Hazel fussed against my chest, her mouth shaping wordless things, and I slipped my finger into her fragile brown hand. She gripped shockingly hard. Her flecks of fingers were almost hot. "Hazel," I said, trying it out. "Hi, there."

Eglantine Blakely's round, worrying face broke into a smile again. "Wrap her in the blanket there, Hallie. Marthe, let's clean you up."

We stepped out the washroom door together, an anti-funeral parade: three women and a small package of minuscule, grasping child. The door to Marthe and Thom's room was shut. I opened it, and at Thom's bedside, James Blakely raised his eyebrows.

"Thom," I said hesitantly. "It's a girl."

Thom's eyes opened, and he struggled upward—winced at James Blakely's "No, wait—"

"When?" Thom asked.

"Just now," Marthe said behind me, and eased through the door. "Her name's Hazel."

"Oh," Thom breathed as Marthe held up little Hazel, bundled in a blanket. She was warm and dry now, half asleep from the hard chore of being born. An unfathomable look passed between them.

"Look what we made," Marthe said softly, and laid Thom's daughter on his chest.

Thom's arms came up, terrified of her small, soft movements and squinched eyes. Hazel wriggled and then settled into his warmth, and his mouth opened in a surprised *O*. He reached out a tentative finger, and she grasped it, all instinct, and held on for dear life.

"Hi," he whispered, stunned, and Hazel stirred at the feel of his breath. "Hi, little girl," he rasped. "I'm your daddy."

Marthe slumped down on the bedside, and Thom wrapped an arm around her waist. "Babe, you look so tired."

Marthe laughed, a thundercrack. "You try pushing a kid out."

It utterly undid him. "I wanted to be here when she was born."

"You are," Marthe said.

"But—"

"Thomas," she said, sharp, and then her voice faltered. "You *came home* to me." Marthe's face, so strong, so angry because it'd kept her strong so long, crumpled into a child's wail.

That shaking, ashy hand reached up. Felt for the tangle of her unbound hair, and pulled it to his chest.

She sagged around her emptied belly, fell into his arms. He knotted them around her, around their small, new daughter, and sobbed.

I backed away from the door, James Blakely following right behind me, away from my sister and the man she loved, their family, their privacies. Downstairs, into the fields, where I couldn't hear them cry.

Heron was perched on the red brocade stool when I opened the smokehouse door again, watching Asphodel Jones like a snake, or a wildfire. I set down the provisions—water, canned carrots, a heel of bread—still dreaming. My arms smelled of newborn child. I could still feel her phantom weight tying me down—pleasantly, forever—to this tenuous soil.

"What took you?" Jones said dryly.

I looked down at him, bemused. "I'm an aunt," I said, and walked out.

TWENTY-FOUR

B UT *HOW?*" HERON ASKED, AND ASPHODEL JONES SIGHED.
"I told you," he said, and cleared his throat. "We
got stuck."

Afternoon stained the smoky sky. The fields were quiet.
Nobody had slept: Jerome Chandler had sighted army scouts
a day's march away from the high towers of their proprietary
ruins. The regiment could not — would not — be far behind.

In the smokehouse, I stifled exhausted impatience. "Tell us
step by step," I said, and let my foot brush the empty soup pot,
"exactly how you got stuck on the other side at John's Creek."

"Jones, you made a deal," Heron said from the corner.

Asphodel Jones smiled grimly. "I'm keeping it. Calm
down."

"There's no *time*—" Heron started, and I shot him a look.
"Tell."

Jones shifted on his blanket. "We were dead," he said simply. "The other disciples never thought you would march into
the wastes. The best outcome was that eventually you'd get
tired of dying, and leave us alone. Let us be with Him, in peace,

to commune with that quiet green heart. It wasn't practical, of course. You never would have."

Heron's gray eyes were darkening, his pupils wide with pain and rage. I reached back, held up a hand.

"But in you all came, and that barricade—it wasn't going to hold anyone back. And that's when *you* showed up." Jones's face, worn and drooping, painfully normal, broke into steely resignation. "You cut it open: the God's heart. It was the thing everyone was sworn to die to protect, our glimpse of all that rain, that other world, and of course, the first thing you did was sneak in and rip it to shreds."

"You were killing us," Heron said, almost too soft to hear.

Jones's eyes went distant; I could guess precisely how many miles away. "I'd made my peace with dying, you know. I knew those months in the wasteland wouldn't last. Things don't: not gods, not people. The world's a wrecking ball, young lady. Don't let anyone lie to you about that."

"Things last," I said, tremulous. "Some things don't break."

Jones shook his head sadly and cleared his throat. "You remind me of my little girl, you know. But she's younger: thirteen, the most beautiful thing in the world." He smiled, faint enough that I risked missing it when I blinked. "When she was ten, she didn't like how the birds died if they stayed too long in winter, so she went around everywhere with seed in her pockets, feeding the robins and finches through the cold. She was so insistent that the cold shouldn't get to win."

My throat went dry. "What happened to the birds?"

He shrugged. "They died. I told her they would; built her a hutch for them anyway. She checked on them morning and night, but they died. I don't know how the robins are keeping now." Jones looked away for the first time. Through the gap in his barricades I glimpsed him for a moment: a pained smile, banked with regret. "I haven't been home since last winter. She's likely a woman already."

You gave up, I thought brutally, with a surge of rage. He'd packed a bag and walked away, and all the regret in the world wasn't going to change that.

"John's Creek," I said again. Insistent. Sharp.

He blinked, and took me in again slowly. "John's Creek. I was going to die. But something went wrong. Or went right, because I woke up inside my God's heart. I didn't realize it wasn't the afterlife until I came upon a few stray soldiers, scratching their fingers bloody on a wall of matted leaves. It went up seventy feet into the sky. They didn't know what they were looking at," he said, quieter, "but I did. I knew the body of our God. The wind was out of Him, but I recognized our offerings to Him in the debris."

"What happened to them?" I asked, and he shrugged.

"Died, mostly," he said: brutal and short. "They bickered and killed each other. Or killed themselves. Or drank the wrong water and screamed themselves bloody. I don't know. I had a job to do. I didn't stay."

"What job?" I asked reluctantly.

Heron shifted on the brocade stool and sighed. "Killing me."

I stared at him. "You're terribly calm about it," Jones said, offhand.

"You're on the floor unarmed, and there's a regiment coming," Heron countered. "I can't get too worried."

Jones grinned. "There's the man who walked right into a storm to kill a God."

Heron flinched. "That's not me," he said, and put a hand to his twisted knife. "Don't get it wrong: I make cheese. I don't *swagger*—"

He was cut short by Asphodel Jones's laugh, wheezing and rich, altogether sincere. "A cheesemaker, hmm?" he said, and, infinitesimally, shook his head. "Don't tell them that," Jones said, almost paternally. "It won't fit the brand-new tales of old."

"Oh, I know," Heron said softly. "I know it won't."

"The hole at John's Creek," I said impatiently. The line of sun was moving, already, across the smokehouse porch.

Jones delivered a sideways shrug. "It was blocked. The body of the God bricked it up. For all I know, it's still there, closing, but nothing can get through."

"Closing?" I pounced.

He cocked an eyebrow at me. "They close," he said patiently, and I bit back on a swear word. He'd *known*, all along, that this was what we were after. He'd been holding it back to torment us—*no*. The eagerness with which he'd made our deal, the way he kept watching, eyes flicked, for our reactions — that wasn't about torment. He didn't have that vicious edge.

Asphodel Jones was *lonely*. And the longer someone would sit with him and be forced to listen, the longer he could keep from being alone again.

"They heal," he said reluctantly. "We worked for months to open the hole at John's Creek wide enough to let the God all the way into this world. And your brother and I worked day and night to widen that pinprick on the shore. We've been scratching it open with our fingers, in shifts, for three whole weeks. It would have closed itself in a few days if we'd let it be."

I stood up. "It'll close itself. You swear?" My knees were shaking with sheer hope. The hole would close itself if we could block it up before the lakelands, infested now, burned to ash.

"Oh, it will. But before the army arrives?" Jones said pragmatically, and I swallowed a sudden rage.

"I have chores," I said to Heron, and stomped out onto the steps.

Tyler was leaning against the wall by the smokehouse door, a long rake in his hand. "How long were you listening?" I asked, and he just shrugged. His face looked absolutely ancient, and his mouth was clamped shut. Heron stepped out the door behind me, shoulders bent, and saw those eyes. And stopped.

"Private Blakely," he said.

"Heron," Ty replied. "Who are you?"

I saw it in his eyes: the lie. *I'm nobody.* Heron stepped down into the snow and closed the door behind him. "John Balsam," he said simply, and bowed his head. "Hired on as a farmhand to have a warm roof for the winter."

"But John Balsam's a hero," Tyler blurted.

Heron flinched.

It didn't stop Tyler. "John Balsam was strong, bright, courageous. He ran up to the whirlwind when everyone else ran away, and he leaped—" Tyler reached out one hand, grasping. "He leaped. He *tried.*"

"I'm sorry," Heron said wearily, and slumped against the doorjamb. "I'm sorry. I'm just . . . not."

Tyler's face crumbled like a child's, and I swallowed. "Ty—"

"Let me by," he said hurriedly. "Just—leave me alone." He propped himself up on his rake and shoved past us down the path, into the farmyard, toward the house.

Heron's face sagged into his cupped hands. "I've disappointed him."

"I'm sorry," I said helplessly.

"No," Heron answered. "We all disappoint eventually." He stumped slowly back up the smokehouse stairs. "I have to change his bandages. I don't want to. I want to leave them. I want to watch him suffer and die."

His gray eyes flickered, not rage, but resignation: the deep pit I felt inside when I admitted to Nat the wrong I'd done.

"That's why I have to change them," he finished. "Apparently there are lines I draw too."

"That's not wrong—" I stumbled. As if I knew what was right and what was wrong.

"I should have never left home," he said again, and shook his head. And went back inside, back to Asphodel Jones.

Thom was napping fitfully when I brought lunch up. Tyler trailed me, desolate still, his arms piled with clean linens. James set down his carding in the bedside chair. "Can I leave you with the kids for a bit, Thom? I need to see what Cal and Eglantine are doing about the sheep."

Thom waved a bandaged hand wearily, and James stood. "I'll leave you to it, then," he said to me and Tyler, and left us together for the first time since we'd left the God's violet world.

I set down Thom's soup with a curious trepidation. There was so much we had to say: a whole summer lost between us that we could never get back. *Why didn't you come home in time?* bubbled up, desperate, and I quashed it. He was here now. And we had more important things to ask.

"Thom," I said, and handed him the soup spoon, "why did you bring that man here?"

Thom's lips parted—and stopped. "What are you doing with him?"

"Keeping him in the smokehouse," I said. "Learning everything he knows about the other world so we can block that hole on the river before the whole lakelands goes down. And we need everything *you* know too: about the war, about the God. Everything."

Thom chuckled bitterly. "I only learned one thing on that walk north: it wasn't even a god."

"What?" Tyler burst out.

Thom smiled, and it wasn't the smile I remembered from summer afternoons when I was twelve or thirteen. It was a vicious Cheshire grin, flecked with pain. "That's the terrible irony of the thing. There are thousands of Wicked Gods in the plains there: hundreds and thousands of those *things* in the grass, whirling like calving tornadoes. They decorate themselves with leaves and flower petals so they're not just pockets of wind.

"It was never a god," he pronounced softly. "It was a wild horse, or a bull cow: some brainless thing that fell through that hole when Jones and his acolytes opened it, got stuck halfway through, and screamed itself raw in the dark."

Tyler's hand clenched around his shirt cuff, around that shining button he'd earned at John's Creek. "But it destroyed John's Creek," he said, barely audible. "Burned it to desert in mere months."

My eyes widened. "It wasn't the wrath of a god," I realized. "Ada *told* us; we just didn't get it then. The god was just so big, and when our air touches them—"

"—they burn," Tyler finished, horrified. "It's a Twisted Thing. It was nothing but a trapped animal all along."

"That's all I know," Thom said simply, and stared down into the bowl of cloudy broth. "All I knew for certain about that world was what Jones saw fit to share with me, and he stopped talking once he realized he'd been the prophet of a false idol."

I swallowed. Here it was, the question, the real one. "Why did you bring him onto our farm?"

Thom bowed his head. "It was a coincidence. We were both going north, so we held conversation on the road sometimes. When we chanced upon each other, we shared a camp. Who he was stopped mattering after a certain point."

"It matters, Thom: he turned against the whole *world*," Tyler breathed.

"It's not that simple," Thom said, and for the first time, he met our eyes. His usually warm brown eyes were burning. "We were two farming men. We were trapped, and dying. We were kind to each other. There is no such thing as an enemy the day you find yourself dying alone."

Tyler's mouth closed so fast I heard his jaw click shut.

Alone, I realized: dying alone in the loneliest place in the world. I'd withstood mere minutes in that green and silent world, locked in with my doubts, my fears, my*self.* Jones and Thom had been there for months on end. *Jones agreed to our deal,* I realized, *because Heron threatened to put him* back.

There was a deferential tap on the door. I turned, and Heron scuffed his worn blue socks on the threshold. "Hallie, I sent for Ada Chandler. She's ready downstairs when you are."

Tyler was suddenly absorbed in gathering up the soiled, bloody sheets. Heron watched him set them in the washbasket with a new anxiety. Tyler was proud of the war, proud of his part in it. But he'd wanted to *be* John Balsam, and that was a different kind of love: one that could turn right into resentment.

"Right," I said, and Thom pushed himself up to his elbows.

"And what are you doing on my farm?" he asked coolly.

"Chopping wood. Fixing fences. Right now, guarding Asphodel Jones," Heron answered. "He's a sad man, that one. He'll say anything so I don't leave, even to the horrible bastard who killed his God."

"But if he knows it wasn't a god . . . " I trailed off.

Heron's eyebrows rose.

"He doesn't want to know anything about his god," Thom said quietly. "It would mean he staked it all on something and was wrong, and some people just don't deal well with the thought that they tried and failed."

I turned away. I didn't want any of them to see me flinch.

"You know, Thomas, you could have stopped him," Heron went on. "He's pitiful. But he still killed all those soldiers. He doesn't feel a speck of remorse."

Thom's humorless grin surfaced and then drowned. "I should have cut his throat in the dark, like an irregular?"

Heron shrugged.

Thom shook his head. "Maybe if I was a hero."

"Nobody's a hero here," Heron said softly.

Thom ran a finger over the long train of his bandages, wrapped like soft leather over a twist-forged knife. "I'm just a barley farmer. I wanted to go home and see my daughter born." He swallowed. "I didn't want to be left alone."

Heron looked down at my Thom with contempt — and pity. "Well, none of us do," he said evenly, and stumped back down the stairs.

TWENTY-FIVE

I FOUND HERON IN THE KITCHEN, FILLING THE KETTLE FOR TEA. Ada Chandler tapped her toes impatiently on the floorboards, raccoon-eyed with exhaustion and inexplicably cheerful. "There you are," she said, and sprang to her feet as I rounded the corner. "That intelligence about the hole at John's Creek is *perfect*. Everything makes sense now. Okay, not everything. But it's *good*. It might just work."

"What might work?" I asked.

"Jerome's measurements were right," she said, all enthusiasm. She was a totally different person on the trail of a mystery: all the restless grumpiness fell away. "The Twisted Things' bodies will block the portal without decaying, like the stones did on the riverbank, if we can brick it up with them—just like that wall of leaves Heron mentioned in John's Creek. And I figured out *why*. The matter they're made of is just slightly chemically different from what *we* are, and from our air. We're alkaline to them. It all makes *sense* now."

I stared. She huffed impatiently.

Tyler came down the stairs with the full washbasket

pressed against his chest. "Tyler," Ada said. "Did you catch that?"

"Don't start again," he said, and she relaxed. "I won't follow it."

"The point is, we're alkaline to them, like — baking soda or lye. For the Twisted Things, being here is like walking through a world of lye fumes," she explained. "Breathing lye. Eating lye. Running through it. Your brother could walk in their world and come out a bit burnt, because the acid levels there — they're like vinegar on a cut. But for the Twisted Things, this place is deadly. That's why they burn here, inside and out."

"Oh," I said, eyes wide. "That's horrible."

"Isn't it?" Ada said, and grinned. "But that's the key. We've had a Twisted Thing in that portal, on a string, for hours now. And it's not breaking down at all. It's blocked the portal, just like we need."

Tyler's head came up. "We could plug it. Stuff it full of Twisted Things, and then it'll close. Just like Jones said."

"Exactly," Ada crowed. "All we need is a mortar to bind them together. A mortar that's chemically acidic enough that it won't burn up on the other side. And then we build a wall, and this is over. It's *brilliant*."

It, I thought, admiringly, *is mad*. Mad enough that it could just work.

"Problem is, we burned them all," Tyler said from the

corner. "Getting enough Twisted Things to fill that hole will take weeks. And they don't stay in one *piece* for weeks."

"So stop burning them," Ada said impatiently. "I'll be ready with my jars. It's either that or we go through that portal and bring down something huge, and I'm no big-game hunter."

Heron and I exchanged a tense look. "There's no time to just save them up," I said. "The regiment's still coming."

Ada scowled. "Then hold them off somehow. Keep them off my site."

"Hold off an entire regiment?" Tyler said from the corner.

"Your uncle's a full sergeant," Ada shot back, and slid her boots on. "Figure it out. We're too close to back out now." She waved, an imperious flip of her hand, and strode out the door.

Heron looked down at his hands and shook his head. "It *was* just a knife," he murmured to himself. It fell flat into the silence festering across the room. "Say it," he said finally.

Tyler set the washbasket down. "The poster didn't look like you," he said, defeated.

Heron smirked. "Of course it didn't. They drew a God-killer. They drew a hero."

Tyler's eyes went bright with humiliation. I fought the urge to throw Heron out of my kitchen and just hold Ty 'til it stopped, to joke about chickens and the bedroom ceiling for the rest of the afternoon. "Stop it," I said, and flung a handful of carrots on the table to chop for supper. "I will *not* watch you two trade potshots until Ada invents her evil glue."

"We can't hold off a regiment," Heron said, sobered now. "Miss Chandler's confidence is inspiring, but they'll come here torches blazing. Like it or not, we *are* harboring Jones now. That's a hanging offense."

"Jones," Tyler said, and pulled a knife from the block for the carrots. "Do you think they'll believe us? That we're going to turn him over to the generals?"

"After how Lieutenant Jackson reacted, I don't know," I said. The problem of Asphodel Jones just kept getting more complicated. I lifted the lid of our soap pot and loosed a stink of crushed mint, lye, and flowers: more of Marthe's normalcy, left on the stove to simmer. The regiment was coming, and we were harborers, but Hazel Mae needed soap. "Do you think when we hand him over they'll give him a trial? Use the law?"

"No," Heron said with the discomfited expression he got whenever Jones came up. "You saw him. He's not the Asphodel Jones they want. They want a raving madman, spitting sand and death and slitting throats by the dozen. He's"—he stopped, with an awful look at both of us—"selfish. Broken. Pitiful."

"That's the second time you've said that," Tyler muttered.

"He is. He's been baiting me," Heron said uncomfortably, and dropped his hands into his lap. "He picks fights because otherwise I don't talk, and the silence drives him mad. And the rest of the afternoon all he's talked about is his daughter: how much he loves her. Every brilliant thing she does—because he knows he won't see her again. I marched into the Great Dust to slaughter Asphodel Jones. I never imagined he would be so *sad*."

I lowered the soap spoon. "The regiment won't *like* the real Jones."

Heron caught my eye, caught what I left unspoken: *Just like they'd hate the cheesemaker John Balsam*. "I don't know," he said carefully, "if he will be enough to keep them satisfied until Miss Chandler reinvents mortar. But I don't have any better ideas."

"Big-game hunting," Tyler muttered, decimating the carrots into round, bright coins. There was a hitch in his voice, a broken, hip-twist hitch that I hadn't heard since he'd asked to court me. He'd rolled his sleeves up, and the glint of his army buttons was no longer visible at his wrists. *He is,* I thought, and I could recognize it now, *heartbroken*.

"We just need something bigger," I fumbled. "Thom said the god's body was big." *Think, Hallie,* I ordered myself, a mere maker of malt and herder of goats. *Don't just give up. Think.* The grease shimmered at the top of the soap pot, casting rainbows across the surface. They shifted under my spoon like patterned skin. Like the hide that was rotting in the river—

The spoon stopped.

"There *is* something big enough to plug that hole," I said quietly. "Beast Island."

Heron whistled, low. Tyler's head rose, slowly and then faster. His eyes were like hazel stars. "Beast Island—it came from there, too. It's—what's her word?"

"Acidic," I said.

"Oh, God, we'd need help," he fretted gleefully. "Boats, rope, a trestle. *Lots* of boats."

"We need," Heron said, "Windstown."

I put the soap spoon down. If I'd been told the air was lye now, that I could never breathe deep again, in that instant I would have believed it. "We can't. Windstown won't come. The things we said to Pitts the last time we were there—"

"They have to," Tyler said.

"I can't. Pitts won't listen; he just puts on his sash and chain and plays God—"

"He *has* to," Tyler repeated, simple, stubborn. "They're our neighbors, and it's the end of the world."

I swallowed and thought of all the worst fears that had come to pass this week: Marthe's face contorted with pain at my lies; Thom, frightened and embittered, bloodying the sheets of his wedding bed; Asphodel Jones in my smokehouse, knowing my name, my face, what made me flinch. My little niece, fists raised and mouth seeking, looking for warmth and light as monsters strode across the land that should, one day, be hers.

"What's one more?" I said, a little hysterical, and Tyler cast me a worried glance. I shook my head. It was a thought for that silent green world, so far outside the humble day to day of living; so far from *seed,* or *plow,* or *goat.* If I was going to live up to the vow I'd made there, I had to not act like my uncle, not act like I was in this alone. I had, I thought with a flicker of sheer panic, to *try.*

"I need a water bottle," I said. "And I need a torch. The light's going to go soon."

Heron nodded. "I'll get them."

"How are we going to get there?" Tyler asked. "The hole's right near the river dock. I haven't *seen* your dock in a few days."

I swallowed. "I'll take the bridge."

Tyler put down the kitchen knife. "You've got to be kidding. It's falling apart. They blocked it off for a *reason,* Hal."

"I'll run," I promised. My heart was already pounding. "Because if I don't, we'll die anyway, and this guy I know told me it was better to try."

"That Tiger guy," he said with just a hint of warmth.

"That one," I agreed, and took his hand in mine.

I didn't have to say the rest. *Hope,* he registered, his eyes alight. Tyler's fingers laced and relaced between mine, seeking restless new combinations. *You're a fidget,* I thought warmly, and leaned into his arm. Tyler took both my hands in his and kissed them firmly, knuckle by knuckle. "Pack your kit. I'll get the cart and drive you to the edge."

"Thank you," I whispered, and Heron came downstairs, water bottle in hand.

I looked up the stairs, at the boards and buttresses of the house we'd kept by never, ever taking a thing Alonso Pitts had sneeringly offered. I swallowed hard. "Tell Marthe," I asked him. "Tell her I'll be back soon."

THE DUST

TWENTY-SIX

IT WAS TEN MILES TO THE FOOT OF THE BRIDGE, EVERY ONE OF them charred and pockmarked with the signs of war. Tyler drove me along the old road in the Blakely family cart as the sun set behind us, tingeing everything red: the fallen trees, the scorched-out hedges, the barns that listed to one side like wounded men. The Twisted Things had desolated the land by the river shore. Ash choked the cold air. The snow heaped, and it was black.

By the time the bridge loomed on the horizon, a sleeping giant, we were silent. Its cords and cables drifted, creaking, in the wind.

"Here," Tyler said, and reined the ponies in. "I'll help with your pack."

I stepped down from the cart and faced the arching road before me with trepidation. I hadn't remembered the bridge running so narrow or so high: a steep hill of metal and asphalt that crested in the middle of the river before it fell away into the dead streets of Old Windstown.

"You're sure about this?" Tyler asked.

"No," I said, and shouldered my pack.

Tyler's forehead crinkled with resignation. "Come home safe to me," he said, and squeezed my hand one last time.

I nodded. There was nothing else to say.

The bridge was wild land: weed-eaten concrete. They had only cleared one lane of it when the old cities withered. Its sides were littered with the rusted skeletons of ancient machines, their workings outside all modern comprehension. They hulked and crumbled in the wind, as inscrutable as the hills: a silent monument to whatever ended our great-grandparents' world.

I swallowed bile and started quickly down the cleared lane, through the high wind that rose over the river, thick with ash.

The bridge was slippery underfoot, the black asphalt slicked with frozen river spray and fragments of powdered rust. I climbed carefully, testing each step against its persistent upward curve. I wasn't yet to the bridge's apex when the sharp howl split the sky.

Dogs, I thought, and turned sharply. Caught in the glare of the setting sun, I saw them pacing, edge-tailed, behind me on the shore. "Oh, great," I muttered, and looked around for a stick, a log, something: the ferals were wild, but they didn't pick a fight unless it was mid-February and they were starving. There was nothing to hand; the bones of the bridge had been picked dry decades ago. Nothing here was anything anyone wanted.

"Well, I did say I'd run," I muttered, and picked up speed. The bridge swayed beneath me like a boat on the water; the roadway under my boot was spidered with cracks. I strode faster. The pavement shuddered, a howl of metal and cord that sent the ferals behind me squealing for the trees. The whole bridge, sinuous, rocked in the too-hot otherworldly wind.

My foot slid. I didn't care.

I ran.

I bent double and scrambled across the endlessly arching bridge, my legs burning, my lungs burning. If it came down, there was nowhere to go. There was nothing to either side but killing winter water. I put my head down and pushed, forced myself faster.

Over the bridge's shuddering beams, against the sunset, the deer-horned trees walked through the river, calling weird and fluting hunting calls. Their leaves brushed the cables one by one, and the metal blackened in their monstrous wake. I heard a creak. A soft ping.

A metal bridge cable as thick as my arm whipped low over my head and crashed into dead metal and glass.

I shrieked, staggered into a rusting, frozen hulk as the bridge shook itself like a wet dog. The wind howled through its ruins, churned the river into roaring waves. The asphalt shook again beneath me, and shards flew everywhere as the second huge cable frayed above me and let go.

I tripped and tumbled, bruising, rolling down the bridge as the cables sang overhead. The roadway shuddered beneath me, vibrating with the endless *snap! snap! snap!* of metal, stronger than anything we'd ever know to make again. The deer-horned trees tossed the bridge to and fro, and I fell between those ancient machines, down the other side. I scrabbled for a hand-hold on the bucking, disintegrating bridge. It reared up, and I landed in something softer, colder. *Snow,* I thought. Weeds prickled my palms. *I'm on the other side.*

Inching and wriggling into the darkness, I lifted my head to the riverside.

The bridge was falling, finally falling. Its broken back arched and split, the girders screaming as the road ripped away. The ground boomed, once, twice, as each piece tumbled into the river. I clung to the soil with my bleeding, aching fingers and shut my eyes as tight as I could.

When I opened them, the river was a disaster of metal. The disintegrated vehicles of our ancestors bobbed through the river, whispering their steel farewells. Around them, the dead bridge ribboned through the water, its concrete flaking slowly. The deer-horned trees called, almost lost, to each other and waded through the river, to the north.

I pulled myself up, breath heaving, and scrabbled to my feet. My knee twinged furiously. I ignored it. *Still alive,* I thought, delirious. *I did it,* and I stumbled into the ruins of Old Windstown.

The dead city behind the Windstown barricade was a maze. The Chandlers had mapped and tamed their home in the ruins on our side of the river, but Old Windstown had been abandoned for a full century, left derelict to the dogs and raccoons while men and women kept to the safe township on the other side of the walls. Trees grew riot through the concrete, buckling up pavement, knocking roof tiles to the dirt. I steered through them, limping carefully, blinded by the scattershot flares of light on the horizon and the scent of distant flames. The Twisted Things had been to Old Windstown. High above me, gutted concrete buildings smoked from their awful wings.

I ducked down and stumbled through the alleys, leaned panting against an ancient redbrick wall. Three raccoons squealed, frightened, and ran out of a door across the street, and the roof behind them creaked and fell in. A flock of spinner birds fled, startled, from its ruins in the other direction: looking for another place to light, another thing to destroy.

I wiped my nose shakily. My fingers came away sticky with blood. The old city sat silent around me, dusty with destruction and smoke.

"You're still alive," I whispered to myself encouragingly, like a good auntie would. I was almost to Windstown: I could see the barricade stretching above the rooftops, keeping out the rot. The militia had a door in it, always guarded, well-attended, for the nights they had to go out and repair the barricade or keep the ferals at bay. All I had to do was *find* it, and I'd be safe in the treed Windstown streets. Minutes from Mackenzie Green's, or Prickett's, or Alonso Pitts.

I tiptoed toward the barricade, around corners and dead ends. It stretched stories high above me, a beacon, a testament to years of keeping civilization alive; keeping the wilderness and desolation out. And then I saw the latest impossible thing.

There was a crack in the Windstown wall.

The barricade that kept Windstown bright and safe gapped open, showing chair legs and bent metal within. I peered through the century-old hoardings and mortar dust. The slimmest sliver of light peeked all the way through.

"We *can't* spare a guard here," a voice floated on its tail. "The fire brigade needs me. There's smoke on Main Street."

"There's smoke *everywhere*, dammit—" I heard, and that voice I recognized.

I raised a fist and banged hard on the wall. "Johan? Johan Prickett?"

The spat stopped abruptly. The wind whistled around me ominously. "Who's there?" he asked. It was definitely Johan, Janelle's other dad, tousle-haired and usually so very mild.

"Johan?" I called. "It's Hallie Hoffmann. I need to get in. Where's the door?"

The silence lengthened. "Ah, *shit*," he said. "You need to get to Cooper Street. Where's that on the—north, Hallie. Go north, two blocks. I'm going for the door, all right? We're coming."

The voices faded into footsteps, and then there was nothing but wind and the rumbling sky. I scrambled against the rough base of the barricade and found north by starlight. It was impossible to count two blocks in the shattered ruins. *They've left,* an old shred of Papa said. *They aren't coming back.*

"Shut up," I told him, and kept moving along the wall.

Heartbeats, seconds, hours later I heard the raised voice: "Hallie?" It was Darnell Prickett, his rich innkeeper's bellow. "Hallie, are you there?"

"Darnell—" I started, joyfully. "Where are you? Where do I go?"

"Hold on," he said, and some ancient machinery creaked, tortured with time. A whole section of the wall buckled open slowly, dust and smoke shedding into the air behind it.

Mackenzie Green poked her head through the opening and reached out both hands. "Child, how in the name of every god standing did you get out *there?*"

"Mackenzie," I said, almost sobbing with relief. "I came across the bridge. It finally broke. It's gone."

Mackenzie's eyes widened. "That's what the sound was. Come on, quickly now," she said, and pulled me through the gate into the safe, bright streets of Windstown.

They were not as safe as I'd left them. Now the neat rows of redbrick houses had scars. Smoke rose over their shingles, fitful and dirty brown. The shouts of the Windstown fire brigade drifted up behind it: the sunset light had segued into the sooty glow of flames. They lit up paper signs plastered on the scarred concrete walls: row after row of John Balsam's ink-drawn face, with MISSING scrawled atop it.

"We have to get you inside," Fatima Prickett said, and I

gave up and let Janelle's practical mother rub heat into my arms. She threw a blanket around my shoulders, and someone found a bottle of something stronger than plain tea. I swallowed what they gave me; it burned all the way down, but it was bracing. My belly squirmed.

"There's no time," I gasped, and handed back the bottle. "There's a hole into the Wicked God's world, wide open, on the river."

"The Wicked God has a *world*—" Fatima started.

"It came from somewhere else, with the Twisted Things —there's no *time*. Our apple orchard's gone, and the back field," I said. "There's a regiment headed this way on the high road."

Johan swore.

Darnell and Fatima exchanged a dark look. "So that's where the Twisted Things are coming from," he said.

"I need to talk to the council," I said, feeling stronger now. "I need to talk to Pitts."

Mackenzie's face shuttered. "Oh, Hallie. That's not a good idea. They're panicking up a storm in there."

"Mackenzie," I said, and grabbed her sleeve. "We know how to stop it. We can close the hole and rescue everything, but we need Windstown. We need to pull together like a constellation—"

She frowned.

My old, proud instincts seized, and I shut my eyes. Pretended, gut-deep, that I was asking Nat or Tyler for a cup of tea, or the salt. Asking something simple, something small from someone who loved me, and was kind.

"We need your help," I said clearly, and swallowed hard.

When I opened my eyes, Mackenzie was watching me, her lips pressed tight together. "All right," she said. "I'll take you to the council. I'll take you up to Pitts."

TWENTY-SEVEN

THERE WAS A HOLE IN ALONSO PITTS'S PARLOR.

The Twisted Things had been here too, and burned during the night. That wall of old-cities windows, his treasured wall of white roses, had melted down to the redbrick frame. Glass lay slopped and frozen on the waxed hardwood, dusted with winter frost. They'd nailed wooden curtains over the mangled ruin, but they didn't keep out the cold. The Windstown Council met in their wool coats, with the lamps up high, and I shivered, standing before them.

This time, they didn't offer tea. Nobody could have stomached it.

"How," Alonso Pitts asked, "did you get in? There are guards on the harbor. They were supposed to detain all boats."

I bit down a reflexive, rising rage. *This is why we never ask you for help, you awful man.* With neighbors like these, you could drown in the river in September and not be missed until June.

No, I told myself, as firm as stone. *Don't think like that. It's thinking that way that left you all alone.*

"I ran the bridge," I said, and tried to keep my voice strong. "It's finally come down. I barely made it to shore."

The councilmen sucked in a collective breath. "We're trapped against the barricade, then," Thao Pa said softly, and ran a hand through his gray hair.

"We've got the boats," Karen Kim reminded him. But her hand tightened on the truncheon at her belt.

"Not enough to evacuate the whole town," Pa retorted, and nerves ran through the room like spiderweb strings.

Panic, I thought. This was what it felt like: weapons and guard postings and hurried conferences in half-shattered rooms. The wind rattled the wooden hoarding against the window frame. "Councilors," I said, "we've been working with the Chandlers. We think we can stop the Twisted Things, but please, we need your help."

Councilor Kim looked down, and I wasn't sure she saw me. Her eyes wouldn't focus on my bruised-up face. "We can't send forces across the river. We're barely holding Windstown together," she said.

The frustration rose up in me. Forget Tyler's talk about *they have to;* he'd never fought Windstown Council. He didn't understand how they really were, deep down: the litany of betrayal the council was and would always be.

"We can stop it," I said, my voice rising frantically. "We have to *try*. The war's not over," I argued, and Alonso Pitts scowled. "The war's in my front yard, right across the river. And we can end it if you pull together and *help*."

Pitts's face set into a furious mask. "The infamous Hoffmann temper. Did you want to slam my door again once you're done telling us what *we* owe *you?*"

I gritted my teeth. *Spite or pride, Alonso Pitts?*

Pride's the Hoffmann failing, James Blakely had said, but even he didn't understand it: The Hoffmann failing was rage, black and absolute. The rage that ate you by inches. The rage that turned you against your neighbors, against your children, made you alone.

I breathed in and summoned, inside me, the quiet place: the constellation of my kinfolk and friends, my steady stars. "No, I don't," I said, soft and cool, "and — I'm sorry we slammed your door. I apologize."

"I'm sure you are *now,* since you want something from me after all."

Silence pooled and froze in that beauteous, ruined parlor. And then Mackenzie said, tiredly, "Alonso, put it away."

"*I* should put it away—"

She held up a hand, and the iron authority she'd always held, her sunburned dignity, stopped his mouth cold. "She's sixteen," Mackenzie said. "You're fifty-three. It's time to be the adult."

"I didn't start this, Mackenzie," he said heatedly.

"No," she answered. "Cyril Hoffmann did. And Cyril Hoffmann is dead in the ground."

I flinched, and her hand drifted down to my shoulder, hesitated, and then patted it awkwardly. "I'm sorry, Hallie.

I truly am." She turned back to Mayor Pitts and said, "Cyril Hoffmann's gone, and nobody was sorry to see him go. He hit his wife and ran his brother off. He treated his daughters like slaves, and this town did practically nothing to stop it. But he's *dead*, Alonso. How long are you going to prove every nasty lie he fed his girls to keep them isolated enough to stay?"

Suddenly my face was very hot; my ears buzzed like a Twisted Thing's, burning, burning. *My father,* I thought. *They are talking about my father like a liar, like a brute—*

The next thought rose and ate the last alive: *They knew everything. They knew it* all along.

I'd had no secrets. I'd had no dignity to protect. All of Windstown had known what went on in the Hoffmann house, and our whole life since—Papa's will, our struggles, six years of isolation and silence—had just been another of Papa's *traps.*

I fought the urge to fly through the door and *run:* north, south, anywhere. Take to the highways. Never come back. No one in that room would meet my eye. No one but Mackenzie Green.

"We tried to help them," Mayor Pitts managed, avoiding my anguished gaze. "We offered land managers to look over the accounts, to take them into town where they could have proper adults about. It wasn't wanted. Everything I offered came up against *no.*"

"That"—I choked up, broken apart, breaking—"wasn't help."

Mackenzie held up her hand again before he could say a word.

My throat clogged. I struggled to push the words free, to put into the world something as fundamental as bread. "Tyler Blakely brought me a cup of tea the other day," I said, and the words hung there uselessly.

"Go on, child," Mackenzie said softly.

"It was the best thing he could've done," I said. "Because he wanted to help me, to give me something. And he asked what I wanted him to do."

And then my head came up, because I had it. I had the root of the trouble between Windstown and Roadstead Farm. "If you wanted to help Marthe and me, you should have asked us. *You* decided what help was, or wasn't, every time. Your help was never what we really needed," I finished, "and the price was always too high."

I looked up at Mayor Alonso Pitts, and he met my eyes with a growing remorse. "We have been doing our best with a bad situation, and sometimes you've got to accept that we've lived a little longer, and know a few more things —"

I fought to keep my hands from balling into fists. "You do, but it doesn't matter if it's *not what we need*."

Alonso Pitts stared at me and then rested one hand on his ruined wooden mantel. His fingers rubbed its burn-scarred polish: a remnant of the old-cities world he clung to so stubbornly. *Never coming back,* I thought. It was gone, like so many other things in the lakelands this wintertime.

"Halfrida," he said, halting, Mayor Hellfire doused and wilted away. "What is it you need?"

Mackenzie's hand on my shoulder relaxed fractionally. It was still a challenge, Pitts still daring me to prove him wrong. But it didn't matter now: I had a niece now, and that farm would be hers. She needed a home to grow up in. A garden to plant. A river to love.

"There's a hole to the Wicked God's world on the riverbank," I said. "It'll heal itself, but not for a little while, not soon enough to stop the Twisted Things from coming or the Great Army from quarantining Roadstead Farm, Lakewood, and Windstown, too."

Councilor Haddad's eyebrows skyrocketed. "Alonso—"

And Mayor Pitts did the impossible: he chopped his hand across the air, leaned in closer to me, and said, "Not now."

I swallowed, thoughts flying. "That was how the war ended at John's Creek. Asphodel Jones and his irregulars made a hole between the worlds there, big enough for the Wicked God to get through—and get stuck, and burn so hot it burned the life out of the land and created the Great Dust. And when John Balsam opened that hole wider, it fell back in and died. It plugged the hole with its body, tight enough to seal the breach until the worlds could mend."

"How do you know all this?" Thao Pa asked. I dug my fingernails into my hands and told my last, most necessary lie.

"From Ada Chandler. From my hired man, and from my

brother," I said, and thought—so I could at least *think* the truth—*from Asphodel Jones.*

Darnell Prickett startled. "Thom's home?"

"He fell through the hole at John's Creek, and he still walked all the way home," I said, tearing up again and, for once, not ashamed of it. "All the way home in the Wicked God's world. When the hole opened on our riverbank, he came out. But now we need to plug it with something so big that nothing can come out from the other side."

"How big are you thinking?" Mackenzie Green asked.

I took a breath. "Beast Island. Ada says it has to be stuff from the other world, stuff that belongs there, that's acidic. Anything of ours will just burn away. But if we push Beast Island in there, we have a chance. We need all the boats," I said, and my voice trembled with fear and desperation. With hope. "And we need rope."

There were too many faces to watch now. There were too many sounds in my ears. I focused on Alonso Pitts, his red-cheeked face, and hoped.

"When?" he asked, shaken.

I swallowed, giddy. "Tonight."

The trip back from Windstown was a haze of ice and water. Mackenzie Green loaded me into the smallest boat in the Windstown fleet, the one that could be best spared from the hasty drive to harness Beast Island with the strongest rope in Windstown. The Thaos took the oars. They escorted me, slowly, from shore to shore by lantern light. I sat in the back of the rowboat as we inched around dead foxes and drowned Twisted Things, and I felt bruises bloom on my kneecaps, my legs, my bad hand.

From the water, I could see the tear between worlds: a shimmering haze of heat that rose above the winter air. It was massive. It hung low in the sky over the gray river and turned it green and white with summer flowers.

Hang couldn't stop staring. His hands stilled on the oars. "Beast Island going to be big enough?"

I don't know, I thought, stunned. *I don't know.*

At the other oar, his sister shook her head. "Focus," she said, and flicked a struggling cockroach-mouse away with the blade of her wooden oar.

The desolation was worse on our own shore: vines choked the shallows and snarled the corpses of winter pike and splayed-out river crabs. I spied the Blakely dock in the distance, a finger of hardy wood still standing in the desolate night. "There," I said. "I can get off there and walk in." They steered me to it, and I pulled myself to my wobbly feet.

"Thank you," I breathed, and hit the Blakely dock running. "Come for first light!"

"Right," Hang said, and cast off nervously. "We'll be there."

I put my head down, picked through the fields, and ran.

There was light in our farmhouse, even this late — the light of a good fire, and warm bread, and someone reading aloud in the parlor. I stopped at the doorstep and held my breath for just a moment. Heard the low murmur of voices and Hazel's mumbled cry, the pick of a finger against a ukulele string.

A home, I thought wonderingly, and burst into the kitchen, into Marthe's and Heron's shocked arms. "They'll come," I said, and fell into the closest chair, dripping with sweat, stinking, safe. "They're bringing Beast Island. They're coming."

We felt the noise before we heard it: a cringing shudder in the ground, a rhythmic banging. Marthe's hand fell to Hazel's delicate skull. "What is that?" she asked, and I slipped out to the porch.

You could see all the land around the river from the house my great-grandparents built at Roadstead Farm; you could see all the way to the falling stars. Down the highway, I saw a mass of small bodies, dark against the snow line, moving like river waves. I squinted. "What's that?"

Behind me, Heron sighed.

"The regiment's here," he said, and we stood together to watch them march toward us, endless soldiers, all in rows. The sky glittered above them, smoke and diffuse moonlight, and somewhere in the dying fields the first star winked out in the sky.

TWENTY-EIGHT

THERE WERE OLD BOARDS IN THE HAY BARN, FOR A ROLLING chicken coop we'd dreamed up three years past and never built. We dragged them out in the light of our perpetually burning fields and nailed the house windows shut. *There might not be broken glass,* I thought as I held them steady for Nat's hammer. *There might not be walls to hold it, soon.* It didn't matter. If we failed, and the regiment scorched our land clean, perhaps we could save the house, the outbuildings. Perhaps Hazel could return here when the land came back, someday.

Marthe sat in the kitchen, Hazel cradled in her lap, surrounded by four generations of our family's striving. We blocked the smoky light, board by careful board. Our most treasured things—Mama's cookbooks, the rose tea-cups—faded under the dim brown of lumber.

Nat dusted her hands on her dress and hefted the hammer. "Where next?" She was still angry at me. Her voice stayed flat even as she shifted my fingers around nails and boards.

"The poultry barn. I'll catch up," I said with not a little

trepidation, and headed for the smokehouse. Everything else was ready. We had to deal with Asphodel Jones.

Heron was out front, facing a split log set tall against a willow tree. In his hands was the old-city gun. "James Blakely rode out just now to meet the regiment," he said. "He'll brief General de Guzman. Maybe it'll buy some time."

I shuddered at the thought. This is what we'd come to: buying time. "What're you doing?"

"Practicing." Heron's hands moved on the mechanism. Inside it, something clicked, and its bottom popped out: a scuffed, black rectangle stinking of oil and sawdust. He checked the rectangle carefully in the lantern light and pushed it back into the handle. "I traded into the Chandlers' grounds for the rest of the bullets while you were in town. We don't know what this might come to."

I stared. This collection of tubes and boxes was more than a hundred years old and insanely precious. We didn't own enough to barter for something like that. "How?"

Heron's face, in the sooty light, was as resigned as an execution. "The man who was asking was John Balsam."

"Oh," I said without meaning to, quick and heartbroken. I could see it unfolding like the seasons: gossip flaring down the roadways, through the townships, across the lakelands until it reached some county magistrate, and then—

There would be delegations. Endless city dances and fetes. Thousands of feet pouring after him wherever he landed to rest, all looking for advice, all with questions.

Questions for the man who killed a god.

"I'm sorry," I said softly, my heart like windows breaking in the storm.

Heron shook his head once. "No. Don't be. It was too important."

He lined up his arms again, braced himself, and *Crack!* spoke the tube as the log split clean in two. I blinked and knew immediately why Ada hadn't wanted June touching this one relic. The weapon in Heron's hands was vicious, formidable. It frightened me with its metal stink.

The man holding it was putting up a brave front, but I knew his moods by now. He looked absolutely lost.

"The poster," I said. "It didn't look like you."

Heron blinked wildly. His hands were rough-knuckled on the old-cities gun. "I know. It was a fantasy. It was a story they told themselves."

It looked more like him than he thought. A version of him who'd never feared, never cried. I shook my head. "It didn't look like you, but I *recognized* you. I recognize you now."

"I'm not a hero," he said, his voice tinged with desperation.

"That's not what I mean," I said simply. "It's because I have good reasons to recognize your face."

He looked at me for a long moment, and then set down the gun and clasped me in a rough hug; breathed in deep and held on for dear life. "You're a good kid," he said thickly, and I heard what he wasn't saying: *You are a good friend.*

"Thanks," I whispered. "You too."

He held me for a handful of seconds and then stepped back, resolute. Head higher, now, against the night sky. He picked up the old-cities weapon like it was tainted, like I had held John Balsam's world-splitting knife.

"Can I—" I asked, and he pulled the weapon away.

"Hallie," he said gently. "Some things aren't for honest people's hands."

John Balsam was the man who had cut the heart out of a god. I didn't try to tell him that he was still, always, honest. "The regiment's here. We have to deal with Jones now," I said, and he shuddered.

"I can't," he said, strained. "Don't ask me to tell a man tonight's the night he dies."

I took a deep breath and nodded. "Okay."

"Okay?" he asked, incredulous.

"You were right before," I said. "It's my farm, and I have to deal with my own consequences." I walked up the steps and paused. "Heron, when do you get to go home?"

He turned away, fast. For a moment, before he'd hid it, his face was as empty as the sky. "I said nobody was waiting for me."

"No," I countered. "You said no one was waiting for you to make things *normal* again. You've got a mother. She's got to wonder where you are."

"Sharp girl," Heron said, and his lips twisted. He set down the weapon and looked at me bleakly. "I don't know. When the legend of John Balsam quiets down. When the army goes home. Never. I don't know."

I turned the door handle. "Don't wait too long."

He raised an eyebrow.

"Home doesn't wait for you, sometimes," I said, and went into the smokehouse to treat with Asphodel Jones.

It was dim inside the smokehouse: old soot and ruin draped over the quiet I'd always known. Heron's things were gone now; the space he'd made for himself looked desperately alone. *Amazing how fast you can get used to things,* I thought, and scuffed into what was once my solitary lair. It moved so quickly sometimes: the way worlds ended, and changed.

Jones was stretched out in his dirty sheet, sleeping. I had a little time.

I tiptoed onto one of my trails, into the heaps of broken things. I kept a lot of things in the smokehouse, but the title to the farm was farther in, around the stack of tangled fishing nets Uncle Matthias had left behind, inside a broken butter churn webbed with dust. In the smallest, darkest corner there was — the most safe.

I reached into the churn with a hand almost twice as big as when I'd first chosen it for a hideaway. The wooden box was still there.

There was no knowing who the box had belonged to; I'd found it here seven years ago, a dark wood thing with half the inlay knocked out. I eased it out from the break in the churn and checked the contents by reflex: Uncle Matthias's spare comb. Two stolen rose petals from the night Thom Clarlund asked Marthe to marry him. The felted doll Mrs. Blakely had made me as a child, kept at my bedside 'til I'd grown too old.

And under them, the copy of Papa's will and land title, folded up together small in the lining. The papers that gave me the right to half of Roadstead Farm.

I brushed them with my index finger. Safe. *It's still safe.* I swallowed hard, closed the box up again, and picked my way out of the junk maze. Jones slept restless on the floor, his cheeks sallow and patched with dreams.

"Jones," I said softly, and he sat up, tangled in the blankets that were likely his deathbed.

"Thom's sister, Halfrida," he said with a faint nod.

"They're coming," I said. "The regiment. We saw them over the hills an hour ago."

Jones flashed his quiet, bitter grin. "Time to hand me over like a sacrificial animal," he said. "I hope it's enough blood to make them spare your houses. I sincerely do."

It was strange: baiting from Jones was almost nothing next to the baiting that was Alonso Pitts. It was so quiet and mild. All the fires in Asphodel Jones's halls had long been quenched. "I know you only do that because you're lonely," I said.

He shrank a little in his skin. He was an old man, I realized; Papa's age, when he died. "You do remind me of my daughter," he said. "She never lets me get away with that either. That's why I built that birdhouse." And just like with Marthe sometimes, I could tell that he meant so much more than I understood, but I couldn't follow him through the cramped byways of his own head.

The words came to me quietly — from the box in my hands, from knowing what was most important in the world. "Does she know what happened to you?"

Jones shook his head. "I'm sure some of the tale's got back to the hill country by now."

No, I translated. *She hasn't a clue.*

The words came unbidden to my lips: *You should go home to your family.* I swallowed them. This time, that wasn't going to work. Asphodel Jones had murdered in cold blood, and there was no way back for him: only military justice and a trial that would end in a long rope.

"We'll come for you when the regiment's here," I said quietly. "But I'm going to take down your last will."

Jones caught his breath. "What are you playing at?"

"Nothing," I said, and sat on the brocade stool. "If we survive this, if the hole closes up like you promised, tell me where you want your ashes and belongings to go. We'll get them there."

Jones pushed himself upright, a tight look on his face. "Why are you doing this?"

I looked down at my box. "I don't hurt people," I said, like a promise: a promise to myself about who Hallie Hoffmann was even to the people she didn't love, didn't need help from, didn't have to impress. To someone whose life she held in her very hand.

I couldn't read Asphodel Jones's expressions: he'd been here too short a time. I'd been too busy juggling catastrophes to know him. "I don't have anything," he said, "not anymore. But what I have I want to go to my little girl, and I want her to know the truth. About where I was. About why I didn't come home. I want her to know I love her the most."

"That's all?" I asked quietly.

"That's all," he said.

You don't deserve to say that after you walked away, I thought, and pulled it back in. My papa had a gravestone. He had been thrown a proper funeral in the family plot, where we'd served a cold lunch and told only good stories about him all afternoon. He had died a painless death in his bed, overnight, blurred with medicine.

If Thom had not come back to us through the endless roads of the Wicked God's world, we wouldn't even have had a body to bury in the soil he'd worked so hard to replenish. Nowhere to visit his memory for the family he'd worked so hard to mend. No vial of ash to end the questions about where, when, how to rest; to let us learn to lock the door again at night and stop listening for a knock that would never come.

Deserve had nothing to do with it. And Asphodel Jones had

a daughter, who was waiting, who would not have a vial of ash to put on her mantel so she could grieve.

"All right," I said through a thick throat. "Give me her name and her township."

Jones's eyes widened. He hadn't truly believed it. Neither had I until the words left my mouth. "Chandi. Her name's Chandika. We lived two days out of Monticello, on a mountain, mostly alone. She's likely with her mother's people now."

I nodded. "South, then."

"South," he said.

I got to my feet and hugged the wooden box to my chest. "We're going to seal the hole in a few hours," I said. "We'll come for you. I'll keep my word."

"I know," said the Wicked God's prophet, and I left him, lonely, in the dark.

Dawn grayed on a farm packed up and boarded up to abandon.

We did the final packing in the cold and spicy air, listening to the branches rustle against each other. It was, if you didn't look at the river, almost peaceful: our last chance to see the place between the river and the road.

We all kept quiet. We took that chance, and remembered every sound.

The Blakelys' cart stood ready in the drive, with Marthe's packages perched in the back: the grimmest crop we'd ever shipped off Roadstead Farm. Eglantine and Marthe handed

Thom up the cart steps, careful of his bandages and his still-peeling burns. "We'll lie you right back down," Eglantine said. "Two steps, Thom. I know you can."

Thom gritted his teeth. *He walked across the shadowlands,* I thought about saying, and just left it alone.

I edged over to the cart once Marthe and Hazel Mae were settled, and folded the darkwood box into Marthe's hands. "Take this?" My own hands trembled. "Take it and keep it safe for me?"

Marthe's eyebrows drew together. "This was Mama's. What's inside it?"

I swallowed, and faced my sister full. "The deed to half of Roadstead Farm."

Marthe looked down at me over the wrapped bundle of Hazel, lashed gently to her chest, and tears sprang to her eyes. *She knows,* I thought in terror and relief. *She knows what I'm entrusting to her.* "I'll give it to you," she said, fierce and low, and tucked the box inside her daughter's blanket. "I will give this right back to you when we get home."

I nodded: left wishing, as always, for the right words to give her, the kind of words that *were* a gift. My hands shook. I couldn't speak.

Eglantine positioned herself by the step. "All right, Tyler," she said delicately. "We'll put you up next."

Ty looked down at the river, and then at me, Nat, and Heron, and lifted his head. I blinked, and then recognized it:

the way a person's body held itself high when it was devoted without compromise to something greater than itself. "I'm staying," he said quietly.

Nat glanced at him and nodded sharply. "Staying."

Mrs. Blakely's calm evaporated. "What? Both of you? *No*."

"Mum—" Tyler started.

"You can't. I can't lose you both—"

Nat stepped forward and folded her mother's hands in her own. "Mum," she said softly. "I understand that if I let my brother die, you will skin me with a soup spoon and spend the rest of your life in black, and it's your worst color, and it will be all my fault."

"That's not funny, Nasturtium Blakely," she whispered. "Not this time."

Nat's face fell for just a moment. "We'll take care of each other, Mum. I swear."

Eglantine threw her arms around her daughter. She reached out, flailed, caught Tyler's shirt and pulled him in. They rocked together, heaving, in a tangled embrace full of elbows and promises. "I have already lost your father this year," she said into that knot, and nearly choked. "You both come home. So help me God, I'll see you both on my doorstep in the morning."

"Yes, Mum," Tyler whispered, and squeezed his mother tight.

I looked up at Marthe: tall and proud, so undemonstrative,

so contained. She reached out and ruffled my hair gently with her free hand. "Be careful, Hal," she said softly.

I swallowed the lump in my throat. "You too."

"Eglantine," Cal said gently.

She disentangled herself from her children with a broken-hearted look and lifted herself up onto the cart.

"Be safe," I said softly, and Marthe took Thom's hand and they drove off Roadstead Farm, into the already-rising sun. We watched them go, Heron and Nat and Tyler and I standing in a row: four flawed bodies, all still frightened but ready. Ready for the thrum of marching feet.

I didn't want to lose this land, but if we did, Hazel would live. She would have parents to love her. She would have, in them, a home. *You cannot anymore,* I told myself, *lose everything.*

I looked down at my hands, at the naked soil of Roadstead Farm. At the fences we'd defended against everyone for years and years. "They'll come, right?" I asked, like an eight-year-old child.

"They'll come," Nat said softly.

They've hated us so long, I thought. And then Heron pointed to the road before us and said, "Look."

Against the sunrise, a column of Chandlers was marching on Roadstead Farm, their lamps held high and blazing, tools strapped to their backs. Ada led the ragged column and waved her hands frantically. Let out a wild war whoop.

"Look," Tyler repeated, and nudged my shoulder toward the river.

I turned, and in the lightening morning, the water swam with sparks: small points of light like bright red fireflies, swarming in the distance, with a huge shadow behind.

"They all came," I said, and the shapes, the shadows came clear: Mackenzie Green standing on the prow of the Windstown ferry, its pilot lantern blazing. Behind her the entire Windstown fishing fleet spread out like candles, like a funeral procession moving stately to the shore.

—and behind *them*, through the steam of a river that was boiling, burning, breaking, a pair of giant, curling horns emerged into the day. Beast Island rose out of the torch smoke, world-tall, floating at the end of three dozen ropes.

"It's time, then," Heron said softly.

I swallowed. "It's time." Tyler reached for my hand and caught it.

I laced my fingers through his and took Nat's hand on the other side. And then we walked, the four of us, down to the wide-rent tear on the river.

TWENTY-NINE

IT WAS RAINING ON THE RIVERSIDE: HOT, WET DROPS THAT smelled of summer thickly dying into rot. They drifted into the winter wind and froze halfway to the ground.

The beach was overrun with Twisted Things: clumped on the sand, swarming around the dead posts of our dock, crawling and hissing and fighting as the stones beneath them smoked and burned. There were Twisted Things *everywhere.* And past them, over the hill and around the riverbend, came the sound of the Great Army's horns.

"You ready?" I asked everyone.

Heron looked at me, at Tyler, at Nat. At Ada Chandler, behind us, with a crowbar in her hands.

"I'm ready," Ada said, "but they have to *listen* to me."

"They will," Ty soothed, and in the river behind us, the first boat touched earth.

Mackenzie Green stepped out of it, her hands wrapped around a thick truncheon. "Good God," she muttered, pale beneath her tan. She looked over her shoulder, uncertain for what might have been the first time since she'd landed in Windstown to take over the general store.

The murmur didn't stop with her. It rippled through the fleet of bumping boats, into Beast Island's veil of steam. Behind her, boat after boat docked: the Thaos, the Masons, the Sumners and Pricketts, the Pitts family and the Haddads, in their too-fine working gear. All the people we knew in the wide world. All the people who had come for us.

The men who'd been at John's Creek with Thom and Tyler clamped their mouths uniformly shut. *This is the war,* I realized. I'd grown so used to this destruction on my doorstep. *This is what they saw at John's Creek.*

"Is it too late?" Mackenzie asked, and I couldn't tell if she was hoping or fearing it was true. The boats bobbed on the shore like lanterns, drifting in on a false midsummer tide.

"No," I said in a small voice, and then summoned up something louder, something I could believe. "No. It is *not* too late for us."

"Let's go, then," Ada said mildly, and the Thaos leaped out of their wooden boat.

The Chandlers rushed in, took sturdy ropes from Windstown hands, and passed around thick leather gloves. "Don't touch its skin," Rami Chandler repeated. "Don't breathe its scent. If you're hurt, fall back." He paused before Councilor Haddad, looked him full in the face, and shook his head. "Dad. Don't touch its skin."

"Rami," Councilor Haddad said thinly, and turned away.

The ropes drew taut, ten bodies to each line. I drew in a breath.

"Heave!" Thao Hang shouted, and every grown man and woman in Windstown and the Chandler village pulled Beast Island ashore.

Birds scattered from their dead nests, and the ropes creaked, strained, pulled the skinned hulk of Beast Island through the currents. It caught in the shallows and dragged, its long paws bent and breaking against the disturbed rocks, and the hefting crew scattered to the back to push, their hands encased in the Chandlers' thick leather gloves. The Pricketts flung blankets, tablecloths, curtains over the beast's wet-furred, stinking haunch and pushed through that smoking shield. I ran to the back and threw in among them, put my shoulder to the blankets on the wet corpse. Smelled their wool begin to burn.

The Twisted Things scattered across the beach, burning and agitated, ducking in and out of the violet light of the open portal. A lizard flicked up its red ears at us and hissed. Councilor Kim faltered. "What *is* that?"

Tyler pulled his shearing knife and brandished it low. "Keep pushing!" he called. "We'll clear a path!"

I shifted my weight against Beast Island's hind leg. "But there are so many of them—"

He smiled at me, his sweet, whimsical smile. "This is what I trained for. Keep pushing, Hal. *Don't stop.*"

He limped toward the snarls of Twisted Things, and he moved like a killer.

Tyler's heavy knife connected with a spinner bird and

ripped. Bones cracked and feathers flew as it let out an out-raged squawk. Nat howled a war cry on his heels and dashed in, her pitchfork high, swinging and swiping anything that moved out of our path. Johan Prickett gave me a frantic glance, and then he was off behind her, silent, eyes narrowed, as focused as a fox.

I traded a frightened glance with Heron. "Keep pushing," he said. *Don't you give up.* I nodded fractionally, and he strode, head high, into the carnage with his twisted knife in hand.

I wasn't a fighter. I wasn't a hero, clearing the path ahead of us with blood and fire as the sun rose high. But I knew how to push, and I pushed, shoulder to shoulder, the endless weight before us. It moved an inch; two inches. We pushed: Macken-zie, with Darnell and Janelle and Mrs. Pitts. "Heave!" Hang called again, and we groaned and shoved, and the body skit-tered another two inches up the scree. One moment at a time, we pushed Beast Island across the beach I'd played on since I was a child. The fumes rose from the blankets, from the body, and I choked. It would never be done. We would never make it.

Tyler slashed fruitlessly at a hissing lizard-fox, and Nat shook her pitchfork at something that looked mostly like wax melting. "Left!" Tyler called out, and Ada Chandler grabbed the lead line. "A little more! Okay, good!"

I leaned in, breath to breath, and pushed with everything I had. The body inched forward, one step, two steps, three.

The tips of those shattered horns vanished into the shim-mering forest, then its head, its torso, its rotted tail.

A drop of rain, soft and sweet with fullest summer, trickled down its length and splashed to the ground. And then the purple light, the light of unfurled leaves, flickered and went out.

Silence pooled over the beach. Not the silence of the quiet place, the place I'd walked through to find our Thom: the silence of a constellation, stars in concert, hand in hand.

"Feel for drafts!" Ada called, and the Chandlers surged forward, plugging the chinks and crannies around it with the bodies of dead spinner birds. The tiny licks of heat faltered one by one. The acid summer of that other world, fading away.

We felt the wind go, together. We tilted our heads up into the sky and watched the bright morning sun reemerge from the smoke that had stained our sky.

A birdcall broke the silence, clear and sharp, and we shook ourselves, together, like we'd spent years underwater. Mackenzie grinned, and then Janelle Prickett, and then the sound of a whole town breathing filled the morning until it burst.

Someone was hugging me. Jerome Chandler, or Thao Cua, or any one of my neighbors who were heaving with tears, with sweat, with shouting as the portal burned itself out. Mrs. Pitts let out a whoop, and then the Sanchez girls picked it up, and we stood there cheering, screaming, dancing in the dead sand under the sunrise sky.

Because we'd done it. We'd all done it.

We'd saved Windstown, and the lakelands, and Roadstead Farm.

Tyler wrapped his arms around my waist and kissed me, full and long, in view of the whole of Windstown society. And there it was, that steal of breath, that flutter Janelle Prickett had described so gleefully. I pulled back and looked full into his face, grinning, crying.

"We did it," I whispered.

"Told you so," he answered.

And then he looked up, and I felt a hesitant tap on my shoulder. "Ah," Nat said behind me, quiet, insistent. "Hal. Ty."

I turned and heard it, felt it: dozens of marching feet, shaking the ground beneath us. I'd almost forgot. The army was coming. The army was here.

The party quieted to hiccups and whispers. "Weapons at the ready, please," Jerome said, and I stared at him.

"You can't be serious."

Darnell Prickett took out his truncheon. Mackenzie Green pulled her filleting knife.

The first of the soldiers of the army that had saved the world came, two-step, down our orchard path.

The Great Southern Army was a wall of sound. They carried horns and drums and standards, wore their polished buttons like regimental badges. The dawn flickered into cacophony as they gained the beach and spread, semicircle, around the tail of Beast Island and the desolated shore.

I realized I still didn't know how big a regiment was. They just kept *coming*: rows of thin soldiers, endless as barley, marching forever through the sand. *How many people died at*

John's Creek? I thought as they stood at attention. *How many, if there are so very many left?*

We watched them come, all of us damp and stinking and small: the ham-handed people of a river town who had just happened to thwart the second coming of a god.

A slight woman came to the fore: brown-skinned, crisp-collared, lines spidering her face. "Who's in charge here, then?" she said in a deceptively mild voice.

"That's General de Guzman," someone breathed, and it set off a new chorus of murmurs. I blinked. General de Guzman was a woman, small, sharp-eyed, and wrinkled — and she was *old*. Older than my papa had lived to, older than my Opa or Oma. She appraised all of us like a general-store keeper: hard-faced with hard living, weights and measures in her eyes.

Alonso Pitts stepped forward. "I'm the mayor," he said, and snuck a look at me. He swallowed. "But it's her farm."

I sucked in a deep, sweet breath of smoky air. There'd be hundreds of witnesses to tell Marthe about this. But it was nothing to being here. It was nothing to hearing it said.

"It's my farm," I repeated, and put some steel in my spine.

She looked me over, and looked at the tail of Beast Island, slumped in a forever sleep where my dock and rowboat used to be. "Explain this," she said. Not unkindly, but not kind.

I cleared my throat, and that's when I felt it.

A full regiment of soldiers leaning in from behind their marching order, memorizing every detail of my tattered coat, my bleeding hands. Firelight glinted in their eyes, and something else. Hunger.

Hope.

I am not a hero, I thought suddenly, piercingly.

Heron looked at the army. And then he looked at me.

"No," I whispered.

But he knew I didn't mean it.

He swallowed hard and straightened his back. Devoted. Uncompromising. Brave.

"Lay down your armaments," he said, his voice reeded with fear, but then louder, stronger. "It's over. At ease. Put them down."

The general squinted at him from before that wall of men. "Who says?"

Heron squared his shoulders. Lifted his chin. He was thin to the ribs, but his jaw was squared, his eyes tired; his face soot-smudged—but looking at our braver, brighter tomorrows.

"John Balsam," he said, and the night went wild.

THIRTY

THE DAMAGE, IN THE END, WAS BREATHTAKING.

The orchard trees would have to be replanted, the far barley field swept of ash and fertilized anew. The riverbank was a melted ruin: hard stone, run together until it sat slick in the winter light. The brush was dying in the back field, around the guts of what was once a hawthorn tree. And the smokehouse—

There was no smokehouse anymore.

In the far field was a tangled ruin of old brick, its roof fallen in, its beams scorched black. It lay like the eldest of the old-city ruins, jumbled in its own old furniture and a dead pile of long deer horns—and, tangled with it, the crushed body of Asphodel Jones. I swallowed hard at the ruin the falling walls had made of his skull. He would never face his justice. He would never be tried.

I stacked the horns into a pile and set them, like a cairn, atop his body to keep the scavengers away. They cast weird, slanted shadows across the fields as the sun crested over the horizon.

The boats had departed through the morning, one by one, fluttering across the river to emptied Windstown. The soldiers were gone, likewise, from what they were already calling the Battle of Windstown-on-the-River. They'd taken Heron with them: John Balsam, God-slayer. Hero of two desperate wars.

They left me with the orchard, and the ruined fences, and my barley field. I walked the land—my land, my one and only home—and claimed it, step by step. "Home," I whispered to the fences, the shattered trees. Safe, now. Free.

I counted up the damage, alone and lonely.

It was Tyler who brought Marthe and Thom back down the highway, on the creaking cart weighed down with everything we could lift and still loved. He coaxed the tired ponies up our drive midafternoon, soot and fatigue smudged under his eyes.

"Oh," Marthe said as her eyes roamed the casualties. Thom ran his bandaged fingers through her hair. It was desolation.

"I'm taking the boards off the windows," I said. "The chickens made it. So did the goats, and the barn cats."

Marthe looked at the hammer in my belt, the dirt on my hands, and stepped down from the cart. She reached into Hazel's swaddle and handed me back my darkwood box. The contents hadn't been disturbed: every little relic was tucked safely in place. The paper with Papa's signature fit crisp as a glove.

"Thank you," I said quietly, and wrapped my weary arms around her.

She held me for a long, long time.

It took less than an hour to unpack. Marthe was upstairs, nursing Hazel in the dim room that was once our papa's. She'd had James move Mama's old rocking chair over: plumped up with a parlor cushion, it looked like a nursery sprouting cautiously in the weeds.

I lingered in the doorway. I didn't feel right, yet, just walking through the privacies of husband and child that had sprung up to surround her, to pull us even farther apart.

I waited 'til she saw me to speak. "How's Miss Hazel?"

"Terrible," Marthe said, and brushed the child's thin curls. "She's always fussing. She never sleeps. If I knew I was going to be someone's Milk Lady for the next year, I'd have sent her right back in."

There was no edge to it. Marthe was tired; I could see the fatigue hanging on her like bracken vines. But she cradled Hazel close, feather-gentle, in her arms.

"Marthe—" I started, and shuffled my feet in place.

"You didn't tell me," she said softly, "who Heron was."

My skin froze. Thom had told her. *Of course* Thom had told her. They were married, they loved each other, and they never, ever lied.

"Marthe, I—"

She shook her head. "Don't even tell me that you didn't know." She looked up from where the baby nursed, busily, in the shadows. "I've known you since the day you were born. You knew."

I swallowed and nodded mutely. I could hair-split, argue, pick at her, but we both knew the truth.

Her eyes stayed steady on me, filled with a dizzying amount of pain. "Why, Hal?" she asked simply.

I swallowed, and sank down in my socks. All I could see was James Blakely's wild face in the fields on the night before everything broke, asking me why I couldn't trust my family enough to let them in.

"I couldn't," I started, and it broke down right past my lips. How could I encompass years of that slow slide into fear, guilt, grief? *I couldn't.* "I am terrible at secrets," I said. "I am terrible at lies. I hate everything about this stupid year." I trailed off. "You don't understand—"

"*God,* Hallie," Marthe snapped. "I don't know what you want anymore—"

With a wail, the baby arched in her arms. Marthe stopped abruptly and cradled her, and then set Hazel deliberately down in the cradle and buttoned her dress back up to the neck.

"I don't know what you want from me," she said again, but lower. "You used to be so *brave,* so loving, no matter what happened. And now you've grown into this . . . stranger, and I can't do anything right."

"You used to be proud of me," I said, low and small.

Marthe's chin whipped upward. Her eyes blazed hot, hard, furious. She reached out for my face, and I pulled away; she reached out again and caught it between her two hands. "Listen to me," she said, looking me full in the eyes. "I am *so* proud of you. I have *always* been proud of you, and I will never stop. Do you hear me?"

For a moment, I was nothing but a body, stiff with shock. A body in a strange, new world, where I could *succeed*.

"But you're *not*," I whispered. "All I do for you is do things wrong. All we do is fight. And I've worked so hard to live up to you, to make you proud, but I'm *so tired*, Marthe. I'm not good enough, and the fields almost went to seed and the beer's late, and four of the chickens died right in the coop, and I couldn't do anything right. I just wanted you to love me again. I just wanted you to never, ever make me leave —"

Somehow I was crying. There were hot tears streaming, blinding, down my cheeks, and salt in the corners of my heaving mouth. Marthe sat with my shaking face in her hands, open-mouthed. "Oh, God, Hallie," she said softly, but it was entirely different now. "Hallie, baby, you're only sixteen."

I looked up, betrayed, but her smile was gentle.

"There's over fifty acres here. You're sixteen years old. No one on earth could ever keep that much farm with two pairs of hands. I never expected you to — God. I never stopped loving you. I'll *always* love you. You're the only family I have."

"But you have Thom, you have Hazel now—"

My sister scowled. "Hallie," she said, "do you remember the night Papa broke the casserole?"

I flinched. I did. I did.

I'd been just eight, and my big sister eighteen, and we were newly alone with Papa's rules, Papa's rages, all the ways those rules changed day by day and the rages flew high when you inevitably broke them. Marthe'd done something so trivial—left her winter coat across the old chair, or forgot to scrub a dish—and Papa's temper exploded, again. He'd picked up Mama's old casserole dish and flung it, sailing past us, against the wall.

I'd looked up at my big sister and her stern, furious face. And saw it, for just a moment, *afraid*.

"You took your hands off your little ears," she said softly. "You stood right between us and *dared* him, eye to eye, to lay a hand on you instead." There was a glint in her eye. Fear, years old, for her safety and mine.

Remembered fear, and real pride.

I saw it before me, sudden as a shudder: He'd stared down at me, my big, raging papa with his heavy meat hands and his heavy red face, and something shrank inside him. Something faded. And he'd turned around and stomped his slow way to bed.

I'd looked at Marthe. And she'd looked at me. And then I threw the most furious tantrum of my life before or after.

That someone had *dared* to make my sister afraid.

"There's no one else in the world who remembers that," she said, and dropped her hands, finally, to the old wood of Mama's rocking chair. They were thin hands, I noticed, for maybe the first time. Thin hands, work-scarred. Strong. "Everyone else in the world, I have to explain that to. What it means to us. What we are. But you and me, we just know it. We know it without words.

"And I know you understand what that means to me," she said awkwardly. "Because you *ran.* You went into that portal and found Thom, as fast as you could, even though it cost something. You didn't wait. You're still not someone who thinks they'll never get to stop walking."

And I finally got it, the thing she'd been trying to tell me all along. The difference between Heron or our uncle Matthias — walking away from disaster after mishap, slow enough to save their strength for the endless road — and what we were.

People who had to turn around and fight. People who *tried,* because we had something to lose. A home.

I choked down another, richer sob. *She* was *telling me,* I realized. She'd been telling me for months: Marthe and I were each other's home. And so was Roadstead Farm, malting and eggs every morning and the cozy routine of chores going on into forever.

She'd told me that she'd always be there. I just hadn't known how to hear it.

I felt it break inside me: the hairline cracks in a fear I'd carried in my gut years too long. All my balled-up ease and kindness broke through the cracks and hatched: kept away so long by the certainty that if I dared love too hard, I'd just lose.

"Marthe," I said, as tiny and high and small as I'd sounded as a child. "I'm sorry. I'm sorry I said those things, I'm sorry I was so terrible to you—"

Marthe's strong face, her bright and sharp and proud face crumpled. She pushed up and wrapped her arms tight around me, crushing the air from my lungs. Letting me, finally, breathe. "I'm sorry too."

"What're *you* sorry for?" I burst.

"You were always such a serious kid," she said softly, and wiped her eyes. "I always knew I was failing you somehow."

"Never," I choked, and held her face close to mine. "Never in my life."

"Yes, I did," she whispered, and hugged me, fierce. "Because I never told you we aren't Papa and Uncle Matthias."

We cried until the last tears shook themselves free, shook onto the dress our mama had worn, the floor our papa had paced, and the million little ways we'd made all those things ours after all.

"This isn't going to be easy," Marthe said when we parted, scrubbing salt from her reddened eyes. "We have to work at this, okay? We'll screw up. We'll backslide. We have to talk to each other, and be patient."

"I promise," I pushed out.

"No," she stopped me. "Shh. It was a bad year."

I nodded.

"A bad year," she echoed for me. "Let's never do it again."

Later, I came downstairs wiping my eyes, lightheaded with the sniffling.

Tyler, busy at the dishes, laid a hand on my cheek. "You okay?"

"Yeah," I said, and gave him a watery smile. For the first time in a long time, I was finally okay.

Tyler stayed through the afternoon to relight the fire in the stove, patch the chicken coop, pry off the boards we'd used to shut the windows. We worked together in silence, hands brushing hands, snow in our hair, soothed by each other's breath pluming through the sky.

Everyone always went to the hayloft to hide. But for now, there was nowhere else, so I lay with Tyler in the dwindling straw inside the old hay barn. An orange cat glared at us nervously and settled into the soft afternoon light. *We should bring them inside,* I reminded myself. So they didn't go hunting until the last Twisted Things had fallen to ash.

Heron found us by the time the sun was westering to evening, when we'd had more than enough time to just lie there, hands and breaths entwined. "You're back," I said, and sat up. Tyler rose behind me, tinged with embarrassment.

"There's straw in your hair," Heron said, bemused.

"I live on a farm," I retorted. "Where's the army?"

Heron sat on a bale, the teasing still in his eyes. "Going home," he said. "Or at least most of them. General de Guzman declared the amnesty this morning, now that they've found me, and most of the regiment packed up for the highway. It's been a long time away for a lot of people."

The taste of inevitability flooded my mouth. "And you?"

Heron looked at the scattered hay bales. "I said I'd fix your wagon wheel," he said tentatively.

I smiled, and then I couldn't stop smiling, bright as sun on snow. "Right," I said, and then he beamed back.

I'd never seen him smile before. It was warm as Sunday morning.

We uncovered Asphodel Jones's body the next morning, from under its cairn of secrets and bone. Tyler opened its eyes with his dirt-smudged fingers, but there was nothing in them.

"What're you looking for?" I asked softly as the breakfast crowd picked their way from the house down to the smokehouse's dusty ruins: James Blakely and Callum; Nat and Eglantine; Marthe, Hazel, and Thom. Heron paced a rut into the ground behind us, looking out over the burnt-down orchard toward Bellisle. To where the bulk of Beast Island no longer blocked the sky.

Tyler shook his head. "There was a picture in Jones's eyes

before, when he was in your father's room. It blotted out the walls, it was so bright."

I swallowed. "What did you see?"

Tyler rubbed his eyes. "Stars," he said. His hand moved in the shattered dust and bored swift dots, jagged and certain, into the cracked earth of my great-grandparents' farm. "Steady stars, on the darkness."

"That's the plow constellation," Heron said. He traced the lines between it with his blunt-nailed finger. "It's a summer constellation. I saw that every night at John's Creek when I looked up."

Tyler traced it over and over, meditative. "He said something that night. I couldn't make it out. I didn't know the word. I think it was a name."

"Chandi?" I guessed softly, and Tyler startled. Jones's daughter.

"What do we do?" Cal asked.

I looked across the newly tumbled, crumbling stones of the smokehouse my Opa had built out of lakelands stone and river mud; across the ruined barley fields and the gray corpse of the hawthorn tree. Thom and I had planned to resurrect that smokehouse. We were going to be the talk of the lakelands. We were going to set Roadstead Farm up for life, so neither Marthe nor I had to worry about how a few struggling acres of land and four barley fields could possibly support two whole families, hers and mine. And no one would have to leave. We'd all have a home, forever, between the apple trees and the high road. That future seemed so long ago: long ago and far away.

"I'm sure the army will want him," James said. "They like that sort of thing."

I shook my head and dragged my eyes along the careless, sleeping bend of his broken body. *I took his last will and testament,* I thought, *because Papa's last will changed our lives; because if Thom hadn't come home, we would have had no vial of ash to grieve over, to let him go—*

"Asphodel Jones has a daughter," I said.

Thom looked up at me. Mild Thom's eyes were steady, and burning with a held-breath hope.

"Somewhere down south there's a girl waiting," I said, quick and low, and then stronger, stronger: "Still leaving the door unlocked every night and a light by the window, because they never found a body, and who knows, he might come back. And the hope's the worst." I swallowed. "The hope means you never stop crying. You just . . . it never stops."

"I'm sorry," Thom whispered.

"You came home," Marthe said lightly, and pressed his bandaged hand to her heart.

"What're you saying, Hal?" James Blakely asked, and his green eyes were piercing.

"Soldiers bring a vial of ashes," I said softly, and placed Jones's corpse-cold hand over his crushed rib cage. "For the families. So we can live life again. We should take him home. We should bring that girl his ashes."

"He's a murderer," Marthe said.

I looked up at her. "But that girl isn't," I said, just like Marthe wasn't Papa. Just like I wasn't Uncle Matthias, after all, but just Hallie. Maker of malt, herder of goats, half owner of Roadstead Farm.

Tyler followed me up the path, through the corpses of our orchard trees, into the December brightness that lasted so fleetingly. "Hal, I have to tell you something."

I stopped. "This isn't about your ceiling."

"The ceiling and I broke up," he agreed, and swallowed. "I can't help mop up the Twisted Things. I can't see anymore."

My heart seized, terrified. "What do you mean you can't—"

"Not like that," he said, and lifted his head.

His eyes were wide and frightened. Light hazel, ringed delicately with green where the sunshine lit them up. There was nothing in them now, nothing and everything.

Tyler Blakely's eyes. Not the same as before he marched the south roads and back, but close enough. The warm eyes I remembered, bright with mischief, bright with loving.

"Tyler—" I started, and my throat caught. "When?"

"This morning," he said. "I saw the Beast block out the light of that sun, and that was the last. I can't help anymore. It's gone."

"I do not *care* about help," I said fiercely, and turned over my scar-pocked hand. "The wounds of the Twisted Things do heal," I marveled. "It takes a while, but they heal."

He nodded, wordless, and fell into my arms.

"Hallie," he said, relieved, weeping from his healed, human eyes. "It's over. I'm home."

SPRING

THIRTY-ONE

WE BURNED ASPHODEL JONES LIKE A BIRD, LIKE A DEER, in a pyre down by the water.

It was a sunny, cold day, but no snow stuck on the land the God's world had scorched into smooth rock. Our pyre stayed clear and dry, and when it was done, we gathered the ashes into an elegant green glass bottle, the color of caught sunshine at the bottom of the lake.

Three months later, when the first melt came, John Balsam packed a bag.

He was stronger now: three months of good home cooking and a warm place to sleep off the endless road had filled him out. And he had boots, good ones from Windstown, and a coat to keep the weather off his back. Gifts, from those who'd fought beside us the day we pulled Beast Island up to shore.

I watched him pack his scuffed leather satchel in the parlor that had become his room through the winter; watched him weigh the things that had sustained him on the dead and lonely road north and tuck them lovingly inside. "Need more space," he muttered, and dumped them out again. There was extra cargo this time, for the journey south: the last effects and promises of the Wicked God's prophet, Asphodel Jones.

There were few enough of them: the container with his ashes, and his ragged hat. His torn coat, laundered and dried carefully. The gold wedding ring we'd found on his finger, loosened by hunger, tarnished sooty black.

And atop them, in a ringing heap, four glinting, shimmering disks: half of Thom's army buttons.

"Do you want these back?" I'd asked Thom. He never wore his. They were hidden in a box in his dresser drawer, behind old socks and ratted undershirts. He walked our ravaged fields with plain flannel and cotton over his burn-scarred skin, closed with buttons the Windstown woodcarvers made.

Thom stopped amid the rows of plowed land, under the birdsong, and studied the buttons in my hand. "Let him keep them," he said, and cast another handful of seeds onto the rich earth.

"Are you sure? He wasn't a veteran."

"That's not the point," Thom said, and dropped more barley seeds into the ground. On his back, swathed and swaddled, Hazel Mae burbled a nonsense word and sang.

I told my niece the story again that night, after Marthe had fed her and she squirmed restlessly, fighting if we tried to put her down. "Hazel Mae Clarlund," I sang into her little ear. "This is the story of the storm between worlds, in the week when you were born."

Our last afternoon I spent with Nat, side by side, walking along the river.

Everyone always went to the hay barn, but right now the hay barn was off-limits: Gus the Third had birthed her kittens, and she stood hissing between us and the mewling litter every time we came in for a forkful. Hazel stared at them whenever she got close, her hands grasping and her eyes big.

"You could come with, you know," I said to Nat, and kicked a rock upstream. "It's horribly improper for a young lady to travel alone with a farm hand."

"Hah," Nat snorted, and kicked another rock to meet mine. "Thank you. But no." She looked straight at me with a sharpness that wasn't furious or frightened, but sober.

"No?" I asked, surprised. Nat Blakely, who was always shoving us toward another adventure. Nat, who broke the rules.

"No," she said, firmer. "Remember? I told you that you always had one foot out the door. You were packed for years. But I've got what I want: good work, and nice weather, and Mum's teaching me the business. Ty's got no head for it. I've got acres to learn if I'm going to be running a whole sheep farm."

"But—"

"It's my home, Hal," she said, and her smile was rueful.

"It's mine too," I promised her. "I'll come back soon."

She nodded, already more distant from me than when

we'd started. "I know," she said, and wrapped an arm about my shoulder. We kept on through the greening riverbanks.

I had packed, the night before, in a new pack, strongly made — not the decrepit one I'd kept packed for years and then lost when the smokehouse tumbled down: four changes of clothes, for all weather, all roads; soap, and a bedroll, and a striker for fires; a bottle for water and a pan to heat it up. And between them, wedged carefully, a darkwood box with two rose petals and a child's doll, and the deed to half of Roadstead Farm.

Because I was leaving on the long road south, but unlike Uncle Matthias, I was coming back.

Heron met us at the poultry barn, Tyler in tow, busy with the last-minute chores we'd promised before setting out into the world. "How's it looking?" I asked, and Heron shook his head.

"Not even close to done," he said irritably. "Before this winter I'd have laughed to think a farm was this much work."

I snorted. It was only half funny. "Townie. So what do we do?"

He gazed out across the greening fields, to the ruin of the changeable river and the edge of the Beast's tail rising above the orchard trees. We'd planted the trees new, from cuttings: their skinny trunks stretched up, smiling, into the thin, bright sun. Heron and Thom and I, together, holding the shovels and steadying the soil. "Bring in help," Heron said, and shrugged. "I can write you a reference for a hired man."

I snickered, and Ty's hammer swung, missed, and re-aimed. I swallowed. Tyler and I had deliberately not talked about my leaving. It was the very worst part, and we'd counted every second together. We'd dodged it for so long.

"We'll come back as quick as we can," I said, and Ty looked away.

Heron looked at him. Looked at me, and sighed. "Look, Private. I was eighteen once too. If you don't want to leave her, just open your mouth and come with."

I flushed. "I'm right here," I said, and Heron shot me a sly glance.

Ty looked up, red-faced, shame-shouldered, but still tall with his own pride. "I can't. I can't walk that fast," he admitted.

Heron studied him and then shrugged. "You in any hurry, Hallie?"

Hope surged beneath my ribs. "Nope," I said.

Tyler's smile opened like a bloom, like the sun. Looked at me. *Yes?* his eyes asked.

I could say no, I remembered, like I remembered every time. No did not mean never. I had to say yes only if I meant it, only if it was true.

I met his eyes. Nodded slowly.

Yes.

"Excuse me," he said, and put down the hammer. "I have to go speak to my mother about a trip."

. . .

James and Cal Blakely came late in the afternoon to give us their farewells, and they came with rucksacks packed.

"You're not coming too?" I asked with a spike of dismay.

Cal shook his head. "South again? Not likely."

James nudged him with a gentle elbow. "We've been meaning for years to take a load of wool with the caravans. Spread our market a little. I thought we'd go north," he said, ever so lightly. "The Sanchez cousins are very curious about handling a flock of sheep, and I hear Black Creek and Kortright are real beauties this time of spring."

Heron's mouth opened, but for once, he had no words. His gray eyes, so reserved, filled with tears. He took James's hand and closed his around it gravely. "Tell her that John Balsam is alive," he said, thick with emotion. "Tell her he's coming home soon. That I love her."

"I will," James said, and cupped his own hand over Heron's. "You've our word on it."

"Thank you," Heron said, strained thin, so very young, and bowed his head to cry.

The afternoon waned into a soft, fitful night, sprinkled with showers and the call of young geese winging across the river. Marthe sat at the table with me, our teacups halfway empty, silent amid the scattered dishes and the warm lantern light.

"It is going to be very strange," she said, "without you here."

The whole thing still wasn't quite real: the pack in my

bedroom corner, the clothes laid out for our morning start, the way I'd drifted out of planting, cooking, chores. It still felt like tomorrow would be a normal day: breakfast around the table with Marthe and Heron and Thom; feed to scatter for the chickens; soft earth to turn, the still-healing earth, while we sang Hazel nursery songs.

"It was all I wanted," I said, and Marthe's head came up.

"What's that?"

I shook my head. A half-remembered thing. Another life. "All I wanted," I said, "was to help bring Hazel up together. The four of us, in our own house, like it was supposed to be all along. Pillow forts and the alphabet and taking turns at sup-per, and now—"

There was a world out there. A world full of homesteads, and cities, and strangers who might give us a meal, a night's shelter, a kindness; who might point us the way to Monticello Town. There were new routines waiting, routines of miles instead of chores, and for the first time, sneaking about the edges, I was *wanting*. Wanting—now that I dared to, now that I had a way to come back—to explore.

Marthe shook her head softly; the smile on her face was wry. "That's the thing about life," she said. "You start off thinking you're doing a small thing: standing up in the face of an argument, or giving three dances to the apple farmer's son from Essex because it'll keep Jeremy Sumner's paws off your backside, and besides, you'll never see him again, right?"

I laughed. Thom's father grew apples. He sent a bushel

basket across the river every year as his anniversary gift to the family that had made a barley farmer of his son.

"You think you're doing something small," she said meditatively. "You never see how large the things you've planted grow until it's too late."

The baby started to fuss somewhere upstairs. Marthe froze, her head tilted up toward those thin cries. A shuffle sounded across the floorboards—Thom moving toward the cradle, murmuring in his deep rumble voice—and she breathed again.

"I have to go with him," I told her, and added hesitantly, "Uncle Matthias went south."

A spark lit in Marthe's eyes: old pain, older than I was. And something else, bright and smoldering.

Hope.

"You tell him to come home," she said roughly, and then surer. "Tell him there's to be no more fighting between blood and blood on Roadstead Farm."

"I will, Marthe," I whispered, and broke into a grin.

It was spring, and my sister and I understood each other, finally, again.

We woke early. The morning was brilliant blue and shining, and it was a long way south to Monticello, past John's Creek.

I washed my face in my basin, and made my bed, and shouldered my brimful pack. There was singing in the kitchen, bright and sleepy through the vents, and Hazel's babbles struck between the notes like rocks in a clear stream.

I planted this, I realized. *I put the seeds of my own leaving into the ground. The good ones and the bad ones both.*

I shut the door and stepped downstairs.

Tyler was waiting at the porch rail. I stopped beside him, and Thom and Heron came in from the fields, moving matched against the sunrise. Heron was taller. It was unarguable when he held his head up high.

Heron shook Thom's hand one last time. "Are you ready?" he said, and I swallowed.

No land beneath my feet. A bag on my back, and another in my hand. The dubious charity of strangers, who might be neighbors or friends after all. I took a deep, long breath.

It didn't matter how much had withered, how close we'd come to the world's end. The goats were kid-heavy in the pen. The trees fuzzed light and green, spring coming in on every vine and bud and branch. Hazel Mae fussed over her breakfast through the open kitchen window, and we had the business of living to get on with.

There were chores.

I hefted the pack and took Tyler Blakely's outstretched hand. "I'm ready," I said.

You could see every bit of Roadstead Farm from my ancient family house on the hill. You could see all the way to the fallen stars. I stepped down from that house and started walking along the grass, through the sweeps and curves that led us out of my little world.

To take a dead man's ashes home.

We walked the gravel path to our open gate and set out, together, a constellation, onto the road.

ACKNOWLEDGMENTS

An *Inheritance of Ashes* was a book that asked a lot of me. I wrote my first book as a writer, but I wrote this one as a person, and bringing your whole self to a book when you are a person, with so much more than books to love, is a harder set of compromises. A lot of people supported and carried me during writing *Above;* for *An Inheritance of Ashes,* a great many people offered, in the face of those more complicated compromises, so much that made such a difference: kindness, experience, and patience.

For all the work, thought, and encouragement that went into fostering this idea, even though the external things didn't work out: Cheryl Klein.

For their patience with a very drafty first draft, and their comments on it: Michael Matheson and Ian Keeling.

Lindsey Shorser and Jeff Yagar, who put up with my occasionally collaring them to go: "Is this cool or stupid?" and reciting random plot points at high speed.

Kelly Jones, Pam McNew, and Jennifer Adam, for taking the time to not only talk about the writing, but to point out some of the things this particular city girl assumed or misunderstood about running a small farm.

Emma Bull, whose wisdom on other projects came forward to vastly improve this one; Merrie Haskell, who generously shared both her insights and experience, and made the way there much, much clearer; and Michelle Sagara West, for her invaluable knowledge and invaluable practicality, and willingness to share both.

Chandra Rooney, for probably a million hours' worth of work dates all over the west end, talking out plot points, talking about positioning, beta-reading chapters that just changed completely anyway, double-checking my instincts on cover copy when it was midnight and my brain stopped working, making me write words instead of bailing to see Batman even though I really wanted to bail and see Batman, and finally, telling me it was going to be okay in a way she knew I'd believe. Which is what the best writing partners do — and the best friends.

The Ontario Arts Council, whose Writers' Works in Progress grant program let me jump face-first into the scary, wonderful life of a full-time writer. Thanks for believing in this book at its very beginnings, and for the chance to, well, take a chance.

My literary agent, Caitlin Blasdell, for knowing exactly where to take a weird little book; Diane Kerner at Scholastic Canada for the immediate and ongoing faith throughout the life of this project; and Anne Hoppe at Clarion, whose patience and enthusiasm were the bedrock that made this manuscript happen—a bedrock that was not excessively dented by teaching one anxious and occasionally very opinionated author the ins and outs of writing on proposal (and a few things about prose clarity and structural tics, besides). Thank you for the immense effort and care put into this book. It has meant everything.

And finally, Philippe McNally, who understands. In the acknowledgments for *Above*, I said that now I understood all those acknowledgment-page stereotypes; what *Ashes* taught me is how a partner who wants you to make good art makes everything suddenly *possible*.

Thank you, love, for doing more than your equal share of a lot of things while I rewrote whole chapters; for the infinite supply of gross deadline snacks; for drawing both the Nope-topus and the capybaras with machine guns, which clearly contributed to my process; for making it clear that time I take away from Us Things for Book Things is not, in your eyes, a favor you do me or a debt to collect; and for, knowing full well that this is going to happen every book, marrying me anyway. I love you like a whole forest of adorable kittens where there is also an astronaut convention taking place. I love you like the sky. Thank you.